Cities of GOLD

Books by William K. Hartmann

Novels:
*Mars Underground**
*Cities of Gold**

Nonfiction:
The American Desert
Astronomy: The Cosmic Journey
The Cosmic Voyage
Desert Heart
Moons and Planets

With Ron Miller:
Cycles of Fire
The Grand Tour
History of Earth
Out of the Cradle

Coedited by
William K. Hartmann:
In the Stream of the Stars
Origin of the Moon
Chronology and Evolution of Mars

*A Tom Doherty Associates book

ay Marcos de niza

Cities of GOLD

William K. Hartmann

A Tom Doherty Associates Book   New York

CITIES OF GOLD

Copyright © 2002 by William K. Hartmann

Edited by James Frenkel

Book design by Jane Adele Regina

A Forge Book
Published by Tom Doherty Associates, LLC
175 Fifth Avenue
New York, NY 10010

www.tor.com

Forge® is a registered trademark of Tom Doherty Associates, LLC.

ISBN: 0-765-30112-1

First Edition: November 2002

Printed in the United States of America

0 9 8 7 6 5 4 3 2 1

For Richard Flint and Shirley Cushing Flint, Coronado
trackers and scholars of the best kind,
and
for Cal Riley, dean of Coronado-era archaeology
in the U.S. Southwest,
and
for Nancy Marble, Don Blakeslee, and Jimmy Owens,
explorers of the Coronado Army campsite near Floydada Texas,
and
for Michel Nallino
of Nice, France—biographer and tracker of Marcos de Niza.

From New Mexico to Texas, and from Seville to Nice, they have
pursued the ancient letters and physical artifacts of Francisco
Vazquez de Coronado, Marcos de Niza, and the other key figures
of the 1500s. Their work helped turn all the players in this tale—
European, African, and Native American—from historical icons
into real human beings who helped shape our North American
world.

ACKNOWLEDGMENTS

Special thanks to the Southern Methodist University Press, and to the New Mexico Historical Review for kind permission to quote from the following works. These references are among the best classic sources of material on the controversy over Marcos de Niza.

Hallenbeck, Cleve. *The Journey of Fray Marcos de Niza.* (Dallas: Southern Methodist University Press, 1949, republished in 1987).

Wagner, Henry R. "Fr. Marcos de Niza," New Mexico Hist. Rev. 9: 159–227 (1934).

Sauer, Carl O. "The Discovery of New Mexico Reconsidered," New Mexico Hist. Rev. 12: 270–287 (1937).

Bloom, Lansing. "Who Discovered New Mexico?" New Mexico Hist. Rev. 15: 101–132 (1940).

Sauer, Carl O. "The Credibility of the Fray Marcos Account," New Mexico Hist. Rev. 15: 233–243 (1941).

Bloom, Lansing. "Was Marcos de Niza a Liar?" New Mexico Hist. Rev. 16: 244–246 (1941).

FRIENDS OF THIS BOOK

Thanks to the following who offered helpful critiques and/or assistance on various portions of the manuscript: Fran Baganal, Sommer Browning, Jaye Caldwell, L. D. Clark, Richard Flint, Shirley Flint, Charles Frankel, my editor Jim Frenkel and his staff at Forge Books, Amy Hartmann, Gayle Hartmann, Mike Hayes, Kathy Kimball, Kathleen Komarek, Paula McBride, Lisa McFarlane, "Michel de Niza" (Michel Nallino of Nice, France), Ron Miller, Elaine Owens, Paul Preuss, Agniezska Przychodzen, James Reel, Kelly Rehm, Cal and Brent Riley, Sam Schramski, Jason Schultz of Reader's Oasis, Jack Scovil, Claudine Scoville, Peter Smith, Sarah Trotta, Stephen and Gloria Vizinczey, Silvia Wenger, Charles A. Wood, and the gracious staff at Zachary's Pizza and at La Indita Mexican Restaurant, both in Tucson, where a writer was allowed to linger with his faithful laptop.

FOREWORD

The first European exploration of western North America, by Spanish adventurers in the1500s, involves a mystery. The reconnaissance was made by Friar Marcos de Niza, who reported his discovery of the "Seven Cities of Cíbola." At that time, Friar Marcos was a well-regarded priest who had just arrived in Mexico from Peru, after witnessing the conquest there. Marcos was sent north from Mexico City in 1538 to investigate rumors of a wealthy northern empire, and he returned in 1539 with confirmation of good lands in the north. His grand success led in 1540 to the vast expedition of conquest under Coronado. Yet something went wrong, and later generations of historians claimed Marcos was a fraud who had lied about his trip. This novel is partly an attempt to unravel the mystery of what really happened. All my quotations from the Spanish participants and later historians, reproduced in italics, are translations of real documents and letters from real people, and are discussed in more detail in the Author's Note. These quotes from the actual participants may allow you, dear reader, to judge whether my solution to the mystery is correct.

Critics . . . have a habit of hanging attributes on you themselves—
and then when they find you're not that way accusing you of sailing
under false colors. . . .

Ernest Hemingway to Maxwell Perkins, 1926
Quoted in *Ernest Hemingway on Writing,*
ed. L. W. Phillips, 1985.

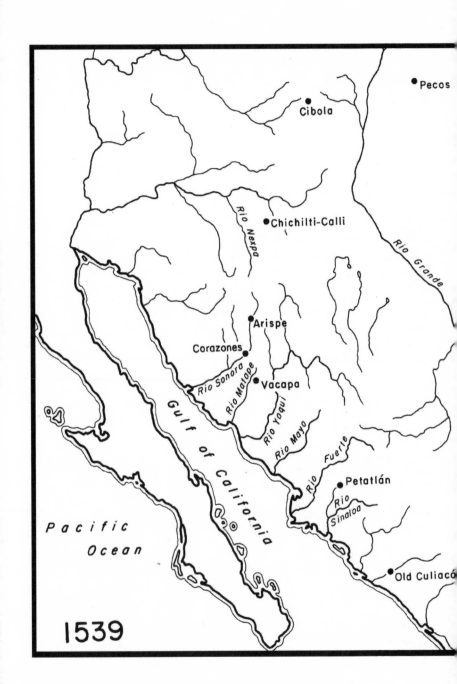

Pecos

Cibola

Rio Nexpa

Chichilti-Calli

Rio Grande

Arispe

Corazones

Rio Sonora

Rio Malape

Vacapa

Rio Yaqui

Rio Mayo

Gulf of California

Rio Fuerte

Petatlán

Rio

Rio Sinaloa

Pacific

Ocean

Old Culiacá

1539

Cities of GOLD

Back Streets of Mexico City, 1542, Two Days Before Christmas

As roosters crowed to raise a reluctant sun, Marcos de Niza shuffled down an alley toward the market of the conquered capital. He clutched his hooded dark robe around his face, and not just to ward off the cold. If he could just get in and out of the market while it was getting started, he might pick up a few things for his Christmas table without being recognized.

A thin screen of morning smoke hung over the city, like a ghostly remnant of Cortés's war of conquest. When Marcos passed through the empty early-morning streets, he always imagined he could hear echoes of the battle, two decades earlier. In this unsavory section of town, some of the ancient buildings still stood in nearly their original form, as built by the Mexica in the days when they ruled the valley. In the rest of the city, most of the pagan buildings had been destroyed during the fighting back in '21. Grizzled veterans of the conquest had told Marcos how the glorious adventure had gone wrong. The Spaniards had to tear down the very houses of the Mexica, not to mention their temples and palaces, to deny them defensible positions as the Christian army fought its way, block by block, back into the city after the notorious Night of Sorrows. Cortés had cried real tears over the destruction of "the Venice of the Indies," the city that many witnesses said was the most beautiful on Earth. People claimed that the old market, the royal gardens, and the emperor's zoo had all been bigger and richer than any similar sites in Europe.

Descriptions of the grandeur of old Mexico gave Marcos mixed feelings. The well-built houses had been decorated with idols and images of horrifying serpent gods. Fortunately, all the paintings of the pagan deities had long since been whitewashed away, but at the tops of some walls Marcos could see the strange, colorful friezes that were only now beginning to fade.

Today, in spite of the flowers that burst out of every crevice, the old market site had become a run-down, odoriferous district of licentiousness. On one side of the great square, the remains of an old temple seemed to radiate an aura of ancient evil across the scene. These days it was being pilfered for building stones. There were rumors that when Moctezuma had been killed, his body had been spirited away along these very streets, but other witnesses from that time denied it. No one seemed to be sure what had happened to him, or to the gold that the Mexican king had amassed for the Spaniards—the gold that had slipped through their fingers during the Night of Sorrows. . . .

Perhaps, thought Marcos, God intended the New World to be a trial for mankind. Many attempts to create wealth from these new, golden lands had resulted in the destruction of cities, souls, and dreams. But he must not let himself grow cynical . . .

He could hardly venture outside his cloistered monastery walls without remembering his own past. Only two years before, on these very streets, he had been hailed as a hero—in line to be the next Bishop of Mexico. But now . . .

Two unkempt soldiers appeared suddenly from a side street. They looked slightly drunk. It was just what Marcos had feared. He tried to step aside into the shadows but it was too late.

"Aha," one of them cried out. "Behold the great explorer." Foul-smelling, he walked up to Marcos and then, with great deliberation, spit on Marcos's robe.

"Why do you act this way, my son?" Marcos said quietly.

"You know why."

The other man laughed as he and his cohort stumbled on down the street. "Just be glad you're a priest, or it would be a lot worse."

Who Was Marcos de Niza?
1537–1949

[Friar Marcos de Niza] is a great religious man, worthy of credit, of approved virtue, and with great devotion and zeal. The friars in Peru elected him custodio. . . . I wrote to him to come here and he came.

Juan de Zumárraga
Bishop of Mexico
April 4, 1537
in a letter about Marcos de Niza, written in Mexico City before
Marcos's journey beyond the northern frontier

[Friar Marcos is a] priest . . . and a religious man, esteemed by me and by my brethren of the governing deputies. We consult about all arduous and difficult matters, and we approved Marcos and held him suitable for making this journey and exploration, because of the aforesaid qualities of his person and also because he is learned, not only in theology, but also in practical astronomy and navigation.

Father Antonio de Ciudad-Rodrigo
Minister Provincial of the Franciscan Order and Marcos's superior
August 26, 1539, in Mexico City, certifying Marcos's
report about his journey

Friar Marcos has discovered another much larger country, 400 leagues (1100 miles) beyond our northern frontier. Many people are moving to go there. The marques, Hernan Cortés, pretends that the conquest of that land belongs to him, but the viceroy claims it for the Emperor, and desires to send friars ahead without arms. He wishes the conquest to be a Christian and apostolic one instead of a butchery. The people [of that new country] are cultured in their dress and in having buildings of many stories. Marcos heard stories of other cities even larger than our own city of Mexico. . . .

Bishop Juan de Zumárraga
Bishop of Mexico
August 23, 1539, in a letter written days after
Marcos's return from the north

Marcos went by land in search of the same coast and country that I had already discovered, and which it is my right to conquer. Since his return, the friar has published the statement that he came within sight of the said [new] country, but I deny that he has either seen or discovered it. . . . Everything the friar says is just the same as what the Indians told me. In enlarging upon this, and in pretending to report what he neither saw nor learned, the said Friar Marcos does nothing new, because he has done this many other times. It was his regular habit, as is notorious in the provinces of Peru and Guatemala.

Hernan Cortés
Conqueror of the empire of Moctezuma
June 25, 1540, in a deposition promoting Cortés's claim to the new lands, after he sent ships to the north in the Gulf of California

It was common knowledge and widely known in [our] camp that Friar Marcos had not seen what he had previously [reported].

Diego Lopez
Soldier in the army of Coronado
describing events of 1540 in testimony given in 1545 at a legal review of Coronado's performance;
document found by Richard and Shirley Flint in the archives of Seville, Spain, in 1998

. . . such were the curses that some hurled at Friar Marcos that I pray God may protect him from them.

Pedro de Castaneda
Soldier in the army of Coronado
describing events of July 7, 1540, when the army arrived in Cíbola,
in a memoir completed in 1596 in Spain

Fray Marcos's accounts have been strongly criticized. . . . He has been treated as an exaggerator, even, to put it bluntly, as a liar, an impostor. . . . [Yet,] as for those of his writings that remain to us, their facts are surprisingly accurate.

Adolph Bandelier
Historian/explorer
1886, in his article, "The Discovery of New
Mexico by the Franciscan Monk,
Friar Marcos de Niza in 1539"

Friar Marcos undoubtedly never willfully told an untruth about the country of Cíbola, even in a barber's chair. . . . Friar Marcos was not a liar.

George Parker Winship
American historian
1904, in his book, The Journey of Coronado

. . . the whole trouble lay in Marcos' perfervid imagination. . . . I decline to believe that he ever saw [Cíbola] unless it was in a vision. . . . He simply magnified everything he heard, one turquoise became a hundred, a small town became a great city. . . . The whole history of the man so far as we know it clearly indicates that he was given to loose statements. . . .

Henry Wagner
American historian
1934, in an article on Marcos

. . . the friar should be remembered, not as a discoverer, but as one of the most successful publicity agents in our history. . . .

It is time that the story of the discovery of the Seven Cities by Friar Marcos be classed where it belongs, as a hoax devised in the interests of [Viceroy] Mendoza's Realpolitik. All that can be credited [to] Marcos is that he was sent out to establish as strong a claim as possible for Mendoza against Cortés, that he got to northern Sonora, but little if any beyond, and that he brought back Indian accounts of [the Seven Cities of Cíbola]. These were dressed up as a claim of discovery that would be useful to Mendoza. . . .

Carl O. Sauer
American geographer/historian
1937, in an article on Marcos

Was Fray Marcos a liar? All in all . . . it is a good old principle that a man is innocent until he is proven guilty.

Lansing Bloom
American historian
1941, in an article on Marcos

The document of Fray Marcos is to be regarded as a political instrument. In order to attain these ends, it becomes a tissue of fraud, perhaps without equal in the history of New World explorations.
Carl O. Sauer, 1941, rebutting Lansing Bloom

It is difficult for me to believe that any careful student of the twentieth century would seriously defend Marcos. . . . I myself know of no other character in all history who, so obviously unworthy, has been so zealously defended. So let us pigeonhole "The Lying Monk" with the other Munchausens of history; but we cannot then forget him, as one writer has recommended, for his fictionized narrative resulted in the greatest exploring enterprise ever undertaken in the New World.

Cleve Hallenbeck
American historian
1949, in his book, The Journey of Marcos de Niza

PART I

THE DISCOVERY OF CHICHILTI-CALLI

"The past was real.
The present, all about me,
was unreal, unnatural, repellent."

RICHARD HENRY DANA, 1859
in *Two Years Before the Mast*, visiting
the booming new city of San Francisco and lamenting the passage of the
old Spanish California he had known
twenty years earlier

CHAPTER 1

1998, France

After I escaped from Arizona to France with my life, my brain cleared. The coolness of Europe was refreshing after the blasting heat of Tucson, where everything seemed too bright, and everyone too busy. If southern California inspired film noir, southern Arizona inspires film blanc. In film noir the titles roll against a backdrop of the city at night, where there are "a thousand stories," but the story that trapped me was not one of those. It wasn't the dark submerged side of the iceberg, but the sunlit apex, the one big tale at the glittering top, dazzling everyone and yet hidden in plain sight like the eye of God atop the pyramid on the back of the buck. Arizona's crimes and misdemeanors happen under a blanched silver sun, when there is too much glare for anyone to notice what is happening.

Here in France I no longer feel crazed by the desert light. I feel safe at last. Which is why I decided to blow Mr. Rooney's cover. And I can begin to understand the string of subtle disasters that linked Marcos de Niza's life with mine. . . .

It's the south of France where I've hidden. Marcos de Niza—Marcos of Nice—came from somewhere around here. The connection between us seems like some thread, mysteriously winding through the labyrinth of space-time. When I fled Arizona, I felt as if the unseen spirit of Marcos guided me here to his homeland.

This is a region of dry hills, not unlike those of Cíbola and

Chichilti-Calli, the lands that Marcos discovered. Chichilti-Calli: I like to use that prehistoric name for my homeland, the region of southeast Arizona, where I grew up. It supports my belief that the present isn't the whole story.

An hour south of my little French town is the Mediterranean, with its unobstructed path out through the pillars of Hercules, leading to America and the constantly reinvented dream of Cíbola—the dream of instant wealth waiting for those who have the *cojones* to grab it. The sea was the shining path that took Marcos to a life he could never have imagined. Sometimes I drive down there in my cozy little Fiat, and hike up a hill and eat my lunch under a scraggly tree overlooking the blue, hazy waterscape, and I think of all the ships that passed this spot during the last three thousand years. Naturally, I focus on the one small ship that took Marcos away from Europe forever.

Was he a thin and earnest young man then? I imagine him on the deck, turning back to watch the blue-green hills of Europe fading in the sea haze. When he looked forward, what was his conception of Amerigo's new world, over the curved edge of the sea? Could he have dreamed of the Inca and Aztec cities? Could he dream that he would be the one chosen to look for the next golden kingdom? What were his expectations when he walked across the gangplank into the unknown soul of America?

Every time I think about Marcos, I get a peculiar feeling, and I wonder if he felt it too: the sensation that you were never intended for your own piece of space-time—your own country, your own century. Suddenly you find yourself out on the end of the sociological bell curve, as if the center had slithered beneath your feet when you weren't looking. All around you, people are saying crazy things. That's the way it seemed to me back in America as my life began to turn weird.

IT WAS BACK IN THE LATE '80S. I WAS MINDING MY OWN BUSINESS in Albuquerque. Kevin Scott, twenty-something city planner, following the American dream. There had been certain difficulties for me in '88, and I had put out feelers for a new job. Out of the blue came one of Mr. Rooney's minions with an offer. He introduced himself as Fred. "In the company they call me Freddy the Fixer. I'm Mr. Rooney's New Mexico rep, among other things."

Freddy the Fixer was bushy-tailed and enthusiastic, as if there was nothing to be ashamed of, working for an Arizona developer. He was a big guy, very neat, in a sport coat and tie. He looked like one of those ex-athletes who end up as sportscasters. "You'll be working for the best, Kevin. When Mr. Rooney puts his mind to a project, it always succeeds."

Rooney's name I had heard before, as I was growing up in Tucson. Never met him, but he seemed to be a presence lurking behind anything that made page one of the Metro section. Sometimes it took a couple of days for his name to surface in a story. "What do you do for him?" I asked Freddy the Fixer.

"Keep my eyes open for opportunities. A little lobbying in Santa Fe or Phoenix when a bad bill comes up before the state legislature. In this business, there's a lot of fires to be put out. But that's not the kind of stuff you'll have to worry about. You'll be back in Tucson, Kevin. Working on one of our biggest projects. You're lucky. Ground floor opportunity. I understand you grew up there. You'll be right at home."

"Why me?"

"Point one: You come highly recommended in city planning. Mr. Rooney made a few calls. He can use you. Point two, this is the part that'll hook you: Our project is called Coronado Estates. It's east of Tucson. Mr. Rooney says you are interested in Coronado."

How the hell had Rooney learned that? My Coronado days had been years before, when I was in college. Anyway, how could someone like me help someone like Rooney? The way I learned it in school, developers created urban sprawl, the planners tried to contain it. We were the yin and yang of the American city. They bought the land, shuffled the papers, and got the rezonings. Sometimes they built the houses, but sometimes they just resold the land to other builders. Their deals were million-dollar deals, which in turn gave them the political clout to keep the system going. Planners tried to maintain livable cities even as the cars poured in from the developers' suburbs and the new residents demanded more freeways, more schools, more water, more police. Developers worried about the present and cash flow; planners worried about the future and livability. It was a losing contest; the developers had the bucks and were always one jump ahead. But we were the good guys. As my professor said, somebody has to represent the trees. "Look," I told Freddy, "I don't think I'm your guy. My work in city planning has been for municipalities. Public interest. You guys are . . . how can I say? . . . the other side."

Freddy the Fixer looked personally disappointed. "Not any more, Kevin. Mr. Rooney, all the homebuilders, they've got the best planners working for them these days." I had my doubts about that. A lot of planners had gone to work for the developers, but they were regarded as having sold out. Talk about conflict of interest.

Freddy was continuing his pitch. "You're a smart guy, Kevin. You know the planning process. You know history. You're perfect. Mr. Rooney wants you. Listen. Coronado Estates will be a whole new town, out near Willcox. Retirement, commercial. Avoids sprawl near Tucson. Helps the rural economy. Win-win. Those little towns out there, Willcox, Benson, Tombstone, they're dying, man. They gotta bring in something new. Mr. Rooney wants Coronado Estates to be good, to respect the history of the area. That's where you come in. We want to have a good plan *before* we go to the county supervisors for approval." He scanned my face for signs. "Look at it this way. You could take a low government salary and review our plan for the county, or you could do the same thing for Mr. Rooney, and make twice as much money. What it does for us is minimize any revisions or extra hearings. The money he saves goes into your salary. How much were you making working for the City of Albuquerque?"

I mentioned a respectable salary for a young municipal worker bee in the 1980s.

"Oh, jeez, Kevin." Freddy's face registered even more disappointment and a flicker of repugnance, as if salaries of that level were evidence of moral flaws. "You can do better than that. Look at your credentials. Kevin Scott. Good track record. Reliable. Good references. What would you think of a hundred-percent raise? Doesn't that sound good to you?"

I was beginning to see why they called him Freddy the Fixer. To make a long story short, he arranged to fly me to Tucson to talk to Mr. Big. I still didn't admit to myself that I'd consider working for a developer, but I rationalized that the interview would be a growing experience. Besides, why turn down a free trip back to the old hometown?

I SHOULD GIVE YOU SOME BACKGROUND. I WAS BORN IN '59 IN THE same little Arizona town Freddy had mentioned, Willcox, dust sink of the universe. Our claim to fame was a caliche-covered dry lake bed on the edge of town, so big it showed up from space. When I was little we moved to Tucson, where my father got a job in the city traffic department, playing out his bit part in the city's explosive expansion. Anglo families like us had been pouring into the onetime Mexican hamlet since the 1800s, when the Yankees bought it from Mexico and put in the railroad. The first trains brought Easterners who tore down the old Spanish presidio fort to get adobe bricks to build their Victorian houses, which still dotted the downtown. I was Mr. Anglo Everyman—six feet, 150 pounds, brownish hair, bluish eyes, pale-ish skin, approaching 30, thinking maybe it was time to get some money in the bank.

I had civic affairs in my blood. Politics, my father said; somebody has to do it. My mother, who had grown up in Kansas, gave me a direct psychological pipeline to innocent ideals of an earlier generation. She placed an overly high value on sincerity. She figured every guy is a good guy in his own mind. She approached every argument with the assumption that the person on the other side was sincere. When the papers caught someone in a scandal, she'd say, "He must have believed in what he was doing." Some of that rubbed off on me.

That mind-set left me unprepared to deal with people to whom sincerity is irrelevant, to whom victory is the only thing that counts. I just wasn't given the parental training to deal with people like Mr. Rooney, who once instructed me that "Sincerity isn't much of a factor when it comes to winning."

When I was ten, I had a boyhood pal, Edward ————. I don't want to use his last name because I fear for him. He knows too much. To be more precise, he's seen too much. In those days, the Apollo astronauts were bringing back pictures of fragile little Earth as seen from the moon. Edward and I were enthralled. We spent that summer firing off little rockets made of paper tubes filled with match heads. We couldn't understand it when public interest suddenly waned after the first few landings. During the first mission, everybody stayed home and watched while Neil Armstrong stepped onto the moon. By the last mission, three years later, nobody cared. We did sociology by standing in the supermarket during that last moonwalk, and discovered that nobody was talking about the adventure. We couldn't believe the customers, looking bored as they bought instant coffee and the *National Enquirer* while men were actually up there walking around among the craters. We were crushed and disillusioned when the Apollo program was canceled for lack of interest.

Still, the pictures from space caused environmentalists to invent Earth Day. We saw the first glimmers of a new, planetary consciousness. That's when Americans resurrected Teddy Roosevelt–era ideas of conservation and city planning. Children of those years, Edward and I in 1977 went to the University of Arizona in Tucson, a.k.a. Great Desert University, a.k.a. GDU, an acronym with various interpretations. We were idealistic; we wanted to do good. College idealists of the '60s had the Peace Corps. Edward and I had city planning. It was a glorious new age, as it always is if you are an idealist in college. Our new paradigm said that urban sprawl was like a spreading grass fire with flames around its edge, leaving ashes in the middle. Civic energy and city budgets struggled to keep up with the new services needed on the peripheries of towns, carving out freeways like fire lanes, and turning downtowns into exhausted ghettos. We were taught the new dream: a partnership between planners, neighborhood associations, and local elected officials to solve these problems before they occurred. It seemed like common sense. However, I failed to realize the passion with which Arizonans of that era equated prudent planning with big-government oppression, antithetical to the all-American goal of life, liberty, and the pursuit of frat-party frivolity.

The fateful event that led to my later disasters was the night Edward and I sat in our little college apartment on Hawthorne Street, and took a pledge to sample as many subjects as we could. We signed up for courses in science, philosophy, history—everything we could fit in. We got interested in writing, wrote sci-fi stories. Edward took up a minor in journalism. We read novels from many countries, and nonfiction about quantum mechanics, assassinations, and amino acids in space. It was the history course that led me to a fascination with Coronado and those first Europeans, clinking and clanking their way north from Mexico into the unknown.

You could call us snobs if you like, but Edward and I recognized we were different from most of the other students, who were satisfied with sex, *cerveza* and Cs. We liked sex, *cerveza*, Bs, travel, hiking, books, hieroglyphics, and the expanding universe. Actually, we liked As. One day came the horrible realization, somewhere in our junior year, that the others were the ones who would soon be running the country and earning all the money. We would be condemned to a lower level of the economic food chain, where new ideas form. Okay, like I said, you can call us snobs if you like.

In 1981, we found ourselves fresh out of GDU, with degrees in city planning. I had a minor in history and ecology. Edward and I spent that first summer doing the free-spirit, neo-hippy thing: bumming around Mexico. We traveled down the mainland coast of the Gulf of California, once known as the Sea of Cortés. We started at the north end, at funky Puerto Peñasco, where the old shrimping economy was being killed off by overfishing, and where seedy Mexican motels with marginal plumbing were just beginning to be replaced by grand new resorts with great cantinas on bright, end-less beaches. Word on the street was that the new money came from American investors and Chihuahuan drug lords. We worked our way south down the state of Sonora into an older time: Kino Bay and Guaymas, sunsets and Seri Indians carving roadrunner sculptures from the last of the ironwood trees. Dumpy little *taquerias* run by kindly people. We talked books and debated politics in the wee hours as the full moon set over the gulf. We enjoyed Dos Equis, margaritas, and college ladies on summer vacation. Eventually we had to head back north, toward real life, but now I remember that Edward on that last day in Kino Bay said he wanted to come back to Mexico and stay forever. Mexico made him want to take up writing, and as soon as he scraped some money together, that's what he'd do.

"The world is changing," he said that afternoon as we sat watching the sea in a beachside cantina. "People will look back and see this century as the great transition. Somebody has to write down what's happening so the next generation can understand it. Future Mexico will never be the same as the country we've just experienced. Even Arizona . . ."

When we got back, Edward disappeared into a planning job in Los Angeles, but I knew he would make good on his dream one day. For me, Mexico was only my moment to let off steam. I admit that during the eighties, when the dream of the New Frontier finally died, I got caught up in the yuppie tide. I got a planning job in Albuquerque and drove my carload of stuff to New Mexico. A year or so later, by some cosmic accident, I found myself married with a Nice House, a Yard, a Dog, and a Gerbil. Two cars. Gasoline. Nightly news. The whole catastrophe, as Zorba called it. If you live that life, you think it's normal. I forgot about history.

Edward and I exchanged Christmas cards every year, saying we'd have to get together soon.

Everything was short-lived. After a couple of years, the bright excitement of young adult life in the Southwest began to fade under my own private cloud of personal stresses: deadlines at the office, arguments at home, and ceaseless assignments to mitigate civic conflicts. Amidst the expanding urban and suburban chaos along the Rio Grande Valley, we had the business community, mostly Anglo, and the Hispanic barrios, and the Native American tribal communities. It was an unholy mix. Anglo businesspeople operate at a higher karmic frequency than the Hispanic communities, and the Hispanics, in turn, operate at a higher karmic frequency than the Native American communities, who operate in the subsonic range at one change per year—a deep frequency that permeates everything without the rest of us realizing it.

It all culminated in an amicable divorce in the summer of '88 and a layoff a month later. I began looking for jobs, which put me on the road to Mr. Rooney.

Oh—the amicable divorce was with the Albuquerque Planning Department. The City Council decided to downsize us. It was my wife who fired me. She also took the dog and the gerbil.

I remember the timing because it coincided with the climax of the presidential campaign. Passions were running high. It made me wonder if statistics showed more divorces during presidential campaigns. This one was especially revolting; the campaign, I mean. The papers were full of debates about the flag, which had lain in some Republican closet for the last four years. Now it was carried forth and unfurled by political marketing flunkies, and the campaign devolved into a debate about whether Mr. Dukakis, the plucky Democratic candidate, loved the American flag as much as Vice President George Bush did. This enabled the candidates and their handlers to act excited about something without having to deal with actual issues. For a few weeks the flag became a transcendent symbol beyond any logical reality, the center of a firestorm, like the sad flags carried into the heart of the battle at Gettysburg. The flag won the battle because everyone knew which party loved the flag the most. After the Democrats lost the election, the flag was folded quietly back into its musty box to rest until it would be needed again.

By that time I was out on my own. After the divorce, I agonized for a long time. Intellectually, I realized our relationship had completed some sort of cycle, had come to a clean end. Still, my failed marriage was a Pandora's box, and every time I opened it, serpents of regret and jealousy crawled out to torment me. Edward knew about it from my Christmas card and wrote to me consolingly. He said his own job and relationships were only so-so. He speculated that his malaise was due to some poison in the car exhaust hanging over Los Angeles. He said he was bailing at last, and heading to Mexico. He said I'd hear from him as soon as he got settled. His parting advice—California advice—was that I should also find a new venue. That was when Freddy the Fixer arrived. Meanwhile, a transitional woman in Albuquerque had renewed my self-confidence. Pandora's box had became a nice piece of furniture in the living room of my life.

A WEEK BEFORE CHRISTMAS, FREDDY THE FIXER LED ME INTO A tall Tucson office building and up the elevator to the sumptuous offices of Rooney Development, Inc. The building was the kind that represented success among downtown financial subcultures the world over. The elevators and bathrooms were full of tacky brass and marble and vinyl imitations of leather. They were derived from the accouterments of aristocracy five hundred years ago, handed down as status symbols in our "democratic" society where all men [sic] are allegedly born equal.

The first thing I noticed as I came out of the elevator was the breathtaking view from the foyer window. We could look down on the shiny blue tile dome of the Polvoroso County Courthouse, a landmark of an earlier Tucson, a city that was proud of its heritage.

The next thing I noticed, as I walked through the glass doors into the office, was the woman in the red dress, who sat behind the desk outside Mr. Rooney's door. She looked as bright and cheery as the packages under the office Christmas tree.

"Oh, that's Phaedra," Freddy whispered, noticing my look. "Everybody wants to get to know her, if you get my drift." He introduced me, and repeated his line in front of her, "Everybody who comes in here wants to meet Phaedra," as if he were saying it for the first time.

She rolled her eyes, big brown ones, as if she had heard it a hundred times before. Then she looked at me. "Hello, Kevin Scott," she said. Freddy hadn't mentioned my name.

Freddy took me back to his small but plush office where my employment papers lay in a neat stack, ready to sign. One of them was a list of Five Commandments. "Mr. Rooney's got these rules of motivation for winning teams," Freddy was saying as he handed it over. "First, there's honesty of communication between employees. . . ."

"You don't have to give me the inspirational—"

"Mr. Rooney would want me to. He wants me to go over all this with the new employees."

"Look, I'm twenty-nine. I've worked with mayors, city councils. . . ." I didn't like business-speak. It reminded me of sermons by TV preachers.

Freddy looked annoyed. "Well, at least take the paper. He wrote these rules himself."

I looked at the next rule. TELL ME THE GOOD, THE BAD, AND THE UGLY, it said. IF TIME IS SHORT, TELL ME ONLY THE BAD AND THE UGLY. I ignored the rest. "Tell me about work," I said.

Phaedra's voice interrupted from Freddy's intercom. "Mr. Rooney's ready."

She ushered us into the inner sanctum. Even on that first day, I enjoyed watching the way she moved, her open, square face, and the way her thick, dark hair fell around her shoulders. She turned to leave the office and Freddy the Fixer excused himself. I imagined him hanging around outside the door, putting the moves on her.

Mr. Rooney's office wasn't what I expected. In contrast to the building, it was surprisingly plain. That's when I realized a law of twentieth-century life in the fast lane: the more powerful the executive, the less clutter on the desk. Have you ever seen a picture of the president with piles of paper on his desk? Alpha males who make decisions that degrade whole communities do it from desks that carry only a phone and an iconic picture of the current wife. On one wall Mr. Rooney had a large, simply framed painting of the Sulfur Springs Valley. Aerial photos of it dominated the second wall, and a large topographic map of the development, the third. The fourth wall was an enormous, floor-to-ceiling window, looking out from the tenth floor across the sunlit city toward the jagged blue Catalina Mountains with their white Stetson hat of listless clouds. The glass was thick and tinted, making the view seem detached from reality, like a live TV picture of breaking news from the KHIP newscam. The glass seemed to filter out various dimensions, leaving only a two-D image as hollow as an empty warehouse. Air entered the room through ceiling vents. A few chairs were scattered on one side around a large table.

The aura of power and success came not from the furnishings, but from Mr. Rooney himself. He was in his early sixties, but looked a decade or more younger. He was tanned, his cheeks ruddy. He looked as if he had just come back from a tennis vacation. When I first shook hands with him, he reminded me of powerful figures on the international news. His smooth skin looked like vinyl. The way he combed his shining titanium-colored hair straight back reminded me of a Soviet party apparatchik in some Eastern European government of that decade; you could tell just from his grooming that his daughters and sons were fated to a life of ease, and that his wife traveled in a late-model car to proper charitable functions, where she would be photographed for the pages of the local journal of upscale pretension, *Sunshine Lifestyle*.

HE CAUGHT ME LOOKING AROUND THE OFFICE AND READ MY expression. He had an uncanny way of reading expressions. "You look like you were expecting something more posh, Mr. Scott." He laughed. The laugh fit comfortably on his face. He seemed very relaxed. "A bigger office, maybe? I never let the office get too fancy. Sometimes, the wrong kind of people come in here and they think I'm making too much money. Politicians. A lot of people these days, they think it's a sin to make too much money; did you know that? They don't realize that the very *possibility* of making too much money is what drives the economy. So they start inventing special taxes and restrictions on your property rights."

Already he was lecturing me about property rights.

"Not you, of course. You wouldn't feel that way. The money we make pays for your job."

"I don't have a job, yet."

"Oh, right," he said, absentmindedly. He smiled and so I smiled. "Well, we're here to remedy that. You're just the guy I need."

"Why is that?"

He paused. I think it was then that he took a shine to me. "You know, a lot of guys in your position, they'd come crawling. But I like your attitude. No guff."

"The good, the bad, and the ugly. Tell you the ugly first."

"Hey, that's good. A lot of guys, they don't read my five rules. But you did, eh? That's one reason I need you around here. But the real reason is, you're perfect for the job."

He started explaining the situation. After a developers' bidding war, he had bought up a huge old ranch out in the Sulfur Springs Valley north of Willcox, and filed a rezoning request with the county, to develop a new town. It would be a satellite community of Tucson, an hour's drive beyond the east end of town. It would be beautiful, stretching from rolling hills down into the grassy flats. There were complaints, he admitted cheerfully. The local ranchers wanted the area to remain rural and peaceful. And then there were the Tucson environmentalists. "Hardly any of them have been out there," he said scornfully, "but suddenly it's important to them. Our goal is to convince all those people that we're doing a quality project." He gestured toward the big painting of the valley. "Nothing stays the same," he summarized. "The challenge is to make changes that people will like."

As he talked, I had to admit that the whole thing was a city planner's dream. It would be far enough away from Tucson to avoid urban sprawl. It would also divert Tucson's growth in a way that would revitalize nearby struggling little towns like Benson, Bisbee, and my very own Willcox. High-end houses with big lots, around the periphery of the development, would mitigate the impact on the adjacent ranches and national forest land.

Mr. Rooney had the initial approval from the zoning commission, subject to some changes in the site plan, but the final approval from the county supervisors was supposed to happen in April, four months away. Everything had to be ready: revised site plan, maps, supporting info.

That's where I came in. "Coronado Estates, we call it. From what I can tell, Coronado's whole damn army probably marched right across our property. That gives us historical cachet. But we've got to document it. I've been looking into it. There's a lot of material we can use."

Developers are fashionably portrayed as narrow individuals because of their obsession with the bottom line, the deal—the money. But Mr. Rooney was different. As he talked, I realized he had educated himself about some unexpected things. He already had the broad outline of exploration in the Coronado era, and he knew some of the historical controversies. I was impressed; but at that time I didn't recognize the difference between knowing and caring.

"What I want," Mr. Rooney was saying, "is someone who can do some research, write up some documentation, show we're sensitive to the heritage of the property. I called up the history department over at the university. Dr. Panofsky and that crowd. Panofsky himself told me about you. You're *perfect*! He's the one that told me you studied urban planning and history, and wrote a term paper for him on Coronado."

"Actually it was Marcos de Niza."

"Marcos . . . oh, the priest. The fraud. I read about him. Conned Coronado into expecting gold in the Seven Cities of Cíbola. They say he made up the whole thing. Clever fellow."

"Yeah, well. . . . He did reconnoiter the route, a year before Coronado."

"Fine. Stick him in there too. Adds color. Mystery. Anything you can do in that direction is good. You can work on the documentation at least half-time. There's some planning and layout issues for you to work on, too. What d'ya say? Nothing's gonna happen around here till after New Year's. You could start in January. Go have Christmas, take a few weeks to get organized then come in for work. New year, new job."

WHAT CAN I SAY? I SIGNED ON. BY THIS TIME MY LITTLE SISTER was unaccountably producing offspring with a dorky husband she had acquired in San Diego, so my parents had moved to San Diego to glory in the grandparenting scene and the beach. It would be fun being in Tucson again, on my own. The money would be excellent. I would actually be able to start laying away some savings. I flew to San Diego for Christmas, flew back to Albuquerque before New Year's, piled my stuff in the car, and headed to Tucson. I was on the road at midnight when the new year came in, crossing Coronado's tracks. I found an apartment and was on the job in January '89, four hundred fifty years to the month after Marcos de Niza moved to Culiacán and prepared to plunge north, into the unknown.

HERE IN FRANCE, FOR THE FIRST FEW YEARS I KEPT LOOKING OVER my shoulder, but then things began to seem normal, safe, and healthy. The keeper of my favorite café, where I come to write this memoir, likes to tease me about being American. "America, oh yes, I've heard of that country. Indistinguishable cars at indistinguishable speeds, but no one can figure out why they want to go anywhere, because all the towns are the same. One of our writers said that. She said no one in America knows how to relax."

His little joke still hurts because I had been one of those unrelaxed people trying to build one of those indistinguishable towns. It was a hard decision, to join Mr. Rooney's outfit, but the job started off just great.

One day early in February, I got called into Mr. Rooney's. "The boss wants to talk about Coronado," Phaedra said. When she ushered me in, she gave me one of her furtive smiles, which seemed to imply there was a story behind this little talk—a story she knew and I didn't. She was nearly as tall as I was. She had great legs.

Mr. Rooney didn't look up, so I scanned the city panorama out his window. I looked for my neighborhood, but it was hard to relate the view in this cool office to my new life on one of those sunny little streets in the distance.

Suddenly I realized he was watching me. "Let's talk about this document you're gonna write," he said abruptly. "It'll be like a position paper. A lot of people in my business, they're *afraid* of the history of their area. A little history can be a lot of *trouble*. People use it as an excuse to avoid trying anything *new*." I noticed that whenever he started selling his ideas, he tended to emphasize one word in every sentence or two.

"I have this *vision*," he continued, radiating pink, polished enthusiasm. "In our project, we don't hide our history, we build on it. We're a quality outfit. You can't just lay out streets and put up houses anymore. There has to be something *special*. I don't mean a gimmick. The development at Starr Pass, for example, they use a fake stagecoach in their clubhouse, 'cause there used to be a stage stop out there. They're on the right track, but I want something real, something people in our area will be proud about. Coronado. All that glamor. *Conquistadores*." He gave it an impressive Spanish pronunciation. "A lot of people use conquistadors and Spanish helmets for a logo, like out at El Con Country Club. But we've got the real thing, right? I mean, those guys actually marched across there, somewhere. Within a few miles. For sure, they nicked southeast Arizona. I've been reading a lot of that history. It's kinda fun, like a hobby. My wife laughs at me."

I couldn't believe it: Were Mr. Rooney and I destined to be co-hobbyists? "Anyway," he was saying, "we can *use* our history. Our company can be a *source* of information about the history of the area. People would get *interested*. Cultural heritage. *Esprít de corps*. Know what I mean? I want people who live there to *care* about the place; they will be part of its continuing *story*."

The bottom line was that I was supposed to get busy reviewing the archaeology and history of the area, document Coronado's route, and write up a summary. Then I was to work with the marketing people to distill it into a brochure. "We'll distribute it," said Mr. Rooney. "We'll state that if anyone wants the longer report, they can get a copy of your original from us. We can publish the whole damn thing if there is enough interest. With *pictures*. Like a *book*. So write it, you know, good." He scowled. "I'm tired of people saying that developers rape the land. We'll show them we *care* about what we're doing. Think of that; a book. That would gain us some *respect*."

"I'll get on it."

He paused. "Back in December, when you were in here for your interview, and you thought my office was plainer than you expected, you remember that?"

"Um . . . yes."

"Some day I'll invite you out to my house. That's where I *pamper* my wife and myself. And that's where I invite my investors, to impress them with our success. The luxuries I've earned. As for the public office, keep it simple. There; that's a little secret for you."

I wondered why he wanted to let me in on a secret of the business. I didn't verbalize this question, but he said, "I'm telling you this because you're a smart kid. You got a good letter of recommendation from Albuquerque, you know. Some kids I get in here, they don't know their ass from a hole in the ground."

I shifted uneasily in my chair while he stared out the window.

"Oh, one more thing. We're gonna have street names centered around Coronado and his boys. Colorful characters from those days. I've already decided we'll name the main street Cíbola Trail, since they were looking for the Seven Cities of Cíbola. But the cross streets could have names of people like Coronado himself, or your Marco fellow. So get me list of more names. What about the guy that wrote the chronicle of the expedition. Castillo?"

"Castañeda. There were other chroniclers, too. After they got home, a lot of them wrote their—"

"Right. Bring me a list, ASAP. Each street will have a decorative plaque about its namesake. People'll be proud to live in our town."

When I came out, Freddy was gone, and I told Phaedra I'd be bringing a list of colorful names. She examined me through narrowed eyes, as if appraising something. Already I was trying to find little excuses to stop by her desk. There she was, every day, outside Mr. Rooney's office in her killer dresses, daring anyone to cross her threshold. "Streets named after interesting historical figures, connected with land," I said to her. "It's good. It reminds me of a European novel I read once, *In Praise of Older Women*. The hero comes from Europe to America but becomes disillusioned by the street names. He says he'd rather live in a town where the streets and parks were named after the region's great artists and poets, instead of mayors, developers, and developers' wives."

It turned out that was the right thing to say. Phaedra looked up from her computer. She actually looked interested! "Who wrote that?" she said.

"Someone named Vizinczey, I think. Hungarian. Anyway, he thought the names should celebrate people who make things that don't lose value with inflation."

She winced. "You don't have anything against making money, do you?"

"No, but I like books. I used to read novels like that. Now that I'm working here, my reading time seems to be disappearing."

She smiled. "Well, if you have anything against making money, you're working at the wrong place. 'Course, the trouble with most of the guys here is, that's *all* they're interested in." She continued smiling, like it was her own private joke, but it felt good that she was smiling at me. Later I learned she was a voracious reader.

In retrospect, a lot of my problems revolved around Phaedra. She was a disturbing presence. Her voice had a strange, wistful quality that made me want to know her past. I was distracted by her dark, auburn-tinted hair, falling around her shoulders. Sometimes she wore it up; it made her neck and shoulders seem exposed. . . . I liked to watch her when she stood up. I found it exciting to meet her dark eyes at the same level as mine.

A DAY LATER I HAD A LIST OF NAMES: MARCOS DE NIZA, ESTEVAN, Castañeda, Jaramillo, Díaz, Mendoza. There were a lot of characters from that era whose names and personalities were known. Casually I dropped off my list at Phaedra's desk.

She looked it over. "Where do you get information about this stuff?" she asked me.

"There are whole books of letters and reports from that period."

"You should show me, sometime."

It was fun flirting with her. Still, for those first months, I held to my quaint belief in the separation of powers: executive and judicial, church and state, business and pleasure.

ONE DAY WE MET BY ACCIDENT DURING OUR LUNCH BREAK AT A little café near the office. We sat in a patio under Tucson's balmy blue winter sky. Around us, at other tables, other couples talked intensely, men and women from other downtown offices, laughing and subliminally negotiating their sexual contracts. She let me a little more into her world by telling me—in hushed tones—secrets about Mr. Rooney. "His father emigrated from Lithuania when the Russians took over after the war. Pulled themselves up by the bootstraps. There's a funny story. His father ran a Cadillac dealership in Fort Worth. The family name was actually Rubi. They were high rollers, and the son, our boss, went into Texas oil speculation in a big way. He went bust just about the time of the Kennedy assassination. His first name was John, and everyone called him Jack, and suddenly people were associating him with Jack Ruby, the nightclub owner who shot Oswald. I think he felt disgraced on all counts. He told me he decided to chuck everything and start all over. So he moved out here to start over in real estate and changed his name to Rooney. Thought it sounded more American. Like Mickey Rooney."

We laughed.

Phaedra looked pensive. "Don't tell anyone I told you. I think it bothers him, that episode. He told me about it once after work when he was letting his hair down. I remember him saying, 'I'm not *that* Jack Ruby. After all, I don't run a sleazy gambling operation.'"

"Actually, he does," I said. "It ain't called land speculation for nothing."

We laughed again.

WHEN IT CAME TO PREPARING THE REPORT MR. ROONEY WANTED, I had a secret weapon. My old term paper about the Coronado period was buried somewhere in my boxes of college stuff. All I had to do was find it.

I rooted through the old cardboard boxes piled in the back of the closet in my new apartment. Other kids threw out their college books and papers ASAP; as you can guess, I had saved mine. I had to cut through eight-year-old tape to get into the box marked HISTORY-SOCIOLOGY-ECONOMICS. The job had taken a new twist. I found myself thinking: it's going to be fun. I would get paid for renewing my acquaintance with those enigmatic Spaniards, and daydreaming about their adventures at the dawn of Euro-American time.

My term paper was there, and some Xeroxes of various editions of old Spanish reports and letters I had used. I riffled through the pages. It brought back memories. The discovery of the Southwest: Coronado's and mine. I loved that old stuff. My paper set the scene as well as anything I could write now.

Understanding the Southwest's first contact between Natives and Europeans requires us to see today's borderlands as the conquistadors did—tierra incognita, beyond their northern frontier. In Mexico City in 1520, Cortés had conquered the Aztecs (or as they called themselves, Mexica, pronounced me-SHEE-ca), with their palaces of golden treasure. In Peru in 1533, Pizarro had conquered the Incas, capturing even more booty.

*America seemed to have cities of gold over every horizon, wait-
ing their turn to be conquered by Europe and Christianity.*

By the mid 1530s, the northern frontier of New Spain was
halfway up present-day Mexico, a month's travel from Mexico
City. No one knew what lay further to the north. For a decade,
many Spaniards had speculated that Mexico might be an
island or peninsula off Asia, and that further north and west
lay the fabled riches of Cathay. In the devastated Aztec capital,
young, would-be conquistadors cooled their heels and dreamed
of new conquests. Bastard sons of great families, with no
chance to inherit the family lands in Europe, they lay awake in
the perfumed night, amid the ruins of pagan temples, dreaming of making their fortunes by finding another fabulous
empire. The resonance of a thousand dreams made a tide. . . .

In 1536, a pivotal event transpired on the frontier. Into Spanish slave-raiding camps wandered four survivors of a 1528
Spanish shipwreck on the Texas coast near Galveston. They
were three Spaniards and a Moor: Álvar Cabeza de Vaca,
Alonso Castillo, Andrés Dorantes, and Dorantes's Moorish servant, named Estevan, sometimes later called Estevan Dorantes
by the Spaniards. Cabeza de Vaca wrote a book about their
epic journey, describing how they had survived for eight years,
wandering among Indian tribes in what we now know as west
Texas and the U.S.–Mexico border. Always they pushed west and
then south, trying to find their way back to the Spanish colonies
in Mexico. In each new region, they established themselves as
traveling shamans, especially with the help of the charismatic,
dark-skinned Estevan, whom they also called "the black."
Somewhere near the present-day border, probably near El Paso,
they picked up rumors of a major trading center, north of their
route. The Indians there gave Dorantes a copper bell, said to
come from this wealthy northern region. The castaways pressed
on, west from El Paso across the continental divide, and then
south through the present-day Mexican state of Sonora, until

they stumbled onto a party of Spanish soldiers, near the modern border of Sonora and Sinaloa, a week or so north of the provincial headquarters in the still-existing town of Culiacán.

The soldiers were troops of a notorious governor, Nuño Guzmán, who operated out of Culiacán, raiding native villages in southern Sonora for slaves that would be sent to mines and haciendas of wealthy Spanish settlers. Guzmán and others had already picked up vague rumors of major cities far to the north. The arrival of the four castaways with their news of a northern trade center confirmed the dreams of the Spaniards about an undiscovered empire in that direction. Dorantes' copper bell seemed to establish metalsmithing in that land. Everyone assumed it must be another city of gold. The news spread like wildfire.

The pages of my report were yellowing. I shuffled through it, marveling that a different me, a decade before, had written this, and how that earlier me had no idea what would come from that act, or how events would link together in strange ways. The paper went on:

In those days Mexico City was governed by an able administrator, Viceroy Antonio Mendoza. This "vice royal", or vice king, was appointed directly by the King of Spain to represent the royal court in the new world. The original conqueror, Cortés, was out of favor, having lost much of the wealth he took from the Aztecs. As early as 1523, the King had appointed a new treasurer to crack down on accounting procedures. Sulking and restless, Cortés moved west, to the coast, and started building ships, exploring what we know as the Gulf of California. He, too, had heard the vague early rumors of cities in the north. In 1535, he established a short-lived colony on Baja California—which was thought to be an exotic island. These naval explorations led to the unofficial name for the gulf: the Sea of Cortés. By 1537, Cortés was building more ships to sail farther up the gulf, an effort now spurred by the castaways' new rumors of a rich empire in that direction. Cortés still claimed that northern exploration was his right, as the original conqueror of Mexico.

Viceroy Mendoza answered these challenges by forbidding any further northward explorations unless authorized by the royal authorities, i.e., himself. This would prevent Cortés from getting the upper hand in the north. After Cabeza de Vaca and his castaways complained about Nuño Guzmán's treatment of the natives, Mendoza also arrested Guzmán. In 1538, the able viceroy appointed a friend, Francisco Vázquez de Coronado, to be the new governor of the province around Culiacán.

At the same time, Mendoza acted to learn more about the mysterious north by sending his own, semisecret land expedition to probe in that direction and check out the rumors about wealthy cities. He wanted no repeat of Cortés's military heavy-handedness or Guzmán's slave-raiding atrocities. In 1536–37, he tried to recruit one of the Spanish castaways, Andrés Dorantes, to lead a small party, but that fell through. Next year, he succeeded. As head of his quiet expedition, he chose a priest of good reputation, Marcos de Niza, who would travel with a group of native allies, and an intriguing guide—none other than Estevan, Dorantes's Moorish servant, who had already shown his mettle in the northern area. Marcos left Mexico City with Coronado in the fall of 1538, with secret orders to explore the northern coast and seek the rumored northern empire.

In September of the same year, Cortés made a countermove. He complained about Mendoza's edict to the Council of the Indies, the Supreme Court of New Spain, noting that he, Cortés the conqueror, already had nine ships ready to sail north and explore the new frontier. . . .

Looking at my old report whetted my appetite for the thrilling days of yesteryear. The reports I had gathered were full of eyewitness accounts of the first European writers in America. Many

Spaniards of that generation, such Cabeza de Vaca, Cortés, Friar
Marcos, Viceroy Mendoza, and Governor Coronado, along with
several of Coronado's soldiers, drafted letters, reports, and memoirs about their adventures. Each document gives a snapshot of life
in the Southwest literally on the last day of prehistoric time.

But where were they when they made those observations? Marcos, for example, carefully described his pioneering journey north
beyond the frontier, in which he reported the first details of the
northern empire. But when he described a river or a village, where
was it? And was he telling the truth? If so, why had he gone down
in history as a liar? Suddenly, I realized that my old term paper had
left me a legacy of deeper questions. In the intervening years, I had
matured enough to appreciate them. What was the story of the discovery of my own land? How did people become labeled as heroes
or villains? What were the real stories behind the sketchy, jingois-
tic histories we had been taught in school?

Mr. Rooney didn't quite realize it, but he had put me right in the
middle of a 450-year-old controversy among the historians. Did the
route of Marcos and Coronado take them into Arizona near our
property? Did Marcos really reach Cíbola as he said, or did he run
out of time and turn back before even crossing the modern border,
as many historians charged? Some of the historians claimed he had
a secret pact with Viceroy Mendoza to concoct a fabrication, in
order to trigger the expedition of conquest. If so, why did Mendoza
and Coronado gamble their fortunes on the fraudulent venture?

Everyone in college said you couldn't make money at history.
Who'd have guessed I'd ever get paid real cash to explore these
mysteries, these early loves?

SOMETIMES AT WORK I'D FEEL PHAEDRA'S EYES TRACKING ME AS I
passed within sight of Mr. Rooney's outer office. Our daily banter
was still mostly about movies, books, and office gossip. She was
always carrying a paperback or two, a best-seller, or poetry, and
she always seemed to be up to date on the latest opinions. She was
the only person I knew who dipped into the ponderous articles in

the *New Yorker*. One day when she told me about a book she was reading, I was able to tell her I had read it.

"You read *that*?" she said, arching one eyebrow. It was as if she never expected to meet a man who had read what she had read. "That makes you an interesting man." I told her of course I was an interesting man, and what's more, she was an interesting woman. Her response was, "Are you messing with my mind, Mr. Scott?" Maybe I was. It was a promising conversation. I began to reappraise my policy about business and pleasure.

CHAPTER 2

Voices from the Past

In the office and at home in the evenings I started rereading some of the old documents. The Spanish of the Coronado era were good yarn spinners. Not for nothing had their countrymen, like Cervantes, helped invent the modern novel in the late 1500s. You didn't need some modern interpreter of popular history to follow the story.

In terms of my assignment, the problem was that those old guys couldn't tell me where they were. Even if you handed them a modern map, they wouldn't know. All they could say was that they crossed a river here, or a mountain pass there. I knew that if I were to create a convincing estimate of Coronado's route vis-a-vis Mr. Rooney's property, I'd need to combine all the accounts by different travelers, compare their different descriptions of the same areas, compare it with modern and historic maps, and add a sprinkling of the latest archaeological research.

Of all the characters in the story, Marcos de Niza was the one who grabbed me from the start, the one who had been called the lying monk. Yet he was a priest, and had a good reputation, at least in some quarters. If he really fabricated the report of his exploration, then why did he do it? You couldn't fault his courage. He was the first European to probe northward into the unknown lands of the modern American Southwest. He became the most controversial figure of the era, a man definitely apart from the others. There had to be a story there. . . .

Not much was known about the guy. There were brief biographical notes by a Franciscan priest and historian, Pedro Oroz, around 1585, based on information available at that time. Oroz said that Marcos was a native and citizen of Aquitaine, a Franciscan province in what is now the south of France, including the city of Nice. Hence Marcos de Niza. Marcos of Nice. No one knows his exact birth date, but it must have been about the same time as the idea of America itself, which was born in European minds between 1492, when Columbus stumbled onto his first island, and 1502, when Vespucci returned from mapping the South American coast.

You see, it was somewhere around my little town in France that Marcos grew up. I might as well admit that I like to think Marcos came from the very village where I am living. As I sit in my café at a little table under a tree and gaze back in time, it's not hard to imagine Marcos, that orphaned French-Italian kid, dreaming his adolescent dreams among the placid cows and grassy hills. He was put in a religious school, and was associated with the old monastery in Nice, whose foundations, marked by a small sign, now lie under a busy intersection. In 1531 he became a priestly emissary from the Catholic world order to a land as new and strange as Mars. In a popular 1507 book about Vespucci's discoveries, the mapmaker Waldseemuller, in northern France, had named the land America. Perhaps Marcos read the book and used the name.

Oroz recorded that after Marcos left Europe in 1531, he landed at the colony on the Caribbean island of Española, and then departed for a post in Peru, which was just being conquered. One of the most interesting documents about Marcos was a horrendous affidavit about what he saw during the Peruvian conquest. This document was published by a famous historian-priest of that era, Bartolomé de Las Casas, a Dominican priest about twenty years older than Marcos. Las Casas was already an archenemy of the New World establishment. He dared to preach the humanity of the Indie-ans—the natives of the new lands, collectively known as the Indies. He attacked the conquistadors for their exploitation of these hapless people. He campaigned against the *encomienda* system, in which individual Spaniards were granted baronial control over whole districts and villages. Theoretically, Indian workers had to be paid for their labor, but in practice, as Las Casas documented, the payments were pitiful and the system degenerated into the age-old exploitation of the have-nots by the haves. Thinly disguised slavery evolved within the rickety legal system. Critics of Las Casas embellished reality, that he was merely a propagandist. They say he single-handedly created the so-called Black Legend, a myth that the conquistadors were crueler than they really were. This remains uncertain. Even if Las Casas exaggerated individual incidents, he seems to have been true to the tone of what was going on.

To buttress his claims, Las Casas collected material from many witnesses, including Marcos de Niza. In his book, published in Seville in 1552, Las Casas says he knew Marcos personally and that he got the Peruvian account directly from him, as eyewitness testimony of what was going on during the conquest of the Incas. Furthermore, Las Casas says that no less an authority than the Bishop of Mexico City himself, Zumárraga, affirmed this to be what Marcos wrote. Marcos's account gives an eyewitness picture of America's first efforts to get rich quick:

I, Fray Marcos de Niza, of the order of St. Francis, commissary in Peru over the friars of that order, who were some of the first Christians to enter those provinces, speak out in order to give a truthful account of certain matters which I saw with my own eyes in that country.

Through various experiences I found out that the Indians of Peru are among the most benevolent people that have been found among all the Indians. . . . They are friendly toward the Christians and I saw that they gave the Spaniards an abundance of gold, silver, and precious stones, and everything asked of them, whatever they possessed or could be helpful. They also received the Spaniards with kindness and honor in their towns, furnishing them with food and whatever slaves they asked for. . . . Their great lord, Atahualpa, gave these Spaniards more than two millions in gold and all the country in his possession very soon after the Spanish entered that country.

Yet, soon after Atahualpa gave the Spaniards his gold, and without provocation from the Indians, the Spaniards executed him. And after him they burned alive his chief general, who had come peacefully to the governor with other principal men of his country. Then, a few days after that, they burned another important lord of the province of Quito, Chamba, though he had committed no fault. . . . They also burned the feet of another lord of Quito, Aluis, and tortured him in other ways, to force him to reveal any additional gold of Atahualpa, a treasure of which it seems he knew nothing. In Quito they also burned Cocopango, the governor of all the surrounding provinces, because he did not give as much as they asked of him. . . . He had come peacefully when summoned by Captain Sebastian Benalcazar. As far as I could make out, the idea of the Spaniards was to leave no lord in that whole country.

I also know of an incident where the Spaniards collected a number of Indians and shut them up in three large houses, as many as these would hold, and then set fire to them and burned them all, even though they had not done the least thing against the Spaniards. One of our priests, Ocaña, rescued one boy from the fire, but along came another Spaniard, who threw him back, where he was reduced to ashes like the rest. The very same Spaniard who had thrown the Indian into the fire, while returning to camp the same day, suddenly fell dead in the road. I was of the opinion that they should not give him a Christian burial.

I also affirm and saw myself with my own eyes that Spaniards cut off hands, noses, and ears of Peruvian Indian men and women without any reason except that it pleased them to do so . . . and I saw them set dogs on many Indians, in order to tear them to bits. I also saw them burn so many houses and towns that I wouldn't know how to recount the number. . . .

Furthermore, I saw that they invited Indian leaders to come in, assuring them of peace and safety, but when they arrived they burned them at once. They even burned two in my presence, one in Andron and the other in Tumbalá, and I could not prevent this act, no matter how much I preached to them.

There were other outrages and cruelties without purpose, which caused great horror; they would take a long time to recount. In God and my conscience, so far as I can understand, the only reason that the Indians of Peru rose in revolt was because of the bad treatment—a fact that is clear to everybody. . . . They determined to die rather than to suffer such treatment.

I also testify that by the account of the Indians, there is much more gold hidden than has come to light, but they haven't wished to disclose it on account of the injustices and cruelties which the Spaniards inflicted on them. Nor will they disclose it while they receive such treatment. Instead, they would choose to die like their predecessors.

In all this, the Lord, our Master, has been much offended and his Majesty has been badly served by the loss of the countryside, which could have furnished a plentiful supply of food to all Castile. In my opinion, it will be extremely difficult and expensive to reclaim it.

I tried to imagine the dark memories that Marcos carried with him when he left Peru and came north toward Mexico in the mid 1530s. In September of 1536, about when Cabeza de Vaca, Dorantes, and the other shipwrecked men were arriving in Mexico from the north, Marcos was in Guatemala testifying at a trial of some conquistadors for the Peruvian atrocities, which must have still been fresh in his mind. Marcos then wrote from Guatemala to the elderly Bishop of Mexico City, Zumárraga, who invited him to come to Mexico City. He arrived by April of 1537, just at the time when rumors of the rich new northern empire were heating up. He must have wondered if the Peruvian excesses were about to be repeated.

ONE AFTERNOON IN MY WINDOWLESS CUBICLE IN A DARK CORNER of Mr. Rooney's empire, I sat down to read my tattered paperback edition of Cabeza de Vaca's book about his odyssey. Cabeza de Vaca and his fellow survivors wrote a first account of this journey for Mendoza in Mexico City. Then he went back to Spain and published his own memoir about the adventure. Cabeza de Vaca's strange family name (meaning "Head of a Cow") was known in Spain, where it had been conferred on an ancestor who facilitated a victory over the Moors by marking a critical pass with a cow skull. As I read Cabeza de Vaca's pages, I tried to put myself into the minds of those old Spaniards, and see what clues I could find about the routes they followed.

The book had been reprinted every decade or so by obscure publishers as a classic yarn of early American adventure. It was the first to describe the prehistoric trade route linking the American Southwest with Mexico—the route that the castaways followed south and that Marcos de Niza and Coronado would soon follow in the opposite direction. So I particularly tried to follow what Cabeza de Vaca said after his party reached what is now west Texas, and worked its way west, north around the Sierra Madre in order to cross the continental divide, and then south through Sonora. Scholars disagree over the exact locations he described, but it was in this stretch that the copper bell appeared. . . .

We continued traveling [in west Texas], skirting a mountain more than fifty leagues inland from the Gulf. At the end of the mountains we found a community of forty houses, where they gave us presents. Among these, they gave Andrés Dorantes a big, heavy copper bell with a face engraved on it, and they showed us much copper and said they had acquired it from other Indians who were their neighbors. When we asked where those Indians had acquired such a thing, they said it had been brought from the north, and that there was much of it there, and that it was greatly prized. We concluded they may have foundries there, and that they may cast metal in molds.

Figuring out locations from passages like this was always tricky. For example, the Spanish used the term "league" as a kind of mixture of distance and time traveled. It was not precise and its usage changed somewhat from era to era and person to person. It was as much a measure of elapsed travel time as of distance. Scholars of the Coronado era pegged it at about 2.5 to 3.1 miles, as used in the literature of the Coronado era.

In a place somewhat farther west, we showed them the bell we were carrying, and they said that in the place it came from, many layers of such metal were underground. It was a thing they held in much esteem. They also said that the houses in that place were permanent. We suspected that the western coast might lie near there, because we always heard that it is richer than the Gulf coast.

This comment turned out to be important. It means they thought the hypothetical metal-rich city-state was on an inland arm of the Pacific or the Gulf of California, somewhere north of their route. This idea seemed to resonate through the next few years, with dire consequences for Marcos de Niza. They were also beginning to hear about strange, cowlike animals, which we can now recognize and translate as buffalo:

Most of the people in that area [west Texas, south of El Paso] had little food and no permanent houses. Continuing west among people who hunted buffalo, we came to the first real, permanent houses. The people here ate beans and squash and were the first we encountered who raised maize. At this point, in order to cross the mountains toward the Pacific coast, we first had to travel 15 to 17 days north along a river, then 17 to 20 days west through higher, hunger-stricken country, where people had no maize to eat but only powdered herbs, almost like straw. In that land they killed many rabbits, which they brought to us. It was more than enough for us. Eventually we came out into fertile country on the maize road.

As I say, neither they nor anyone later knew where they were. Most scholars think the "first permanent houses" were small pueblos now known to have been along the southern Rio Grande. The jog fifteen to seventeen days north would have been a trip up the Rio Grande to the area known even today as The Pass, El Paso, which has always been one of the easiest regions to cross the spine of the continent, without hitting high mountain ranges. The seventeen to twenty days west then took them roughly along the modern Mexico–U.S. boundary until they hit the maize-growing villages dotted along the north-south river valleys of the Sonora-Arizona border. What they called "the maize road" to the south, into Sonora, was the age-old trade route which Marcos and Coronado were soon to explore in more detail, in search of the metal-using empire that had produced Dorantes' bell. Cabeza de Vaca resumes at the point where they had first reached the maize road.

When we came out of the twenty days of poor high country and reached this fertile land, we found permanent houses where much maize was stored. The Indians there gave us a great quantity of both maize and its flour, along with squash, beans, and cotton blankets. We gave all these things to the people who guided us there. With these supplies, they returned to their lands, the happiest folks in the world. . . .

Among the houses in this region some were made of earth, but the others were made of reed mats. From there we went on to the south for 100 leagues [about 250 to 310 miles]. Along this way, we always found permanent houses and good supplies of maize and beans. They gave us much deer meat and many cotton blankets, better than those of New Spain. They also gave us many beads and some corals from the Pacific coast, and many fine turquoises, which come from the north. In a word, they gave us everything they had. In one town they gave me five emeralds made into arrow points. I asked them where they got them, and they said they were brought from some mountainous country toward the north, where they bought them in exchange for parrot feathers. They said there were towns there with many people and very large houses.

So, according to the news brought into Mexico City by the castaways, the putative northern empire not only had copper but also turquoises, emeralds, and permanent towns with large houses. Later archaeological evidence suggests the "emeralds" were turquoise. Nonetheless, the totality of these rumors must have sounded very good to conquistadors in Mexico.

The black, Estevan, talked with the Indians constantly. He found out about the direction we needed to go, and what towns there were. . . . In all these lands, the Indians who were at war with others quickly became friends so they could come and greet us, and thus we left the whole land at peace. We told them by signs, so that they could understand, that there was a man in heaven whom we called God, who had created heaven and Earth . . . and that we had him as our lord. . . . We found in them such a disposition to believe, that if there had been a language in which we could have understood each other more perfectly, we would have left them all Christians. They are a well disposed and intelligent folk.

In the same village where they gave us the emeralds, they gave Andrés Dorantes more than six hundred hearts of deer, opened, which they always have in great abundance as food. So we called this village Corazones (the Village of the Hearts). It is the gateway to many provinces that are on the Pacific Coast.

If those who go from the inland to find the seacoast do not pass
through here they will be lost, because there is no maize along
the coast itself. But along the maize route, through these vil-
lages, there are more than a thousand leagues of populated
country, with good supplies of food.

The people along the maize route sow beans and maize
three times a year. There are three kinds of deer as well as per-
manent houses. . . . There were pueblo structures with about
twenty joined houses, similar to ones in the country we had left
behind. The pueblos were compactly built so that there was not
one house here and another there, as in the villages of reed mat
houses, which we later saw again in the area farther south that
had been pacified by the Spaniards.

Geographically, the maize route was the north-south strip
between the coastal deserts and the mountain crags. The
Goldilocks Effect applied: It was neither too hot nor too cold, but
just right. The "permanent houses" seen by Cabeza de Vaca's party
in northern Sonora were of special interest to them and to their listeners in Mexico City, because the slave-raiding Spaniards on the
north frontier of New Spain had hitherto encountered only poor villages of flimsier, reed-mat houses. The "permanent houses," however, were built up of stone and mudlike plaster, and some were
even multiroom, multifloor structures. They were thus seen as evidence of higher cultures farther north.

These particular pages by Cabeza de Vaca also gave the first
description of the town of Corazones, which was to become a
major landmark. Coronado would later establish a garrison there
for his army, and it became a pivotal point on the route from Mexico to the mysterious north. Virtually all historians place Corazones
on the Sonora River, in the central part of the state of Sonora, near
the sizeable modern town of Ures. The identification is based partly
on geographic descriptions of the "gateway," a gorge northeast of
Ures, where the Sonora River empties out onto the drier coastal

plain. A short distance downstream from there is the current capital of Sonora, called Hermosillo.

Corazones. Hearts. I liked that. *Corazon* was the most popular word in all those Spanish songs that played in the background of every Mexican restaurant in Tucson. Everything tied together.

It was easy for me to link Cabeza de Vaca's text to the next few years of exploration. After Cabeza de Vaca and his companions reached Mexico in 1536 and told their story, Viceroy Antonio Mendoza and Hernán Cortés began their frantic race against each other to get more information about the northern kingdoms. Although the castaways had traveled south along the trade route, it seems clear that they had gathered little solid information about the north, and neither they nor the Spanish court in Mexico City had any real idea of the nature of any native cities in that direction. Somebody had to be sent north to see if Cabeza de Vaca's "maize route" was just a trail between dusty villages, or if there really were rich cities at its north end—and if so, how they might be reached. In a letter to the King of Spain in 1539, Mendoza himself tells how he began to promote a northern reconnaissance.

After Cabeza de Vaca's party arrived in Mexico City, one of the castaways, named Andrés Dorantes, joined my court. I engaged him close at hand, supposing he would be able to do great service for Your Majesty. I employed him to take a party with forty or fifty horses, and search out the secret of the northern regions. Even though I provided all things necessary for his journey, and spent money to that end, I found that the matter had been broken off. I don't understand why this happened, but the enterprise collapsed [in 1537].

At this point, as a result of all the contacts and preparations that had been made, I still had the black Moor, who also survived the journey with Dorantes. Also, there were certain slaves

I had bought, and certain Indians whom I had gathered together, who were born in those northern lands. [In the fall of 1538] I ordered all of these to go north with Friar Marcos de Niza and his companion, another Franciscan Friar. I chose Marcos and his companion because they were well traveled, experienced in working with such parties, and had great knowledge of the affairs of the Indies. They were men of virtue and conscience, for whom I arranged a leave of absence with their superiors in their order.

So they traveled [from Mexico City] with the [new Governor] Francisco Vázquez de Coronado, to the city of Culiacán, which is the last province subdued by the Spaniards in that direction, being 200 leagues from the City of Mexico.

So the northern exploration was underway from Mexico City in the fall of 1538. Heading toward the northwest frontier were Marcos, his Franciscan companion named Honorato, the moor Estevan Dorantes, the new governor, and their party of servants and aides. In December 1538, when the newly-minted governor, Coronado, arrived with Marcos de Niza at Culiacán, on the Spanish northern frontier, they found the Indian population in chaos. A letter by Coronado to the King, dated eight months later, July 15, 1539, gives a vivid account of what happened next.

The Indians had been wandering the mountains, because, after the unlawful attacks of Guzmán and his slave raiders, they had neither houses nor agricultural fields. They are now beginning to rebuild their houses and plant their fields. They have also returned to their old village sites. . . .

I brought with me to this province a friar of the order of St. Francis, Father Marcos de Niza. Viceroy Mendoza had recommended that I send him inland. At the viceroy's command in your Majesty's name, he was to travel by land and explore the coast of this New Spain, in order to learn its secrets and gain knowledge of the provinces and peoples that now are unknown.

In order that Marcos might travel safely, I first sent some Indians, chosen from those who had been freed from slavery, to the towns of Petatlán and Cuchillo, nearly sixty leagues [140–180 miles] north of Culiacán. I asked them to recruit some native Indians from those towns and tell them not to be afraid, since your Majesty has ordered that no hostility, bad treatment, or enslavement be allowed toward them. In view of this, and the fact that the messengers themselves were free— which astounded them—more than eighty men came to see me.

I took pains to explain to them your royal will, namely that for now you want merely for them to become Christians and recognize God and your Majesty as their lords. After that I commissioned them to take Fray Marcos and a black farther north, into the interior of the land. The viceroy bought the black for this purpose from one of those who had been ship-wrecked. His name is Estevan.

The Indians did this, treating them very well.

Viceroy Mendoza's letter, the one I quoted earlier, gave more details about the beginning of Marcos's expedition. Everything fit together. The Indians were excited at being freed from Spanish attacks, and the Spaniards were excited about gaining new knowledge of the lands to the north, where populous cities of wealthy and unsaved souls might lie.

The Indians who came to visit Governor Vázquez de Coronado said they wanted to learn about these Spanish newcomers, who gave them so much happiness, and who allowed them to return to their homes, to plant maize for their sustenance. After all, they had previously been driven into the mountains for several years, living like wild beasts for fear they would be made slaves. They said they and all their people were ready to do whatever was now commanded.

Coronado pleased them with his kind words, and gave them food, and had them stay for three or four days, during which

*the Friars taught them to make the sign of the cross, to learn
the name of our lord Jesus Christ. They sought to learn these
things with great diligence. After these days, Coronado sent
them home, telling them not to fear, but to live quietly. He gave
them clothes, beads, knives, and other such things which I had
supplied for this purpose. The Indians departed well pleased,
and said that whenever he would send for them, they would
come and do whatever he commanded.*

*The entrance to the northern lands being thus prepared,
Friar Marcos and his companion went forward, with the Black
Moor and other slaves and the Indians I had given him.*

Marcos was armed with secret instructions that had been written
by the viceroy and handed to him by Coronado on November 20
when they were on their way to Culiacán. The instructions have
survived in the Spanish archives. They not only show Mendoza's
concern to learn about the rumored northern empire and to free the
Indians from slave traders, but also give many clues about the
effort to explore the northern coast.

*Tell the Indians that I send you in the name of His Majesty, to
see that they are well treated, and that he grieves because of
the wrongs they have suffered. From now on they will be well
treated. Anyone who does evil to them will be punished. Assure
them they will no longer be made slaves or removed from their
lands, but will be free, and that they should put aside any fears
and recognize God, Our Lord, who is in heaven, and the King,
who is placed on earth by God to govern it. . . .*

*If, with the aid of God, you find a route to enter the country
beyond, you shall take with you Estevan Dorantes as a guide,
whom I order to obey you in all that you command. If he fails
to do so, he shall incur penalties. . . .*

*Francisco Vázquez de Coronado has with him the Indians
who came from the northern lands with Dorantes. If it seems*

advisable to both of you, take some of them in your company, and employ them as you see fit to the service of Our Lord.

You shall always arrange to travel as securely as possible. Inform yourself in advance if the Indians are at peace or if some are at war with others. Give them no occasion to commit any violence toward you, which would be cause for punishing them, and would thus, instead of doing them any good, be to the contrary. Take much care to observe the following:

- *the people who are there, if they are many or few, and if they are scattered or live in communities;*
- *the quality and fertility of the soil;*
- *the climate of the country;*
- *the trees and plants and domestic and wild animals;*
- *the nature of the ground, whether rough or level;*
- *the rivers, if large or small; and*
- *the minerals and metals that are there.*

If there are any things that you can send or bring as specimens, bring them or send them, so that His Majesty can be advised of everything.

Always inquire about the coast, because the land may become narrower and in the country to the north some arm of the sea may enter the land. If you come to the coast, bury letters about noteworthy matters on selected promontories at the foot of some prominent tree, and on such trees make a cross so that it can be seen. Likewise, on the largest trees at the mouths of rivers, and in situations suitable for harbors, make this same sign and leave letters, because if we send ships, they will be advised to look for such signs.

Having noticed Cabeza de Vaca's speculation that the wealthy northern cities might be on an inland branch of the sea, I could now see between the lines what Mendoza was thinking. Already he had

ideas about sending a naval expedition (his own, not Cortés's!) to
conquer the north or at least to supply an army that would be not
too far inland. It was thus important to learn the coastal configuration and how close the northern empire was to the sea. Later I was
to find that most historians, who think of the Coronado enterprise
entirely as land expeditions, had missed this point—which was to
influence the destiny of Marcos de Niza.

Later I was also to realize the importance of another instruction,
designed to give Mendoza an edge in his competition with Cortés:

> *You shall arrange to send information by Indians, telling
> specifically how you fare and what you find. And if God is so
> served that you find some large settlement, suitable to establish
> a monastery and send friars to undertake Indians' conversion,
> send information by Indians or return yourself to Culiacán.
> Send such information with all secrecy, so that whatever is nec-
> essary can be done without commotion, because in bringing
> peace to that country, we look to the service of Our Lord and
> the good of the inhabitants.*
>
> *Although all the land belongs to the King, you shall take pos-
> session of it in my name for His Majesty, and you shall execute
> the signs and acts of possession that appear to you to be
> required for such case. You shall also instruct the natives that
> there is a God in heaven, and a King on earth to govern it, to
> whom all must be subservient.*
>
> *Don Antonio de Mendoza*

Not only Mendoza's instructions survived but also a receipt of
the viceroy's above instructions, signed by Marcos de Niza himself.

> *I, Fray Marcos de Niza, of the order of Saint Francis, affirm
> that I received a copy of these instructions, signed by the most
> illustrious lord, Don Antonio de Mendoza, viceroy and gover-
> nor of New Spain, which were delivered to me by Francisco*

Vázquez de Coronado, governor of this northwestern province of New Galicia. . . . I promise faithfully to fulfill these instructions, and neither to contravene them nor exceed them in anything, now or at any time. . . . I thus sign my name, the 20th day of November of the year 1538. . . .

Fray Marcos de Niza

After the departure from Culiacán on March 7, 1539, the first days of the expedition were happy ones. Armed with his royal instructions, Marcos marched north on foot into the unknown with Estevan, Honorato, their Indian friends from Mexico City, and their new Indian friends from the region around Culiacán. Coronado stayed in Culiacán, to deal with the natives, stabilize the town, and begin his own exploration toward rumored silver or gold mines in the mountains to the northeast.

Marcos's hardy band was feted at each new village. Marcos himself set the scene in his *Relación*, or report of his travels, which he submitted immediately after returning to Mexico City nearly six months later, in the late summer of 1539:

With the company of the Indians who had been freed, I took my way toward the town of Petatlán, receiving on the way many hospitalities and presents of food, roses, and other such things. The Indians built huts for me of mats and brush in the regions where there were no people.

In Petatlán, I rested three days because Friar Honorato was seized by illness, and I found it advisable to leave him there. Following the instructions, I pressed on with Estevan de Dorantes, the black, and some of the freed Indians and many people of the region, who, in all the places we reached, arranged for me great hospitality, celebrations, and triumphal arches. Along the road after leaving Petatlán [I gained information about the islands near there and then] I pursued my way through a despoblado for four days.

Despoblado was a word I liked. It meant a depopulated zone, usually between the populated river valleys. We ought to use this word, I thought. You still pass through *despoblados*, driving through the western U.S.

Marcos, meanwhile, was still near the coast, enthused about his prospects, in spite of the loss of Father Honorato in Petatlán. That village was already known to the Spanish, named from a word that referred to the reed mats used to build the small houses. Marcos and Estevan plunged on through the *despoblado*.

Indians joined me from the islands and towns I had passed. At the end of the four-day despoblado I reached other Indians who marveled at seeing me, because they had no knowledge of Christians from New Spain, since they have no dealings with those below the despoblado. They gave me joyous receptions and much food, and they tried to touch my robe, calling me Sayota, which is to say, in their language, "man from Heaven. . . ."

It was good to hear Marcos telling the story himself, but at every stage I wished he had put in more detail. Apparently there once were additional records of messages that Marcos sent back along the way, which have now been lost. For example, the Franciscan friar-historian, Fray Toribio de Motolinía, apparently used copies of Marcos's messages to write in 1540 about Marcos's life on the trail.

When one of the two friars took sick soon after crossing the frontier, the other, with two interpreters, followed the road which led to the coast, which he found open and in use.

After a few days' journey they reached a land inhabited by poor people. These came to the friar, calling him a messenger from heaven, and touching his person and kissing his robe. Day after day they accompanied him on his journeys, three hundred or four hundred persons at a time, and sometimes more.

When it was time to eat, some of the Indians went to hunt game, especially rabbits and deer, which were plentiful. Those who were expert hunters captured as much they wanted in just a short time. They served the friar first, then divided the game among themselves. In this way, the friar traveled onward. . . .

But now, according to Marcos, the route turned inland.

[After passing the region where they called me Sayota,] I went on three days through country inhabited by that same tribe, by whom I was received in the same way. Then I came to a fair-sized settlement that they called Vacapa, where they made me a great reception and gave me much food, which they have in abundance because their land is irrigated. From this town to the coast is forty leagues [about 100 to 124 miles]. Because I found myself now so far away from the sea, and because it was two days before Passion Sunday, I decided to stay there until Easter in order to send messengers to reconnoiter the coast.

As I read the old documents, I kept looking for clues that might reveal Marcos the man. Could this guy really be a fraud, as so many of his critics charged? This account sounded perfectly straight, upbeat, enthusiastic. If he lied about parts of his trip, where did the lies begin? Did Mendoza's request for secrecy really imply a dark conspiracy with the viceroy? Sure, Mendoza asked Marcos to report in secret, but that was because he didn't want Cortés to get enough information to start his own conquest of the north. So far, in my reading, I saw no sign that Mendoza's instructions or Marcos's report were anything other than what they seemed—a sincere attempt to unravel the mysteries of the new frontier.

CHAPTER 3

March–April, 1539
The Man from the Sky Visits Vacapa

Sunday, March 23. Marcos de Niza sat under a tree on the bank of the main irrigation canal above the Indian town of Vacapa, in the heart of the unknown land north of New Spain. He was a sinewy man, with a hawklike face and dark, darting eyes that had seen as much of the world as anyone alive: Avignon, Rome, and the pope. Cuzco and Atahualpa, Lord of the Incas. Mexico City, and the ruined temples and canals of Moctezuma's beautiful capital, Tenochtitlán. He had talked to the surviving lords among the Mexica, who had witnessed the epochal meeting of Moctezuma and Cortés, their strange months of joint rule over the ill-fated city, and the final tragedy after *La Noche Triste*, the Night of Sorrows.

Tragedy: the prime mystery of God's world. Marcos had seen more tragedy than anyone would want, yet his eyes were crinkled with smile lines. By temperament and necessity, he looked on the bright side of things. That habit was his answer to the mysteries God posed. His skin was dark with days of sun. At forty-four, he was muscled and scarred from a lifetime of walking. His gaunt physique made him look taller than he was. His grey robe was beginning to fray. He was already considered old by his friends, but he felt ready for whatever God would bring his way.

His journey was going well and it was good to rest after the recent long days he had spent on the trail. Too bad that Honorato had fallen ill in Petatlán, but the young priest would still be useful: He had promised to wait in Culiacán and relay any messages to the bishop and the viceroy.

Although Marcos had been led through long stretches of dry country, this irrigated river valley was shady and pleasant, and the townspeople of Vacapa seemed happy and well fed—good candidates for conversion. Still, Marcos was disappointed that this first major village in the unknown land showed no signs of stone architecture or metal working. The houses were constructed around a frame of rough beams, on which were lashed small sticks and reeds, woven into panels that made the walls. In some of the sturdier homes, these were plastered over with adobelike mud, making the more permanent, flat-roofed homes that Dorantes and Cabeza de Vaca had described. But the climate was apparently warm enough that people did not bother about sealing their homes against the weather. Marcos was also disappointed that the people had no knowledge of any rich kingdom to the north. His Indian interpreters and servants from the Valley of Mexico, led by his chief servant and acolyte, Juan Olmedo, had learned only that native traders often passed through this town. Where were they going? "To other towns" was the only answer he could get—spoken as if the answer was, after all, obvious.

From here on toward the north was *tierra incognita*. Cities? Mountains? Cannibals? Monsters? What about the virgin warriors of apocryphal tales? Many of the young soldiers in Mexico City believed that the storied Amazon queen, Califia, would be found in the north, ruling her empire of women. In contrast, certain scholarly friars told a legend about seven bishops who had escaped the Moors in A.D. 725 and traveled to Lisbon, and then sailed west across the sea to a land called Antilia, where they had built cities and established Christianity. Antilia might lie in the northern lands. Still others said that the lost tribes of Israel might have settled here. The navigator, Vespucci, had shown that a huge landmass lay south of the Indies, and many thought it must be part of Asia. Bishop Zumárraga, in Mexico City, along with most other scholars, reckoned that Cuba, Mexico, and all the Indies lay off the east Asian mainland, and that the fabled palaces of Cathay, described by Polo, were somewhere to the northwest. Marcos reserved judgment. After all, that's what he had been sent to find out.

Instead of speculating, he took one thing at a time. At every stop, he gave thanks for the reliability of his aides, guides, and interpreters. Juan Olmedo was especially useful, now that Honorato had been left behind. Juan had grown up in the city of Mexico. Marcos had to scold him constantly not to use his old name, Eagle. He had been only a young fighter, hardly more than a boy, when Cortés sacked the city in '21. He was one of the few young Mexican warriors to survive, and had been baptized into the church. Under the influence of Marcos he had become a lay brother. He was proud of being given the Christian name of the great gospel writer, but he still seemed secretly proud of his heritage as one of the Mexica who had ruled the valley of central New Spain. The Spaniards in Mexico City had given him the name Olmedo, because he had lived with an uncle from that town. He was a sober and quiet man who had traveled with his uncle as far as Compostela—so he claimed—before the Spanish came.

He had sad eyes. The Franciscans had drafted him into service as a translator and advisor on dealing with the natives, and he was the first choice as an aide to go on this trip. With his Mexican pride, Juan tried not to show surprise or even interest in the strange peoples they were encountering. Privately, in conversations with Marcos, he maintained that they were mere savages, but Marcos could see Juan's keen intelligence at work, soaking up information.

It was Juan himself, with the help of the ill-starred Fray Honorato, who had interviewed the provincial Indians in Vázquez de Coronado's frontier outpost of San Miguel de Culiacán, finding the ones worthy of the expedition north. From this group Juan himself had selected their chief translator, Tall Man, an Indian from a village that Guzmán had raided for slaves. The natives said that Tall Man was good with languages and had traveled far to the north in his youth. Now, he was a wiry old man with missing teeth. He had already picked up some rudiments of Spanish from his year in Culi-acán. In serious interviews along the way, Marcos talked to Juan, Juan talked to Tall Man, and Tall Man talked to the local Indians.

Tall Man, along with several of his friends, loyally followed Juan everywhere, and was mesmerized when Juan had bragged about how he had been Christianized, and was almost a Spaniard himself. Tall Man was a good candidate to be recruited into the body of Christ. Marcos had him targeted to be his first convert in these pagan lands.

Marcos had confidence that if anyone could ferret out news about the rumored northern empire, it would be Juan and his team. Even now, Juan and Tall Man were in the village, gathering information about the trading routes west toward the coast, east toward the mountains, and north toward the unknown.

Marcos snapped out of his reverie and glanced up at the sun, which was now high in the south. He was waiting for Estevan. Where had the infernal Moor gone? They had agreed to meet when the sun crossed the meridian. Marcos scanned the dome-shaped reed huts in the distance across the shallow river, but could see no sign of his unruly servant.

Estevan. Was he a blessing or a curse? He was acting less like a servant every day. He and his master, Andrés Dorantes, along with the other two survivors of the Narváez expedition, had all gained fame throughout New Spain when they appeared in '36 out of the wilderness—but it was charismatic Estevan that people gossiped about. Andrés Dorantes had told Marcos how Estevan, eyes gleaming maniacally from his dark face, would travel ahead of the others, dressed in feathers and pagan clothes, carrying shamanic gourds and rattles, paving the way for their triumphal entry into each village along their way. Marcos felt respect for the men's survival skills, but also felt concern for the way they had established themselves as shamans among the pagans, with Estevan taking the lead. When they had met Guzmán's slave raiders, they had been followed by an adoring Indian throng, two hundred strong. Preying on Indian superstitions, they had cured Indian illnesses and raised themselves in the Indians' eyes, but Marcos was suspicious of their conceit, their condoning of superstitious magic. What was the cost to their souls? Estevan had gone so far as to claim, blasphemously, that in making their cures, they had worked miracles. Their journey had been dangerous in more ways than one.

Taller than most Spaniards, well muscled and handsome, he mesmerized everyone. He hid his crafty mind behind a grin. In theory, he had embraced the church, but there was always a question of whether he meant what he said, or whether he was mocking them all with his cleverness.

Now, Marcos had seen Estevan's powers firsthand. In the villages along the way, Estevan made friends with all the Indians, greeting them with smiles and songs and little dances, waving his rattle and making his two greyhounds do tricks. Marcos had to admit that the man was brilliant. He always grew closer to the people than Marcos himself. Often during his own travels, Marcos had noted that the more education a man had, the less he could talk to ordinary people. Conversely, Marcos had seen simple farmers thwart the foolish logic of learned clerics. Uneducated people like Estevan often had more congeniality and common sense. Was he feeling jealousy? No, he would not compete with Estevan. A man of God needed to be a man apart from the common fray, a detached observer. . . . At least that's what he told himself.

No one watching them would guess that the Moor had submitted to Viceroy Mendoza's order to represent the kingdom of Christ on Earth, under Marcos's leadership. Estevan wore his cross but would not part with his rattles and feathers, arguing that the Indians revered such symbols. Also, he loved to amaze the Indians with his command over the trained dogs. Marcos was dependent on Estevan in many ways, and had to humor him. But was he in fact making a pact with the Devil?

And then there were the women. Estevan was always quick to find the most comely young women in each new village. Some of the governors of these towns indulged him, bringing shy daughters out from their beehive-shaped reed-mat houses. Marcos tried to forbid the practice. He recalled an incident on the first day in Vacapa, when the Indian men in the village had come to him, laughing. They pointed to young women, working in the fields, and made obscene gestures toward their genitals. They were offering the women to him. Marcos stammered a negative response. His own servants explained that the Vacapans treasured their women, and that with honored guests they had a tradition of sharing happiness. It was not only the friendly thing to do, but also an honor. Estevan had already accepted; why not Marcos? The Indian men had walked away, shaking their heads in puzzlement. He hoped that his refusals had given him some sort of exalted status. Or were they simply insulted? There was so much to explain to them.

After Honorato fell ill at Petatlán, Estevan had became a different man, acting as if he had his own plan for the journey, whereas in fact the viceroy's orders had stated very clearly that Estevan must obey Marcos in all things. Yet there was never any overt rebellion. Estevan was too clever for that. It was as if for the first time the Moor had become his own man, on a par with any Spaniard. When Honorato announced he would stay behind, Estevan seemed to sense that there was one less layer of Spanish authority over him. It was as if some secret power was growing in him, the closer they got to the northern lands where he had first gained his reputation as a magician.

Suddenly Estevan was approaching along the canal that diverted water from the river upstream. It was as if Marcos's musing about the man had conjured up the reality. There was a young village woman with him, of course. So that's what he'd been up to! Estevan was shooing her away, pointing back to the town. Marcos knew that Estevan would be trying to make her understand that the Father did not like to see him with women from the villages where they traveled. Marcos felt little satisfaction as he watched the woman skip away across the field and dance into the river, splashing gaily and waving back to Estevan. Marcos could see her smile; surprisingly white teeth gleaming in a pretty face. Many of the women here were quite . . . He put the thought aside.

"Ho, Father," Estevan smiled a familiar greeting, his eyes flashing. There was no doubt about Estevan's ability to charm anyone. His dark skin gleamed with the water the young woman had splashed on him, and his dark, wet hair curled close on his head. As his hair began to dry, its peppering of strange, premature gray was emphasized in spite of his youthful thirty years of age. Estevan was fully a hand's breadth taller than Marcos himself. "You see, I sent her back to the village. I did not bring her to bother you. I came alone, as you said."

Estevan seemed to be mocking him, in his characteristic way. Estevan was the most cheerful sinner he had ever known. Had God brought Estevan all this way for some special purpose? Marcos realized he was always fighting some feeling of awe for the Moor, who seemed to exist outside the ordinary world.

"Estevan, sit down. Listen to me. How many times have I talked to you about these women?"

The lanky Moor picked a spot on the sand and folded his legs under himself, like a large bird. "Do you like the gift she gave me?" He puffed out his gleaming chest. He was wearing a large shell pendant, carved in the shape of a frog, inlaid with bits of turquoise. The pendant covered the small silver cross that he also wore around his neck. Estevan's Spanish had an odd accent, not just from the African lands across the Mediterranean; it was as if his language as well as his beliefs had absorbed mysterious influences during the years he had wandered in the northern wilderness.

Marcos frowned as he struggled to put aside his old complaints against Estevan. He had important business to conduct, and there were times when it was better to look the other way in the face of provocation. "We must think about other things than the women and their gifts," he said lamely.

"But Father," Estevan answered, "you are a priest of God; I am only a humble man as God made me. . . . God wants me to have my life. Besides, we must please these Indians. I know these people. It would be an offense to reject the girl given by a chief." He smiled slyly and Marcos could never understand if he meant what he said. Marcos was used to plain speaking. Estevan seemed to be able to speak and mean three things at once.

"This is wrong, Estevan. This is sin. You are going to get into trouble."

"Trouble?" Estevan scowled fleetingly. Then his enigmatic smile returned. He ran his hand across his large, gleaming forehead and through his damp hair. "In my life, I have learned to survive trouble. Being taken from my land by my people's army, then captured by your people's army, then being a slave, then being taken across the great Atlantic Ocean in a ship—I can survive anything. I've been shipwrecked, enslaved all over again by the Indians, and still learned to make friends with them. All those nights stuck in their stinking huts serving them; what do you think I thought about? I studied them. I learned their dreams, and that gave me the power to rise above them. I crossed rivers and mountains and deserts. I have led one hundred lives and survived each one. Father." He added the last word, as an afterthought.

"You risk the sin of pride."

"Would you have been able to survive such trials?"

"It would be as God willed it."

"A simple answer."

"Are you sure you know these people so well? They are very different from us."

"Look. Everywhere, they welcome us. They carry our supplies. They make flowered arches for us to enter their villages. Some of them, I believe, are friends of the people who met my master Dorantes and me when we traveled south near this region three years ago. Their hearts went out to us." Estevan winked at Marcos. He was full of double meanings. He was probably making a joke about his sexual life, and he had made a pun on the fact that Dorantes and Cabeza de Vaca had used the name *Corazones*— Hearts—for a village somewhere near here, where they were honored with a feast of hearts of deer.

"I am a great healer in their eyes," Estevan continued. "Remember, if I may say so, Father, we have to find the joy that these people want and give it to them. That is my secret. Give them joy and—"

"But of course. That is why I preach to them about God's love for them."

"But you also preach about the damnation of evil souls."

"Of course, that is part of—"

"You frighten them and puzzle them. Give them joy first." He shook the gourd rattle he had been carrying. "Then they will love you and follow you."

Marcos had sent out explorers, and planned to wait until Easter for them to return, but he could not stand the thought of Estevan working his way through all the young women of Vacapa. He had a plan.

"Estevan, listen to me. We are farther from the coast than we have ever been on this trip. The chiefs tell me that we are now several days inland, and the trail to the north will continue to move farther from the coast. Remember our instructions. Viceroy Mendoza wants us to explore not only the northern lands, but also the northern coast, in case there are good harbors. This morning, after mass, I sent out three parties of the Indians from this village, together with some of the Indians that came with us from Mexico and Culiacán. They will explore toward the coast in different directions. I will wait here until they return. Meanwhile, as for you, you must take our Indian allies and travel northward, to advise me what lies ahead of us. It is a great responsibility, Estevan. I want you to leave today. It is not good for you to sit idle in this village like a rich nobleman."

"Yes, Father." Estevan's eyes gleamed with the thought of adventure.

"I want you to go no more than fifty leagues—six or seven days. Visit the next villages. Ask about the lands and cities still farther north. Tell them I am coming to bring peace and good news to them. Get all the information you can."

"Yes, Father. Do you want me to come back to you here?"

"If you find a good village, you can wait for me there, but you must send me a message about what you have learned."

"But, Father . . ." Estevan could neither read nor write.

"Here is how you will send me messages." Marcos pulled a small white cross, the size of a hand, out of the deerskin bag he had been given in the village. At the sight of the cross, Estevan said "Ah. . . ." He loved symbols. Marcos winced at the thought that Estevan saw the holy cross as a talisman to project mystical power over the Indians. He continued, "If you find Indians who know of a better land farther north, send messengers back with this cross. If they know of rich cities, make me a bigger cross, two hands in length. And listen, if they say it is a great kingdom, such as Mexico, then you can make a still larger cross and send that to me. Do you understand?"

"Yes, Father."

"It is very important that we learn as much as we can. We must see if we can confirm the rich country you and Dorantes and the others heard about. And find people who can take us there. Find out if the route is through good country or bad. The sooner we learn anything, the sooner I can report back to the viceroy."

"I understand. Somewhere ahead I may come to the villages where I was known three years ago. It will be a joyful—"

"Estevan, listen. You must not go too far ahead. We must not get separated. The success of our expedition depends on our prudence. We must not let something happen to us before we get our news back to the viceroy. When you reach a good spot, wait for me there."

"Yes. Wait," Estevan repeated, fingering his new frog pendant. His whole body radiated excitement about getting back on the trail. He was like a hunting dog that sensed a new quarry and could not be restrained.

LATER THAT AFTERNOON, MARCOS ACCOMPANIED ESTEVAN TO the trail leading upstream, north from Vacapa. It was time for Estevan to leave. With them were a dozen men from Vacapa, plus Tall Man and five of Marcos's best guides who had come with them from the south. Crowds of Indians from Vacapa stood around to watch; word had spread of Estevan's imminent departure. Estevan was dressed gaily for the event, with small bells on his armbands and a metal helmet he had been given by Vázquez de Coronado himself. Marcos knew that Estevan would put away his most gaudy apparel once he was on the trail, only to don it again when his party approached the next major village. The Indian women of Vacapa wore white paint on their faces, which seemed to mark some ceremony of parting. Estevan had with him his two Castillian greyhounds, who ran up the trail and back, sensing the excitement of the departure. The dogs were larger than the mongrels of the village. "Indian dogs," Estevan had said once, contemptuously, "they know nothing."

Outside the north edge of the village, Marcos clasped Estevan's hand before he left. "Remember," said Marcos, "send me messages and then wait at some good spot on the trail."

Estevan's face still had its intelligent, slightly mocking look. "We will meet soon, in the north," Estevan said.

Marcos stood, feeling there was something else he should say. "And don't forget to pray every day," he called out. "Pray for humility and safety."

"It's all right, Father," Estevan called back. "You worry about unseen things of the spirit, and I will worry about the things of this earth. Then we will come out all right." He looked very wise at those moments, not like his frequent role of the mad alchemist, which he adopted when he put on a show for the Indians. In another moment, Estevan and Tall Man and the others disappeared where the trail followed a bend in the river, before Marcos could think of an instructive response.

After Estevan departed, Marcos thought about the lectures he had given Estevan, about the sins of pride and arrogance. Yet he had to examine his own conscience in this regard. He was beginning to understand how easy it was to enjoy the adoration of these people. In the villages of the last two weeks, he had been greeted not just as a liberator, but as if he were an angel of the Lord. The people had swept the paths with small brooms, and erected arches overhead, twined out of branches and decorated with feathers and spring flowers. As he passed through the arches villagers had reached out to touch him, feeling his garments and even his body as if to see that he was human. "*Sa-yo-ta*," they had murmured.

Tall Man and Juan, after conferring with the natives, had passed along the interpretation: "It means 'man from the sky.' They say they have a story about holy men from the sky. When they touch you, they are drawing power and goodness from you."

Marcos shook himself out of this reverie. Enough of these idle thoughts. He was not here to wallow in adulation. He had a mission to accomplish.

STILL LATER IN THE AFTERNOON, MARCOS TOLD THE CHIEFS OF Vacapa that he wanted to make marks in his leather-bound trail-book, marks about their village, largest of the towns in this peaceful, green valley. Of all Marcos's activities, "making marks in his book" was the one that caused greatest wonder. Adults and children gathered around him in a semicircle to watch as he sat on a rock and wrote.

"What is he doing?" The question went through the chain of interpreters they had established since leaving Culiacán.

"Explain it to them," Marcos said to Juan.

Juan swelled with Mexican pride. He tried to explain writing, working back through the interpreters. "The Spaniards, they have a system of making marks that represent ideas. In Mexico, we, too, had a system of making little pictures that stood for happenings. Like the pictures you paint on the rocks near your villages. Except our pictures are in a certain order, on sheets of leather or paper, like the sheets in the Father's book. When we look at them, we can tell a story. But the Spaniards, their system is more complicated. Their marks don't represent pictures. They represent sounds."

"So this is a way to take a story out of the mind and put it away in this . . . book," one bright young man repeated. Then he looked puzzled. "Why would anyone want to do that?"

"If you make the marks in the book, then another person can

look at the book later and understand what you said, even if they never heard the story before. When you write your ideas in this way, they don't disappear like smoke in the wind."

"But we learn our stories from our elders and tell them to each other. That way, everyone remembers the same story. Surely it is better to have a story in your mind than to have it wrapped and hidden in a leather box."

Marcos interrupted. Juan needed help. "A great lord in Mexico has sent us on this journey. If I write down what I learn here, I can wrap it up and give it to one of my servants to carry back to our lord in Mexico. Then he can understand what we have seen, even if something happens to me."

"But you could tell a runner and the runner could tell him."

"What if the runner makes a mistake? This way, I know that my lord will see exactly what I have to say."

"A runner could say exactly what you have to say. The markings cannot. They would depend on how people interpret them."

The Indians from Vacapa finally lost interest in the argument and went away, shaking their heads and talking among themselves.

AN HOUR LATER, MARCOS HAD FINISHED WRITING AND THE small, leather-bound book lay on his lap desk. He sighed, contentedly. The trailbook was, he reflected, the most priceless item in his possession during the journey. The daily notes—days traveled, descriptions of rivers and villages—would be the basis for his letters and eventual formal report to the viceroy. Such records would give the viceroy the justification he needed to launch an official expedition to claim the northern country. It was only with the viceroy's backing of such an expedition that Marcos's Franciscan brothers could enter these valleys and begin the conversion of these smiling but pagan peoples into God's embrace.

Viceroy Mendoza, the wise governor, had understood the excesses of the past and promised Marcos that this new venture, the conquest of the northern empires, would be different. Mendoza's face had hardened as he swore that it would not be like Cortés's blundering rape of Moctezuma's once-beautiful capital in the previous decade. It would be done in the name of the King and Christendom, not in the name of the rapacious few.

Marcos believed him.

He leaned back against his tree and thought about the first Indians he had seen, servants in the port at Española, timid with that haunted look in their eyes. He must not forget that the real treasure of the New World were the natives themselves. During his visit to Rome, in the grandiose painted meeting halls of the Vatican, he had sat through a learned debate by explorers, scholars, and priests of the Holy Church, about the true nature of the Indians. An amply fed cardinal represented the strictest faction of the church, and often seemed to demolish the other debaters merely by his zealous tenacity. "The Indians that Colón found are not truly human beings with souls. Look at them! Look at the reports and the diagrams by Colón's artist. They are animals. They have neither clothes nor souls. This alone justifies their being pressed into our service in the New World."

"But," said a young priest who had served in Cuba and was sitting with several recently returned explorers, "their servitude is odious. I have seen fine young men among the Indians, worked to exhaustion and despair."

"Your observations may lead you into error," said the cardinal. "Remember that Jesus, the Christ, was sent to bring God's word to his chosen people. The world was thus divided by this one stroke of God's will: There are Christians and there are infidels. History after Christ has been a fifteen hundred–year struggle between the two. God's assignment to true believers is to triumph, to create civilization. Even the years themselves were labeled *anno domini* so that Christ's soldiers can be aware of the progress of the battle. Is it really so easy for you to think that naked, animalistic infidels deserve to be treated as equals to the best Christians?" The cardinal was growing red in the face. "You forget that they are weak and lazy! Look at the reports! They live in dirty villages with grass huts! Without knowledge of God, they are inclined toward slothfulness and many sins of the flesh. They need examples of virtuous behavior to look up to, which they will see as they work for the good of Spain. We must be like a stern father, who makes his children work for their own good. They must learn the value of labor. They must learn that a fine house or a fine village, with markets, blacksmiths, clothiers, and so on, does not come from idleness. We must help them help themselves."

One of the explorers spoke up. "But the markets of Tenochtitlán, when Cortés conquered it, were grander than those of Europe!"

"Pagan markets! Next to temples where human sacrifices occurred. Do you think we have not read these reports? You are in grave peril, my son, if you presume to compare those lands with ours, where God rules. You cannot *give* the blessings of civilization to them; they would merely become dependent on us. They must work under the tutelage of God and His Majesty, to *earn* civilization in order to appreciate it. Perhaps if they learn these lessons, God will eventually transform them into humans."

"But," said the young priest, excitedly, "Bartolomé de Las Casas wrote that when our people conquered the Indians in Cuba, they—"

"Ah, the famous Bartolomé de Las Casas," the cardinal sighed as the reformer's name came up—inevitably—in the debate. "We are familiar with him. He alienates himself from the nobles and conquistadors by writing a hundred letters about poor Indians. Make no mistake. He is a man with dangerous ideas. His ideas sound Christian when you first hear them, but it takes reflection to see that his ideas would lead to social chaos. Poor and ignorant savages would be treated as if they were as good as religious gentlemen of noble birth. Remember, our Lord said, 'The poor you have always with you.' Therefore, our job is not to correct poverty, which is impossible, but to lead the poor into the blessed light of the church."

Marcos had read several of the impassioned sermons in which Las Casas argued that the Indians were capable of reason, but the story that stuck in Marcos's mind was one Las Casas himself told him one day when the two priests stood in the ancient market plaza of the Mexica, where the old pagan temples had been dismantled, stone by stone, to provide material to build the new cathedral. "In the early days," Las Casas said, "I used to see Indians come into the square, all wrapped in their blankets with only their eyes showing. They would stand at some distance from one of our silversmiths, pretending to see nothing, while the silversmith worked. And then they would go off to their houses and make the article as well or even better! Merely from watching! They would bring their pieces back to the market and sell them to whoever would buy. They copied thousands of our objects faultlessly. Even musical instruments. Flutes, oboes. I saw one make a good sackbut starting with a candlestick! Pretty soon, our people made nothing in front of an Indian, for fear their businesses would be ruined. I've written this story down in my *History of the Indies.*"

It was true. Marcos had seen many beautiful works made by the Indian craftsmen after minimal instruction.

The tide had finally begun to turn in favor of Las Casas and the natives. Late in 1537, not long after Marcos arrived in Mexico from Guatemala, word arrived from Europe that Pope Paul III had issued a papal bull giving God's will, which, to the dismay of many of the New World's conquistadors, echoed Las Casas. Marcos remembered the Pope's words of hope. "The Indians are truly men. They are capable of understanding the Catholic faith. They are in no way to be deprived of their liberty or property." God's will, as delivered by the Pope, should have ended the matter. But these words were only volleys of ink, fired in the middle of what Marcos felt would be a long war.

Here, in Vacapa, in the boisterous play of the children, and the smiles of the young mothers, Marcos had seen for himself the simple humanity of the natives, who had not yet had the privilege of meeting the virtuous Spanish. These people had heard vague rumors of unrest in the south, but they said none of them had ever seen Christians. But because of this their faces were not haunted like the Indians in Cuba; they laughed easily.

MARCOS LOOKED ACROSS THE GURGLING IRRIGATION CHANNEL, TO the cottonwoods along the river, their leaves dancing in the sun. The rivers were like avenues through the desert. The dream of Las Casas might yet come to pass. He could imagine that some day these lazy green river valleys would be the sites of bustling missions surrounded by orchards and vineyards, adjacent to peaceful Indian towns. How could it be accomplished? The flimsy pagan temples with their turquoise inlaid idols would be torn down and cast into the river. The painting of heathen symbols on pots would have to be controlled, along with the carving of animals and demonic symbols on rocks. The Indians would be taught to speak only Spanish and to abandon some of their more revolting sexual practices. Meanwhile the canal systems could be enlarged, and the fields expanded across the fertile valleys. Cows and other livestock could be introduced, and mission gardens.

Here, far from Mexico City, Marcos could allow his musings to drift into more delicate territory. Some of Marcos's Franciscan brothers said not so secretly that the church hierarchy in Europe was becoming bloated and corrupt, leading to heresies, like Luther's in Germany, and the formation of new orders, like the Jesuits, in '34. Many Franciscans were excited by the idea that the New World offered them a chance to establish their own perfect world. While other orders claimed certain parts of the Indies, the Franciscans dominated central Mexico and the lands to the northwest. God had given them these lands for a purpose. Their goal must be to use the Indian souls and lands to create an example for the rest of the world. "From the grapes in *la viña de Dios* we are making wine"; that was their saying about their work. Mexico was "the vineyard of the Lord."

Already, the Franciscans were holding grand, open-air services and getting thousands of conversions. Perhaps whole Indian towns could be rebuilt along the lines of ideas suggested by Bartolomé de Las Casas, with clean dormitories, common fields and work areas, productive mines and foundries, and communal kitchens, preferably before too many Spanish settlers arrived. The Indians would not be managed and taxed by individual big landowners, as had happened elsewhere in the Indies. Instead, their towns, administered by the Friars, would be at some distance from the Spanish towns. Commerce would flourish between them. There would be a just system of taxation on both, to maintain roads and the king's courts, where all would have equal rights of appeal. Horses, wagons, and cavernous, cool public buildings with massive walls—these were wonders the Spanish could bring to these people! In turn, the Indians could trade their ceramic vessels and bring to the markets crops, cotton, and metal products, all taken from their own fields and lands.

Marcos remained prudent in public and private about these new ideas. He believed that dreams were the first step toward progressive reality, but who could say whether a happy life of commerce could flourish some day in the fertile valleys of the north?

When he had been in Rome, he had visited the pastures on the edge of the city, where cows grazed among grand ancient columns and statues of the ancient Roman forum. Nearby, scavengers sold old blocks of marble and burned pagan statues to produce quick-lime, and merchants of religion had set up stalls to sell indulgences to pilgrims who came to see the old temples. What it taught Marcos was that there had been more to this world than he knew in his time. Proud civilizations could come to an unexpected end. Any dream of a perfect world was a fragile thing.

THE SUN WAS MOVING ON. MARCOS FOLDED HIS TRAVELING LAP desk and set it aside. He would rest just a few minutes more. Disquieting thoughts passed through his mind. When he came through Compostela with Coronado, rumormongers said that Cortés had already built more ships on the southern coast, and was preparing to sail north, to claim the rumored northern empire himself. Without the justice that could be delivered to these lands by Viceroy Mendoza and the church, these valleys could be doomed to the kinds of atrocities Marcos had witnessed personally in Peru. The thought conjured up a ghastly image. One of the two Peruvian chiefs, who had been burned at the stake in front of him—who had talked with Marcos as a friend during those few short months they had known each other—looked directly at him as the fires were being lit at his feet. It was not a look of fear. It was a look of great wisdom and pity, the look that one of the holy martyrs might have had. And then the smoke had covered his face. . . .

Marcos wondered if anyone could ever understand God's creature, man. One night in Mexico City, he had discussed these things with the great conqueror Cortés himself. It was on a cool night near the gardens of Xochimilco, shortly after Marcos had arrived in Mexico City in '37. Marcos was no friend of Cortés, but the old soldier, ever seeking new alliances, had invited him to a chat in the golden glow of a Mexican sunset on the patio of the conqueror's fortresslike villa, built by loyal Indian servants.

"Your Indian allies built you this beautiful house, from your own designs," Marcos pointed out to Cortés. "In turn, you clothed them and fed them, and brought them to Our Lord Jesus Christ. Obviously you trust some of them." Marcos discreetly did not bring up Marina, the comely Indian woman of the burning eyes, who had been taken as a translator by Cortés before the attack on the Mexica, and had become more than Cortés's friend. "So why didn't you order your armies to work with all of them, just as you work with these? Why do the *conquistadores* love the laws of war more than the blessings of peace?"

Cortés set aside his glass of Spanish wine that had come in a great keg across the sea and up the long road from the coast. "In the first place, I tried to work with Moctezuma. I had him in the palm of my hand, but his priests and nobles turned him against me. In the second place, excuse me, Father, but you see only as much as you want to see. A ruler has to see everything, the good and the bad. If I proclaimed only friendship, a smile an easy hand, or if I told my officers, 'Never strike our Indian brothers,' well, yes, of course you are right: Many of the Indians would come to us smiling and kiss my robe, the way they kiss your robe. But I have to deal with things you do not have to deal with." Cortés sighed. "What you miss, in your churchly wisdom, is the wisdom of the streets. In every country there are not only good people we wish to accept into the Mother Church under His Majesty's rule, but also bad people who would hate us. The doves of peace and the eagles of war, who seek their chance to prey on the doves. You dream about the doves, but my job is to deal with the eagles.

"If we unclench our fist, somewhere in the hills the cousins of our Indian allies would speak against us, the way Moctezuma's priests spoke against me. 'These Spanish,' they would say, 'they are but a few. If we rise against them now, we can throw them out.' And what would happen if we let those ideas go unpunished?" He drew his finger under his bearded chin. "Always we Christians would be under attack. The quiet arrow in the dark. Ambushes on the road to Compostela. . . . No, the soldier learns that life is not so simple as you priests would like. If you would conquer a population, whether for the king or for God, you must make sure it stays conquered. A hand that is cut off for insolence will not put a dagger in your back. The garroting of a rebellious chief, in the square in front of his countrymen, establishes who is in charge, who holds the scales of justice."

Cortés's expression changed. "It is hard to order an execution, Father, even when it is justified by sacred and secular law. You know, there have been nights when I could not sleep. Nights when I have had to order that one of our own men . . . as an example to the others, you understand. . . . Listen, nothing is easier than to return to Spain as a failure. Nothing is easier than to attack this empire and then lose it. The king and the court, and the people who write those weighty volumes of history that you prize, they do not waste their time writing about the captains who fail—what princely fellows they were, how they did the upstanding thing, what gentlemanly restraint they showed on the day they were defeated.

"Father Marcos, do you understand me?"

* * *

THURSDAY, MARCH 27. THE LIGHT OF THE HIGH AFTERNOON SUN played through the leaves of a massive cottonwood outside Marcos's brushy domed hut, built for him by the Vacapans at the edge of their town. Among the neighboring huts, Marcos could hear the incessant *swish, swish* of the stone mealing bins, which the Indian women used to grind corn. He had just finished mending his robe when there was a commotion outside.

"Father, Father, come! It is news from Estevan." It was Juan. Marcos crawled from the low hut, thinking to himself that this could be a pivotal moment. Had Estevan found something?

In front of the hut stood Tall Man, the most trusted of the Mexican Indian translators, who had gone north with Estevan. Tall Man's missing teeth were on display now: He was grinning from ear to ear. Proudly he held in front of him a cross— not the small white cross Marcos had sent north, nor even an arm-sized cross that Marcos had told Estevan to send if he had great news. This cross was much larger, made of carefully cut thin poles. Its foot rested on the ground; it was as tall as Tall Man himself! The top was nicely carved in Estevan's flamboyant style and had a feather attached—a touch that would ingratiate the Moor to the Indians, but which he certainly knew would irritate Marcos.

"Father," Tall Man said in his broken Spanish, "Estevan bids me to tell you, you must come north at once to join him. On the hour. The news is very great." He spoke carefully, as if he had rehearsed his speech. "Ahead is the greatest land in the world. The people of the valley where Estevan is, they have been to that land, and Estevan has sent one of them back to talk with you. Bring all the interpreters."

The group had already collected in the dusty plaza of the village, sitting in a circle on mats under a thatched ramada. The messengers had brought a burly, aging man, gray of hair and painted in a pasty green pigment. He squatted in the shade of the ramada, chewing on a piece of dried meat. He had the look of a wise man. His name, they said, was Traveler, and he was said to know all the dialects of the northern provinces. He spoke haltingly with Tall Man, who then conferred with Juan. There was much groping for the nuances of certain words. With frustrating slowness, the story emerged in Spanish.

"I've been instructed by the great lord, Estevan, to bring this message," the old man was saying. "To the north a great province with many cities. These cities are all in one country, governed by one lord. People from my valley often make pilgrimages there during the trading season. I myself have been there. They say you are interested in this place. I can tell you all about it."

"What is the name of this place?"

"The name of that place is Cíbola. Ci-bo-la," he repeated the syllables carefully. He went on excitedly, enjoying the attention of the villagers. From what Marcos could gather, Cíbola was the main trade destination for the Indians visited by Estevan.

Traveler had a wrinkled, kindly face. He looked very patient and wise, and was strikingly agile and strong for his apparent age.

"This community of Cíbola, it is bigger than this town of Vacapa, then?" Marcos had asked him, waving his arm toward the huts of the village.

The old man listened gravely to the interpreters, and then apparently asked them to repeat the question. Finally he broke into peals of laughter, rocking back on his heels so that he almost lost his balance. He said something to the other Indians, who burst out laughing as well. "Oh, Father, who is not my father, you do not understand. Cíbola is the most wonderful thing in the world. Bigger? It is a great city. It stands in one place, year after year, not like villages you see here in this valley, which shift location from generation to generation, like country people moving to a new water hole. In Cíbola, the houses are made of stone and earth." He took a twig and sketched rectangles in the dirt, one atop another. "They are so great that one house is on top of another. This town," he gestured disdainfully at Vacapa's plaza and brush huts, "is not even a poor anthill in comparison to Cíbola."

As they talked, Marcos came to understand that the houses of

Cíbola rose several stories tall. "The people in my village, a few *jornadas* north of here, we have made a few houses of stone and earth, as tall as two men. But even we live mostly in houses of brush mats. The houses of Cíbola are still much greater than we can make."

"What about wealth? Is there gold? Precious stones?"

"Oh yes, precious stones. The lord, Estevan, asked me to show you these." The man reached into a little leather pouch at his belt and held out three polished aqua-colored stones, as if in proof. They were turquoise. "These are good luck stones from Cíbola. Very fine ones. They protect us on journeys and even in town. We wear them, as you see," he fingered his single-strand necklace, "and we have the best ones in our temples, but in Cíbola, they have so many that they work them into the doorways of their best houses."

"And what else? You say you yourself have been to this place?"

The question went through the translators with many gestures. Hands waved in the air. Traveler gestured to the north with his chin; he held up his fist and opened and closed it rapidly six times in succession pointing to the afternoon sun with his other hand. More slowly, the answer came back in Spanish. "Yes. I told you. I have been there. To get there from my country, we travel for thirty days. It is a major trip. People go only during the trading season."

"And you say there is not just one of these cites?"

"There are many cities in the northern province. More than the fingers on one hand." He held up seven fingers. "This many. Different sizes. There are also empty cities in that land, cities where no one lives now. And beyond the first seven cities, more cities in other provinces."

Seven cities? This number rang a bell in Marcos's mind. Could they be the fabled colony of the seven bishops, the Seven Cities of Antilia? If so, the northern discovery might be a land where Christ already ruled among the Indians! Still, a land with six or seven cities and more beyond—it could be a description of

Cathay. The great Khan himself might be waiting to welcome him!

Three or four days before reaching Vacapa, some Indians, looking at Marcos's samples of metals, had picked out the gold and said that some Indians in a valley in the inland mountains to the east had earrings and small implements of that metal. Marcos had been tempted to go there, but now breathed a sigh of relief that he had kept his eye on the main goal in the north.

Marcos could hardly contain his excitement. This trip could be the grand climax of the all voyages of Atlantic discovery, the final link to the wealth of Cathay! "And these cities? Have there ever been white men there? Men like me? Our people have legends of seven cities built by men like me." He decided to leave out the complication that the Earth was proving to be round, and that Polo had reached Cathay and the Indies by traveling east from Europe, not west.

Traveler laughed and laughed again, until tears came to his eyes. "You are very strange. How could there be more men like you? There are seven cities in this province of Cíbola. But I tell you, they have never seen anyone like you or Lord Estevan." The others giggled about this. "We trade with these cities, and they trade with the other provinces, under other chiefs even farther away. And no one has seen strange people like you."

Marcos held up his crucifix. "Have you ever seen anything like this, in this city of Cíbola?"

The old man looked at it closely and skeptically, and shook his head in what was clearly a negative gesture, even before the translators had finished. "This is a strange fetish. This man looks very uncomfortable. Why should I see something like this in the north? Every clan has its own fetishes. Your fetishes are different, even among yourselves. You are a very strange man. You are very different from your friend." Cautiously, he touched Marcos's arm. And then rubbed it, inspecting his fingers. "This is not paint. Your skin is a different color, then. You are a very strange people, each with your different color, but I think you are a good man." The old man clapped Marcos on the arm with a big smile. Like Tall Man, he was missing more than one tooth. He also seemed to be missing the tip of each ear. Marcos studied him intently as the man grinned. The man was so full of praise for Cíbola that Marcos doubted all his stories could be true. Sometimes, in traveling, one has to take the local tales with a grain of salt, he reflected.

The interpreter broke in. "Estevan, your servant, he says you should come away this very hour, to join him so you can both go to this great place."

Then Tall Man looked at him guiltily, and Marcos was suddenly filled with foreboding. "What is it, my son?"

"I think that Estevan, ummmm, he will not wait long for you. He likes to be on the trail." Tall Man looked like he expected a blow from a cudgel.

"He will not go on. I told him to wait for me."

"That is why he say to come now, at once, on the hour. He expects you will catch up with him. He said, ummmm, he wants to explore the route further. He says that to sit on one's rear end is not good. He says you taught him that." Tall Man started to smile at this joke, but then thought better of it.

"But I have to wait here for the scouts that I sent west, to tell me about the coast."

"Yes, Father."

"Didn't you remind Estevan of his orders? Didn't you tell him not to go on?"

"Yes, but the orders are between you and him, Father. And Estevan has a strong spirit."

GOOD FRIDAY, APRIL 4, NOON. MARCOS STOOD IN THE PLAZA OF Vacapa and admired his handiwork, the chapel where he would tell the Indians about Easter. A fat Indian dog lay at his feet, looking on skeptically.

Marcos had taken a risk by converting and consecrating a native shrine. Perhaps he had been too forward, and should have accepted the Vacapans' offer to build him a new chapel on the edge of the village. But, in practical terms, it was better to make a bold statement by co-opting the pagan structure with a Christian church, right here in the midst of the village. Boldness was the way to succeed. This was the way Christ drove the money changers out of the Jewish temple, and Cortés had torn down the shrines of the Mexica to erect Christian chapels on top of them.

The ceremonial structure which the Vacapa villagers had allowed him to convert into a chapel originally had arrows embedded all over the outer surface, so that it resembled a giant porcupine. The walls outside and inside had been plastered and decorated with turquoise and other colored stones, brought as offerings and attached with resin. Some were worked into intricate patterns. Feathers and colored stones decorated the three interior posts that supported the roof. Colored tapestries, like blankets, had lined the back interior walls. They were woven with wool and cotton, dyed in various colors and woven into fantastic jagged patterns, such as a demon might design. In the center had been an altarlike table, with a large ceramic frog figure, inlaid with more bits of turquoise. It seemed to give off a blue gleam in the dark hut's interior, and gave Marcos an uneasy feeling.

In converting and consecrating the shrine, Marcos had removed the idol. An elder of the village had carried it off with a scowl. Marcos also stripped away the hangings, and the feathers and turquoises fixed to inner wooden posts. They were of uncertain significance, but pagan intent. With the help of several young natives, who seemed to revere their new visitor, Marcos enlarged the doorway of the hut, so that it was more like a canopy under which he could stand and preach to the crowd that would gather in the plaza. Upon the inside table he placed a sacramental cloth and outside the door he placed a tall cross, which he had painted white with pigment obtained from women making pottery.

There had been grumblings about his changes, mostly from the old men and women who gathered to watch, but the grumblers were in a minority. Most of the villagers looked on him with a sense of wonder. Marcos had spent days talking with them about Christ, the gospels, and Rome. The Indians who had accompanied him from the south explained to everyone that Marcos was a great teacher and liberator, come to tell them wonderful stories full of good tidings. Joyful acceptance, and a troubling tendency toward licentious celebration of unpredictable life, had won out over skepticism.

EASTER, APRIL 6. THE EASTER MORNING MASS HAD GONE WELL. The Indians, he had learned, loved stories, and word had spread that on this day Marcos would tell a grand story. People had assembled not only from Vacapa, but from nearby villages as well. Speaking slowly and simply through his own interpreters, including Juan and Tall Man, Marcos had explained about the greatest Lord of all, who had come down to Earth from his home in heaven, far away in the sky. He had come in the form of a man but he was really the Son of God. Because he was the Son of God, it was fitting that he had been born not of an ordinary woman, but of a virgin maid.

His Indian audience looked perplexed, but enthralled. Marcos plowed on. However, this Son of God, named Jesus, had a stepfather, who made tools of wood, much as the Indians did. The Indians smiled at that. The virgin and the stepfather, Marcos told them, had raised this Son to be a good man, and eventually the Son began to speak out about the things of God. He preached many messages from God, about how the humble, simple, and honest people of the Earth have within them the truest spirit of God, and how they must therefore love and help each other. As a result of these preachings, this Son of God had been assassinated by evil men who did not want the ways of humility to replace the ways of the rich and powerful.

But all was not lost. God, the father of all people, who still lived in heaven, knew that the people of Earth, even here in the village of Vacapa, were weak and tended to disobey His laws. In spite of this, God loved them, especially those who lived in harmony with His ways. To demonstrate this the Son of God rose up on the third day after his death, and walked out of his tomb. He went up into the sky and returned to heaven, where he protected all his followers from then on. This day, Easter, was the very day it had happened, many, many generations ago.

Marcos explained he himself was a follower of this God, who still lived in heaven. Furthermore, God in his mercy had promised to let everyone who believed this story come and live with him in heaven after they died, in eternal happiness. At this, the Indians in the crowd murmured among themselves. "Live in the sky?" they asked. It was all true, Marcos reiterated. Heaven was a celestial realm, beyond the sky. Scholars had proved that the sky consisted of seven crystalline spheres, centered on Earth. These spheres carried the moon, the sun, the planets, and the stars in their various courses. Many modern scholars thought heaven corresponded to the outermost realm of the universe, the seventh heaven, beyond the crystalline spheres where the planets moved. Anyone—even the poorest person—could live in that seventh heaven some day, but only if he accepted the story about this Son of God. If he did not, he was marked as an enemy of God, and there was a place for him far below the earth, full of fires and fumes, where he would be taken after he died, and tortured forever.

The Indians had watched and listened. They seemed deeply impressed by the story.

NOW, IN THE MIDDAY EASTER SUN, MARCOS WAS PREPARING TO explain to the Indians about the governance that Spain was offering them. Marcos was mounting a small painting of the king and queen on a post in the plaza when there was a commotion in the distance. Juan came running to find him. "Father, messengers have come!"

What was this? More good news from Estevan?

It was something else. First, the Indian scouts had returned from the coast, with news of additional islands. Marcos dutifully attempted to write down the strange names in his book. The coast was dry and continued on toward the northwest. Secondly, three Indians had come from the east, saying they had heard of the black and white strangers who wanted to meet them. These visitors were heavily tattooed in multiple colors. One, who seemed to be the leader, had shoulders that were entirely blue. They studied Marcos as carefully as he studied them. In truth, Marcos was chagrined to sense their disappointment at seeing only one white man among a group of Indians—a plain, thin man in a light robe of gray wool. Parleys with the interpreters yielded the information that these visitors, too, knew of Cíbola. To Marcos, the important fact was that news of his expedition had spread to a different province in a matter of days. This confirmed that the Indians in these northern lands communicated from one province to another, and they had a good trail network.

To emphasize the blessings of this fine Easter day, God seemed to be blessing Marcos's every effort with success. With his news about the fabled northern empire, even Estevan had partially redeemed himself. Tomorrow Marcos would leave Vacapa, race north, and catch up to the Moor. He sent Juan to announce to the villagers that there would be one final ceremony this evening, the reading of the acts of possession and the *Requerimiento*, the legal document which would explain and formalize the extension of Christian Spanish rule to this area.

Marcos glanced again at the large cross of sticks that Estevan had sent back. That simple cross seemed destined to lead to discoveries that would rival Mexico and Peru! Many a spring day he had spent as a boy on the dry hills above the blue Mediterranean—hills not unlike these, where he had wondered at the strange ships and sea captains and travelers of the past who must have plied those waters and brought incredible tales back to their own people. Now he was in that company.

In the early evening of Easter, the Indians of Vacapa gathered in the dusty plaza. They had been in a festive mood during

Marcos's entire visit, and they clearly understood that this was a climactic moment. The men wore three, five, and even ten strings of turquoise, and the lords of the town wore elaborate feather crowns and feathered capes over their shoulders. The women had donned their cleanest cotton shifts and had shaded their eyes with dark brown pigment.

Marcos realized he had come to care about these cheerful people, who had waited so long in this dark part of the world for the light of the celestial realm to beam down upon them. During his morning sermon, he had already announced the good news that their Spanish brothers would welcome them into the Christian world, under the benevolence of the king's beneficent representative, Viceroy Antonio Mendoza.

Even as the Indians were still gathering, he read quickly through the acts of possession, claiming all these lands for the Spanish Crown, and had Juan and even Tall Man sign their marks on the form as witnesses. These acts were a Spanish legal necessity, not intended for the Indians. And now came the *Requerimiento*, which was a different matter, a message directly for the native population.

When the people had assembled, he took the portrait of the king and queen, which had caused much wonderment among the people, and carried it through the crowd as his interpreters explained that these good-hearted royal people were supreme lords of the Spanish, and that they lived far across the waters to the east, and that they had sent a message specifically to the Indians. He unrolled the scroll he had carried and began reading, pausing for the interpreters to struggle with the concepts. Spanish scholars from the royal court had correctly predicted that some of the native tribes would have trouble understanding the nuances of the legal and philosophical concepts, and yet everyone agreed that in the name of fairness this proclamation must be read in every newly claimed land. Some lawyers argued that if the natives could not understand the proclamation, it was merely a measure of their own backwardness, not the fault of Spain. The first part of the *Requerimiento* echoed some of the material he had gone over in his morning sermon.

On behalf of the King, Don Carlos V, and his Queen, subduers of the barbarous nations, I, Marcos, his servant, notify and make known to you, as best I can, the following. The Lord God created heaven and earth, and made one man and one woman, of whom we are all descendants. But because of the multitude that sprang from this original man and woman, during the five thousand years since the world began, it was necessary for some men to go one way and some another, dividing themselves into many provinces.

Over all these nations, God appointed one man, called Saint Peter, to be superior to all men in the world, so that all should obey him. He was to be head of the whole human race, no matter under what law or sect people might live. God commanded him to put his seat in Rome, the spot most fitting from which to rule the world. From there he should judge and govern all Christians, Moors, Jews, Gentiles, and all other sects. This man is called the Pope. The men who lived in the time of Saint Peter regarded him as the most superior person of the universe, and so also they have regarded all others who have been elected to serve as Pope after him.

One of these Popes has given all these islands and mainlands—all the Indies and Mexico—to the aforesaid King and Queen, and to all their successors. This is spelled out in certain legal writings, which you can see if you wish.

Therefore, their highnesses, the King and Queen, are lords of these islands and this mainland, by virtue of this decree of the Pope. Many of the inhabitants of these lands, indeed almost all to whom this proclamation has been read, have accepted their highnesses as their lords, in the way that subjects of a king ought to do, with good will and no resistance, when they were informed of the aforesaid facts. They also received and obeyed the priests whom their highnesses sent to preach to them and teach them about our holy faith. They have all become Christians, and their highnesses have joyfully received them, commanding that they be treated as subjects of Spain. Thus, as best

we can, we ask and require that you think about what we have
said, and take whatever time you need to deliberate about it,
and that you acknowledge the church as the ruler and superior
organizer of the whole world; and the Pope as high priest; and
the King and Queen of Spain as our lords and as the lords of
these lands, since the Pope has designated these lands to
belong to the King and Queen of Spain.

The Indians had grown very quiet, listening to the translators.
The air was still warm, and Marcos paused to take a drink of water
as the translators struggled on. It was the next part of the *Requerim-*
iento, the final two paragraphs, that sometimes got touchy. He
paused a bit longer, and looked up at the now-serious faces.

CHAPTER 4

March, 1989; Tucson

Marcos spent March beginning his journey north, and I spent March 450 years later tracking him. You can see why I began thinking about how his life paralleled mine. Around us both, vast forces were in motion, seeking fortunes just over the horizon.

MARCH 1, 1989. THE HEARING ABOUT OUR DEVELOPMENT PLAN was still scheduled before the county board of supervisors in April, and Mr. Rooney needed my report before that. It would be part of his ammunition. Word on the street was that questions would be raised at the hearing about our impact on the valley ranchlands and adjacent national forestlands. Our strategy was to demonstrate our concern for the land, the history, the future.

"Find out where Coronado went. I want the real thing, Mr. Scott," Mr. Rooney would tell me. "Good scholarship. We don't want somebody poking holes in our story, right? But you realize, it adds to the project if we can show that Coronado went somewhere near us. I'm sure you understand."

It didn't worry me, his implied pressure. Most scholars already agreed with his idea that Coronado came near our area. All I had to do was write it down. What was the problem?

The problem was that I was getting hooked on Marcos and Estevan and Coronado and the rest of them. Where did they go? What did they find? Was Marcos a fraud? I wanted to convince myself, not Mr. Rooney or the supervisors.

I had already started trying to write the report, but the more I got into it, the more I wanted to follow the loose ends, which were all over the place. The books and papers I needed were all in the university library: ancient Spanish texts, old translations into English, and scholarly journals full of argumentative papers about Coronado esoterica. I had to get over there and immerse myself. For too many weeks I had been letting my other office assignments get in the way.

On the rainy Wednesday night of March 1, I found myself driving to my old stomping grounds at the Great Desert University. The evening rain surrounded my Honda Prelude with a darkness so deep that the white lines on the pavement had dissolved in black liquid. Streetlights reflected dimly in distorted puddles of water, smeared by the streaks on my windshield. Wipers in Tucson were like smoke detectors; by the time you needed them they were too old to work. The weather elevated my mood. Anyone from the Sonoran Desert loves rain.

Given my profession, I didn't just drive the streets, I judged them. I chose Tucson Boulevard because it was less crowded than the main drags, like Campbell and Speedway. "Speedway" Boulevard. It was named back in the '20s or '30s when some sons of a local real estate family used to race their cars out in the desert on what was then a dirt road. Speedway; what a joke. It was already out of control by the '80s, one of the first streets to go, with cars struggling from light to light every afternoon. Under the impassive sun, they backed up for blocks at major intersections, like exhausted beasts. Tucsonans kept voting down freeways that would carve up the city and destroy old neighborhoods to service the new ones out on the edge of town. The heart of the city was preserved, but the suburbs and their new cars just kept coming. Population was going up, water was going down. Traffic was getting awful.

It made me think about my job. Tucson, since 1950, had been a one-industry town, and the industry was buying up land, getting it rezoned, and selling it to builders of subdivisions. The wealthiest businesspeople were not captains of industry but a handful of development and real estate executives. They made enough money to get their people into city, county, and state governments, to keep the system going.

Phoenix, the capital, lay ninety miles to the north across a desert *despoblado*. It was twice as big as Tucson, and already getting smog alerts, which should have been a warning. But for some reason Phoenicians thought that being the New Los Angeles was a cause for pride. Gated, eight-cylinder enclaves with grassy lawns and tree-lined avenues were tastefully segregated from four-cylinder neighborhoods with dusty yards and no garages. Growth was the mantra. In contrast, Tucson was schizophrenic, occasionally passing tighter zoning ordinances during odd years when the developers lost control of the city council. The theory was to control sprawl, and preserve open spaces around the city, but was all for naught. The state legislature in Phoenix, citing private property rights, routinely overturned these bits of social engineering, which they viewed as an insult to the American way of life. They did this, of course, on the days when they weren't touting local government. Rednecks in suits, the legislators regarded it as their mission to save the state from creeping Tucson socialism. Tucsonans talked about quality of life; Phoenicians talked about cost per square foot. Frustrated neighborhood activists in Tucson looked toward the Phoenix Philistines with fear and loathing, and kidded about seceding to form the new state of Baja Arizona. They resurrected the joke San Franciscans used to tell about L.A.: What is the difference between yogurt and Phoenix? Yogurt contains an active culture.

On Tucson's rare rainy nights, nobody thought about all that. The streets were full of drivers who didn't know how to handle wet pavement. An occasional police car would blare past me on the way to some fender bender. Drivers on Tucson Boulevard seemed less hysterical than on the main drags; they spaced themselves at decent intervals, swinging around the huge puddles. Our desert city hadn't bothered with adequate storm sewers. If a rain lasted more than twenty minutes, Tucson Boulevard, like many of our streets, turned into a streambed.

As I drove, I mused about what the land had looked like to Marcos, back in the days when there were no cities. To be more honest, I mused about Phaedra. She and I had started going out to lunch together in February. As a matter of fact we had already gone out once to a movie, the newly restored rerelease of *Lawrence of Arabia*. I loved it. I wondered if Marcos felt the same guilt as *el Aurens*, who found himself cast in the role as a messiah to the Arabs during World War I, and then found himself caught up in their betrayal at the Versailles peace conference.

"Where were the women in that film?" asked Phaedra when we came out.

"But—"

"Just kidding. It was wonderful. Peter O'Toole was wonderful. And Omar Sharif. Mmmmm." She stood back and examined my psyche with her x-ray vision. "You liked that, didn't you? You look exalted." Then she gave me a kiss. In the next week we progressed to postlunch kisses in the car. What was all the fuss about mixing business and pleasure, anyway? Life's too short to pass up attractions, office or no office. We were consenting adults. Whose business was it anyhow? Kenneth Starr hadn't been invented yet.

Each week I learned more about Phaedra. Her background was lapsed Hispanic. Her grandparents on one side had moved north from Sonora to New Mexico early in the century.

There was Indian blood in there somewhere, and Anglo blood too. One of those sprawling Hispanic families, mostly scattered around the lower-to-middle rungs of the socioeconomic ladder. Her parents had ended up in Denver, where she was raised. When her parents broke up, Phaedra's Hispanic mom moved back to the sun belt, where you didn't have to deal with rain and snow. There was an ex-husband in the story, but he had mercifully split to L.A. after a semi-amicable divorce. Broken marriages, a bond to share. There was a 5-year-old daughter, too—Amber—but she was not Phaedra's. Phaedra had no kids. Amber belonged to Phaedra's sister who had also been married. That marriage had collapsed, too, and Amber spent a lot of time with Phaedra and with Phaedra's mom while Phaedra was at work. The sister had a part-time job; she and Phaedra were raising Amber as if it were a joint project. "Amber depends on both of us," she said. "We both had marriage melt-downs. Sisters are more reliable than husbands."

Phaedra and her sister had each gone to both the local junior col-lege and to the university before and during their marriages. But when the marriages imploded, they had to leave college to support themselves and their joint daughter, not to mention help their mom. Phaedra had great native intelligence. She was full of ideas and dreams. She said she had always loved books. It was scary how educated she had become without ever graduating from the U. There were Pd.D.'s who should be so smart. But in the country we've built, you need paper certificates to certify wisdom. So Phae-dra, unable to afford the time or money to go back to school, labored on as the indispensable assistant in Mr. Rooney's office, dressing smartly, struggling to get ahead, wondering where her life was headed, pulling herself up by her own high heels.

She was cheerful there every day, but in her private moods, she railed about support-staff salary, precarious health care, lack of safety net, and absence of child care options for her and her sister. The old single-mom story. "The American family is dead," she'd say. "We're entering the neo-neolithic. You need a network of rel-atives and friends to raise a kid."

She acted like Amber was her own child. "I'm part of her net-work," she'd say. I was wondering if I wanted to be part of the net-work. Or if I'd be admitted, even if I tried to get in.

THE RAIN HAD STOPPED BY THE TIME I ARRIVED AT THE BIG RED-brick university library. I liked that building. Out in front, in those days, on a grassy knoll, was a wonderful sculpture of a young woman playing a flute. Most of the other outdoor sculptures on campus were formalisms exuding twentieth-century art department credos that art should make a political statement. Attitudinous constructs in sufficient quantity were supposed to shock the bourgeoisie into renouncing materialism. Anyway, the flute player exuded warmth and creativity and pleasure, and I paused to say hello to her.

I went inside. The old books were all there, waiting for me. I looked at the checkout records. Hardly anybody had checked them out since I had used them ten years before. Big empty tables offered clean surfaces and invited productive work. I found the very table where I had written my term paper. It carried me back in time. I had been smitten by a woman student who used to study there. I would sit there, pretending casualness, thinking that sooner or later she would drop her pen or something, and that would lead to one of the great romances. She never did drop her pen.

Now, ten years later, my table looked a little more worn, like I did. I half-consciously fantasized that another woman like the first would come along. This time I was better prepared. The university was wonderful. Nature, in her wisdom, kept turning out new women students with smiles on their faces, wave after wave. The library was like a garden where flowers bloomed, year after year. You didn't have to do anything. I felt a little guilty about watching them; but still, Phaedra and I hadn't exactly formalized our relationship.

I WORKED HARD THAT NIGHT. IT WAS STRANGE TO SIT AT MY TABLE and imagine the earlier me who had sat in the same spot, and who was now as much a ghost as Marcos himself. Was my own spirit somewhere in that room? Can you be haunted by your own ghost?

The more I read the more fascinated I got. All these stories that no one else knew. Most American kids hear about the pilgrims and Daniel Boone and George Washington, but no one told us about Marcos de Niza or Estevan Dorantes or Francisco Vázquez or Viceroy Mendoza or Bartolomé de Las Casas, the very human and variously flawed heroes of the Southwest, and how they lived their saga generations *before* Plymouth Rock got stepped on.

At first I made quick progress. Some of it had to do with place-names in our region, which helped me document the route. Marcos's report, unfortunately, didn't give many place names, but Coronado's army chroniclers gave lots of names. They said they came to the famous native town of Corazones, and several of them mentioned that it was in the valley of "Señora," which is why earlier historians had located Corazones on the river now known as the Rio Sonora. The army then followed that river valley north through various Indian towns. One mentioned an Indian village of "Arispa" in that valley, and another called it "Ispe." This had to be the modern Mexican town of Arizpe, on the Rio Sonora just south of the border. It was significant to the Spanish, and became a regional capital in the 1700s. Based on these place-names, most scholars accepted that the army came up the Rio Sonora, past modern Arizpe, heading right for southeast Arizona.

Some of the best geographical reporting came from a Coronado army chronicler named Jaramillo, who said that after the army came up the "Señora" River, they marched four days farther north across deserted country to a different river the Indians called the Nexpa. They continued a couple of days north along this river downstream—an important clue, since few rivers in this area flow north. Then, as Jaramillo wrote, they "departed from the stream, turning right." This was pretty easy to reconstruct. If you come north from headwaters of the modern Sonora river, in Mexico, you cross empty grasslands a few miles south of the border and then you hit the headwaters of the San Pedro River, flowing north into Arizona. The San Pedro is the next valley east of Tucson. You wouldn't go too far north on the San Pedro because it leads into rugged country. You'd turn right and go around the mountains on a flatter route. The "Nexpa" had to be the San Pedro.

I took inordinate pride in knowing the original prehistoric name of one of our rivers. I decided then and there to combine my historical life with my love life, by going out with Phaedra for a hike on the San Pedro, to see what it looked like. Funny euphemism, "going out." In this case it was apt, since we'd be hiking. We'd see one of the rivers as Marcos and Coronado had seen them. In Tucson, the water table had been pumped so far down that our Santa Cruz "River" looked like the Okie dust bowl during the depression; but the San Pedro—that was still flowing, still natural. Its banks still had trees.

THE NEXT DAY AT THE OFFICE, I SUGGESTED TO PHAEDRA THAT WE could go for a hike. "Along the Nexpa River," I said. She said she never heard of it. I smiled mysteriously and said it was the real name of one of our local streams, and I would take her there. "It's not like the Sandy Cruz," I told her. "It's got water." She checked her calendar against her activities with her sister and Amber, and agreed to a date on an upcoming Saturday, the 11th.

You see, in spite of the library of temptations, I was still concentrating on my Phaedra option.

IN GENERAL, I LIKED MY JOB JUST FINE, IN SPITE OF MY INITIAL MIS-givings about working for a developer. Obviously, I was enthralled with the part of the job I'm telling you about—the researching of Coronado's route relative to our property. As for Coronado estates, there was not much to complain about, from a planner's point of view. Everything was well thought-out, and, after all, it was not classic urban sprawl, as we kept reminding ourselves. My first specific forebodings came from a conversation I had around this time with Mr. Rooney. He'd call me in about one thing or another, and then, when he was in a good mood, steer the conversation toward philosophy, as if he enjoyed having a small debate. We could actually argue, within unspoken guidelines. On this particular occasion, he got into the private property issue, the favorite hobgoblin of Arizona politics. He let his hair down and said the real issue with Coronado Estates was whether a land owner "out in the middle of nowhere," as he put it, would be free to develop his property as he pleased.

I said something about being responsible to the larger community.

"Who's that?"

"Surrounding towns, people in Tucson, the environment . . . For example, there's the whole question of managing the water table in the whole valley, and encroaching on national forest land."

"We don't encroach on national forestland."

"But if we put high-density housing up against the forest boundary, then you have dogs and hikers encroaching on wildlife and—"

"The only people we're responsible to are our buyers and our investors. The park does its thing inside its boundaries and we should be free to build as we like within ours."

"What do you mean, 'free'? We already accept limitations. You can't build an asbestos plant in your backyard. John Gardner, the guy who built up the Peace Corps, said 'Freedom and responsibility, liberty and duty: that's the deal.' That's what I'm talking about. Where's the long-term conscience?"

Maybe I overstepped the guidelines of our little discussions, but Mr. Rooney didn't blink. "If some builder wants to worry about public land and can offer a better value, let people flock to him and stop buying our stuff. It's a free market. That's how the people are served best."

"But in the long term we may all end up with a ruined valley, no water, damage to the wildlife population. You start to apply that on a global scale, you get a planet with rich CEOs and crummy living conditions and no resources."

"That's what they teach you in planning school, isn't it?"

"Sure."

"But what they leave out is that if starts to happen, the market will respond. Look at rubber during World War II. When it got scarce, we invented a synthetic substitute."

"Why not apply the intelligence that God gave us, ahead of time, instead of blundering into—"

"'Ahead of time' means a planned economy. Entrepreneurial freedom—that's what'll save the world."

"Jesus loves me, this I know, for the Bible tells me so."

"I beg your pardon?"

"I had a teacher who used to point out how free market theory was becoming a mantra to absolve business people of guilt."

"I think it's time for you to get back to work." That time I overstepped the line.

I HIT THE LIBRARY SEVERAL MORE AFTERNOONS THAT WEEK. I poured over my old Spanish friends' letters. It felt as if they had been mailed to me in the 1500s and had just arrived. The information kept adding up. If the army turned east off the Nexpa, it must have taken them directly toward our property. One possible route was to turn north up the Sulfur Springs Valley, in which case they would have gone directly across Coronado Estates! Even if they bypassed the Sulfur Springs Valley, they couldn't have missed us by more than a few miles. Mr. Rooney would be ecstatic. I sat at my table basking in triumph. Now all I had to do was fill in some details and finish writing up the report. I decided to go over to the venerable student union to grab some dinner.

It was strange and nostalgic, spending time on campus, getting dinner at the student union. Sometimes I found myself daydreaming about my own days here, how I had arrived wondering what my future would be. Now I had slipped through time like a salmon swimming upstream. I was here, in the future, and it was the past I thought about.

In the old days at the student union, I would pick up one of the loaner copies of the *New York Times* in the reading room, or visit the art gallery, or listen to professors argue at tables next to me in the several restaurants. It was my first exposure to the outside world of ideas. Now, I learned that budgets had been cut, the art gallery was to be closed, and the restaurants were being replaced by Pizza Hut and McDonald's franchises. Mr. Rooney would have loved these signs of free enterprise—even universities were participating in the country's economic progress.

If I had memories from my few years on this campus, what must it be like for the old professors, who had spent a lifetime here, every day passing the site of early triumph or disaster or secret foible? It was not like working downtown, where offices moved as leases expired. It was like living in your own private garden, which went on and on, and would outlive you. Here was the corner where you had that accident with the bicycle; here was the auditorium where you were applauded for your speech after you won that prize; here was the conference room where you were denounced in some faculty meeting the following year. Here was the tree under which you sat with some lover. How did it feel, as you got older, as the campus transformed into a catalog of memories, where the aged buildings were maintained in changeless permanence, and the students grew younger and younger?

One day I had an epiphany. Facts that I had known since grade school suddenly clicked into a larger framework, like wandering atoms suddenly snapping into a crystal lattice and making a new state of matter. I saw that those few centuries of exploration toward America, from the Vikings to Coronado, formed a unique moment in humans' relation to the planet itself. During those brief centuries, two branches of humanity met for the first time after a million years of wandering. One branch of humanity had spread east out of Africa across Asia, Mongolia, Alaska, and down into the Americas. The other branch took the other route, north out of Africa, up across Europe and finally west across the Atlantic. Finally they met. In other words, humanity had wrapped around the finite globe and was meeting itself for the first time in all of history. Those few centuries marked the "moment" when we humans finally closed our global frontier. Marcos was an eyewitness participant: the first European to reach cities built by the Asiatic wanderers who had reached the American Southwest.

How strange, then, that Marcos's book moldered on the university library shelf, forgotten by everyone. Questions kept pounding in my brain. Why was I the only one who had checked it out in ten years? Why did school children never hear of it? Enthralled by TV superheroes, they knew none of the adventures that had happened on the soil beneath their feet.

It was like some sort of Buddhist enlightenment, my odd and sudden sensation that we were immersed in an exploding pageant of history. Whole centuries were as important as weeks—even in ordinary daily life. From then on, I began seeing everything in a different way. Everyone else around me seemed immersed in absurd, forgettable daily details, failing to see the overall reality. They were like a beginning painter, who looks at a scene with eyes too wide-open, and tries to render too many details without seeing the big patterns that make beauty. A seasoned painter squints and sees masses of color and light, and renders the larger reality; and then concentrates on only a few telling details. In the same way, I sensed that daily urban reality blocked out the big patterns that could lead to enlightenment.

It was a good realization, but it made me iconoclastic. As I followed Marcos and Coronado day by day, and as I thought about great tides of time, I got deeper into the habit of making comparisons with what was happening on the same dates during our own glorious century, just 450 years later, as culled from the newspaper. Daily facts took on ineffable connotations.

March 7, for example, was a big day for both of us. Marcos says on the first page of his *Relación* that he set out from Culiacán to find the northern empire. March 7 was filled with omens and portents in my own year of 1989. Believe it or not, the sun was partially eclipsed in Tucson! I resisted the urge to believe it meant something, but when several of us stepped outside the office to view the eclipse through special mylar glasses, Phaedra let her hand linger on mine as we passed the glasses back and forth. Then she said she was really looking forward to the hike. So I knew the future would be interesting.

There were other omens on Marcos's departure day of March 7. A huge solar flare disrupted communications, and the Soviets said they needed more proof of damage to the ozone layer before agreeing to ban freon. Page four of the paper said that a group of scholars, investigating Biblical texts, had decided that Jesus didn't ever actually say he'd come back and usher in a new age. I wondered what Marcos might have said about that. Meanwhile, the Tucson City Council was looking into lowering fees on the city's ubiquitous golf courses, built to meet the needs of the exploding population of sun belt retirees. The paper reported that Mr. Rooney's lawyer was at the meeting, arguing that golf courses should be counted as part of the natural open space allotment required by new zoning ordinances in each new development. Golf courses were our new "nature."

The next day, March 8, the temperature broke a 29-year-old record by reaching 88.

EVERY FEW DAYS I'D WRITE OUT FRAGMENTS OF MY IDEAS AND bring them to Phaedra, who would type them into her clunky '80's computer. She'd give me printouts, which would become my building blocks of my report to Mr. Big. In those days, we didn't carry laptops. Why didn't I just finish the report and be done with it? The trouble was, as I said, I was fatally caught in the web of historical puzzles. As usual, the controversy about Marcos attracted me most. He was the key figure, since he had first proven the existence of the Seven Cities of Cíbola, yet there were all those claims that he hadn't done what he said he had done. But the more of his stuff I read, the more I grew to like the guy. There was even a sense of humor in his report. And I admired his open-heartedness and raw courage, setting off into the unknown with no insurance policy. It was my entertainment, figuring out what he had really done— better than TV, more fun than Nintendo. It never grew dull because it drew me on, as if by its own secret power. I was as happy as a gumshoe with wiretaps on his chief suspects; which is what I was, except that the alleged crime of conspiracy and concealment was 450 years old. I was beginning to think of it as My Case. The Case of the Fraudulent Friar.

The key clue in pegging Marcos's positions during his mysterious trip was the location of the one village he described by name, Vacapa. There was some ambiguity in the date of his arrival, due to usage in those days of the term "Passion Sunday," but it

appears that it took him 14 days (or possibly 21) to get from Culiacán to Vacapa. He stated clearly that he left Vacapa on April 7.
Given these statements, the position of Vacapa calibrates the
timescale and travel rates needed for the rest of the journey. The
locations suggested by historians for Vacapa looked as if the
scholars had thrown random darts at a map of Sonora. Some said
it was at the far south end of Sonora, only a few days north of
Culiacán. Others put it at the north end of the state at the border
with Arizona.

The scholars who liked the southern position were the ones who
argued that Marcos didn't have time to make it all the way to
Cíbola. By the 1800s, the location of Cíbola was clearly known. It
was the pueblo of Zuni, in west-central New Mexico. Coronado
himself had confirmed this. To put Vacapa at the south end of
Sonora and then ask Marcos to reach Cíbola/Zuni and return to
Mexico City in the time available was like putting a ladder in a hole
and then realizing the top wouldn't reach the roof. However, putting Vacapa that far south, where the slave raiders had operated,
ignored Marcos's comment that the Vacapans hadn't heard of the
Christians.

The scholars who put Vacapa at the north end of the state, near
the north end of the Gulf of California, ignored Marcos's comment
that he had to travel about two more weeks north to reach the latitude where the Gulf ended and the coastline turned west.

So Vacapa had to be in the middle. I checked out what the old,
ghostly me had written in my term paper. The logic still seemed
pretty good:

*The mystery of the location of Vacapa is tied to the location of
Corazones, the prosperous "Village of the Hearts," named by
Cabeza de Vaca's group after they were given a feast of deer
hearts. Corazones, in the center of Sonora somewhere near the
modern town of Ures, is the linchpin in locating the scenes
recorded by the early explorers. When Marcos and Estevan
traveled north in 1539, Marcos did not specifically record pass-*

ing through Corazones. If he had recognized it, he probably would have mentioned it, since it had been emphasized by Cabeza de Vaca's party. But Marcos did describe a very similar feast in a village a few days's journey north of Vacapa, which suggests this was the general region of Corazones. Furthermore, Coronado's chroniclers mentioned a place name, "Vacapan," apparently in the vicinity of Corazones, supporting the idea that Marcos's Vacapa was nearby.

As I compared the old documents, I soon discovered other clues about Vacapa. In Corazones the natives told Cabeza de Vaca that they knew about Cíbola and traded there, but in Vacapa the natives were not able to tell Marcos about Cíbola. So Vacapa was probably a bit south of Corazones. Sure enough, Estevan encountered people who knew of Cíbola only two days north of Vacapa. All this indicated that Vacapa was just a few days' journey south of Corazones.

A river named Rio Matape and a modern town called Matape are located there. In some early references it was spelled "Matapa." The modern name may be a descendent of the name Marcos rendered as Vacapa, and Matape may thus be the region of Marcos de Niza's lost village. Another village called Sayopa is about thirty miles southeast of there, on the Yaqui River. This name may be a ghostly echo of the name *Sayota*, by which the natives of the same tribe as the Vacapans referred to Marcos three days before he reached Vacapa.

I soon discovered that if I put Vacapa in that area, near the Rio Yaqui or Rio Matape, in central Sonora, the rest of Marcos's timetable made sense. I also discovered that, in spite of historians' seemingly random placement of Vacapa—or perhaps because of it—at least one of them had actually picked the same location I did, near Matape/Sayopa.

With Vacapa pegged, the documents began to hang together even better, and some of the attacks on Marcos himself began to look less reasonable. Each day, as I read the letters and reports, Marcos and the other characters became more real. That's the great thing about civilization; things are handed down, and you can share adventures and ideas with ancient friends. I developed this feeling that those guys lived closer to the ground than we do, closer to the basics. They were out there in the original, raw, beautiful country, while we are insulated from seasons, storms, heat, cold, smells. You can see how I continued to get more detached from what everyone else was mistakenly calling normal life: offices, cars, cities, smog layers, and dinnertime TV intoning news reports of mayhem.

ON SATURDAY, MARCH 11, PHAEDRA AND I HEADED OUT TOWARD the Nexpa. We drove east, happily chatting about inconsequential office gossip. Beyond the city, everything seemed more open. A half hour away, the sky was a brighter color of blue, like blue light shining through a blue opal shade. The Empire Mountains were low brown hills and the Whetstones made a pleasing profile of sharp ridges and blunted peaks. They were speckled with low vegetation, the gray-green color peculiar to Sonoran Desert plant life. Fat creosote bushes, happy after the winter rains, were scattered evenly across the rolling plains, as if they had been dropped from airplanes. Between the mountains you could see for miles: long, pale, green-tan vistas running out toward blue mountains on the horizon.

Out here, the land was so timeless that—with my new enlightenment—it seemed to exist in all moments of time simultaneously. You could hear the music of the land in your mind, great contrapuntal fugues with chords made out of simultaneous melody lines drawn from different eras. I almost asked Phaedra if she could hear it, but I was afraid I wouldn't be able to explain what I was talking about. She and I were just one note in the whole symphony.

At one point I tried to explain my emerging attitude. "For example," I was saying, "when the Europeans came here the land was a common resource. The Spanish brought in land grants from the king; one man was given 'ownership'"—I made little quote marks with my fingers—"over vast tracts, and of course the right to pass it on to his children. In ten generations the land of North America went from common resource to private commodity. Did you ever think how weird it is that Mr. Rooney can buy big pieces of land and build houses on them—and it's all just a private deal?"

"It's not so private. There's the planning and zoning commission, and approval by the board of supervisors. They could turn him down."

"So the commission turns down the deal, to save the green space near the city. Mr. R. just waits a few years until he has a pro-business majority on the board. Then he comes back and tries again. Eventually, *poof!*, the land is gone and he's built houses on it. Rezoning denials are just temporary. Building is permanent."

"People have to live somewhere."

"There's too many people."

"So join Planned Parenthood."

"Doesn't it seem weird to you that all Rooney does is sit at his desk and make telephone calls and sign papers, but he's the one who gets rich? Does he actually produce anything?"

"He told me once he had never built a house himself. He said he doesn't have any carpentry skills. Isn't that funny? I think it's funny."

To get to the hiking trail, we had to drive through Tombstone. It had a sign marking its elevation as 4500 feet and announcing a "Historama" narrated by Vincent Price. There were entire tourist shops devoted to Wyatt Earp. We didn't stop.

"Mr. Rooney wants to put in a history center," I said to Phaedra. "Do you think he'll want a 'Historama'?"

"What *is* a historama?" she laughed.

"I don't know, but I don't think I want one."

"We aren't going to be putting in anything if we don't get final approval from the board." Everyone in the office was preoccupied with our final hearing, now six weeks away.

South of Tombstone, we could see a white object hovering high over the blue Huachuca Mountains, like a UFO. It was a tethered aerostat balloon. I had read about it in the paper. It carried radar and was installed by some agency to keep watch for drug-bearing planes heading into the U.S. from Mexico. The drug runners followed a new trade route in the sky, only a few hundred feet above the old one where Marcos had walked.

WHEN WE REACHED THE RIVER, THE AIR WAS GETTING WARM already.

"This isn't the Nexpa," she said. "This is the San Pedro."

I explained to her about the old name, how it had been reported to the first Spaniards as the local name for the river, and how it had thus survived from prehistoric times.

"I like that, Kevin Scott," she said. "You've got a direct telephone line to the past."

The rippling stream was thirty feet wide and maybe eight inches deep, floored with pebbles and sand. We had brought old tennis shoes, to walk in the avenue of cooling water. A row of giant cottonwoods, big as cumulus clouds, lined the banks, making an enormous shady avenue. The voluptuous deciduous branches were much brighter than the scrawny desert vegetation; they seemed almost Day-Glo green. Standing in the middle and looking down the stream was like looking down the aisle of nature's gothic cathedral, with giant arboreal pillars sweeping up to a vaulted green roof. In the trees, the birds were constantly singing, nature's free choral concert. A few hundred yards on either side of the cottonwoods was a bosque of scruffy mesquite, and then the desert. The sacramental liquid water, the lime-green gothic arches, and the choir of birds projected sensuality in the midst of the dry brown vistas.

Phaedra projected sensuality, too. Her blouse was splashed with water, and she'd kick the water up on me, too, every once in a while. She was talking about how beauty couldn't last, about how we should enjoy it while we could. The upstream town of Sierra Vista was growing fast, she said, and the prediction was that in a few years its pumping would lower the water table and this stretch of the river would be dead. "You can designate a river wildlife preserve if you want," she lectured, "but if the water stops coming in at the uphill end, you lose your river. And in Arizona, if you don't have a river, you don't have wildlife."

She should have been named after Cassandra, not Phaedra. Her talk about the river cast a pall over the beauty of the scene. I asked her how she knew about the dropping water table and she said she had been going to Sierra Club meetings.

"Really? I mean, isn't that a little . . . status inconsistent?"

"Mr. Rooney likes me to go. He wants me to report what's going on. He likes to get different perspectives. He likes that in you, too. He says you open new horizons for him. He laughs about it."

"Yeah? I thought I was an ordinary worker bee."

"Amber would like this," she added dreamily, waving at the trees. "I look at this river and realize it may be gone by the time she grows up. But as Mr. Rooney says, everything changes. There'll be something new to see when she's my age."

The sun was blasting down, the air was warm before noon, and it felt good to walk in the riverbed with our feet in the cold, clear water, so I put gloom out of my mind. The water was only a few inches deep, and the riverbed was covered with little stones that sparkled in a hundred earthy colors. The water continued to splash on Phaedra's shorts and blouse, and even the scarf she was wearing, kerchief-style, around her neck. It made her look even more sexy than usual. She knew it.

Part of her fascination as a woman was that every time you thought you knew her, some new twist came up. To her credit, when we talked, she steered conversation away from any serious details of office politics—at least at the beginning. "Did you know," she said at last, "when Mr. Rooney named our place, he did a survey and found most people don't know about Coronado? It almost stopped him from using the name. We did a little poll, and got comments like, 'It's a baseball team, right?' Or 'Isn't it a high school?' The ones who've heard of Coronado don't know what he did. They are amazed when you tell them he went as far as Kansas."

When we stopped under a cottonwood to get the lunch out of my backpack, she fished a worn paperback out of her own pack.

"By the way," she continued, "why haven't you finished that report by now?"

"I'm trying. Everything I learn connects with something else."

"You're a slow mover, aren't you?"

Before I could make a move to set the record straight, she waved the book. "Here, I brought something for you. There is an interesting point you could make in your report."

I liked it, that she wanted to help me with my report. She handed me the book. It was *Cadillac Desert,* published in 1985. It was a history of the west and how we're doomed because we're using up the water. "This is a case of the right book at the right time," Phaedra said. "That's the key to success. Writing the right book at the wrong time gets you nowhere." She opened to the page of reviews. "Look. The *Washington Post* says this book is ' . . . wonderfully researched . . . timely and of national importance.' And the *L.A. Times* says it is 'well-written history and analysis, thoroughly researched. . . . ' And here, look." She pointed at a page. I looked over her shoulder. Her hair smelled wonderful and fresh, like spring. "The *St. Louis Post-Dispatch* said it's 'beautifully written and meticulously researched. . . . '

"Okay, okay, I get the idea."

"Yeah? Well, listen to this." She started picking out fragments of lines in the first pages of the book. "In 1539 Coronado set out with a couple hundred men . . . into the uncharted north. His objective was Cíbola . . . legend said the houses and streets were veneered with gold and silver. All he found somewhere in northwestern Arizona, were—get this—savage people living in hovels, perhaps descendants of the Hohokam culture. . . ."

She looked at me, challenging me for a reaction.

"What?" I had been watching her, instead of listening.

"Almost every sentence I just read is wrong, according to your stuff. Coronado rode north in 1540, not 1539. The north wasn't uncharted because it had been reconnoitered the year before by your hero, Marcos de Niza. Coronado had a thousand men with him, not a few hundred. But the others were Indian allies and didn't count as real men either to the Spanish or, apparently, to 1980s authors. Like women secretaries in our society." She paused and gave me a challenging smile. Then she turned back to the book. "Cíbola was a multistoried town, not a bunch of savages in hovels, and as for 'savages in northwestern Arizona,' Coronado and the main army never even went to northwest Arizona. And neither the inhabitants of northwest Arizona or New Mexico have anything to do with the Hohokam; the Hohokam lived here in southern Arizona and northern Sonora and built canals and ball courts."

She gave me a smile as bright as the sky. "There. Aren't you impressed?" She closed the book. "I don't mind the guy making a few mistakes, since history wasn't his real subject, but what irks me is that the critics from the greatest papers specifically praised his meticulous research. Nobody has time to check facts. Bandwagon effects are more important than content when it comes to book sales."

"The world is crazy." I wondered why we were talking about economic analysis.

"Anyway, it applies to you, because you could point out how the Coronado story has been distorted, even in modern accounts."

She saw the look on my face and gave me a little kiss, too quick for me to kiss her back. "I'm sorry, I don't mean to lecture you. Let's walk a little more." She put her arm around my waist and we splashed down the stream together.

We came around a slight bend where there were some massive rocks on one side, and a grove of cottonwoods on the other.

"Look," she said, pointing at the rocks. "Indian petroglyphs."

We went over to look at the rocks. An imposing weathered outcrop, the color of dark molasses, rose behind some thorny bushes. Ancient hands had pecked away the dark surface stain to make lighter, ghostly figures: mountain sheep and grids of lines, and a crosslike figure, with knobs on the ends of the crossbars. There was a stick figure vaguely like a standing man with arms held up menacingly, but looking perhaps more like an angry lizard. The mountain sheep marched among the other figures, kind of cocky, with their horns swept back in streamlined curves over their bodies.

"I wonder what these symbols meant," she said, dreamily.

"They aren't writing. Modern people try to make language out of petroglyphs, but that's not what they are."

"I know, but they must have meant something. Maybe totems, or clan symbols."

"Or doodles."

"I think they had some mystic meaning we can't know. I think we'd be surprised if we knew their story."

"Who can say?"

She kissed me again. This time she lingered. *We* lingered.

We moved to the secluded clearing beneath the trees across the stream. The birds sang overhead and the dappled light made glowing spots on the sand as if God had spilled drops from his bucket of sunshine. Phaedra pulled me to her. I pressed her against one of the huge cottonwood trunks. She took off the scarf she was wearing and suggested some games we could play with it. We did, but that's another story. Like I said, she was an interesting woman.

Later, trying to replay every event of that hour in my mental hard drive, I realized that I kept seeing the lizard man over her shoulder. He was standing across the river like a voyeur, watching us. He seemed to shift position slightly on the rock, every time I caught his eye, as if he were about to break out of the rock and come after me.

AS WE WALKED BACK TO THE CAR, PHAEDRA STARTED MUSING about Mr. Rooney's impending zoning problems. She said an unlikely coalition of ranchers and environmentalists was beginning to organize out in the valley to oppose our project because of its impact on their neighborhood. They said it would create a leapfrog pocket of urban sprawl and change the entire nature of the valley.

The coalition was unexpected, she added, because the environmentalists had spent years fighting the cow-running ranchers. Now, they were becoming best buddies. They were threatening that if our zoning was approved by the county supervisors, they would circulate a petition to get a public referendum to overturn the supervisors' vote. "That's what I hear at my Sierra Club meetings."

"Sounds like you're caught in the middle. Do your Sierra Club pals know you work for Mr. Rooney?"

"Oh," she said playfully, "I'm a double agent." She pulled her now-wrinkled scarf across her face and gave me a femme-fatale look, like one of the Bond girls. She was good at that. "Really, I want to be on the right side of this. At those meetings, they call us names, you know. I don't like it. They think all we do is destroy the land with tract houses." She looked as serious as I'd seen her. "They don't take into account building for the future. I try to focus on that. I bet people complained in the old days, too, like when they tore out medieval hovels to build cathedrals." She paused and picked up a bright red pebble from the streambed. Its color faded as it dried, as if we were destroying its beauty by looking at it. Then she skipped it across the water. "I need to keep this job," she added, "but I try to understand all sides. I want to be a well-rounded person."

"You are a well-rounded person."

She ignored my leer.

"Listen," I said. "I think about this stuff, too. What bothers me is, it's all driven by some land investors making a buck, not by what's best for the country. And yet they make a national religion out of their right to do it. Did you know America is using up its best river bottom agricultural land with urban sprawl? It's because most cities were originally started near rivers and farmland. Who speaks for preserving the farmland?" I looked up at the blue sky. "I guess I'm torn, working for Mr. Rooney."

She scowled. "You professional guys with your successful careers and BMWs, you can afford to sit around and philosophize, then you move on to another job if you're unhappy, with a big raise. For me, I can't imagine a job that's much better. If people like me try to move on because we don't like what we see, we get branded as troublemakers. If push comes to shove, I need to take care of myself first, myself and Amber. And . . . well, it all gets too hypothetical. I don't want to talk about it."

"I don't have a BMW," I said.

"A lotta people in our company do."

We walked farther down the river toward my lowly Honda, and she put her arm around my waist again and leaned into me as we splashed along. There's a unique sense of wholeness and completeness in walking arm in arm with a happy lover, with the cottonwoods arching above on each side, and the sunlight falling down through the leaves as soft as a spring rain. Now that I look back on it, I think the Universe programs us to go out and find a partner to lose ourselves in, so that we can experience at least one day of that wholeness.

I SPENT A CERTAIN AMOUNT OF TIME THAT MARCH MUSING ABOUT how to use my brilliant research to get ahead in the pecking order at the office, which still seemed important in those days. Over lunch, Phaedra continued to tell me that Mr. Rooney had taken a shine to me. I was the starry-eyed kid that he was going to convert into a realist, in his own mold.

Also, during one of these weeks in middle or late March, I did something else that would have ramifications later. I wrote to Edward ————, my college buddy. True to his dream, Edward had left his planning job in Los Angeles. He had taken a long car trip, doing freelance articles along the way for various papers and magazines about environmental issues in the West. We had stayed in touch only intermittently: letters and late-night phone calls. Then he dropped even further out of the rat race. He had gone back to Mexico. His Christmas note said he was in Phase IV of his life. There was the kid phase, the formal education phase, the roosting phase, and now the exploration phase. He said I was probably going through the same phases. He had taken his savings, arranged to live cheap, and was going to write what he called the great Southwest novel. He had given a post office address in a little town outside Mexico City. So now I wrote him and told him about my job, and how I was going to be the great expert on the discovery of the Southwest. I told him about my friends, Phaedra, Mr. Rooney, and Marcos. I asked him to drop me a line and tell me the latest.

ON THE LAST DAY OF MARCH, WHILE MARCOS WAS STILL IN Vacapa, the headline story in our paper was about the bodies of six men and three women who had been tortured and stuffed down a well and a septic tank on an abandoned Sonora ranch, not far from Marcos's route. An AK-47 was found in the ranch house. Residents in the nearby town of Agua Prieta were quoted in Mexican understatement. "It is not tranquil here anymore."

Other interviewees were more specific. "At night gunfire is heard routinely. The drug wars are going on."

One day as I passed through Mr. Rooney's outer office for my Phaedra fix, she said, "Hey, Mr. Scott. Why don't you come over here. I've got something for you." Mr. Rooney always had this tradition of calling people "Mister" around the office, but when she did it, it always sounded like flirtation.

"What?"

"I was just talking to one of our lawyers who was there when Mr. Rooney bought the property. The people who sold it bought it from the family that ranched out there originally, around the turn of the century."

"So?"

"They said there's a rumor the original family had found old Coronado stuff on the property."

"Yeah?"

"Yeah."

I didn't want to let myself get too excited. "There's a lot of old Mexican stuff out there in that valley. Mexican cowboys from the 1800s made knives, machetes, horse gear. . . . People find that stuff, they always think its from an old conquistador."

"Look, there's more. Do you want it or not?" She pretended to pout.

"Sure."

"I didn't want to say anything till I tracked it down, but I've been calling around. The owner from the original family, he died, but his brother still has a ranch down near Lochiel; he's got an unlisted number, but his nephew works here in Tucson, in the Sears garage at the Buena Vista Mall. The name is Carlos. I got his number. You could talk to him, see if you can learn anything about the kind of stuff they found out there."

I took the number.

CHAPTER 5

Marcos Reports News of Cíbola

For a while I kept the telephone number of Carlos on my dresser and postponed making contact with him. I felt there was more payoff in old documents than in old ranchers. My relationship with Phaedra energized me; I was throwing myself into my work. By late March I was getting into another mystery about the Marcos route. It was the key problem about Marcos: How far north did he get? He claimed he made it all the way to Cíbola/Zuni, but the charge against him by many historians was that he didn't get farther north than the modern-day Arizona-Sonora border region, where they claimed he turned back after gathering enough facts about Cíbola to concoct a convincing story about the rest of the trip.

When I went to the library to visit with Marcos via his report, he was his usual, breezy self about his trip through the villages where he received descriptions of Cíbola. Although these villages were somewhere in central and northern Sonora, hundreds of miles from Cíbola, the people gave him clear and—as it turned out—accurate descriptions of the northern city. No doubt about it: The prehistoric trade networks and information flow were excellent!

I enjoyed the way Marcos revealed his excitement at what he was learning. In spite of all the naysayers, everything he wrote about this part of the trip seemed simple and straightforward. To me, it rang true. I started back at the point where Marcos was about to leave Vacapa.

The Indian that Estevan sent to me in Vacapa told me so many wonderful things about the northern land that I withheld judgment until I could see these things myself or get more information about the place. He said that the distance from where he had left Estevan to the first city of that province, a city he called Cíbola, was thirty days' journey.

I think it is worth recording here what this Indian said. He stated that there are seven very great cities, all under one governor. The houses, of stone and lime, are large, the smallest being of one story with a terrace or porch above. Others are of two and three stories, and that of the governor is four stories. In the portals or porches of the main houses are worked many designs of turquoises, which he said are plentiful there. The people of these cities are very well clothed. He told me many details of the cities, and of other provinces even farther away, which he said were even greater. I asked this Indian many questions and found him to be of very good intelligence.

I gave thanks to Our Lord, but I delayed my departure from Vacapa until my coastal scouts returned, assuming that Estevan would wait for me as I had arranged. They arrived on Easter Sunday with descriptions of the coast. I give the names of the islands and settlements in another document. . . .

That other document is one which, alas, has never been found. It's unclear how many names or how much geographical information it had. Its existence may explain why the main *Relación* is so sketchy on specific place-names. In the *Relación*, Marcos, like any newly-returned traveler, seemed primarily interested in recounting his adventures on the road.

I left Vacapa the day after Easter on the same road Estevan had followed. I received other messengers from him, with another cross the size of the first, urging me to hurry, and declaring that the land we sought was the best and greatest thing of which he had ever heard. Those messengers told me more details about things the first messengers had described. There was no difference on any point, but the information was clearer.

I traveled that day and two more days, the same jornadas that Estevan had made, at the end of which I reached the people who had given him the information. They affirmed it was thirty jornadas from there to the first of the seven cities. I obtained accounts of Cíbola not just from one, but from many of them. They went on and on about the grandeur of the houses, and their style. They affirmed that beyond the seven cities are still more kingdoms, and gave their names, such as Marata, Ácus, and Totonteac.

I asked them why they went so far from their homes to visit Cíbola, and they told me they went there for turquoises, hides that look like cowhides, and other things. Of these goods, the Cíbolans had a large quantity. I asked what they exchanged for them, and they told me it was their own sweat and manual labor. They said they traveled to the first city, called Cíbola, and served there by tilling the ground and other work, and in return were given the cowhides and turquoises. All the people of this town wear fine and beautiful turquoises hanging from their ears and from their noses, and they confirmed that these stones are worked into the principal doorways.

They also told me that the clothing of the people of Cíbola is a cotton shirt, reaching to the foot, with a button at the throat and a large tassel that hangs from it, and with sleeves of constant width, top to bottom. To me, it sounded like a Bohemian or gypsy style of dress. They say they wear belts of turquoises, and that over these they wear the shirts; some wear very good blankets and others wear the cowhide garments, well processed, which they hold to be the better choice and very plentiful there. The women of Cíbola are clothed and covered to the feet in the same manner.

*These Indians received me very well and took great care to
learn the day I had left Vacapa and thus my travel rate, so as
to plan the food and shelter that would be necessary for me on
the road ahead. They gave me some of the hides, so well
tanned and dressed that they appeared to be the work of very
cultured people, and they said all these had come from Cíbola.*

*Next day I continued my journey. . . . I reached another set-
tlement where I was well received by the people, who wanted to
touch my robe. They said people from their village had gone
four or five days' travel ahead with Estevan Dorantes. Here, I
came upon a large cross erected by Estevan to indicate that the
news of the good country was getting better and better. He left
word that I should hurry, and that he would wait for me at the
end of the next despoblado. At this place, I erected two crosses
and took possession [of the land] in compliance with my
instructions from the viceroy, because it appeared to me that
this was a better land than that through which I had passed
before.*

I liked the fact that Marcos recorded the Indians of Sonora traveling all the way north to Cíbola in order to work and bring back
rewards to their families. It meant that the problem of migrant
laborers crossing the border to El Norte was prehistoric. It also
meant that Marcos had been traveling on well-established trade
routes, not struggling through uncharted wilderness, as some historians of the 1940s seemed to imply. At that time, not even scholars
could imagine that the "primitive Indians" had such well-
established trade networks. The well-used trails would have
allowed him to travel faster than the historian-critics imagined.

Marcos was also criticized for saying that the people of Cíbola,
i.e., the Zuni pueblo, had jewels set in their porches. But I soon discovered that three centuries later, in the 1880s, a Swiss-American
ethnographer, Adolf Bandelier, roamed the Southwest and proved
that Marcos was right about this! He compared Marcos's *Relación*

to the work of Frank Hamilton Cushing, a colorful explorer and ethnographer who lived in Zuni for nearly five years in 1879–84, when Zuni was still similar in appearance to the Cíbola of the 1500s. I found this passage in Bandelier's article, "The Discovery of New Mexico by the Franciscan Friar Marcos de Niza in 1539," published in French in 1886.

Turquoises and all sorts of green and blue stones . . . were a fairly common ornament among the natives of Zuni. In Zuni, as in all the New Mexico pueblos, there are great numbers of them. What the Indian informants told Marcos about the turquoises set in the doorways at Cíbola was absolutely true. This custom persisted from ancient times. As Mr. Cushing discovered during his stay in Zuni, they set small stones of this kind in the wooden frames around the entrances, through which they passed by ladders, especially in the estufas or meeting places. Today the custom is falling into disuse.

The Bandelier/Cushing remark about the variety of green and blue stones may explain why the Spanish referred to some of them as emeralds.

I WAS JUMPING AROUND AMONG THE CENTURIES. BANDELIER clarified some other issues in his article. For example, he agreed with other scholars that the prized "cowhides," which villagers traded from Cíbola and which Marcos encountered as far south as central Sonora, were really buffalo hides. Cíbola traded for them from the eastern pueblos, who in turn traded with Plains Indians. Bandelier and other scholars agreed that the very name, Cíbola, was a native word that referred to buffalos, and its use extended into Sonora. The fact that the Seven Cities were known far and wide by that name attested to fact that people from Sonora were trekking great distances to trade for the products that came from the great beast of the plains. Summarizing his studies in 1886, Bandelier exonerated Marcos and his reporting skills:

> *As for the seven-story houses, it is unnecessary to mention that in Zuni, as well as in Taos, some pueblo structures still exist today with at least five stories. . . . So the bold exploit of the friar from Nice resulted not only in the discovery of New Mexico, but also in very accurate accounts of the customs and lifestyles of its most interesting inhabitants. . . . I believe I have shown that these reports were consistent with the truth.*

It's a free country. Everyone seemed to have his or her own opinion of the friar from Nice.

CHAPTER 6

April, 1539
On the Trail

M*onday, April 7.* At the end of the first day north of Vacapa, the Indians from that town led Marcos to a well-used dry campsite at the sheltered base of a hill. The smell of rabbit stew and mesquite smoke from their tiny cooking fires was sweet. Marcos was glad to be back on the move again. The Indians would not let him do any work. As they cleared the camp, he sat with his trail-book and reflected on the events of the previous day. Happily, he remembered the Indians' rapt attention when, during the Easter mass, he had been able to describe to them, for the first time, the truth about the nature of the Universe. After mass, Traveler, the old man who had been sent by Estevan with the news of Cíbola, had come to visit Marcos in his hut. Traveler talked earnestly with Tall Man, who translated haltingly. "That story you told us this morning, many of the people think it was a strange story."

Well, Marcos had to agree, it was a strange story. The greatest story.

"I think you believe this story. I want to see and hear what happens next with you and your story. I will follow you," Traveler said. "I know the tongues of the peoples in different provinces to the north. I will help you to speak with the men who live there."

It was a great victory, that Traveler would accept his word and join him. Bishop Zumárraga once said that God had offered the

New World to Spain as an opportunity to defeat Satan. Each act of friendship was a step. Zumárraga had talked about this vision with Marcos, late at night, over wine. The church could work with Viceroy Mendoza, said the bishop, and together they would accomplish a great thing. "Las Casas worked it all out, you know." The Bishop moved painfully to pull down a leather-bound tome, labeled *Memorial of Remedies for the Indies*. "He wrote it long ago, in 1515, when he was irritating everyone about the conquest of Cuba. It shows how to build a perfect country among the Indians. Las Casas took this book all the way to King Ferdinand. Now everyone in Europe is talking about such ideas. Here, look," the bishop said, rummaging around his dusty shelves. "I've got another book, by an Englishman, Thomas More. *Utopia*, it's called. It's got the same ideas, about building a perfect city. Published in '16."

The bishop chuckled, took his seat and a sip of wine, and continued. "There's a funny story about it. Las Casas says Ferdinand sent a copy of his *Memorial* to Prince Charles in the English court and that Thomas More just copied it and published it as his own, changing a few words like the name of the island to Utopia. Maybe it's true. But you know Las Casas, always telling outrageous stories."

As Marcos sat staring into the fire later that night in the Indian campsite, he struggled with his next challenge. It was the conflict between the need to reach the newly reported kingdom of Cíbola and the need to gain more information about the coast. The coast lay to the west, while everyone agreed that Cíbola was inland, to the north and east. Marcos remembered his last talk with Viceroy Mendoza in the new stone palace in Mexico City. Mendoza had speculated enthusiastically about the unknown geography of the new land. "We know that the coastline runs northwest from New Spain," he had said with a gleam in his eye. "But what we do not know is how far it goes in that direction. Maybe . . ." He had looked out the window across the smoke-shrouded city, as if the horizon could reveal some secret.

There was no need for Mendoza to spell it out. If the coastline turned inland, and if the conquest could be conducted by sea, then he faced extreme political danger with the marquis, Hernán Cortés. Cortés had already explored parts of the sea that lay off the southwest coast. He could send an army north on his ships, which the conqueror had continued building during the last few years. Everyone knew Cortés was itching to capture the north for himself. People said he resented the appointment of Mendoza as viceroy, after Cortés himself had conquered Mexico. As with every political argument, there were those on the other side. They said Cortés had bungled the conquest and deserved to be replaced by Mendoza. He had lost most of the Aztec treasure and destroyed their city in the process. Still, if Cortés landed on some beach near Cíbola, read the formal acts of possession, and claimed the northern empire for himself it could turn into a disastrous *fait accompli*, beginning a new cycle of exploitation before Mendoza could establish a stable government and before the Franciscans could establish their dream of a new society. Mendoza's words still rang in his ears: "If you learn that the northern kingdom really exists, remember that the information is for my ears only."

THAT NIGHT, AS MARCOS WAS PREPARING THE BLANKET HE USED for his bedding, Juan Olmeda, his aide, stepped out of the darkness. "Father, come away from the fire. There is something you must see."

They stepped into a clearing, away from the flickering shadows. Marcos stepped cautiously, trying to watch for cacti in the dark underbrush. "Look," Juan pointed, "up in the sky. A new feather-star."

Marcos peered upward, letting his eyes adapt to the blackness. Yes, he could see it, a hazy star low in the sky, with a faint glow fanning up away from the horizon—what the astrologers called a comet. It was like the one he remembered seeing in '31, and again in '33 when one of them shone brighter than Jupiter, drifting among the stars from night to night. This one had a strange, forked tail.

Juan looked worried. "Did you know there was such a star when your great general, Cortés, came to our city?"

"Juan, come sit with me by the fire."

This was an unaccustomed intimacy. Juan looked hesitant, but he sat, carefully, on the other side of the small fire. Marcos studied his fine features. It seemed clear that he was of higher character than the others; Marcos marveled at how nobility could appear in every race.

"Tell me about the conquest, Juan," Marcos said. "Tell me about what happened in Mexico when the general came."

There was a long silence as Juan stared into the fire. "I cannot," he said finally.

"You were a warrior . . ." Marcos prompted.

Juan sighed. "I was young then. I had been to our best school, trained to become an Eagle warrior." Juan's eyes darted around and seemed to come to rest only on some empty piece of the evening sky. "The feather-star in the sky in those days—our lord Moctezuma and his priests said it was an evil omen. You know that we Mexica took the Valley of Mexico from earlier people, who took it from still earlier people. There are many cycles like that in the world, and Moctezuma thought our cycle of mastery over the Valley of Mexico might soon end, because of the bad omen of the feather-star. Moctezuma became very discouraged about the future of the Mexica. He said the feather-star signified the return of our god called. . . . Well, I mean, he said it signified changes."

Marcos was aware why Juan was afraid to mention the old gods. Only months ago, Bishop Zumárraga in Mexico City had tried several Indian nobles before the Inquisition for keeping alive the superstitions about the Mexica's heathen deities. One of them, a governor and ringleader of a native village, had been scheduled for execution after Marcos left the city.

Marcos had heard how Moctezuma expected the return of their strange god Quetzalcoatl, the feathered serpent, who had departed generations before, and how he foolishly suspected that Cortés was the returning deity.

"At first," Juan continued, "Moctezuma sent wizards to cast a spell on the Spanish army, when they were still on the coast. When it had no effect, that's when he decided they were gods."

Marcos had heard that during Cortés's march toward Mexico City from the coast, Moctezuma seemed paralyzed, wavering between military action to confront the intruders, and welcoming them with open arms. His main strategy was to send messengers requesting the visitors to go back to the coast, where he tried to placate them with gifts of gold and feathered capes. Many of Moctezuma's nobles had tried to talk him into more decisive action, but by the grace of God, Moctezuma had stuck to his beliefs. Cortés, to his credit, did not succumb to the temptation and blasphemy of claiming to be a god. Instead, he sent word to Moctezuma that he was only a man who represented the Spanish king, who, incidentally, would be pleased to accept the gold of Moctezuma as a token of friendship. As always, Cortés, with his early training as a lawyer, brilliantly played the odds. He recognized that the Mexica had many enemies among the nearby cities they had conquered, and so he recruited an army of a thousand disgruntled natives to assist his small band of a few hundred Spaniards. In this way he marched to Mexico City, and was personally greeted by Moctezuma.

Marcos returned to the conversation with Juan. "But what about the fighting between your people and our people? Is there some way things could have worked out differently?"

A pause again. "At first, our lord Moctezuma welcomed your lord Cortés. He came out with all our nobles to meet him on the southern causeway leading into the city. I saw it myself. It was a great day. They gave each other necklaces. Moctezuma hung pendants of gold and garlands of flowers on Cortés, and gave a speech saying that their meeting had been prophesied, and that he recognized Cortés as the god who had left our city long ago. We believe the General Cortés saw his advantage at that very moment. From then on, he always spoke deviously. He said he had come as a friend. It was a good speech but it was all false."

Juan paused and smiled sheepishly. "Can I tell you something else?"

"Yes, everything."

"I remember that when our people heard him speak, well, we were hearing Spanish for the first time, and everyone said what a savage-sounding language this was. I remember my father and my uncles saying 'Who are these barbarians with their strange speech and their animallike hair?' You have to excuse me, Father, I am being frank. What seems curious to me is that your people thought we were barbarians, but our people, from the nobles to the peasants, thought that *your* people were the barbarians."

Marcos smiled ruefully into the fire. "Maybe our greatest goal, as we travel north, is to change those kinds of perceptions."

"Anyway, Cortés and his officers then shook Moctezuma's hand and patted him on the back. Everyone was happy at this great event. Moctezuma led them into the city, and gave them the royal house as a residence, across the square from his own palace, near where the viceroy's palace is today.

"Soon after that, Cortés said that Moctezuma and our lord Itzcuauhtzin, of Tlatelolco, must move in with him as his guests. Cortés said it all in very fine words, that the Spaniards were hosting them. The nobles were against it, but Moctezuma said that he and Cortés would be as brothers. All the formalities and niceties were observed, but people soon began to see Moctezuma was more a prisoner than a guest. People began to gather in the plazas to complain. Then the Spaniards fired a cannon in front of their quarters, which frightened everyone. No one had seen anything like that. That night there was anguish in every home, by every hearth in the city. Men told their wives and their children about the ominous events, and everyone wondered what would happen."

Juan paused and let out a sigh. Marcos had heard parts of this story before from veterans who had served with Cortés, but the campfire intimacy offered a chance to hear it from the native point of view. Cortés had managed to establish a precarious coregency with the pagan king, but the details of the final tragedy had always eluded Marcos.

"The next day the Spaniards told Moctezuma's court of the great quantities of supplies they needed, chickens and other food, fire-wood, cooking pots, and so on. The chiefs protested to our king, but Moctezuma said they should honor the Spaniards' wishes. So they did. Then the Spaniards asked about the treasures of the city, and Moctezuma himself led them to see our national treasure house called Teucalco. He walked with the soldiers through the streets to Teucalco, and the Spanish soldiers always formed a ring around him, with their weapons at hand, pretending to protect him and be his escort. But really, they were guarding a prisoner. When they came to the treasure house, it was a travesty. Your soldiers fell upon everything, laughing, tearing the beautiful featherwork from the gold standards and shields. They fought over the gold for themselves, and built a fire and burned the rest. I did not see this but many of our people did.

"Next they went to Moctezuma's own storehouse at the Palace of the Birds, and the same thing happened. My father was in attendance at that time. He saw it and he said the soldiers were laughing and crying out like little animals, when they saw the treasures there. They slapped each other on the back and became slaves to their own appetites, he said. You have to understand, at the Palace of the Birds, everything belonged to our king, it was tribute to our nation. There were rings, necklaces with rich stones, ankle rings with golden bells, crowns. But the rough soldiers put the things into their own pockets and bags, as if it were their right.

"In spite of these happenings, the people continued to bring food to the Spaniards, because Moctezuma ordered it. All our people were still frightened. Everyone still pretended we were friends. Many weeks went by. One day, many weeks later, came the time of year for the great fiesta in honor of our god Huitzuilopochtli . . . our old god." Juan paused, and gave Marcos a timid smile. "You realize I am not blaspheming, I am just trying to tell you what it was like."

"Yes, yes, go on."

"General Cortés had gone away to the coast. People say some Spaniards were coming to arrest him because he was exceeding his authority by marching inland to conquer us. Anyway, he took part of his company with him, and left only part of his force in Tenochtitlán, under the authority of one of his captains, Pedro de Alvarado. Our people called him 'the Sun' because he dominated everyone each day. Everyone says 'the Sun' was an evil man, and so I always wondered if the outcome would have been any different even if Cortés had stayed in the city. Well, anyway, 'the Sun's' soldiers became very nervous and fearful, living in the midst of our city, because they were few in number and missed their clever lord Cortés."

Juan fell silent again.

"What happened?"

"This is hard for me. . . . You see, there was a young woman, a maiden. . . . We were to be man and wife. At the time of the festival of Huitzuilopochtli, many of us gathered in the temple courtyard—the dancers, the priests, many of the young men. She was there, helping to prepare for the dances. Then the Spaniards came to watch. They said 'the Sun' wanted to learn about our ceremonies. You understand . . . it was part of our religion in those days. The Spaniards stood by the doors, at the gates to the courtyard, blocking the exits. I was there. . . ."

Juan stopped. He turned away from the dying fire. Marcos could not see his face in the shadows. Finally, he got up. "Forgive me, Father. I cannot . . . I cannot tell this story." He walked away quickly into the shadows with his head down. Marcos could see that his shoulders were racked with sobs.

FALLING ASLEEP THAT NIGHT, MARCOS CONTRASTED JUAN'S VIEW of the conquest with that of the Spaniards. He remembered more of his talk with Viceroy Mendoza, before leaving on his quest. Mendoza was a civilized man, and therefore spoke in circumlocutions. "I know you are aware of the, hmmmm, excesses that some of our men may commit when their baser passions are aroused. They're like animals turned loose in a new pasture. Guzmán's slave-gathering rampages near San Miguel de Culiacán are just one example." Mendoza paused, then drummed his fist on his big table, an impatient gesture. "The King's interests will be rudely served if some of these so-called gentlemen are allowed to have their way in the north. Imagine the consequences if our captains raise their own armies. Slave raiding among the poor natives is bad enough, but unprovoked confiscation of land and attacks on wealthy cities along our northern frontier could lead us into a whole century of warfare, with disastrous consequences for the treasury. Who knows how powerful the northern empire we find might be? If the northern peoples are offended by our actions, and retaliate . . ."

Mendoza got up and walked to his window, staring for a moment at the scattered new Spanish buildings across the plaza, rising from the rubble of the Mexican city. "What if they are more powerful than we are? Our position here in New Spain, Father Marcos, is by no means secured just because we have conquered the Mexican empire so easily. No one likes to talk about it, but it was mostly luck that gave Cortés his victory over the Mexica," he said. "Moctezuma, the fool, refused to fight us. When the Mexica began to arm themselves, it was too late."

Mendoza gazed for another moment at the bustling plaza and then turned back to his desk. He picked up a small parchment. "Look. This is something I wrote down. It is from an amusing book that I have been reading, from the bishop's library. It is called *The Ruler*, by some Florentine named Machiavelli. He gives instructions for those who would govern. I copied down some of my favorites. He warns a viceroy to be careful of his wealthy nobles. Listen, here is a good one. 'The nobles have more foresight and are more clever than the rest of the people, and so they always act in time to safeguard their own interests, and they always take sides with those who they expect to win.'"

Marcos laughed. "He seems to have got that right. They seem to spend all their time carving out their own empires instead of serving God and king."

"Yes, and they are doing it right now! Our nobles are organizing against our long-term interests. We must act carefully. I am sure you understand that I must make choices about how to proceed, and the sooner the better. The marquis Cortés is already building ships to sail north. And Don Francisco Vázquez de Coronado, whom I am naming governor of the northwest—even he urges me to authorize him to go north at once. Everyone is pressuring me. And not just here in Mexico. I have received word that Hernán de Soto has a license from the king to explore west from Florida, and that even now he is preparing an expedition. This could bring him into the lands north of us, where he, too, might make a claim."

Viceroy Mendoza went on, stroking his black beard, and growing more animated. "On the other hand, if we should be able to gain information about the north before any of our hotheaded friends, we could, um, serve the king's interest. And, of course, your interests— the interests of Rome. Do you see what I am driving at? A quiet and prudent exploration, under the king's sponsorship. Then an *orderly* conquest. We will start with the Indians whom Guzmán enslaved. I know you have opinions on that point. We must make them understand that they are free, and slavery is not our Majesty's desire."

It was just what Marcos wanted to hear.

"Next, we must end the vague rumors about northern cities," Mendoza went on. "Vague rumors are always counterproductive. They make more heat than light." He opened a cabinet next to his desk and took out a round bell of gleaming copper, inscribed with designs. "This is the very bell Dorantes brought back from the north. It proves that they work in metal, but what does it prove about their wealth? Our young cavaliers lie about idly here in Mexico, drinking, causing trouble, and dreaming of the next great conquest. The whole situation will turn to chaos if we cannot move forward with plans based on concrete reality. If chaos happens, it will be my fault, in the eyes of his Majesty, and you Franciscans won't look too good, either. That's why I am sending you north. The bishop, Zumárraga, agrees; he has recommended you. He speaks highly of you, you know. Between you and me, I would say he is grooming you for great things. But you must carry out this assignment successfully. You will be my eyes and ears. You must learn if the northern empire exists, where is located, and how to reach it. This expedition has not been officially announced, you understand."

Mendoza paused, considering his words. "Only Bishop Zumárraga knows about this expedition, and the head of your own order, Father Ciudad-Rodrigo. Tell no one about it, even your brothers in your order. Some of them have very loose tongues. I will test you with this secret for a few weeks and see if I can trust you. Remember, I have my spies. Then you will go north with the new governor. When you come back, talk to no one but Ciudad-Rodrigo, the bishop, and me. You will write a report and submit it through Ciudad-Rodrigo to me. We don't want it circulating to others who might attempt their own ventures, like packs of wild animals.

"You must make this trip along the coast, where we can get some idea of the prospects of naval exploration. That way I can learn what we're up against with Cortés and his ships. You will start with rumors but come back with facts."

He continued more cordially. "You and I, Father Marcos, can help each other. You Franciscans want to save these Indians. And I want to govern a peaceful kingdom—to send word to our Majesty of new provinces, full of riches, pacified, Christianized, ready to be mined and opened for settlement, able to send back wealth beyond what that spice merchant, Señor Colón, ever dreamed of. Common interests, Father. Interests that will be corrupted if the northern empire falls into the wrong hands." Mendoza, suddenly as still and enigmatic as one of the Mexican idols, stared at Marcos intently, his dark eyes burning brightly. "I am sure you understand me, Father Marcos."

FALLING ASLEEP IN HIS HUT AT VACAPA, MARCOS COULD NOT SUPpress a private smile. The marquis Cortés had said the same thing. "I'm sure you understand." Everyone in Mexico wanted him to understand them. . . .

And tomorrow . . . From what Estevan's messenger had said, Cíbola was just thirty *jornadas* from the next village. His journey was half complete. Another month on the trail and he would walk through the portals of the mighty city, the Babylon of the north.

WEDNESDAY, APRIL 9. AS MARCOS HIKED ALONG THE TRAIL, HE thought about the surprising world that was being revealed in his lifetime. There was something comforting about the similarities and differences he had seen in different countries. All over the world, towns were dotted along rivers, joined by roads and trails. Governors in each town. Children playing. Women baking bread. Emptier country in the hills, where wild animals roamed. Everyone tended to focus on the differences in customs, yet certain patterns seemed fundamental. Sometimes on this journey he felt like he was approaching the answer to some great question, except he was not sure what the question was.

Now they were three days past Vacapa, passing through deserted hills, where the shrubs were sparse. Several Vacapan men had joined Marcos's own party, and he could see them all, strung out along the trail ahead of him, carrying his food and the packages of gifts to be given out in Cíbola, along with his own kits of trail supplies, his writing box, his vestments, wine, and other materials for the mass. The first day after Vacapa had been the hottest so far, and Marcos's throat had grown dry, but an overcast on the second day led to a cold wind, and a refreshing rain that swept down on them in fits and starts from the mountains on the right. The rain was inadequate to make the streambeds flow in the little gullies between the hills, but the Indians knew the locations of catchment ponds in the rocky hills.

On the trail, Marcos struggled with a new problem. He wanted to send a message back to the governor and the viceroy, reporting the good news about the existence of Cíbola. But could he trust the Indians' reports and the embellishments sent by the impetuous Estevan? The flamboyant Moor was known to exaggerate for effect, and perhaps he had picked messengers of like mind. Marcos decided he would wait until he himself could reach the villages of the people who claimed to know of Cíbola. He was close on the heels of Estevan, now. Each of the last two days they had come to well-used camp spots, where the guides poked around and announced that Estevan had camped there.

Late in the day they came to a strong river, flowing west, toward the sea. On the bank, the guides found three natives of that valley, fishing along the riverbank. The natives explained through Marcos's translators that there was a place one hour upstream where the river was shallow enough to wade across. These three looked different from the natives to the south; their hair was longer and tied back; they had rows of small spotlike scars on their right cheeks.

There was much conferring and gesturing between the guides and the three strangers. They pointed to the north, east, and south and made many drawings in the damp sand. While the Indians parleyed, Marcos paused on the stream bank to refresh himself. First he enjoyed the taste of the cool water, and then he splashed his face and washed the caked dust from his feet. He leaned against a table-sized rock and watched the Indians. They always seemed excited at the prospect of a new visitor. Finally, Traveler, Tall Man, Juan, and several others of Marcos's Indian allies came to him.

"They say that in order to follow the main trade route, we cross the river, then go upstream along this valley, which then turns directly north. There say there are large towns along that valley."

"Then they know of Cíbola?"

"Oh, yes."

"What is it like? Do they confirm what Estevan and Traveler told us, that they have big houses there?"

They put their heads together, like women gossiping. Finally Tall Man reported, "They have not been there but people from their villages have. They say it is the greatest place known to them, but that you should ask others in their villages, who have seen it."

"Let us go, then."

"But you have ordered us to stay close to the sea when possible. They say that to do this, we should cross this river and go then downstream a short distance, where there is another river valley that leads north. It is west of the first one, parallel to it. If we go up that one, and then northwest across the hills for a day, we will come to a different valley, which runs west, where it is just a few days to the sea. That valley also has villages, and those people can tell you about the coast, as well as Cíbola. After that, we can go upstream in that valley, it will take us back to the main Cíbola trail. That route is only a few *jornadas* longer but you will learn more about the sea. Do you want to go that way?"

"Which way did Estevan go?"

"Along the western valley. He knew you wanted to stay on the coastal side."

At least the Moor had done one thing right! "How far ahead is he? Is he waiting for me in that valley?"

"He is just a few days ahead. These people say that he arrived here three days ago, but he pushed on to the first village because people there had heard of him and they wanted to meet him." Tall Man winced and made a sad expression, knowing this would displease Marcos.

It did. One reason for ordering Estevan to wait was not just so they could travel together, but also so that Estevan could advise him about the location of the village the castaways had named Corazones. It should lie near this latitude.

"Do these people know the village where Estevan and the others stopped three years ago, the one they named after the feast of deer hearts?" Marcos asked the guides.

"Father," Juan answered, "we asked about that because you and Estevan said it was important. But these men don't know which town it was. They say deer hearts are a sacred delicacy in all these valleys."

"No one here met Estevan or the others three years ago?"

"No. We asked them, and they said they heard stories of strange men of many colors, appearing in the last few years. Who is to say if these are stories of your friends, or rumors that have come from farther away?"

Marcos reflected on this. "I think Corazones lies in the eastern valley, because Estevan said he came into these lands from the east and north. But we must follow the western route, because the viceroy wants us to learn about the coastline."

AFTER THEY CROSSED THE RIVER, MARCOS RAN THROUGH HIS conversations with Estevan about the now-elusive town of Corazones. "At the feast in Corazones, they gave us arrowheads of green gemstone, like emerald," Estevan had said, excitedly. "With those emerald points, the Indians could make powerful magic."

"Estevan, you know that is blasphemous," Marcos had told him. "There is no magic that comes from men—only the wonders that God decrees and the evil tricks of the devil."

"Well, I mean, the Indians believed they were magic, which meant we could use them to exert our power over them. Don't you see? If the people believe that you have magic power, it's the same thing as having it. It isn't blasphemous if you don't believe it yourself."

More it seemed that Estevan was deliberately rushing ahead, against instructions. Was the lure of fame and turquoise enough to explain Estevan's behavior? Or was there something else that Estevan knew and was not telling? Would Marcos ever catch up? If so, he would give the Moor an earful.

THURSDAY, APRIL 10. IN THE AFTERNOON, MARCOS RESTED IN THE first village in the new valley. Estevan's disobedience began to seem a minor setback compared to the wonderful news Marcos obtained by interviewing numerous Indians, individually and in groups. There could be no doubt that Estevan's basic news was true. The great city called Cíbola really did exist, along with other cities where people lived in multistory houses and traded in turquoises and other goods.

Marcos could wait no longer; he must send a message back to confirm the great discovery. It had been more than three weeks since he had left Honorato recovering from his illness in the village of Petatlán. Now it would be Honorato's duty to take the message on to Mexico City. Marcos wrote feverishly on a page cut from his trail book.

Honorato!

*There is great news, as you will see from the letter I will
enclose. Your duty is to take this letter to the Governor,
Vázquez de Coronado, and then to make sure that this news is
taken directly to our Father Provincial, Ciudad-Rodrigo, so that
he can take it to the viceroy. I hope you are fully recovered.
Remember that we are ordered by the viceroy to report these
things only to our superiors, for the glory of God and the King.
See to your vows and remember that God has chosen us humble friars to open the pathways to this great new country.*

On a separate page he drafted a more formal report. Once again,
he cautioned himself not to overplay his hand. Surely within
another week or two he would know much more about Cíbola, and
could send more complete news. For now, he must only alert his
superiors that success was at hand. He paused to do some quick
additions in his head. If he sent this message now, and if Honorato
carried out the instructions with dispatch, the news of this land
could reach the viceroy in Mexico City as early as June. He wrote
as much as he could be sure about.

April 10, 1539.

*To His Excellency, the Governor Francisco Vázquez de Coro-
nado, and to His Excellency, Viceroy Antonio Mendoza,
through the Father Provincial Antonio Ciudad-Rodrigo.*

*In accordance with my instructions, I have the honor to send
this message of good tidings from the northern lands. Here, I
find myself in a fertile country with many well-watered villages,
and I have received news of rich and prosperous lands farther
to the north. The people along the way have treated Estevan de
Dorantes and me well, and they show great zeal to learn of
God's grace and the love for them shown by the viceroy and
our King. They say that in the lands to the north is a great
country with several cities, including a great city called Cíbola.*

Beyond that are other prosperous lands. They also say that those cities have great houses that reach several stories in height. I am still gathering information about that country. Surely its grandeur must be the source of the rumors we have heard, and it seems sure that the copper bell brought by Dorantes comes from those lands. I understand that Cíbola lies thirty days north of here. They say it is a journey across mountains. I will push farther ahead to find the route to these lands.

Marcos put aside his book. That should be enough. He smiled, visualizing the excitement with which the viceroy would read these words. If the news leaked out to members of the royal court they would salivate like dogs about the idea of a new conquest! Mendoza's apostolic conquest would be only a matter of time.

FRIDAY, APRIL 11. MARCOS ASSIGNED TWO OF THE BEST SERVANTS from Culiacán to take his letter back down the trail to the south. He explained the content of the message, how they must take it back to Honorato, if they found him in Petatlán, or if they could not find him, to the governor himself in Culiacán. He read the letter to them: once, twice, three times. He made them each repeat the content. By their trade, they were used to memorizing, and each of them soon had the message held safely in mind. If anything evil happened to them, or to the original copy, at least one of them might get through to deliver the basic message. He explained how they must tell none of the other Christians about these discoveries, according to the orders of the viceroy himself. Finally, Marcos sealed the letter with wax and an imprint of his ring.

He sent the messengers on their way, hanging a cross around the neck of each member of the party to protect them from the evils of the road.

THAT NIGHT THE COMET WAS STILL VISIBLE.

"It is a very bad portent," Juan said. "As I told you, Moctezuma and his priests saw one of them just before Cortés arrived. It signaled the downfall of the Mexica. I am afraid of this sign. . . ."

"Do not listen to the astrologers," Marcos said as they returned to the fire. "It is not the stars that rule our fate. Scholars say that comets are some kind of glowing vapor high in the air. God in his mystery puts these things among the celestial spheres for us to see. We have to trust his plan."

Juan wrapped himself in a blanket and they sat, watching the celestial apparition. It did not twinkle like the other low stars, but seemed to glow with a soft, impassive light, as if ignoring their earthly concerns. "Do these scholars understand how the moon and planets and stars move around the Earth? It seems there many mysteries up there."

"There are crystalline spheres that surround Earth and hold up the heavens. I have heard scholars debate certain ancient writings of the Greeks, who tried to measure these things. Ptolemy mapped the paths of planets around the Earth. Aristarchus tried to measure the sizes and distances of the moon and the sun, using eclipses and angles and various principles of Euclid. Eratosthenes measured the size of the world. In our generations, there is a new interest in these things. But one must be careful. I've heard cardinals of Rome accuse the Greek philosophers of humanism. After all, they were pagans."

"What does that mean, humanism?"

"Putting ourselves before God. Assuming that, somehow, by reasoning or measurements, we can unravel His secrets. Only the scriptures tell us the true secrets of the world." Marcos paused, scanning the stars. "Still, Eratosthenes seems to have got it right, about the size and round shape of the world. They say Colón relied on his writings when he sailed west and discovered these lands."

They were silent for a long while. Finally, Juan added a few twigs to their smoldering fire.

"Juan, I know you do not want to talk about what happened when Cortés and the Spaniards killed your people. But maybe you can tell me this. Cortés lost much of the gold that he tried to take from your people. What happened on that night?"

A faint smile flickered for a moment across Juan's face, a restrained expression that betrayed his former Mexican nobility. "Your people call that night *La Noche Triste*. But for us it was not a night of sorrow; it was our greatest moment against the invaders." He was silent for a long time, as if debating whether to go on. Marcos remained silent as well. He had learned that etiquette with these people required patient listening. "I told you how General Cortés and his men were holding our lord Moctezuma and another important lord named Itzcuauhtzin in the palace in the middle of Tenochtitlán, pretending it was out of friendship and protection. Moctezuma kept trying to give them what they wanted, thinking a real friendship could grow. Our nobles advised a stronger posture, but Moctezuma wouldn't listen. Finally our nobles began to abandon him, saying the nation would be ruined. That was after the festival of Huitzuilopochtli—the thing I don't want to tell you about. It was when Cortés was away at the coast, and Alvarado, 'the Sun,' was in charge, and there were only a small garrison of Spanish in the city. Anyway, our side was talking about what to do next, at the end of that terrible festival day, when the Spaniards brought Itzcuauhtzin onto the roof of the palace to speak for our king. He said, 'Mexicans! Our king Moctezuma sends these words, that we must end this fight, that these Spaniards are too strong for us to resist. He tells you to realize that if the warriors continue this fight, it is our own people who will suffer, especially the aged, and the poor people, and innocent children. We cannot prevail against the Spaniards.'

"But at last the Mexica became real men. They rose up and shouted 'Who is Moctezuma? We no longer take orders from him!' They began shooting arrows at the roof and the Spaniards had to raise their shields to protect Itzcuauhtzin!

"After that, our city was in chaos. Our lords argued among themselves and tried to organize a resistance. But then after a few weeks Cortés returned from the coast with new soldiers and it was too late to throw out the Spaniards easily. Moctezuma still urged calm, saying that Cortés would punish Alvarado 'the Sun' and restore good will. But no one paid attention to him anymore. We closed the market and cut the food supply to the Spanish. Mexican people coming and going from the palace with messages were seized by other Mexicans and accused of collaborating with the Spaniards, and were killed in the streets. We also attacked parties of Spaniards who dared to venture onto the streets, and eventually we attacked the palace itself. This time the Spaniards brought Moctezuma himself to the roof to speak, but our people greeted him with a shower of stones and he was hit several times. Some people say he died from those wounds but others say he was killed by Cortés's officers. I did not see it." Juan shook his head. "Moctezuma was a bad king, because he failed to protect us, but he was right about the Spaniards. You were stronger than we were."

"We had cannons."

"But we outnumbered you. Each day during that period, our army secretly gathered its weapons and grew stronger, while the Spaniards used up their supplies and grew weaker. Even with their allies from the villages that used to be our vassals, the Spaniards knew their position was impossible. There they were, in the middle of our island city, in the middle of the lake! The Spaniards whispered among themselves and conspired about how they could escape with our gold. Then came the night you call *La Noche Triste*. The Spaniards tried to flee by darkness."

"What happened next?"

"You have to remember, the Spaniards had been ordering our noble families to bring them all their valuable goods. Our nobles brought statues, sacred images, and vessels of gold, our jewelry of turquoise, and the finest feathered capes. But the Spaniards cared only for the gold. They had piled it in the palace where they were staying, in a special room. The rest, our sacred items, they burned in huge fires in the plazas. To understand it, you have to think how you would feel if we took your sliver chalices from the altars and burned your Bibles and the sacred paintings. My father said they talked about how our gold would make them nobles when they returned to their own land—as if nobility could come from treasure instead of the other way around."

"But that night . . ."

"That's what I was trying to tell you. They had to figure out how to get the gold out of the city. The problem was, they tried to carry it with them. They made a plan. When it was dark, they crept out of their palace, and down the avenue toward the nearest causeway that would take them across the lake and out of the city. Each soldier was carrying as much gold as he could." Suddenly Juan paused. "People say that in your land, across the eastern sea, a man's nobility is judged only by the amount of gold that he stores in his treasure chest. . . . Is that true?"

"Just some men. Other men know it is riches in the heart, that allow them to be happy."

"Gold itself is worth nothing. So why would your soldiers fight for it?"

"You know very well we exchange gold for work or for goods. So men who store up gold can get many possessions."

"But why would other men accept the gold as payment, when it is worth nothing?"

"Because, well, because everyone believes in that system. It's the same as when your people trade macaw feathers to northern villages. Is a macaw feather worth anything?"

"Yes. The people in the north need macaw feathers to honor their gods in their ceremonies. Gold is not like that. Your people want the gold not to honor God but for itself."

"Go on with your story."

Juan looked sad, as if some great truth had just slipped from his grasp.

"Well, before dawn, the Spanish soldiers were creeping down the street in the dark, like rats. But there was a woman—she was a friend of one of my aunts—she was going down to the lake to get a jug of water for her sick child. She saw them sneaking along the streets and she cried out, 'Ho, Mexican people, the enemies are escaping!' After she screamed the warning, a soldier of Cortés ran to her and slit her throat. But it was too late. The cry went up all around our city. Our Eagle warriors grabbed their weapons, and poured forth from every house. Some of them blocked the causeways out of the city. Others ran for the boats and rowed out into the lake, firing arrows at the Spaniards as they tried to enter the causeways. Many of the soldiers of Cortés were killed at once by arrows shot from the boats or the house roofs, before they reached the causeway. Others were pushed off the causeway in the hand-to-hand fighting, and were drowned by the weight of their packs, before they could free themselves. Still others threw their gold from the causeways into the lake, trying to escape with their lives. Much gold disappeared into the waters that night. Some people say it is still there. Others say our priests recovered some of it." Juan smiled briefly. "They say your Christian army ran like dogs."

Marcos said nothing.

The comet and its neighboring stars were sinking toward the horizon. Juan grew grim again.

"In the following months, General Cortés bided his time in the hills outside our city, rebuilding his army. He even built boats. Eventually he came back out of the hills and surrounded the city, with his boats in the lake and his army at the end of each causeway. He ordered us to surrender. Our nobles said no. So the Spaniards fought their way into the city across the causeway, but we attacked them in the streets, from our roofs. So the next day they fought their way back in, attacking the first houses they came to and tearing them down, so we had no roofs to fight from. Each day they came further into town, tearing down more houses as they came, and then retreating at night. Eventually they destroyed Tenochtitlán, because as long as there were buildings standing, we fought from the rooftops and corners. People say Cortés was sad at this destruction, and begged our people to give up. If I may say, Father, the city you know today is only a ghost of the city that I knew as a boy. They say Cortés had hoped to give the city as a present to your Spanish king—the most beautiful city in the world. But in the end, he conquered only a ruin. Your people claim they are building a grand new city there, but to our people, it seems to get worse every year.

"By the time Cortés came back, the priests and nobles had taken most of the remaining gold out of the Spaniards' treasure room and hidden it. I don't know where. Most of the rest was lost in the lake during *La Noche Triste*. After your people subdued my people, I became a Christian because I concluded that there was more power in your ways than in the old ways of my people. But truly, Cortés never gained back the fortune that he had during those last few days in that treasure room in the old palace."

Marcos knew the rumors, that Cortés had salvaged some of the gold for himself and a few trusted officers. He was still in trouble with the king, since he had accounted for only a fraction of the total. A general without adequate gold was a general in name only. People said this was why Cortés had left Mexico City for the west coast, to invest his remaining wealth in new ships, to find the next rich empire. Mendoza's friends joked that Cortés was good at arriving but not so good at staying. Already he had started a town on the Island of California, across the sea to the west. He had brought back pearls from there, but the effort had come to little. In order to restore his personal glory and rehabilitate himself in the eyes of the court, Cortés needed a new, greater victory—a quick victory over the good viceroy Mendoza and his long-term ideals.

CHAPTER 7

April, 1989
The Outsider

I was still seeing Phaedra. "Seeing," another funny euphemism. I was still trying to figure her out, wanting to get further into her life. When I came to the office each day, she was the one I wanted to see. During those springtime lunches in shady patios, and those spring evenings when we couldn't keep our hands off each other, we shared everything. We took walks. In certain Tucson neighborhoods at that time of year, orange blossom perfume hung in Tucson's evening air, thick enough to wade through.

There was always something to talk about. Books, movies, Mr. Rooney's foibles, Amber's progress, the impending zoning hearing, or the latest coup of Freddy the Fixer, getting some vote to go Mr. Rooney's way in the state legislature. Phaedra had her own struggles. She lived on the border between the long-term world— the world of my recent religious conversion—and the grittier short-term world. One moment she might talk about disparities in twentieth-century world consumption. Another moment she would be talking about "doing what you have to do" to pay the rent. But she always said my long-term world was basically a luxury, indulged in by people who had "made it."

The daily news still seemed full of ironies and portents. For example, on Saturday, April Fools' Day, the newspaper carried pictures of a pageant at Tucson's old San Xavier Mission, celebrating the arrival of Christianity in the Southwest with Father Kino in the 1690s. Marcos, who had arrived about 150 years earlier than Kino, was, as usual, forgotten. The same paper reported that on the other side of the border, Sonoran police had arrested nineteen suspects in connection with the drug torture-killings in Agua Prieta, the little town where it was not tranquil anymore. It was just south of the border, along the route pioneered by Marcos. I wondered how he would have felt about what our generation was doing in the region to which he brought what we are pleased to call civilization.

THERE'S ALWAYS A STORM GATHERING, SOMEWHERE. OUR PROJECT was turning from private enterprise into a publicly visible enterprise. Mr. Rooney and his aides fumed about this. Phaedra continued to report rumblings among environmentalists and the local ranchers out near our site.

In the bars of Willcox rumors started about Indian ruins on our site. Our surveys confirmed it. Mr. Rooney called me in. "Did you hear we have an Indian site out there? It's not much. You have to look to see it. Stone foundations, pottery sherds. We gotta be careful about that. 'Course, it's private land and we can do pretty much what we want. But out at Rancho Sonora, they got a lot of bad press when they destroyed *their* Indian site during the construction phase. Temple platform, a court for some kind of prehistoric ball-game, the whole works. They thought they were safe because they had done all that damn mitigation archaeology and given the best relics to the state museum. Trouble is, they didn't take into account *public opinion*." I could tell from the way he said it that he regarded public opinion the way gangsters regard the police department; he didn't really believe in it, but it was good to have it on his side.

He stared out the window for a moment. "What I'm thinking is, we could nip this in the bud. Turn it to our advantage. Make a little park out of it. *Community heritage center*. First class. As long as it doesn't use up too much space. To get good press, we could include it in your report. Glossy, with pictures; what the Native Americans were like when the Spanish came through. Pictures on the walls of the clubhouse. We could commission paintings. Historical *authenticity*." He was waving his arms now, indicating the sweep of history. "Work up some ideas on that."

THE RUMORS OF OUR INDIAN SITE BEGAN TO CIRCULATE IN TUCson. It became scuttlebutt in the back halls of the county building. Somewhere in the first few days of April the county supervisors announced that they wanted more time to gather opinions on the project, and our hearing was postponed from the April to the May meeting. Mr. Rooney was furious, but the delay made me happy because (a) it gave me more time to fine-tune my report, and (b) I naively figured that the more time we had to improve our development plan, the better.

By the end of the first week of April, I completed a basic rough draft of my report, but every day or so I would adjust it, adding a new reference or a new supporting argument, or following some loose end. At my big table in the library, I fantasized about the report being published in the form of a book with Mr. Rooney's blessing, timed to coincide with the opening of the project. I'd be the toast of the town. Phaedra would admire my talent. Later, when the papers called to ask for a comment about my Pulitzer Prize, I'd cough modestly and say it was nothing, just some research I did in my spare time.

It was then that Phaedra made her first complaint about my habits—an important date in any relationship. "You're spending too much time in the library."

"I'm improving the report. Besides, it's interesting stuff. But I'll be done soon, and then we'll have time to—"

"That's not what I mean. You're getting detached from reality."

I didn't have a good answer for that one. To me, reality was beginning to seem an okay thing to get detached from. Drug murders, ecodisasters, surreal news reports, the whole *fin de siècle* mess. The library was a refuge. Elsewhere, things were humming along everywhere in their usual unpleasant way. Three more bodies had been found at the Agua Prieta drug murder site. The Exxon Valdez tanker had vomited its black cargo onto the beaches of Alaska. The morning paper was getting less and less fun to read.

At the same time, it was getting more fluffy and surreal. That was the period when the once-respectable news media were slowly transformed into an arm of the all-pervasive, intergalactic entertainment industry. On April 7, the headline was that gasoline prices had topped a dollar. The paper treated this in the new journalism's empty and dualistic way. The reporter quoted consumer complaints that this price was too high for the hardworking commuter, then quoted an environmentalist claiming that the price was not high enough to represent the associated costs of urban air pollution, fossil fuel depletion, traffic congestion, etc. A politician's complaints about the high gas price was carefully matched by the remark that European gas prices were several times higher and Americans should realize how lucky they are. This use of one quote from each side was called "balance." News stories like that always seemed to cancel themselves out, like a positron and electron colliding and annihilating themselves. You ended up with a tidy neutral event. Life went on.

In an interview, John Le Carre said that a spy and a novelist are similar in that they observe everything around them with a sort of detachment. I didn't think I was a spy or a novelist, but that's the way I was starting to feel. In my case I think there was also, fortunately, a sense of mordant amusement. Deep down inside, I still figured all things will pass.

ONE DAY I REALIZED I WAS FAR ENOUGH INTO THE HISTORICAL material that I was doing original research, putting old things together in new ways and seeing things that others hadn't seen. I decided I should discuss my results with some of the university scholars. When I tried to find someone to talk to, I learned that my subject fell into an academic no-fly zone: There was a history department and an archaeology department, but the Coronado period lay in a chasm between them. It was an accident of academia. The history department cared only about the "Spanish colonial" period, after the Spanish got established in the 1600s and left enough records to "do history with." The archaeology department defined its field as ending the day before the Spanish arrived. Archaeologists derived ancient lifestyles from mute bones and sherds. If someone wrote it down in a living language, it wasn't archaeology anymore. Besides, the Coronado-era eyewitness descriptions were considered vague and untrustworthy because no one knew exactly where Coronado's army was. To complicate things, in the late 1980s, some sort of hyper-conceptualist post-contextual neo-revisionism meta-bullshit was the academic mode du jour, according to which no early written document meant what it said, because it was a product of zeitgeist-derived semiotics. A village was no longer a village, but a part of a regional socioeconomic polity linked to its cultural framework through subliminal mytho-historic constructs. If Marcos wrote "I talked with three chiefs," it was no longer a traveler's attempt to report a conversation, but a politico-psychological construct whose meaning was exceedingly complex.

I went to see my old professor in the history department, Dr. Panofsky, for whom I had written my fateful term paper. He was sympathetic. He smiled at me across a desk piled with enough paper to saturate a landfill. The papers in the bottom stratum had certainly been there when I took his class a decade before. After he listened to me, he said it was possible, with all my reading, that I might find some info that others had missed. But I should not expect widespread interest from others in the department. He explained empathetically that I was an amateur, and as for other scholars in the university, they had their own specialties, not to mention classes to teach and faculty committee meetings to go to; they wouldn't take me seriously unless I came up with something spectacular. If I did come up with something spectacular, I should call him first.

In short, I couldn't get anyone interested in paying attention to what I was doing.

*   *   *

Next week I went to see Carlos, the nephew, at the Sears garage. I thought it was all a wild goose chase, but I wanted to make Phaedra happy. That's what you do when you get romantically involved with people: crazy things you think might make them happy.

The Buena Vista Mall was a place I usually avoided. After half an hour there, I found that the consumer goods were all screaming at me, and I began to fear for my sanity. The garage was at one end of the main madhouse. Institutional waiting rooms. Frayed chairs and a frayed TV. I had brought a book, because one of my secrets of life is always to carry a book. But the TV was on and I couldn't read. A mother and her 5-year-old son were there. The mother read the frayed magazines, and the 5-year-old tore around molesting things. Neither one watched the TV talk show, which involved guests hurling insults at each other as the audience cheered them on like Romans at the circus. The cheers were on cue, like laugh tracks on old radio shows. It made the audience seem Pavlovian. I was exasperated at first, having to wait amid the bedlam, but then the madonna and child left and I turned off the TV so I could concentrate.

I had just started to read when the little boy pranced back in. A strange thing happened. This child, who had paid no attention to the TV when it was on, was now transfixed; forgetting whatever carnage he had planned, he stopped in his tracks and stared at the empty, sickly green screen. Had he never seen one turned off before? He walked over tentatively, reached out his hand and touched it; it was like the obligatory, reverent scene of touching in a Spielberg movie: boy touches alien, boy touches airplane, boy touches silent TV.

When I finally talked to Carlos, he said his uncle, Steve, lived on a ranch southeast of town and had found Coronado's helmet. That's what his family called it, Coronado's helmet. Unlikely, but from the description it sounded like it could be from that era.

"Uncle Steve, he's kind of . . . well, an old-timer. Like from the old west, you know? But he's okay. He's Anglo. On my father's side. If you're interested in that stuff, you ought to go have a look. Uncle Steve had some expert look at it. Said it could be real. He has it stored away somewhere."

"Where?"

"On the ranch." He was writing down a telephone number. "It's down near Lochiel, on the border. It's really nice down there. I used to go there when I was a kid. Now, there's no time for that, what with fixing cars, and . . ." He smiled ruefully and gestured past the stacks of tires and past the parking lot toward the street, with its zooming cars. He was about my age, and seemed very earnest about his life.

I figured I had to check it out. If it was real, and I could learn where it was found, it might clinch the route. Even if there was nothing in the story, I'd have a chance to see the high grassland country south of the section of the Nexpa where Phaedra and I had played. That country was probably the *despoblado* that the Spaniards reported between the Rio Señora and the Rio Nexpa. Somewhere along there was where Marcos unknowingly stepped across the invisible line that constitutes today's border, entering the present-day United States for the first time. Strange to think there was a time when that invisible latitude line, which figures prominently today in talk of illegal aliens and drugs, had no significance at all.

I called Steve. At his suggestion, we decided to meet that Sunday, the 16th, in a bar in Patagonia, southeast of Tucson. We had to postpone it until then. We both had taxes to finish. Saturday was hell, trying to thread my way through the last of the forms. You know your country's in trouble when the first quarter-page of a government paper is a paragraph about the Paperwork Reduction Act.

THE BAR IN PATAGONIA WAS OLD, DARK, AND DECORATED IN nuevo old west, with saddles, bridles, spurs, coils of ropes, and license plates. This had been real ranch country, but you could see in the decor the collision between the old ranch types and the new yuppie/horsey set starting to move down from Tucson. We spent the first beer over small talk, whereupon Steve invited me to follow him in his truck, up to his place in Lochiel, the smallest spot on the border, to see what he had to show me.

I followed Steve up the winding road at a snail's pace. He had lots of time, I could tell. I figured this was another opportunity to look at the country where Marcos walked. The road climbed slowly into a beautiful countryside, with wide plains of foot-high golden grass, dotted by scrubby trees. Occasionally we crossed little creekbeds; some of them actually had water in them. It was hard to understand what the water was doing there, where it came from, and why it didn't evaporate.

This was a hidden bit of Arizona, not the Arizona you see in the tourist brochures and calendars. The landscape was different from the rocky hillsides and tall saguaros around Tucson. It looked like the paintings of old California, very quiet, very peaceful, with hillsides of golden grass. It seemed far away from the world of oil spills and gas prices and traffic jams.

Lochiel was no more than a few scattered houses and a wide spot in the road, nestled against the U.S.–Mexico border. They used to have a crossing checkpoint there. Now, it's closed. Turns out, back in the thirties when they were preparing for the 400th anniversary of Marcos's walk, somebody else had beat me to the conclusion that Marcos had come through here. There, beside the road, under a windmill, was a giant concrete cross, a memorial to Marcos de Niza, saying this is where he crossed into what we optimistically call the United States of America. The sign might have been right. It might have been within a mile of here. It might have been this very spot. I mentally nominated it for a prize as the least-known monument to the most ignored explorer in U.S. history.

Steve's house was there, a mile or so back in the hills. He suddenly drove faster once we got on his dirt road, like a horse heading to the barn. I followed him, trying to keep up with his flying cloud of dust. He wheeled into the yard. Like many ranch porches in southern Arizona, Steve's was lined by old metates and manos and other examples of what my granddad used to call Indian relics.

Presiding over his porch, Steve fit his role as an old-time rancher. His bushy gray mustache made him look like a character actor in a Western. He was aware of this. "This here's the north end of the Cananea Grasslands," he said, waving his arm at the general surroundings. "Extends down into Sonora."

He motioned for me to sit on the porch. "Wait, I'll get you a beer." Through his window I could see bookcases, some chairs, a handmade coffee table with a glass display case with what looked like a collection of old cans. I waited in the late afternoon shade, marveling: People don't realize this other Arizona exists, this timeless, high, pleasant grassland in the southeast corner of the state. Time stands still here in the afternoons; the period from 3 P.M. to 4 P.M. lasts two or three hours. The sun pauses in the sky, and the very plants hesitate in their photosynthetic processes. Then finally the bushes and rocks give up waiting for something to happen. They get ready for night and wonder if, perhaps, something will happen the next day.

Steve emerged with two cans of cold Simpatico. As soon as we started talking on the porch he said, "You boys from the city think an old coot like me ought to be called Jeb, and be poorly educated. Well, I put in my time at the university, just like you. Got a master's out of that place. Didn't improve my respect for academia." He smiled at some private memory.

"But you've got books."

"Books, that's a different story. You can learn everything from books, if you know how to find the right ones. But academics . . ." He spit off the porch into the bushes.

We were about to hit it off on the subject of books, and it made me wish I had asked Phaedra to come along. My momentary silence gave him a chance to start free-associating. "That's why I live out here. You can see things straight. People live in the city, they're knee-deep in shit but they don't know it. They convince themselves it's clover. Out here, you really are knee-deep in clover."

He never told me what field he got a degree in.

"How'd you get interested in this Coronado stuff?" he asked me.

I told him part of the story, about doing the term paper, and how somebody had asked me to write up what I had found. I didn't really tell him about Mr. Rooney.

"It's interesting," he mused. "Didja ever think about what those Indians thought, when Marcos and Estevan, or Coronado and his boys, came marching over that horizon there, into their villages? It reminds me of this guy I met, what he said about civilizations. He was a space alien. I ran into him one day, out on my back forty."

My brain just edited out the word "space." I figured he was talking about one of the Mexican migrants, who passed routinely back and forth along these back roads, in spite of the best efforts of the U.S. Border Patrol.

"He started giving me this big lecture about contacts between civilizations," Steve was saying. "That's when I started not to trust him. He said whenever you have a contact between two civilizations, one of them always gets destroyed." Steve paused to rummage for tobacco. He took his time about stuffing it in his old, charred pipe. "Of course, it's true, I suppose. You only have to look at history. But it was the way he said it. Cold, like. The guy had no compassion at all. 'Whenever two civilizations meet, it's merely a contest to determine which one has the longer history of technological development. They meet; sooner or later they try their weapons on each other; the ones with the best weapons win. The others sink out of sight. It's happened many times throughout the history of the galaxy.' That's what he said."

Steve got his pipe working. Blue clouds of smoke wafted across the porch as the scrub oak in the yard hissed with gentle winds. "He was very serious about it. Very grave, you know? 'It's happened many times throughout the galaxy,' he said. 'Whole planets are littered with debris of lost civilizations. I've seen them.' That's how he put it."

About that point in the conversation I started not to trust Steve himself. I wondered what I was doing there. But Steve continued, as if he had all the time in the world. Which he did. "Talk about archaeology! The debris that guy's seen must be a helluva lot more interesting than Coronado's helmet."

"About Coronado's helmet," I said. I wanted to get him off UFOs, or whatever he was talking about. Maybe he was crazy. I had a sinking feeling there was no helmet.

"You know what I think?" Steve said. "I think they put that big Marcos monument in the wrong place. Coronado and them boys were out in the San Pedro Valley, east of here. Since that helmet was in the family, I read all about that stuff. Coronado was down there with the water and good grass for the animals, not up here in the hills. Since Marcos was the pathfinder for the expedition, he woulda been down there, too, charting where the grass was."

"But, um, according to Marcos's account, just before he got here he made a side trip west to explore the coast." I felt nervous about contradicting Steve. "So he might not have been coming up the San Pedro. He might have been coming back from the coast, trying to rejoin the main trade route. So he might have crossed around here."

Steve paused, considering. He was all graciousness. "Say, that's interesting. That might be right." He shook his head and blew a large cloud of aromatic smoke that seemed to hang about the porch.

I felt I had scored a point. I began to think that if he was reasonable enough to consider my ideas, he might be okay after all. "About the helmet your grandfather found. You still have it?"

"It was passed down through the family. Don't get so damn impatient. That's what I was telling you about. This alien, or whatever he was—he's a lot more interesting. And he has a bearing."

"Alien."

"I'm not talkin' wetback, you know. I'm talkin' honest-to-God space alien, from some other star system. Asked him where he was from, once we got into the conversation. He just laughed. 'There's no way to tell you. There's no frame of reference.' That's what he said. 'No frame of reference.' Interesting talking to him. Looked just like us, except maybe the skin was smoother, almost hairless. And he was thin. Kinda short. Not too short."

"A space alien, and he looked like us?"

"He laughed about that, too. He said, 'It always amused us that your world expected people from other worlds to look like monsters.' See, he pointed something out to me. Obvious when you think about it. It's called convergent evolution. You can have radically different species, but they evolve to the same appearance if they've got the same function. Like in the ocean for example. Sharks are fish, but dolphins are mammals. Radically different histories, but they came to the same form. And there was some prehistoric amphibian that had that shape, too. That's the way it was with his people. Toolmakers. Opposing thumbs. Stereo vision. With the right clothes, he could've passed among us. At least with sunglasses. Interesting eyes. Kind of big, and sort of yellowish green. Reminded me of the grass in the right season. . . ."

"If he was so like us, how'd you know he was a real alien?"

"I saw the goddamn spaceship comin' in, that's how. Jesus. What did you think?" He spit off the porch again in disgust. "Landed at the base of the hill." He pointed toward a hill beyond the trees. "About a mile or so. I was sitting right here. Saw this glaring thing, coming down from the sky. About midnight. Then there was a glow beyond the trees. Hiked over to see what it was. Took my gun. Didn't actually see the ship on the ground. Met him, instead, walking out of the woods. It was late at night. Last summer. We came back here to the porch. Talked until dawn. He was sittin' right there where you're sittin'. Want another beer?"

"Uh, sure." He had cases of Simpatico in a cooler inside the house. "So you never saw the spaceship," I called after him as he went into the house. "I mean on the ground?" I figured I had to let him talk it out.

He returned with the beer. "Damndest thing. It took off the next morning. Right up into the sky. Hardly any noise. Naturally, I didn't have my camera ready. It was round, kind of spherical with a projecting turret on the top. More like the one in *The Man from Planet X* than a flying saucer." He looked at me. "Oh. Guess you wouldn't remember that one. Fifties. This spaceship comes down in the Scottish moors. Well, anyway, mine wasn't silvery, like in the movie. It was green. Bright green. Damndest thing. That's why I didn't tell anybody. Nobody would've believed a green spaceship."

"So why you telling me?"

"Who else am I gonna tell? Anybody around here, they'll think I'm crazy."

"So you don't have photos or anything. Any proof . . ."

" 'Course I got proof. For one thing, it left prints in the ground. No burned area or radioactivity or anything like that, but three deep holes. Conical. I photographed them and then I staked it out with a big tarp over it. They all looked the same, the holes. About a foot deep. Poured plaster in one of them, to make a permanent cast. And I left the others so somebody might make measurements *in situ*. There might be something in the soil. Whatever is there, it'll be preserved pretty well under those covers. Anyway, what's the use of telling anybody? None of your scientists at the damn university would believe it. They're too busy writing to Washington for grants; no time to study what's under their noses. Anyhow, sure as hell don't want a bunch of fools with doctorates pokin' around here, know what I mean? Also, I'm telling you because you're interested and you're sharin' a beer with me. Some people, I can tell, they got a head for listening. Other people, scientists for instance, they just compare what you're saying with their theories, and then call you a liar if it doesn't match."

He started fussing with his pipe again, tamping down the tobacco with a little silver tool and looking satisfied.

"So, about that helmet," I ventured.

"Oh, hell, okay. I'll show it to you. But don't expect me to let you take it down to the university for testing. I refuse to show it around in public. First thing you know, the government people will come in here with some search warrant and take it away, and it'll end up in the museum instead of here, in the family."

"There's no law that would let them do that."

"They're passin' more laws every day, sonny. Big government."

We went inside. There wasn't much family left, as far as I could tell. Above the bookcases, the walls were lined with old Fred Harvey posters from the Santa Fe Railroad days, and a photo of Truman signed "To Steve, with thanks for you conscientious assistance." I never got around to asking him what the Truman connection was. He had a lot of books. Old ones and new ones. Odd juxtapositions. "Mark Twain and Karl Marx and Milan Kundera, side by side," I observed. "You're probably the only guy in southern Arizona who's got a shelf arranged like that."

"You don't see the connections?"

"Well. . . . How do you mean?"

He puffed a mighty blue cloud, with pride. "Sure as hell ain't arranged alphabetical, I'll tell you that." Without a word more about the books, he led me farther back into the dark house. I bumped my head on the low lintel of a back room. "I grew up in this room," he said. The room was full of boxes, an old chest of drawers, magazines dating from the sixties, dog-eared Sears catalogs, and an old bedstead piled with blankets. He took down a worn box of heavy cardboard from a closet shelf. As soon as he opened it I could see a dull gleam. Reverently he lifted out the helmet.

I felt a shiver rise up my back. It was not the classic helmet of conquistador paintings, with side shields and a top crest, but merely a skullcap-shaped piece, with a tiny sagittal ridge. There were some holes along the side, as if for lacing in some padding and a chin strap. It matched perfectly the kind of helmet worn by many of the ordinary soldiers in Coronado's army.

There were smudges of rust, but there were still shiny surfaces. There was also a little tag of heavy, worn paper, tied through one of the holes, with a faded inscription in old cursive: "Found in the hills east of Kennedy's Well, N. Sulfur Springs Valley. J. M. McCallister. October, 1893."

"It's a goddamn conquistador's hat, that's what it is. Don't tell me it ain't Spanish, 'cause it is."

"This is amazing."

"I told you."

"Was there more? I mean, did your grandfather find anything else with it?"

"This is all I've got. I never had much chance to talk to grandaddy about it. My daddy said that my grandaddy used to tell him he found it in a little cave or overhang, up in the mountains. No bones with it. It was in a little cairn of rocks. I used to imagine this old Spanish guy was up there hunting or something, and set it aside, and never came back to get it. Or maybe he was killed by Indians and they set it aside in a shrine as magic material. If you read your Coronado books, you'll find out that although the Indians loved Marcos when he came through going north, they were pretty mad at the Spanish by the time Coronado arrived a year later. Maybe they killed him."

"Where—"

"I don't know exactly where it was."

"Kennedy's well. . . ."

"That was an old ranch location, out in the Sulfur Springs Valley. East of there, that'd put it up in the Pinaleños somewhere."

"So it was found in the hills above the Sulfur Springs Valley?" I was frustrated and excited at the same time. Steve's description put this find within a few miles of our land, on the mountainside overlooking the development. But Steve's story was all hearsay. Nobody would be able to track this down. Anyway, who would believe somebody who started talking about flying saucers? Arizona old-timers were notorious for trying to pull the leg of a greenhorn. Still, the find sounded authentic. The chronicles talked about soldiers seeing mountain sheep in the southern Arizona part of the trip. The soldiers might have been up in the hills, looking for game. "Some scholar ought to look at this thing."

"I told you: Hell, no."

"Can't I at least photograph it?"

"I don't want pictures getting out. It's been in the family for eighty years. Didn't seem to cause the end of the world, nobody knowing about it."

"Don't you care about it? About history? You seem like a knowledgeable guy."

"Of course I care about history. That's why I've preserved my grandaddy's stuff. We go way back in this area, my family. My grandaddy homesteaded out here. And my daddy took over after that. You couldn't tear a book about Spanish history out of his hands. That's why he was one of the ones promoting the Marcos monument here."

"I thought you said it was the professors from the university."

"Well, now, I have to admit, they had a little help from the local boosters. Wouldn't you rather have a national memorial next to your property than have it out in the middle of the San Pedro Valley?"

"People ought to know about this. I mean, who's going to hear of it, locked away in your house? If you pass on—"

"What do you mean, *if* I pass on? Do I look immortal? Look. When I croak, my attorney will let the university boys come up here and look at this thing. I care about history, but history can afford to take its time. I tell you, when the scholars get here, they'll be more excited by the alien landing site I told you about. That was the biggest thing in my life. But if I try to go public about it, they'll just laugh me off the land. Lock me up somewhere, like as not. C'mon back out on the porch." He left the helmet lying on the bed.

I tried to memorize the shape, the dimensions, the exact gleam of the old metal.

"The thing is," he said as we walked down the hall, "people in the backcountry around here know a lot more of the history of this state than the professors do. You have no idea. It's just, they don't have to publish reports in journals to make a living. They just tell whoever they choose. It gets passed along, one way or th'other."

I studied the inside of the house as we walked back out toward the porch. It was plain and practical, not full of knickknacks like a city house. I could believe that all the houses along the old road through Lochiel had their own strange secrets.

When we got out on the porch, Steve went on, "What I wanted to tell you was about what that alien said. Like I said, it's all connected. He never should have landed his ship on the property of someone whose family knew of Coronado. See, late that night, we started walking back toward his ship and he was telling me all this stuff about how the history of the galaxy proved that inferior civilizations got wiped out every time they met an older civilization. But then I realized, that would mean the first civilization in the history of time would be the only one to survive. I asked him about that. All the ones that came later, on planets of younger stars—did you know stars have different ages?"

"Yeah. I learned that in an astronomy course," I answered.

"Yeah, well, according to what he was telling me, any younger civilization of a younger star should perish at the hands of the oldest one."

"How did he answer that?"

"He said: 'Not necessarily. Sometimes civilizations get tired. They lose interest in things. Their technology falls into disuse. One day they confront a civilization younger and more vigorous. And they find to their surprise that their technology is no longer superior. But it is very rare. As for you,' he said, 'you are doomed. But it is some time in the future.' He looked me in the eye and then he kind of looked at the sky with those yellow-green eyes. He seemed amused.

"And then I got to thinking. Can you imagine some village of Indians, back in the 1500s? And Coronado's army comes riding through. And the Indians send out their biggest, strongest warrior. The one who's twenty-five years old, and six feet tall, and never been beat by anybody, wrestling, wenching, bashing people over the head with a stone ax, or fighting with arrows. They send this guy out to tell Coronado to go away. This guy starts brandishing his arrows. He's never been beat, see, and the whole tribe is watching him, and he knows nobody can lay a glove on him, and he's twenty feet away from the Spaniards. And Coronado watches him coming, and figures he has to make an example. Coronado nods to one of his few *arquebus* men. Bang! And this guy, this hero of the tribe, turns back toward the tribe with a puzzled look and blood gushing out of his chest, and falls to the ground dead, without a word. Can you imagine what that did to those people?"

I raised my eyebrows and frowned sagely, trying to look like I was participating in the conversation. I didn't know where this was going. "Well, I think on the northward march Coronado was trying to be careful not to antagonize the Indians. I don't think he would just—"

"That's when I shot him; the alien, I mean. Let him have it, right out there in the forest. Figured, why let him go back to tell his people about us if they had that attitude. He didn't even know I was carrying a gun. I fixed the son of a bitch. Him and his superior civilization. I must say, I liked the look of surprise on his face. You want another beer?"

"Um, no, thanks." I tried to get up casually. He had said the alien took off in his ship in the morning. This guy was all over the map.

"So, listen, if you ever change your mind about showing that Spanish material to some experts . . . I mean, I'd really like to bring some people up here. You've got my phone number on my card—"

"I told you. After I'm gone. You bring anyone up here before then, I'll deny everything. Hey, aren't you going to ask me about the spaceship?"

"Yeah," I said, standing on the edge of the porch. Suddenly I was afraid to turn away from him. "Tell me about the spaceship. I thought you said he took off the next morning." I was feeling panicky.

"Nah. You don't listen. Like I told you, *the ship* took off the next morning. I never said he was in it. I figure it was on some kind of autopilot. I'm sure he was alone. I sat up the rest of the night, till dawn, right here on the porch with my gun, waiting for the rest of them to come after me, but nobody showed up. He musta been the only one in the ship. Buried the son of a bitch out there near his landing site. Figured that's the least I could do for him. Don't worry though; the grave's well hidden. But it's my ace in the hole to prove the story. I'll leave instructions how to find it, in my will."

After I left his ranch, I sat in my car under the Marcos monument and made some sketches of the helmet as I remembered it. Steve might be a flaky misfit who believed in flying saucers, but his artifact was real.

The more I thought about it, the more I began to wonder which one of us was really the misfit. People who believe in flying saucers with humanoid space aliens may be the majority in our society. Where did that leave me? You don't have a lot of people running around trying to reconstruct the journey of Marcos de Niza.

An hour or so later, I slipped back and hiked through the woods in the direction Steve had pointed. I did find his big tarp, carefully staked out, and under it were the two conical holes and a third hole filled with plaster. Well, just because a guy can dig holes and pour plaster doesn't mean he wasn't spinning a spin tall tale. And just because a guy spins tall tales doesn't mean his grandfather didn't tell the truth about an artifact.

WHEN I GOT BACK FROM TALKING TO STEVE, PHAEDRA TOLD ME that the office had been called by a reporter known for sniffing out controversy before it happened—or to be more accurate, a penchant for creating it where it did not exist. He was writing a feature about Coronado Estates.

Everyone in our office waited apprehensively for the article. It came out on Wednesday morning, the 19th, which was the supervisors' meeting day—the day our hearing had originally been scheduled. It focused on the beauties of the valley, the reality of urban sprawl, the destruction of solitude, how much more traffic our suburb might generate on Tucson streets, and who stood to gain from our plan. In passing, it mentioned "reports of Indian ruins" on our site, but the emphasis was more on politics than on archaeology.

The slant was that, with the hearing delayed, the public now had an extra month to find out what was "really happening." It was a formula piece. There was an interview with the head of the chamber of commerce in Willcox, about how our new town would revitalize the whole community, and an answering interview from a Sierra Club spokeswoman, who said that our development would destroy the character of the area and would impact the national forests in the mountains east of the valley, which she said were already threatened by construction of an astronomical observatory. The article promised to keep readers posted on this important story.

Meanwhile, on the same day, the temperature broke 100 degrees; it was the earliest date ever recorded for triple-digit temperatures. As our local TV weather anchors used to say, the ice on the Santa Cruz River had broken.

THAT NIGHT, I HAD A DREAM. IN MY DREAM, THE PARALLEL streams of history in America and Europe get out of synch by a mere five hundred years—a small glitch in their ten-thousand-year histories. As a result, the Aztecs, a.k.a., the Mexica, develop better technology than the Europeans. Moctezuma, having conquered the surrounding city states, gets curious about their stories of Quetzalcoatl, the god who sailed away into the eastern sea. He builds a navy and sends the warriors of Quetzalcoatl east with crossbows and cannons, in the name of God and king. They discover Dark Age Europe. The court of Spain falls to the Aztecs, who ally themselves with hordes of Moors and march on Rome. Rome falls, and St. Peter's is torn down to build a pyramid. The Pope is sacrificed along with various kings and princes, and the old European books are burned in great fires. The old tombs in the Gothic cathedrals are broken open so the Aztec scientists can study the customs of the savages.

CHAPTER 8

Marcos Tells About His Side Trip to the Coast

During the last days of April I kept burrowing deeper into Marcos's itinerary. I was trying to see where his 1539 route matched the Coronado army's route of 1540, and where they were different. Aside from locating the Spanish route, I kept getting sidetracked by the fact that these archival documents were the only eyewitness accounts of prehistoric life in the Southwest. After the Coronado expedition, the Spanish didn't come back for another thirty or forty years, and by that time everything had changed because germs are mightier than conquerors. Spanish diseases, against which the natives had no immunities, worked their way north and infected the villages, either with Coronado's army or a decade or so later. The social order changed and native populations declined by the 1580s. Prehistory had been lost forever. So the observations by Marcos and the Coronado army chroniclers were unique time capsules, our only source of information on ancient lifestyles and trade routes as they had existed until the Europeans arrived.

Marcos himself was terse about native life when he hurriedly wrote his *Relación*, but he and Cabeza de Vaca apparently passed additional details to the first American historian, Bartolomé de Las Casas, who included them in Chapter 67 of the massive "apologetic history" he published about New Spain around 1560. In one passage of *Apologética Historia*, Las Casas described the weird religious practices in central Sonora. It starts with a description from Cabeza de Vaca:

> *Cabeza de Vaca and his companions arrived in a town where they were offered as much hospitality as if they were the peoples' own relatives or parents. They were given 600 open hearts of beef to eat, and for this reason they named this town Corazones. It seems the people of this region use hearts for sacrifices to their gods, as well as eating them. Cabeza de Vaca, when he arrived in the town, saw ceremonies celebrated as follows. They put many animals, such as deer, wolves, birds, and rabbits, in front of a large idol. With a background of music by flutes, they cut them in half and took out the hearts, and with the blood they bathed the idol, and then they hung the hearts around their necks. When they celebrate this sacrifice, they prostrate themselves in front of the idol as a sign of great reverence. In the whole province of the valley of Sonora, they sacrifice only the hearts of the animals.*
>
> *They also have two fiestas in which they have much music and singing, and in which they celebrate sacrifices with great happiness, ceremony, and devotions. One fiesta is in the time of sowing the crops, and the other is at the time when the crops are harvested. There must be other ceremonies that the Spanish travelers didn't see in the short time they were there. It seems that some sign [about scheduling these ceremonies] may come to these people from the sun worshipers in the provinces of Cíbola.*

The last lines fit with later records from nineteenth-century ethnographers, that the pueblo sun priests in what is now New Mexico carefully observed solstices and equinoxes in order to schedule ceremonies and agricultural plantings. In his next paragraph, Las Casas continued with material he apparently got from Marcos, which includes details that Marcos didn't mention in his own *Relación*:

A well-known ecclesiastic of the Franciscan order, Fray Marcos de Niza, also arrived in this valley of Senora and entered into the principal town. The head of the town received him on behalf of the entire valley, and extended his hands toward him, and then rubbed his entire body. After this, in another town, six leagues from there toward Cíbola, was the principal chapel or temple, which was called Chicamastle, where that chief goes to offer his sacrifices. There was a very tall temple made of stone and mud. At this temple there was a stone statue full of blood, and many animal hearts hung around the neck. Also around this statue were many bodies of dead men, with their intestines taken out, dried, and placed on the walls. They must have belonged to people from that valley who had died, and this was their tomb.

This passage might be taken to mean that Marcos passed through Corazones. At first I thought it was an argument against my theory that Marcos had been farther west, trying to check out the coast. Then I realized that Las Casas gave no date for these observations. Marcos might have seen these things when he passed through Corazones on his return from Cíbola in 1539 or as he guided Coronado north in 1540, or on his return from the Coronado expedition later in '40. Anyway, it gave an exotic glimpse of "organized religion" in the legendary town of Hearts.

The problem with Marcos's own *Relación* is that it gets extremely vague and poorly phrased, in terms of the routing and timing after Marcos left the village of Vacapa. The *Relación* was not intended as a road map, but more of a chatty documentation that the viceroy's man had obtained information about Cíbola and made claims on the land. It gave numbers of days here and there, but Marcos seemed more excited about describing the increasingly prosperous villages and the news of Cíbola than about reporting a route. He may have deliberately restricted the routing details to a more private document prepared for Viceroy Mendoza, to keep

Cortés's boys from learning the way. Anyway, Marcos himself picks up the story as he tries to catch Estevan a few days north of Vacapa, probably on or near the Rio Sonora.

I continued five days in the province of the people who gave Estevan the first information about Cíbola. All along the way, I found well populated settlements where I was received with fine hospitality and receptions. Here I found many turquoises, the hides that look like cowhides, and always the same report of the country ahead. . . .

At one town, I received messengers who were natives of that locality, but who had gone ahead with Estevan. Estevan overloaded them with messages about the grandeur of the land, urging me to make haste. At that town, I also learned that after two more days' journey, I would reach a four-day despoblado, where the only food was what they could carry and store in shelters. I went on, expecting to meet Estevan, because he had sent word that he would wait for me.

Before reaching the despoblado, I came to a fresh, cool town, irrigated, where I was met by a number of people, both men and women wearing clothes of cotton and the cowhides, which they liked even better than the cotton. All of them wore ornaments of turquoise which they hang from their noses and ears. . . . Among them was the lord of the town and his two brothers, very well-clothed in cotton and ornaments, and each with necklaces of turquoises on his neck, and they brought me much meat of deer, rabbits, and quails, plus maize and meal, all in great abundance. They offered me many turquoises, hides, handsome bowls, and other things, but I declined everything, which has been my custom since entering the country where they have no knowledge of us.

I was dressed in a habit of dark woolen cloth, given to me by Francisco Vázquez de Coronado. The governor of this town and other Indians touched my habit with their hands and told me the natives of Cíbola were clothed with similar material. I laughed and declared it could not be true, as their blankets were of cotton.

But they replied, "Do you think we don't know the difference between what you wear and what we wear? We're telling you not only that Cíbola is full of this cloth that we wear, but also that in a nearby town, Totonteac, they have some small animals from which they take fiber and make cloth like yours." They said those animals are the size of the two Castillian greyhounds that Estevan had with him. I was surprised about this, but I could not learn any more about their genus.

The next day I entered the four-day despoblado, and at the place where I stopped to eat, near an arroyo, I found huts and sufficient food. And at night again I found huts and food.

At the end of the four days I emerged into a well-populated valley. In the first town many men and women came to meet me with food. They all wore many turquoises that hung from their noses and ears. Some wore necklaces of turquoises like those in the town on the other side of the despoblado, except that those were only one loop, while these were three and four loops. The women were dressed with . . . very good skirts and blouses. These people had as much knowledge of Cíbola as we in New Spain have of Mexico City, or in Peru they have of Cuzco. They particularly described the style of the houses, streets, and plazas in Cíbola, like people who had been there many times. . . . I remarked that houses of the style they described, several stories high, seemed impossible. To make me understand, they took soil and ashes and mixed them with water, and showed me how they placed the stones, and how the edifice was built up, placing stones and mortar until it reached the required height. I asked them if the men of that country had wings to reach the upper stories; they laughed and explained the concept of ladders to me as well as I could explain it. They took a stick and placed it over their heads, saying this was the height from one story to the next. . . .

Here, [nearly two weeks after heading north out of Vacapa] I

learned that the coast turns abruptly to the west, though it had
been running to the north. As a change in the direction of the
coast was a matter of importance [as stated in the viceroy's
instructions], I wished to learn about it, and so I went to view it,
and saw clearly that, in latitude 35 degrees, it turns to the west.

This coastal visit was one of the main controversies of Marcos's
account. Did he really have time to do it? Was he spinning lies or
putting a propitious spin on the truth? It was the old problem: is the
glass half full or half empty? In support of Marcos, he was basically correct about the geography. The coast does turn west, forming the north end of the Gulf of California in this general region.
Raising doubts against Marcos, the time available for a westward
jog was marginal, and he got the latitude a few degrees too high.
Many Spanish latitude measures at this time were a degree or so
too high, but Marcos's was a degree or two higher than would be
expected from the techniques in those days. So Marcos's critics say
he never made the side trip to the coast, but rather fabricated this
whole episode.

One of the strongest critics was the geographer-historian Carl
Sauer, who analyzed Marcos's *Relación* in the 1930s and concluded that most of the journey reported after Vacapa and the initial
news of Cíbola was a deliberate fraud. Sauer made a valuable
analysis of the main route used by later parties traveling between
Culiacán and the north country. He said Marcos should have followed that route, which was well inland. Sauer then had to conclude—in a circular argument—that Marcos wouldn't have had
time to make a side trip to the sea. The logic bothered me. Marcos wasn't following Sauer's instructions, but rather the
viceroy's, which were to get information about the coast. Sauer's
problem was that instead of looking for evidence that might
reveal where Marcos actually was, Sauer simply attacked Marcos whenever the priest's account didn't fit the scholar's theory.
Here is one of this "objective" scholar's typical passages about
Marcos.

The paucity and confusion of data as to terrain, as to direc-
tion, distances, and . . . latitude, make this easily the worst
geographic document on this frontier, and indicate either that
Brother Mark was an amazing dunderhead or that he indulged
in deliberate obfuscation. . . . If we subscribe to the old theory
that he was an arrant swindler, it is perhaps more charitable to
leave him in that role, rather than have him also a fool who
had no business to wander about in strange places.

Even if Sauer was too harsh toward Marcos, and his logic was
no good, I had to admit that Marcos did not have enough time to
map the coastline in detail. Furthermore, as Edward and I had discovered during our peregrinations in Mexico, the coast in that
region was truly hostile, a region of sun-blasted barren sands,
pathetic vegetation, and dry riverbeds. More importantly, there is
no one place from which you could "see clearly that the coast
turned west." My conclusion was that as he worked his way north,
Marcos had chosen not Sauer's eastern route, but the more western
valleys, and that he had indeed made some sort of foray to gather
news of the coastline's orientation. Sure, he relied partially on
Indian accounts of the coast. Was that so bad?

I wondered if his linguistic construction, "I saw clearly that the
coast turned west," was a conveniently vague idiom, in the way
that we would say "I saw that it was true," to mean "I came to
understand that it was true."

EVERYONE DUMPED ON POOR OLD MARCOS. ALWAYS THERE WAS
this conflict between the two possible portrayals: the openhearted
storyteller, or the scheming fraud. Somehow, to me, he still didn't
seem like someone who was concocting an elaborate hoax. I liked
his chatty little anecdotes, like the story about the ladder.

I turned the question around. If Marcos was basically trying to
tell the truth, then how could the historians be so wrong? Were
they merely overzealous, like a sleazy lawyer trying to "win" a
case at the expense of some innocent defendant? And why should

a search for the truth be like a game, in which someone wins and someone loses? I went back to the critics one more time. Let them take their best shot, I thought. Let them show me what I was missing. The ambulance chasers cut Marcos no slack. Here's Cleve Hallenbeck, from his 1949 book, making his summation to the jury:

> [Marcos's] claim of having visited the coast from the Sonora Valley is also demonstrably false. He spoke of this "visit" as though the trip occupied only a few hours, although at that time he could not have been within 100 miles of the Gulf. . . . Others have insisted that Marcos must have visited the coast because he had been instructed to do so. Such students have not examined the viceroy's instructions carefully. Marcos was not instructed to visit the coast. He was told to "inquire always for information" about the seacoast, and, if perchance he came to the coast, to leave evidence of his presence. He could have obtained information from the Indians, and clearly all the information he did get was from that source. The rest he invented.

Hallenbeck was disingenuous at best. Marcos's overall record clearly indicated the side trip took days, not hours. Furthermore, it is clear from the viceroy's instructions that a major purpose of Marcos's trip was to get the maximum information possible about the coast, to prepare for a possible naval expedition to the north, and to defuse Cortés's claims to the coastal regions. Hallenbeck was really stretching to claim that the viceroy's instructions on what to do "if you come to the coast" were evidence that Marcos had *not* been told to look for the coast! In Sauer's breezy summary of 1937, "his account of the coast is faked, a translation of hearsay into his own observations." Poor Marcos. Having been instructed to inquire about the coast, that's probably exactly what he did, and for his troubles he is called a fraud.

Still, the whole thing was frustratingly vague. I kept wondering why my reading of the documents was so much different from the "real" historians readings. Had I missed something?

THE HEARING ON OUR PLAN WAS NOW SCHEDULED FOR MAY 24. The heat was on. I say "our" plan. I had developed a craftsmanlike pride in the thing, in spite of my reservations about Mr. Rooney's philosophical attitudes.

Only the library seemed cool. If Marcos had the stamina to walk across prehistoric Sonora and Arizona, I should at least have the stamina to finish my research. A lot of things were adding up. The fact that Steve's helmet had apparently been found in the hills above our property gave me private encouragement that Spaniards of the Coronado era had been near there, but it wasn't something I could use: an artifact owned by a guy who wouldn't show it in public and talked to space aliens didn't inspire confidence. Besides even if it were perfectly authenticated, a doubter could argue plausibly that it might have been traded by Indians from some point three hundred miles away. Still, the evidence from the Coronado documents had convinced me that Marcos in 1539 and the Coronado army in 1540 had marched right up our valley.

CHAPTER 9

April, 1539
By Sea to Cíbola?

Tuesday, April 15, late afternoon. This was the last village of this valley. Tomorrow they would enter the four-day despoblado that led to the valley close to the sea, where he could learn more about the coastline.

Here in this village, where he would pass the night, they were preparing a great fiesta for him. Marcos admitted to himself that he looked forward to the feast after his spartan days on the trail. There would be deer meat, maize, squash, beans from village fields. And the hearts of the deer—*corazones*. Even if the town named by Esteban's castaway friends was not in this valley, the customs of all the neighboring valleys at this latitude seemed to be the same.

Days before, the townsmen, hearing of his imminent arrival, had set out into the hills on a hunting expedition, and returned this morning with twelve deer and many rabbits. Upon his own arrival, Marcos had been disturbed that the carcasses were not simply cut up in the homes, but were collected on a raised platform in the middle of the village, in front of the plastered, turquoise-studded structure that passed for the local temple. Here, as feathers were waved and turquoise-decorated maces were set in receptacles in the shrine's doorway, the animals were cut open. Marcos turned away from the bloody proceedings as they invoked the names of their pagan gods. He prayed that the Lord would accept his own sacra-

ment later—a civilized, Christian act, in which he would wave the
cross on high and bless the food in the name of the Virgin Mary,
who he hoped would look down benevolently on the foolish superstitions of the Indians.

More Indians filtered into the town throughout the late afternoon, coming from nearby villages to see the strange visitor.

Before the feast came the time to meet with the village chief,
who had already delayed the meeting for an hour, for effect. He
was surprisingly young, a muscular, handsome man, with his hair
pulled back in a red leather band. His eyes darted back and forth as
he spoke, as if he were on the alert for some threat or advantage.
Around his neck were eight or ten heavy strands of turquoise
nuggets and a large shell, incised and inlaid with tiny turquoise and
garnet bits, in an intricate design. There was a nasty, fresh-looking
scar on his upper right arm. He was the youngest native governor
with whom Marcos had dealt, and he had a charismatic aura,
almost as strong as Estevan's.

After an initial introduction, the chief seemed friendly enough.
They sat together on woven mats, outside the chief's house. Here
was a chance to ask: Did the chief know the whereabouts of Estevan?

The chief paused before answering the question, staring
unblinkingly at Marcos, as if appraising him. Speaking through the
usual team of interpreters, he answered, "Oh, yes, I know exactly. I
sent guides part way with him. He has taken the trail northeast,
inland, the trail toward Cíbola."

"Did he not speak of waiting for his master?"

"No, no. On the contrary. He was in a hurry, excited to keep
going. Perhaps," the chief said with a mysterious smile, "for a man
like that, it is best that he move on and not wear out his welcome.
He is a man of many powers and many purposes."

Marcos tried to gain information about the surroundings. The
young chief said he knew about the sea, and had been there. "First
you go four days to the next valley and then go down that river a
few days. I will provide guides from my village. That valley is a

good one, but the land downstream, at the mouth of that river, is a great desert. The people in the next valley can tell you as much as you want to know about the coast because they go there to get salt and shells for trade." He showed off the shell bracelet on his wrist. "The trail through that valley is called the salt trail. You can take it upstream, to the northeast, to join the Cíbola trail. Perhaps there you will find the lord Estevan waiting for you."

Marcos's guides had whispered to him, through Juan, about this chief. Only a year ago, there had been terrible strife in this village. The locals said the elders had lost their powers. Some months before Marcos arrived, the young chief had overthrown the old chief, who had died a month later under mysterious circumstances. His bones were still enshrined in a nearby temple, and the new chief was regarded with fear and awe.

Marcos broached the subject carefully. "They tell me there has been unrest here."

"Oh, yes," the young chief described with gusto, "there was much strife in this whole valley. We have had five dry years because the old men of the village in this valley, they failed to honor the gods. It was time to restore virtue. The men from my village led the way. There were those who resisted, but when we defeated them, they were sent to be sacrificed in the great temple at Chichi-Maxtl, in the next valley. Now they are happy, living with the gods."

Marcos winced. "We do not believe in sacrifices. We—"

"They tell me your gods also have great temples," the earnest young leader continued. "Perhaps we could form an alliance. I could teach your people about our religion. It is the way of truth, that keeps the heavens and the seasons in harmony."

Marcos hardly knew whether to laugh or recoil in horror. It was ludicrous that pagans should presume to teach Christians about religion!

AFTER THE FEAST, MARCOS MADE HIS WAY TO HIS HUT BY THE light of a first-quarter moon. He shielded his eyes from the moon and peered into the sky. The comet had moved to a new position among the stars. Its tail was many times the width of the moon. It was a strange apparition. He tried to convince himself there was nothing in what the astrologers said about evil omens. . . .

WEDNESDAY, APRIL 16. THEY WERE ON A GOOD TRAIL ACROSS THE *despoblado.*

A great drama had played itself out in that last valley, Marcos reflected. All these valleys must be full of stories that would never be written down, never told. It put him in mind of his old question, why God had created this other world, across the sea, where dramas and passions were somehow disconnected from the real world, God's Christian world. It was almost impossible to imagine life and emotion existing here for generations, without the Spaniards even knowing about it. What was God's point, having pagans live in remote lands where no one knew of their existence until now? It was like the philosopher's story of the tree falling in the forest with no one present. Did it make a sound?

His faith in the goodness of these people was shaken, he realized. Human sacrifices in these idyllic valleys, just as in Moctezuma's capital! What other perversions were hidden in this seemingly idyllic land? He knew some people said he was naive. Had he been too optimistic about the people of these northern valleys? In Peru, someone said of him, that "Marcos polishes the apple that contains the worm." He remembered the tales told by the old-timers who had come to Mexico with Cortés—how the pyramids in Mexico City had been topped by stinking temples where the blood-encrusted priests of the Mexica cut out the hearts of sacrificial victims demanded by the Mexican religion. Old soldiers told the story of the fearsome day when they fought their way to the top of the main pyramid on the central plaza, and how Cortés himself had smashed one of the bloody idols in the summit shrine. Fortunately, Cortés had been able to follow this act of bravado by cleansing the pagan chapel and installing an image of the Virgin Mary, to replace the broken and obscene statue. Would he, Marcos, be so lucky?

Was he journeying toward a grand new Christian conquest, or was he simply traveling further into the darkness, away from God? The question brought to mind the scholarly arguments that had raged in Europe when he was in the seminary. Even before Las Casas had made the issue famous, the Dominican father, Antonio de Montesinos, had preached in the Indies in 1511 that the Spanish settlers were living in mortal sin because of their enslavement of the Indians.

"Are they not men?" he had asked in his most famous sermon. "Do they not have rational souls?" In the presence of King Ferdinand himself, Montesinos debated the point with the university professor, Juan Palacios Rubios, who cited Aristotle's dictum that some peoples might be "slaves by their own nature," and argued that the Indians were destined for servitude and in need of correction. That debate resulted in the Laws of Burgos in 1512, a kind of compromise stating that the Indians must be made Christians and compelled to attend church, and also that their old houses and habits should be destroyed, that they should be forbidden to dance, and that one third of them should work in the mines. These laws reflected the view that God gave the New World to the Christians in the same way that He gave the lands of Canaan to the Jews.

Professor Palacio Rubios remained very influential at court and went on to write the *Requerimiento*, which he said would calm Christian consciences, even though he admitted that some Indians might not understand it when it was read to them. Bartholomé de Las Casas had once remarked that when he heard of this logic, he didn't know whether to laugh or cry. Still, Marcos reflected, it recognized the progressive view that the Indians deserved dialog and explanation.

But always there was that nagging question. Did the Indians truly have souls? There was the controversial theory of Paracelsus, back in '20, which Marcos had heard as a young monk in the monastery of Saint-Croix, back on the sunny beach at Nice. According to that view, God had made two Adams on different sides of the Earth, and that descendants of the other Adam, these

Indians, did not have human souls. Thus, according to the theory, they could not be saved. Church fathers in Rome had finally rejected the idea, but they had never seen the extent of human sacrifices and other dark practices. If Paracelsus's theory carried even a tiny grain of truth, Marcos knew, all his dreams would be in vain and the dangers would increase with every step of the way, as he journeyed farther into the soulless pagan wilderness. . . .

For the next few leagues along the trail, Marcos visualized the bodies of sacrificial victims, and he struggled to put the dark thoughts out of his mind.

SATURDAY, APRIL 19. MARCOS AND HIS PARTY HAD BEEN MARCH-ing four days across sun-swept hills toward the northwest. The mornings were cool and magnificent for walking, but each afternoon grew hotter than the last, and the land grew more arid.

Marcos paid no attention to the afternoon heat. He was in a better mood. Each day, he marveled at the air in this northern desert land. It had a brightness to it, as if the air itself was luminous. The sky was blue, day after day, and even the muted olive green of the vegetation had a clarity and sparkle. In some inexpressible way the light was different from that of the valleys behind him, where shady trees crowded the rivers. The cloudless sky gave everything a sense of openness and portent. This shining air gave him a feeling that he had escaped from Satan's lair among the evil temples of the last province. After all, he thought, all peoples—even the Spanish Christians—had their evil excesses, but that did not mean they were inherently evil people. He began to develop a strange thought: that every man, instead of being good or evil by nature, was a victim of the traditions he inherited. Only God could lead each human being out of his own particular darkness.

Ahead of him, on the trail, there was some commotion among the Indian guides. They were reaching the crest of a low, gravel-strewn ridge. The trail passed a cairn of stones as high as a man, rising around the base of a dying saguaro from which feathers fluttered. The Indians were pointing ahead, to the northwest. They were laughing among themselves.

Marcos's heart leapt. Perhaps it was the sea, visible in the pale distance. He joined them. No, it was not the sea, but a beckoning green valley, perhaps three leagues away. He could see a ribbon of spring-green cottonwoods, the telltale sign of a watercourse. A wisp of smoke at the edge of one thick cottonwood grove suggested a village.

The Indians were each throwing a stone on the cairn. "They are thanking the spirits," Marcos's guide explained, "for bringing them through the *despoblado* to this good valley." The guide offered him a pebble and the others paused to look, expectantly.

"It is good to give thanks. I will thank the Great Spirit, who is my Father, who lives high in the sky overhead," Marcos told them. He knelt, saying a prayer. He laid his stone on the pile, but then reached into his trail bag for one of the small crosses he carried, and laid it carefully on the top of the pile, above the pagans' stones.

He hoped the Indians would learn by this example of piety. The men watched him in silence and then headed down the slope. To each his own, they seemed to be saying to themselves. Ahead of them, on the slopes, along the trail, were patches of spring flowers, scattered like small carpets. Really, it was delightful country. Surely no great evil could dwell here, in all this celestial light.

SUNDAY, APRIL 20. THEY ARRIVED AT A LARGE VILLAGE WHERE the river turned its flow from south to west, toward the sea, as prophesied. Smaller irrigated villages were scattered half a league apart along the broad valley. The people seemed prosperous and content with life. Many of them wore jewelry of turquoise and shell. They had earrings, nose ornaments, bracelets, and well-worked cowhide moccasins that they said came from Cíbola in exchange for their shell work. In the previous valley, only the chief had worn more than three strands of turquoise, but here, many of them wore multiple strands of the sky-blue gem around their necks. Marcos could not help but notice that the closer he got to Cíbola, the more prosperous the people.

Now that the existence of Cíbola had been abundantly confirmed, one last question about the northwern empire hung over everything. Late in the afternoon he called some of the villagers together to try again. He showed them his samples: a gold nugget, a gold nose plug of the Mexica, some copper ore, a small copper bell from Michoacán. "Do you know material like this? Metal?"

The Indians grew very somber, almost reverent. "Not in our village. There are people in other lands who have it. . . ." Metal, they explained, was a very strange and magical material. They seemed almost afraid of it.

"Then you've seen metals like these before?"

"Oh, yes." Then enthusiasm would give way to caution. "Sometimes."

"Where? Where does it come from?"

"Who can say? It is a magic material. Traders sometimes bring it from the south."

"Yes, but what about from the north?"

"Not very often."

"Do they have it in Cíbola?"

"Some people say so. But they say many things about Cíbola. Our people have not seen it there, but the priests and magicians there have many powers and things that our people do not understand."

Another man spoke up. "I've been there. Yes, they have some of this. Some of them like to brag to us that they can make it and we cannot, but as for me, I think they get it in trade. But you must understand, they do not explain anything to us. They are very proud, those people. They treat us like bits of dirt, but we are glad to work for them in exchange for their wonderful goods."

An old man approached, who also said he had been to Cíbola and who seemed to have a more philosophical bent. Marcos made him examine the samples. "People say that people in Cíbola offer metals like these in trade," Marcos prompted him. "Where does it come from?"

"It is magic. It comes from the underworld."

"Yes, yes, I know, but after it comes from the underworld—who fashions it? Do they use it in Cíbola?"

"Cíbola, ah, yes." The old man got a dreamy look. "There is metal in Cíbola." He picked up the copper bell. "The people of Cíbola decorate their dancers with these. I have seen it."

"And tools? Do they have tools made of these metals?" Marcos reached into his pouch again, eagerly. "Like this knife?"

The man shied away and put up his hands as if he had been threatened with Marcos's little knife. "Metal is used to make sacred implements and beautiful, shining things. But as for ordinary tools, they come from the stones of the Earth. I mean good materials, like flint, and obsidian. You don't have to worry about competing with the spirits of the underworld when you use flint and obsidian."

"What about this?" Marcos held up the gold nose plug. "Do they have this yellow metal?"

The man held the object close to his eyes. "Yes, I've seen it there."

"Ah . . ." Marcos breathed excitedly. "And do they have much of it?"

"Mmmmm. A few pieces. Like this. They use it for ceremonies. And sometimes the women wear it, as trinkets. They say some women there will stay with you if you give them metal like this, or feather capes." He smiled knowingly at Marcos. "But I think there is not as much as this other metal." He held up the copper bell. "This metal is more valuable."

THE OTHER QUESTIONS MARCOS PUT TO THEM CONCERNED THE seacoast. The villagers spoke of the great water several days to the west down the river, but rolled their eyes and indicated it was a difficult journey. Marcos had hoped the sea would be closer, within sight, or only a day downstream. He told them he wanted to see it. One villager took a stick and carved a channel on a little slope in the dry soil. From a small brown *olla*, he poured some water into the uphill end. The water ran down the gully and sank into the dry dust. The Indian pointed emphatically to the now-drying damp spot. "The river runs out of water before it gets to the sea. There is little water or food in that direction."

"And the coastline—does it continue north?"

There was much gesturing and arguing over the meaning of the question. "No. A little north of here, it turns toward the summer sunset. All that country, it is a dry desert. No one goes there except when we make special trips to collect salt and shell, which we trade to all the people who travel here from the inland towns, just to get these things from us. In any case, the towns downstream from here are only poor villages with ignorant people, not fine towns like we have here. The better sort of people don't go there. Maybe you would like to stay here and spend your time with us. People say you tell interesting stories."

"No, I am sorry, my new friends. I cannot stay."

Marcos was now torn about how to spend the next days. On the one hand, if the coast turned west, instead of inland, it was important to verify this information so that he could hold his head up in front of the viceroy. On the other hand, to the northeast, Estevan was probably still marching gleefully toward their goal.

After mass, and after praying for guidance, Marcos made his decision.

TUESDAY, APRIL 22. MARCOS MARCHED AT A FAST GAIT DOWN-stream, toward the sea. The thing to do was to complete this seaward trip as quickly as possible. The path soon became more difficult. The vegetation was more sparse and desiccated. The weather seemed hotter and the once-welcoming sunlight was now turning into a harsh glare. Even the banks of the river lacked shady trees. Sometimes he and the guides would wade in the middle of the shallow river to cool off, but it slowed their progress.

In the late afternoon, Marcos left the riverbed and walked a parallel course nearby, to understand the rest of the countryside. It was a rock-strewn desert, ablaze with yellow-blooming, hemispherical low bushes with strange, bluish leaves. Now they were encountering masses of spiny cholla cactus, glistening and standing like malevolent demons, as high as a man. Bristly and unforgiving, they were Marcos's least favorite plants. Only a moment after having this thought, he accidentally swung his hand against one of the projecting cholla buds. It came off, glued to his hand by a hundred daggerlike thorns. In a blaze of pain, he cursed his stupidity. His fingers had wrapped around the spiny segment. He had to sit by the trail for half an hour while one of the Indians, a young man who wanted to be helpful, patiently pulled off the thorns with an ingenious clamshell tweezer. The pain of each needle coming out was excruciating and Marcos thought of Christ's crown of thorns. Marcos sweated, and tried to concentrate on the landscape around him. Ahead, there was still no view of the sea, only low brown hills on the western horizon. The river had turned into intermittent trickles interspersed with stretches of dry, sandy bed.

The young man knew how to ingratiate himself. He was perhaps seventeen, discovering his manhood. "You should let me be your guide," he said. "I know all about this land."

"All right, lead on."

IN THE LAST HOUR OF DAYLIGHT, THEY CAME TO A DESOLATE-looking village, which the Indians said was the last permanent town.

"What lies beyond?"

The young man spoke up again, through the interpreters. "Sand."

"And the coastline?"

"Not far ahead." The guides, including his young friend, conferred. They faced the coast and gestured in a northwest direction. "There is a place," they concurred, "another day's travel, where you can climb a mountain and see the waters far in the distance. We can point out to you, from there, where the coast turns west. Along that coast, that is where the salt is."

"But perhaps somewhere beyond that, farther to the north, are you sure there is no place where the coastline turns back to the east, toward Cíbola?" It was a hard question to ask, but he had tried it several times.

"No, no, no. We already told you. It turns toward the summer sunset a few *jornadas* north of here. To the north and west is only an endless dry desert. It runs on for several more *jornadas* to a broad river, much bigger than our river. You need a raft to cross it. It is called the Firebrand River, because the reeds that grow there are good to make torches that can burn all night. But it is bad country, dry and rocky. There is a race of giants who live there, but we have little trade with them."

"But perhaps that river offers access to the inland country?"

After prolonged discussion and sketching in the sand, he learned that some of its branches ran inland, but not to Cíbola. One branch ran east to a province they called Chichilti-Calli, where it crossed the Cíbola trail, but that place was fifteen days south of Cíbola, across a *despoblado*. This was important information. Perhaps the viceroy's ships could follow that river inland to reach the Cíbola trail.

As the sun set in the west, a spectacular full moon rose in a band of dark purple along the eastern horizon. Marcos paced up and down the village until the last light of dusk had disappeared. A wind from the seaward direction came in as he walked by moonlight into the desert, away from the fires of the village, and faced north. The comet was still faintly visible. He scanned the rest of the sky. There was the star he sought, the pole star, a third of the way up the northern sky. With a hanging pendant and a sextant, he attempted to measure the zenith angle. The wind and the lunar glare made the measurement difficult. Fifty-seven to fifty-nine degrees. That meant the altitude of the pole star, and hence the latitude, was thirty-one to thirty-three degrees.

Sitting under the stars, Marcos pondered his situation. The Indians had been absolutely truthful in everything they had told him about the trail. Their report on the coastline, repeated by many individuals in different villages, must also be correct. The coastline must turn westward a day or so north of his position, at about thirty-four or thirty-five degrees latitude. The only chance for the viceroy's ships to approach Cíbola would be sail inland along the rivers.

To cross still drier and more hostile country, merely to glimpse some tiny part of the coast, now seemed pointless. What was now more important was to return to the Cíbola trail, in hopes of catching Estevan. He could report truthfully to the viceroy that he had made a serious effort to discover the coastal configuration.

He scanned the sky once again before returning to camp. Was the comet beginning to grow smaller and fainter, or was it merely shrunk by the glare of the full moon? Somehow the presence of the comet seemed to complicate his trip. Perhaps its disappearance was paving the way for his triumph at Cíbola.

THE NEXT MORNING, HE WAITED IN THE SHADE OF A LOW ramada while Juan gathered the group of travelers around him. Impetuously, he stood up to address them, accidentally banging his head on the low, brushy roof. "My apostles," he told them with a smile, "now it is time to turn around. We are going back." He pointed east.

There was a buzz of conversation among them and much shaking of heads in wonderment at this man who made fitful trips in different directions. They began to gather up the packs.

"No, wait a moment. First I must perform the acts of possession." It was crucial to the viceroy that the entire coast be claimed in his name. Marcos began building a cairn of rocks, and sent out Tall Man to gather the best scraps of wood to fashion a worthy cross. "If you can finding nothing good enough, then dismantle one of these ramadas." He rummaged in his pack and pulled out his copy of the *Requerimiento*, as required by law.

Half an hour later, his legal duties were done and he was on the trail. Once and for all, like a lodestone pointing north, he was facing in his proper direction, toward the great city of Cíbola. He picked up the pace. As he walked along, he smiled with anticipation at the country ahead. A tiny, pale cloud hung above the distant eastward mountains.

MONDAY, APRIL 28. THEY HAD TRAVELED NEARLY A WEEK BACK upstream, northeast along the coastal valley through many prosperous villages. In the most recent village a man had appeared who was his most important informant yet, an Indian named Two Macaw Feathers, who had actually grown up as a resident of Cíbola. Attracted by the fame of Marcos's party, he had come from a nearby village asking if he could join the expedition. Two Macaw Feathers was no longer young, but like many middle-aged men here, he had the robust health of a survivor, and a great store of knowledge when he was in the mood to share it. Already he had told Marcos that the lord of the Seven Cities designated a governor in each of the towns. Then, with a rueful smile, he had admitted that he had quarreled with the governor of his own town, which Marcos understood to be a town called Ahacu or Ahacus. Two Macaw Feathers had been exiled, fleeing with traders to these regions, south of the fifteen-day *despoblado* that separated Cíbola from the province of Chichilti-Calli. The man was vague about the cause of the quarrel; it seemed that he had violated some religious taboo associated with the seasons. As he asked to join Marcos's party, he tugged on the sleeve of Marcos's robe. "Perhaps with you as my advocate, I can obtain my pardon with the high lord of Cíbola." Be that as it may, Marcos was looking forward to more long talks on the trail with this man who had actually lived in Cíbola.

Every day, it seemed, the image of Cíbola grew more rich. It must be a great metropolis, as full of grandeur and political intrigue as Mexico City itself.

Now they were heading northeast along what the Indians called the salt trail, a path that took them across a few-day *despoblado* to join the main Cíbola trial. They were crossing grassy, empty hills. His party made an impressive sight, strung out along the path in their now-standard order. In the front were the new guides who had joined him from the last valley. Then came admirers from various earlier valleys he had visited, chatting happily and carrying many of the supplies. Next were the interpreters, including Tall Man. Closer to Marcos hovered some of the one-time Eagle warriors that Mendoza had assigned to him, as if forming a protective phalanx around him. They were mostly quiet men; he never knew what they were thinking. The idea of a protective phalanx had become irrelevant; there had never been the slightest hint of a need for protection in this land of friendly, wide-eyed people.

Suddenly he noticed Juan, Tall Man, and the youthful, would-be aide who had pulled out the cactus needles, standing beside the trail. They were waiting for Marcos to catch up. The young man was smiling at him. "Look, I am carrying the heaviest pack. I am your best apostle."

Juan nudged Marcos. "He wants me to tell you," he said, gesturing toward the youth, "that tomorrow when we drop down into the next valley, we rejoin the main northward trail to Cíbola, and maybe Estevan will be waiting for us. It is the last place he can wait for you, because there are no towns after that."

"We will see." Marcos would rather have talked to Two Macaw Feathers.

"This young man has other news for you," Juan added disdainfully. "He says it is a secret."

"So, let him speak."

Through Tall Man, the young guide spoke excitedly, drawing himself to his full height. "I can tell you many things," he said. He seemed to have a quick intelligence. "I know the country toward Cíbola. My father took me on that trail twice when I was merely a boy. After the next valley we will travel a few *jornadas* to the land of Chichilti-Calli, where you will see many wonders, and then we must travel fifteen *jornadas* beyond there to reach Cíbola—across mountains." The young man was beaming at him, and began to relay a story, with Tall Man translating laboriously to Juan. "I heard from the others that you were asking questions about shiny stones—what you call metal."

"He says he knows about metals in Cíbola," Juan interjected.

"He told us they have metals of all colors. I think he is trying to tell us he has seen gold there!"

"Gold! In Cíbola?"

"Show him your samples," Tall Man suggested.

Marcos was already fumbling for his bag of samples. He showed his gold nugget and the golden nose plug from Mexico. Tall Man needed no prompting, and was already quizzing the young man about whether he had seen anything like this in Cíbola. The youth nodded excitedly, jabbering to Tall Man and Juan.

"Father Marcos, you will like this news," Juan exclaimed. "He says they have much gold in Cíbola, traded from the south, like the one you have here, but also many other objects."

"But why has no one else been able to tell me this so clearly?"

Juan and Tall Man relayed the question and there was a pause. The man looked around furtively, and then glanced at the sky. Finally a long answer poured out.

"He says most of these things are not used in public. The priests and elders of Cíbola sometimes wear belts and necklaces of gold, but they keep them hidden, to use in ceremonies. He says not everyone knows about this. He says only he has seen these ceremonies. He says different clans in Cíbola have different secret ceremonies and ceremonial objects, but he can introduce you to people who know about such things."

"Praise God! This is wonderful news!"

"He says if you let him be your personal assistant when you reach Cíbola, he will help you find it. He says if he is your assistant, he will be great in the eyes of the people in Cíbola and they would not dare to withhold anything from you or from him."

The closer he got to Cíbola, the more everyone wanted to be his friend. "First, I must ponder this news." Marcos patted the young man on the back and motioned to Tall Man to send him to the group of guides at the head of the party. As they started to move forward, Marcos called after Tall Man good-humoredly. "And go find my friend, Señor Feathers. Wait with him by the trail for me. I want his version of this story."

When Marcos found Two Macaw Feathers and Tall Man waiting by the trail, he recounted the story told by the young guide. Two Macaw Feathers listened, soberly. Marcos pressed him: "Why have you not told me about this gold?"

The man from Cíbola studied Marcos for a long moment. "You have asked me many questions and I have given you the answers," he said at length. "You seem like a man of some refinement and experience, as if you had come from Cíbola itself," he said. "You are not like these country people who live around here, so surely you see that the young man, who is too young to be a real guide, is just making up stories. He wants to tell you what you want to hear, so he can be your assistant, like your friends Juan and Tall Man. He is jealous of them. If he had that position, it would give him much status when we reach Cíbola. He is the kind of man we call a pack rat. He sneaks into your house and collects bits of your life, using truths and lies all mixed together, in hopes that he can use them someday to further his own ends. Do not listen to him."

This business of gold was frustrating. Still, he realized that if a stranger came to ask him about the sacramental vessels and holy treasures of the church, he himself would likely not give very direct answers.

"Then you say there is no gold there?"

"I told you. There is gold, but only a few little ornaments obtained in trade from the south. The people of Cíbola are more fond of the bells made from the red metal you call copper, which they also bring from the south. It does not bend so easily and lose its shape."

"But you yourself have asked me favors. You want me to help clear your name with your governor. Which one of you should I believe?"

"I tell you the truth," Two Macaw Feathers replied haughtily.

Marcos changed the subject. "What kind of man is the governor of your town?"

Again the answer came back through layers of translation. "An ill-tempered man . . ." Two Macaw Feathers began to enumerate a long list of faults. Obviously he was obsessed by the events that led to his exile.

"What about the lord of all the Seven Cities? What kind of man is he?"

"Stern, of great nobility. He never laughs. He is wise and so the people listen to him with respect. He will not meet with you at once. He will make you wait, to show respect. His voice sways our council, which is made up of the other governors and the priests of the various religious societies. They meet in the largest *kivas* of Cíbola, on the days of the festivals. Often he comes to the town where I lived, Ahacu, which is the most important of the cities."

"Some of the other towns are larger," one of the other Indians interrupted. He was a trader who had been to the province of the Seven Cities.

There was a minor squabble. "Well, yes," said Two Macaw Feathers, "but Ahacu is the best and most important."

"Tell me about Ahacu," Marcos broke in.

"It has many terraces and plazas. There are fertile fields and happy people. The women are very beautiful," he said with a knowing smile. "More beautiful than these poor women in these lands here. They have culture and confidence. They can talk about interesting things. And they have beautiful dresses of white cotton and of supple leather. You should see how they fix their hair."

Men are the same everywhere, Marcos thought to himself. The man had obviously been away from the city for too long. "Tell me about the priests and temples."

The man continued with enthusiasm, "Cíbola has many priests, of different clans. For example, the sun priests. Our stone buildings are tall, not like the miserable plastered brush huts they have here in these lands south of the mountains. In the top rooms of our buildings, the priests observe the comings and goings of the sun, and they have paintings on the walls to tell them the seasons, and the walls have decorations of turquoise. The buildings of Cíbola have many terraces and patios, even on the upper levels." Two

Macaw Feathers claimed he had seen buildings with ten stories, but Marcos noticed that, like the man he criticized, the man was eager to please. The more interest Marcos displayed in the buildings of Cíbola, the taller they became.

He wondered if he should send another message to Vázquez de Coronado and the viceroy about these conversations. The worst mistake he could make would be to send messengers back with claims of wealth that later turned out to be false. He had to fight his own urge to exaggerate good news. Cortés had once told Mendoza that Marcos had a tendency to hear music in the hiss of a viper. But Marcos was always impatient with men like Cortés, who were cynical and hard-bitten, and talked only about problems. Wasn't every fact pregnant with possibility for good? Facts were not like stones, but like vessels; they carried meanings and implications. In any case, he must not send back a message that might discourage interest in settling these promising lands. He decided to wait till he reached the next valley, where the people might tell him something more definite.

THURSDAY, MAY 1. "NEXPA," THE LOCAL INDIAN SAID, WHEN Marcos asked him the name of this new valley—the last populated valley before they reached Cíbola. It was late afternoon when they reached the first village. As the sun sank behind the trees, the temperatures began dropping, and a pleasant breeze wafted across the stream. Marcos sat on a rock writing in his trailbook near the brush hut they had thrown together for him, at the edge of the village. The villagers sat on their haunches, watching curiously from a respectful distance.

"Nex-pa." Marcos wrote the word phonetically in his trailbook along with a sketch map and an arrow showing the direction of the river flow. This was important, because the modest stream was flowing not in the southerly direction of all the previous valleys, but north. Where did it go? Like the other little rivers, it was not wide enough to be navigable, but maybe it emptied into a tributary of the great Firebrand River, which could give the viceroy's ships access to the Cíbola trail.

It had been an eventful day. The local villagers had met him in a grove at the river, erecting their arches of thatched branches, under which he passed into their village to the accompaniment of their strange, not-quite-tuneful flutes and drums. Marcos marveled at how the Indians' arches of boughs mirrored the arched doorways of the great buildings of Europe. He shut out the thoughts of the Old World; they brought a longing for the modern life, beautifully prepared food, candles, books, the excitement of the cities, his old friends, and his lost youth. No, he must keep his thoughts on this new land, so full of potential for Christendom.

Marcos recorded in his book that shortly after he had arrived in this village, a delegation of three men of the village had sought him out. They said they had news from Estevan. They had befriended the gregarious Moor when he passed through only eight or ten days before, and they had gone with his enthusiastic party four days farther north and east on the road to Cíbola. Estevan sent them back to meet Marcos and report that they had reached the beginning of the long, final *despoblado*, stretching for fifteen *jornadas* over mountains to the land of Cíbola. Estevan, they said, was a good leader. A real man, one of the translators added, making lewd gestures to convey the meaning, and then cowering under Marcos's disapproving glance.

"Estevan is very happy with what he has discovered," the translators added. Marcos winced at the word, "discovered." It should have been Marcos himself, making these discoveries. The translators continued the story. "Estevan said to tell you: Everything the locals said about the trail has turned out to be true, all along the way. Estevan is sure that Cíbola will be the wondrous city that has been described to us. He sends you a personal message, too," they said. "The message is: 'I cannot wait to get there.' He says he will continue preparing the way for you, like John the Baptist in the wilderness. We do not understand what this message means, but he says you will understand it."

Marcos was furious at this. The Moor always pretended to be

following orders with enthusiasm, while he really followed that bright, devilish mind of his own.

This village, on a terrace above the river Nexpa, consisted of a cluster of thirty brush-and-mud-covered huts with slightly depressed, plastered floors. The inhabitants wore many strands of turquoise and shell ornaments—more than he had seen elsewhere. There was a network of tiny irrigation canals branching off from the river through the fields, where the villagers raised their maize, beans, and squash. Within a small fenced area near the village center one a small shrine decorated with turquoises, feathers, and the skins of snakes, and a kind of altar inside displayed a turquoise-inlaid effigy in the shape of a turtle. Marcos averted his eyes from the idol.

LATE THAT NIGHT, HE AWOKE WITH A START. HE HAD FALLEN asleep thinking about Las Casas's idealistic plans, but in his sleep some angel of caution had been whispering in his ear—"the enemy who can defeat Las Casas is the sin of greed." What did it mean? The clean simplicity of the desert lands had been making Marcos contemplate greed in the last few days. As a youth, he had lived in a simple white-plastered monastery cell. It was a modest life, and good. That simple life left him unable to understand the overpowering drive for acquisition that he saw daily among the soldiers and administrators in the New World. Could people not see that goods merely brought responsibilities and unending chores? Houses to be cleaned, servants to be managed? In the modern world, Christian governors like Mendoza were setting up plazas, fountains with good water, and beautiful churches, and even the lowest citizen could choose the few necessary things that he needed, and thus live a life of simplicity and happiness, taking pleasure in God's creation, yet everyone seemed driven to make their lives as complicated as possible. No matter how many constructions and inventions might improve life, men and women always began to feel they needed more elaborate things to make them happy. The Indian village brought this problem into his mind again. The Indians here lived what some would call poor lives, with only a few strands of turquoise, brush huts, and fields of beans, yet they smiled and laughed more than the brash Spaniards of Viceroy Mendoza's court, who spent their lives trying to outmaneuver each other, competing to acquire land, gold, the finest new clothes from Spain, and books from the new printing press that Bishop Zumárraga had set up in Mexico City. Among those few who had married, the wives wanted ever finer houses with more servants than their neighbors. Lust for property and possessions was the prime mover of the modern world. In such a world, was it possible to free oneself from the desire to acquire?

A worse question was troubling his dreams. He was coming to believe that there were good men and vile men among the pagans just as there were among the Christian Spaniards in the rich courts of Mexico City or even Rome. If this was true, it meant that virtuous behavior toward others came more from what men learned at their mother's knee than from exposure to the holy church. Was this a riddle, some test of his faith? Was it the Devil whispering in his ear, that pagans could live happily in this universe beyond the word of God? To quiet his mind, Marcos repeated to himself that improvement would come to these peoples' lives after the future missionaries brought them Christianity.

Marcos stuck his head out the door of his hut and scanned the sky. The comet, having slipped into the morning sky, was definitely fading. As if to interrupt his midnight idyll, two dogs erupted into a fight in the plaza. After the battle died down, Marcos fell back into sleep.

MAY 2. MARCOS'S PARTY CONTINUED NORTH, DOWNSTREAM along the Rio Nexpa. In the midday, with the sun beating down, they came to the largest town yet seen on this pleasant little river. It had perhaps fifty of the little brush houses, neater than in the first village. There was a low plastered wall around the heathen brush temple, which stood on a small rise. Under ramadas in front of the houses, Indian women were grinding meal. The chief of the town came forth with a crowd of followers to greet Marcos. He was a wizened old man with many strings of turquoise around his neck, and more hanging from his nose and ears—enough, it would seem, to make him topple over. He wore garments of finely dressed hide, which Marcos could now recognize as the type of cowhide traded from Cíbola. Many others in his party wore similar attire.

The chief made a speech after his happy greetings. There were nods and murmurs of assent among the smiling villagers, who had gathered *en masse* around the extended mound where the chief stood. Much discussion ensued among Marcos's squadron of translators, who passed the comments back and forth among themselves, until Marcos grew impatient. Before deigning to tell him what had been said, they seemed to debate endlessly over fine points of language, like the old Jewish scholars Marcos had met in Florence.

Tall Man delivered the final version, breathlessly. "He says they welcome you to this village and that they believe you are a great man. Your co-chief, Estevan, has told them about you. He was here with us three days. Already, he has taken a large party with him, more men than I can count, and some of their women. The chief says that still more now want to go with you. They will come from villages throughout this region. They want to see your arrival in Cíbola because the people there will be astonished when you and Estevan arrive."

Co-chief? Marcos thought.

"He says that they understand from Estevan that you are a man sent from the heavens and that they want to help you. This is the last village before you reach Cíbola. In order to reach Cíbola, you must cross the country to the east and north of here for four days, through what they call the province of the Red House, or Chichilti-Calli. He says that before you leave for Chichilti-Calli and the *despoblado*, you must stay here for five days, so they can gather emissaries from the nearby towns." The chief's jewels clinked as he kept nodding through this speech of the translator, as if he understood and agreed with everything. "If you stay here, the people here will prepare the food and clothes for the journey, and they will serve you along the way."

"What will they do when we get to Cíbola?"

The question was translated. The chief and the men around him were all smiles. "They will trade. They will gain much respect when they arrive with you. There will be many festivities. The local people will return with many goods, and the people in Cíbola will remember that we are an important province, because you came here first. They say it will make them a province to be reckoned with."

"I cannot wait that five days. We must hurry and catch up to Estevan."

After the question was translated, the answer came back. "They say they can be ready in three days, but no less." Marcos accepted the offer. He hated to wait while Estevan moved to the north, but these days in the last village would give him a chance to prepare a final letter to the viceroy before entering the great *despoblado*. At least Estevan had waited three days himself, and would pull no further ahead than he already was.

THE VILLAGE, LIKE THE OTHERS, WAS ON A TERRACE ABOVE THE river. Even before he arrived, they had built a hut for Marcos and a campsite for his party in a grove of trees on a small beachlike peninsula where the river curved, just downstream from the village itself. Across the river was an outcrop of brown rock, with several petroglyph carvings. "These are symbols of our clans," one of the villagers said proudly. "The sheep, the lizard . . ." The more Marcos sat by his hut and studied the artwork on the rock, the more he was disturbed by the pagan images, and the strange, manlike lizard, who seemed more a demon than a lizard.

MAY 3. MARCOS SPENT THE DAY INTERVIEWING THE INHABITANTS and talking to people who had begun to appear from villages several leagues away, including the next valley to the west, which was said to be very populous. He would ask them questions, talking to one person at a time in the shade of the trees, in front of his hut, with the soothing water babbling nearby. Still he worried about confirming the precise truth of the great empire to the north. Always the answers were the same, relayed through the interpreters. Cíbola was a mighty kingdom, and beyond it lay other kingdoms: Ácus, Totonteac, Marata. In Cíbola you could meet peoples from these other kingdoms, traders who brought products from all over the world. These included not only the strange cowhides, but also wool from Totonteac, cotton shirts, blankets, and beautifully painted pots with intricate designs.

As for gold and other treasures, the answers were still mixed. Everyone agreed that turquoises and copper bells were used for decoration and ceremonies, and golden trinkets were among the trade goods, but Marcos could never get anyone except the dubious young guide to tell him about priestly rooms of golden treasures, the kind that Cortés found twenty years ago in the Aztec capital of Tenochtitlán. Nonetheless, even in this region he had seen signs of mineralization on rocky hillsides and in arroyos—rocks of the type that might yield silver, lead, copper, or even gold itself. Two informants from the village told him of slablike outcrops of silvery or coppery native metal, in some hills somewhere west of here.

But what should he write to the viceroy? He pondered and prayed over this question. It would be foolish to emphasize that he had no firm proof of gold. And yet it would be just as foolish to promise that gold would be found. It was better to say nothing about this until he had seen the truth with his own eyes.

Back at his hut, at the bend in the river across from the lizard rock, he carefully cut some pages from his trailbook and devoted a morning to writing a letter to be dispatched back to the south.

Esteemed Viceroy: I have the honor to report to you news of the grandeur of the lands 150 to 200 leagues by my reckoning north of San Miguel de Culiacán. I have reached these fertile and populous regions after eight weeks of travel through many inhabited valleys as I described in my earlier letter. These lands lie on the road toward the great kingdom of Cíbola, of which I sent word in my last message. God be praised that the people of all these lands are very friendly. They welcome us and show desire to learn about Our Lord Jesus Christ, and about his Royal Highness, the King, in whose names I have erected crosses and performed the acts of possession over these lands as requested by your Lordship.

The best lands in this region are irrigated and fertile valleys along the rivers, which run north and south along the Cíbola road. There are many villages half a league apart in these valleys. These fertile lands could support many more people, both horsemen and settlers. These Indians in these lands wear many jewels of turquoise, and have small houses made of brush and other more permanent houses made of mud-adobe, but they have few other riches. However, they say that the people of Cíbola are much richer than they are, and well-cultured. Everyone agrees in describing the huge permanent houses of stone in Cíbola, saying that these rise four or five stories in height, or perhaps even more. The people here have many trade goods from Cíbola, including finely worked leathers like cowhides, and silky shirts of fine cotton. I send your Lordship two examples of these garments with this message. The people also say they have seen some metals in Cíbola, but I am still trying to determine what kinds.

As for the coast, it runs to the north-northwest, parallel to my route for most of the distance. I departed from the main Cíbola road and traveled some days west of here to the coastal region. I learned that the coast turns west at this latitude, around 35 degrees. Some say that a great river enters the sea in a desert at that latitude, and that a branch of that river comes inland a few jornadas north of where I am now.

After I learned about the coast, I returned to the main road and reached this province where I am now. The river where I am is the first I've encountered that flows north, and it must empty into the one that I mentioned. The next few jornadas cross a region called Chichilti-Calli, and might be accessed by ships along one of the rivers I have mentioned. I will continue to investigate with great alertness whether it may be possible to establish a port to help reach these northern lands.

From here I understand that I will cross a province of four days, and then cross the river into a mountainous despoblado of 15 days to reach Cíbola. I will leave tomorrow. I will also send this message tomorrow. From the fact that I am now 19 days south of Cíbola, and that I may stay a week in Cíbola to learn of its customs, it may be estimated about roughly 45 days after you receive this message I myself will return to Mexico to report to your Highness. Perhaps it will be a bit more because I am slower than the Indian messengers—but after I visit Cíbola I will return to you with haste. In short, I may see you by late summer with much more news, if God continues to give His blessing to this undertaking.

He read the letter over and over. He had emphasized the fine attributes of these lands that he had already seen with his own eyes, and that was something he would never have to deny. As for Cíbola, even though his mind reeled with images of a great capital of wealth and power, he had not promised anything beyond what he knew.

He sent for Juan and three of the best Mexican allies to come to his camp at the bend of the river. "Juan, I have something very important to ask of you."

"Ask and I will do it."

Marcos explained about the importance of sending messages back to Coronado and the viceroy. "One important message was the one I sent to Honorato just after we learned news of Cíbola. I told him to be sure that it got back to the viceroy. He may have taken it himself. Now it is your turn. This is the most important message yet, and you are the one who must carry it back."

"All right. I will go." Juan was always stoic, but Marcos could sense his disappointment at not being part of the final approach to Cíbola.

"It will be a great honor. They will be glad to see you in Mexico City."

"Yes." Juan paused. "I have been thinking. I want to tell you . . . about what happened that day in Tenochtitlán. You asked me about it. Perhaps I can tell you before I leave."

"Yes."

"I will come tonight."

THAT NIGHT THEY SAT IN THEIR SMALL ENCAMPMENT. THE SMALL fire cast flickering light on the rocks across the river, where the lizard-man, faintly visible, seemed to dance grotesquely. Juan stirred the fire carefully. When Marcos came to the fire to sit, Juan took a deep breath. "Father, the reason I want to tell you the rest of my story is so that I can ask you a question about what is happening in the world."

"Tell me."

"Your army had been living in our royal palace, as I told you, and it was time for one of our festivals. My young woman was there. I can still remember her, Father. I can remember her smile, and how it felt when she embraced me. . . . You can't understand this because you don't love women."

"No, Juan, you are wrong. I love women and I can feel desire. There was a woman once, when I was younger, back in Savoy. . . . But it is not seemly to tell you. You know that we priests have renounced the passions of the flesh so that we may better serve God. We have to transform desire into something different."

"But my woman . . . she was my whole life in those days. Everything I did, secretly it was for her. When I went away from the city, she was the one I was coming back to. Then . . ." Juan fell silent. In the distance, crickets chirped to celebrate the oncoming summer. "Everything was so different in those days."

"Tell me the story from the beginning, Juan."

"You remember I told you the Spanish said they were curious to see the festival of Huitzuilopochtli, and so the young warriors who were to dance all felt this was the way they could show the Spanish that we were a people of culture, to be taken seriously. The first activity was for the women to prepare the *chicalote* seeds and other foods for the festival." Juan's voice broke and he paused. Marcos waited for him. "My young woman was among them. The Spanish soldiers came into the temple patio where they were working, to see these young women. They would come right up to them to stare and smile, but then go back inside without harming them. The women were terrified. It was as if they were being inspected, like animals. This went on for several days. But the preparations continued.

"On the day of the festival, everyone gathered in the patio of the temple, and the Spaniards came out to watch, again saying they wanted to learn about these rituals of ours. The great statue of Huitzuilopochtli was uncovered. Meanwhile, some of our captains said to each other: 'The Spaniards have attacked people in other towns, whenever they wanted to have their way. We should not dance in front of them defenseless. We should hide our weapons close at hand in case we need them.' But Moctezuma himself sent a message to them, 'Do you think we are at war with these people? No. I tell you, we should trust them, to show them they can trust us!' So the people agreed that if they danced with all their hearts, the Spaniards would marvel at the beauty of our rituals and would treat us more like civilized equals. Our great captains led the procession and our young untested warriors, like me, were at the end. And the music started, and the people were singing the songs, and the warriors began dancing." Again, Juan broke off his narrative and stared into the fire. It seemed that the stars themselves moved across the sky while Juan sat, expressionless.

"What happened then?" Marcos said gently.

"The Spaniards had made their own evil plan in secret. They said they were Christian, but . . ."

"Just tell me what happened."

"More Spaniards came out of the palace, as if to watch the ceremonies. They took up positions at each entrance to the temple patio, the Canestalk and Eagle Gates, and the Gate of the Serpent and of the Mirrors. They put three or four soldiers at each main gate so that almost no one could escape. Then they rushed at the dancers and the celebrants. They had swords and were carrying shields, and our people had only sticks of wood. One soldier slew our captain, who was leading the dancers, and another hacked at our statue of Huitzuilopochtli, raining as many curses on him as blows of the sword. Other soldiers ran to the three drummers and hacked off their arms. Blood spurted everywhere. I saw them cut off the head of one drummer with one blow of the sword. The head rolled across the patio.

"They were stabbing and hacking at the celebrants, even striking them from behind. It was terrible, Father. Our temple became a slaughterhouse. Heads were split open. I saw one of our men trying to flee, tripping over his own entrails before they finished him. But there was no place to go. The Spaniards blocked the gates and cut down those trying to climb over the walls. Some people ran into the communal houses along the side of the patio and hid, but the Spanish hunted them down in a few minutes. A few of us escaped by lying among the bloody victims and pretending to be dead. When our people who had been shut out of the patio heard the clamor, they rushed to help us. That is when more were killed. I ran to find my sweetheart. Later, I learned that she was among those who rushed against the Spaniards and were cut down by crossbow arrows." This time Juan got it out without faltering. "She was killed coming to help me when I was escaping through the window. It is my shame—I will never live it down, Father. I lived while my sweet woman died coming to fight for me. It is the worst thing of my life, the thing that I carry around with me and never forget."

Marcos was horrified into silence. He was not sure he could promise that Juan would meet his unbaptized betrothed, one day in heaven.

Juan pulled himself together. "In the next hours after that, the counterattack by our warriors was so fierce that the Spaniards retreated to the palace. We tried to carry the bodies of our dead back to their homes, but some were hard to identify. It was the death of our nation—the worst thing I have ever seen."

Marcos was silent for a moment. "But now your people know God and Jesus," he said at last, as gently as he could.

"Yes. Now we know God and Jesus."

Something in his tone . . . Marcos almost pressed him on it, but a small voice told him that Juan had suffered enough. "You never told me how you grew up after these events."

"During the final battles, I was wounded, and my aunt spirited me away on a boat across the lake to her sister's village. A year later, our village was drafted by the Spaniards to be servants and workers. I was lucky, because the Spanish priests took me into their service as a translator. I lived in the little town they called Olmedo, in Jalisco. That's why some of your friends call me Juan Olmedo. One of my jobs was to explain to the priests, your brothers, about the Mexican gods and places of worship, and the ancient texts of history. They would ask me questions about our gods and then get very angry when I gave them the answers. They wanted the answers so they could kill the gods, destroy the temples, burn the ancient texts, and punish anyone who still practiced the old ways." Juan paused, looking solemn. "It is a mystery to me."

"What is?"

"Whenever our people conquered another people, we demanded tribute, slaves, victims for the sacrifices that had to be made. These were sacred things. We called these 'wars of flowers.' In the battles themselves, no one tried to kill anybody. Our clubs are not even designed to kill. Our goal was to capture warriors for the sacrifices to the gods. To live with the gods is an honor. Warriors understood what was expected, and the life of the people on both sides went on. But your people, when they conquer, they actually want to destroy us. You have taught me that God wants men to believe only in Him. But why did this require destroying everything? Smashing our buildings and statues, melting down our gold ornaments, executing our priests and poets as criminals, burning our books? Once we were defeated, were we still such a threat to you?"

Marcos stared into the fire. The wind had died and the small flame hardly wavered. Slowly it waned. "I have no answer for you, Juan. God does not always reveal his purposes. Sometimes he tests us, even if we have tried to follow his way. That is all I know."

"That is not very much."

"Hush, Juan. Do not risk blasphemy."

Juan put some more small sticks on the fire.

"I do not know why these things happened, Juan. I think we can only try to do our best at each moment, even though evil is around us. As for this moment, I think our purpose is clear. What we must do is send our message of discovery back to the viceroy. Cíbola is a mighty kingdom."

"If you tell that to the Spaniards, everything I have just described to you will happen all over again!"

"No, Juan! That is wrong! Everything you have described was twenty years ago. Now civilization has arrived! You know that the viceroy is a good man. There are many new ideas in the world today. I have told you about the ideas of my brother, Father Bartolomé de Las Casas."

"Do you really believe these good things will happen?"

"I believe that the viceroy will send people north to pacify the province of Cíbola, and the kingdoms beyond. By now, God willing, he already has our earlier messages. You will be a very important person in the court of Mexico City, if you successfully deliver this last message."

THE NEXT MORNING, JUAN AND THE OTHER THREE WERE READY to leave. Marcos clasped Juan's arm, one last time. Moments later, they were gone, around the bend in the river. Juan was a good disciple and would have a place in the history of the church in Mexico. Fortune seemed to smile on him. Marcos prayed that no danger would befall him, and he imagined meeting Juan again in Mexico.

Marcos visualized the viceroy's pleasure at his report, and allowed himself a short dream of how he himself might be back in Mexico by August. Strange, this was the first time he had reversed the direction of his imagination, projecting himself back to Mexico instead of forward to Cíbola. He felt a warm glow of pleasure at the thought of sipping wine and telling stories of his adventures and discoveries.

CHAPTER 10

April/May, 1989; Tucson
Marcos and Me

I arose each morning to the sounds of the cars waking up across the city. In the last days of April, the midday sun was no longer slanting down at a gentle angle. Instead, it was beginning to beat down from high overhead, glaring back off the pavements. The green-barked palo verde trees around the city were starburst explosions of tiny golden flowers. At Rooney Development Inc., the historical richness of our property was turning into an embarrassment. Coronado, Coronado, Coronado. The albatross around our neck. News of the ruin on our property had exploded among the anti-sprawl activists and history buffs of Tucson—the people who, to use Mr. Rooney's phrase, wanted to keep the world the way it was.

I had nearly finished the report but I worried about what it said. The problem was compounded by the ruin. I had to deal with an interesting fact that I haven't even mentioned yet. Coronado's army diarists said that after they left the Nexpa River and traveled east for a few days, they camped at an abandoned, ruined building named Chichilti-Calli. It seemed to be a famous camp in a good spot, the jumping-off point for the final fifteen-day *despoblado*. They stayed there a couple of days.

At first I discounted any connection between that story and our "ruin." In the first place our site was not what most people would call a ruin. It was little more than a few alignments of rocks and low mounds. Secondly, I knew there were others of these "ruins" in southeast Arizona. But as I looked into it, I learned that various pueblolike structures had been built in Arizona around 1300, and that, generally speaking, they had moldered into low mounds of mud and rock alignments marking wall foundations, and ours was in the right place. Suddenly the question blew up in my face. What if our obscure ruin was the remains of the one, the only, the original ruin mentioned by Coronado and his army? To look at it the other way: How could I prove it wasn't?

Everyone in our office was distressed one morning at the end of April, when the paper's lead article in section B was headlined DEVELOPMENT THREATENS RUIN. The article obsessed about bulldozing and paving native sites. The reporter hadn't got as far into the story as I had, and hadn't yet discovered the Chichilti-Calli angle— the idea that this might be a unique site associated with Coronado. She merely pointed out that modern civilization, after settling Arizona in the late 1890s, had already methodically destroyed most of our archaeological patrimony. Dozens of prehistoric ruins in Arizona, from Phoenix to Tucson, had already been plowed under by Anglo farmers, or scraped away as developers' housing tracts blanketed the once-fertile river valleys. Our generation's duty, said the paper, was to see that it didn't happen again to the last pristine sites. I agreed.

Reporters were already calling our office asking for interviews with Mr. Rooney. He called several of us in for a strategy session. It was like a political campaign meeting. We needed to develop the party line. He did most of the talking. He said the article was misleading because there were no freestanding walls to bulldoze. It was just a bunch of foundations and debris. As for our construction, we might smooth out some low mounds of debris, but we would actually be covering some of the ruins and preserving them. That sounded flaky at first, but he cited a school of archaeological thought that held that in private developments, if there was not time or money for full investigations of sites, then instead of doing rushed excavations and half-baked interpretation, it was better to pave over ruins, thus preserving them for future centuries.

In an interview the next day, he said as much. He also put out the word that we would turn the main ruin into a park, with a museum in the community center.

The museum idea was turned against him. The need for a museum, said the reporter the next day in her article, proved the historical importance of the area. Mr. Rooney responded the following day that other ruins in southeast Arizona, on unprotected ranchlands in the middle of nowhere, were being vandalized by four-wheel-drive vandals from the cities. Our plan would document this particular ruin and put it in a controlled environment with a "heritage center" that we were planning. The opposition cried "nonsense:" The more people in the area, the more vandalism. Building on it was not the way to save it.

I was beginning to understand what it must be like to work in the White House as the president tries to talk his way out of the latest disaster. The papers loved it all. The law at that time gave builders pretty free rein with prehistoric sites on their own private property, short of digging up Indian burials. Unscrupulous developers had been known to destroy everything, before anybody could get wind of it. Of course, we would never do that. Would we?

I told myself I was on the right side. Mr. Rooney had proved his interest in history. His talk of a community heritage center convinced me that our little park would be the natural culmination of the conflict. I would help design it, and it would preserve a piece of prehistory. I dreamed of a grand opening ceremony, where a Mexican delegation, an American delegation, and a delegation from Cíbola/Zuni would look to the future of the relationships among the three cultures, and say, "Okay, where do we go from here?" I imagined Mexican and American tourists mingling at our museum, a generation hence, saying to each other, "This is where our two histories first came together." In my more elevated moments, I thought that it might even serve to reverse the trend that was making our border look more and more like a reverse Iron Curtain, designed to keep people out. Barbed wire and walls we already had; all we needed now was towers with machine guns. Sure, I was optimistic, but you have to start somewhere.

IT WAS ABOUT THAT TIME THAT MR. ROONEY GOT HIS CITIZEN OF the Year award from the chamber of commerce. It was a splashy do, up at SkyView Country Club, at the top of Skyline Drive. I had rarely been that far up in the foothills. The road gave a superb vista of flowering palo verdes against a backdrop of the twilight-lit Catalina Mountains' crags. Along the club driveway, the saguaro cacti had sparkly lights draped over them. Mr. Rooney kindly invited me to escort Phaedra to the event. She was at her most exquisite, with a long black dress which had a marvelous slit up the skirt. She was very happy that evening. I pulled up in front of the green-tiled entrance to the club, behind a Mercedes, and was checking out the signs to self-parking when Freddy the Fixer came out to meet us, gesturing at the eager, young, white-shirted men clustered around the door. "Use the valet parking. It's on the company tab. After all, what are college students for?" We all laughed, including the kid who came to park the car.

I enjoyed seeing the stares that Phaedra drew from men and women alike as we walked to our table. It was a gift she was able to give me, those stares. She enjoyed exhibiting herself and I knew she would be turned on by it. Freddy led us to a table just below the ornately set head table on the stage. There sat Mr. Rooney, the mayor, a local car dealer, the owner of a local ad agency, a couple Republicans from the board of supervisors, and other Tucson notables. At the end of the table, I recognized Tony Beecher, our company attorney and patrician dean of Tucson developer lawyers. Mr. Rooney smiled at Phaedra and me, as if acknowledging that this was the best of all possible worlds. We smiled back.

Phaedra pointed out that the only women at the front table were wives of the power figures. "That's Mrs. Rooney, on his left," she whispered. It was the first time I had seen her. Mostly, I remember her striking middle-ageish fitness and her superb tan.

"They are the Ladies Who Lunch," Phaedra continued.

"What?"

"They come downtown from the foothills and have lunches, to organize benefit galas and keep the various cultural boards running. Art museum, Arizona Theater, the opera. They are the people who keep the arts going."

"What about the artists?" I said.

"You're funny, Kevin Scott," said Phaedra.

"Somebody has to have the money to buy their stuff," Freddy said.

"On election contribution forms," she whispered to me, "they fill out their occupation as 'Philanthropist.' I helped Mrs. Rooney fill out hers and her friends' in the last city council election."

"Very modest. Like listing your occupation as 'War hero.' "

The huge windows along the side of the room displayed a breathtaking sea of lights, twinkling down in the valley. I imagined the thousand stories going on in the city below us.

When they gave Mr. Rooney his medal, the mayor gave a speech about how the citizens were giving him this award to thank him for making the city what it is today.

During the applause I looked around the room at the tuxedos and the velvet. Lots of velvet. Velvet drapes and velvet dresses. "If it's a citizens' award, where are the ordinary citizens?" I whispered to Phaedra. I was still trying to be funny, in my sardonic way. Freddy heard me.

"Down there in the valley," he said, gesturing toward the picture window, "where the billboards grow. Ha ha." Freddy was a card.

I noticed Phaedra didn't laugh. She lived down in the valley.

"It's pretty nice up here," I agreed, in desperation.

Freddy leaned over toward us conspiratorially. "Mr. Rooney had to pull a lot of strings to bring this off. By the way, he wants to see you and Phaedra tomorrow. There's important work for you to do."

*   *   *

IN THE AFTERNOON OF THE NEXT DAY, MR. ROONEY CALLED
Phaedra and me and some of the other younger staff members into
his office, and urged us to try to find out what we could about what
the opposition movements was doing. "Keep your ears to the
ground. You know, the Sierra Club, the neighborhood groups. We
need to know what people are saying."

I shot Phaedra a look. She didn't look back. She was very professional, in the office.

"You people," Mr. Rooney was saying, "are more likely to hear
things than me or Tony." Tony Beecher, his lawyer, had been
spending a lot of time at our office. I had seen him at the award dinner, and he was handling the preparations for the hearing. He was
sitting quietly on one side of the office, like a court wizard. Unlike
the rest of us, he was wearing a suit and a tie. He had the face of a
mortician, contrasting with Mr. Rooney's expansiveness. Mr.
Rooney went on venting against the opposition. "The thing is, the
ruin is bad news. It's too late to get rid of it."

"I've heard some talk," Phaedra chimed in. "Some people say if
we win our final zoning approval from the county supervisors, the
opposition will organize a referendum. They'll get it on the ballot
and overturn the supervisors." There was something funny about
the way she and Rooney acted. Were they trying to keep secret
what she had told me, that he had *assigned* her to go to Sierra Club
meetings, where she had heard this?

"Greens, No-growthers," Mr. Rooney said. "Those people don't
care about *truth* or *due process*. They only care about stopping anyone from building anything *new*."

"God help us if they find some little bug out there, on the endan-
gered species list," said Tony Beecher.

Mr. Rooney sent me back to the library with orders to find out
more about other ruins in southern Arizona and their relation to the
Coronado route. I was supposed to have the whole report done in a
few days. I could see that now, in this geomagnetopolitical storm,
my mission statement had reversed polarity. In contrast to my orig-

inal orders, the "right answer" now from Mr. Rooney's point of view would be that Coronado never got close to Coronado Estates. Not that I was planning to change my answer. I was living in some grand madhouse, where the facts remained the same but their meaning changed week by week. There was a personal angle: If the missing ruin was ours, the environmentalists would crucify us, and I would no longer be the heroic historian-planner who added a sense of place to Coronado Estates, but just another heritage-raping developer's lackey. Was this the way Marcos felt, when things started going wrong?

In my fortress of solitude, the library, I zeroed in on whatever I could find about Chichilti-Calli. Its name came from the Nahuatl language of the Aztec/Mexica, the same language that gives us words like "coyote," "peyote," and "hurricane." "Chichilti" came from the same root as "chili," and meant red. Chichilti-Calli meant "Red House." The chroniclers reported that this name referred to a famous camp spot on the Cíbola trail, a mysterious ruined building or fortress that had been built by earlier people. The Spaniards also applied the name to the surrounding region and to a nearby pass through the mountains.

I liked knowing old stuff like that. It was like knowing the name of the Nexpa, or that the term "big wheel" came from the old days of carriages, when the richer folks could afford carriages with larger wheels, which gave smoother rides. The Nahuatl origin of the name was one more piece of evidence that a well-used trade route went from Mexico to Cíbola—the route that Marcos discovered.

Of all Coronado's chroniclers, Captain Juan Jaramillo gave the best geographic information about Chichilti-Calli's location. He's the one who described how, after the army hit the Rio Nexpa, they marched two days farther north "down" the river and then "turned right" for two days before coming to the base of some mountains. He went on to say that this is where they learned of the ruined red house and a mountain pass with the same name. About a day after that, they crossed the mountains to a deep river with grass for the horses, and then headed north or northeast into the final, fifteen-day *despoblado*. I followed this on a map. If they headed north two days on the San Pedro and jogged east a couple of days, it would bring them practically to our entry gate. Continuing north out of our valley, they would have crossed Eagle Pass, traversed today by a lonely dirt road which comes down into the valley of the Gila—Jaramillo's deep and grassy river. Once you cross the river, you head north into the high country of the Gila Mountains and the White Mountains: the final, fifteen-day *despoblado*.

Marcos's report added complementary detail. He said that when he reached the last populated valley before the final wilderness—the San Pedro/Nexpa—the villagers told him he'd have to cross a four-day stretch before entering the fifteen-day wilderness. The four-day stretch from the last populated valley makes no sense by itself; why not add it to the fifteen-day *despoblado* and speak of a nineteen-day *despoblado* after the last town? The answer was that those four days took you east across the rolling, yucca-studded grasslands that were geographically part of the Nexpa natives' own region, the province of Chichilti-Calli. These four days involved the same stretch that Jaramillo remembered as a two-day jog east to the base of Chichilti-Calli pass, and then a day or two northward across the pass to the Gila River, which marked the beginning of very different, mountainous country north of the Gila. The Coronado army chronicles repeatedly confirmed this division of the landscape, remarking how things changed north of Chichilti-Calli. The soldier named Pedro Castañeda, who wrote a memoir of the expedition twenty years later, recalled that "at Chichilti-Calli the character of the country changes again, and the spiky vegetation ends. . . . The rest of the country is wilderness, covered with pine forests." The chroniclers reckoned the journey in three stages, each stretched from C to shining C: Culiacán to Corazones, Corazones to Chichilti-Calli, and Chichilti-Calli to Cíbola.

Frustratingly, Marcos himself didn't mention Chichilti-Calli by name, but Castañeda specifically said that Chichilti-Calli had been discovered by the friar, and that Indians of the area had gone to

Cíbola with Estevan. So both Marcos and Estevan must have stopped there, which was to be expected since it was on the main trade route to Cíbola.

It all added up. East of the San Pedro, south of the Gila, Coronado Estates lay right in the middle of the Chichilti-Calli province.

As for the ruin itself, native informants told Coronado's party that it had been built years before, by warlike strangers who came from the north. Pedro Castañeda actually recorded a local tradition that the strangers had broken away from Cíbola. He said the abandoned structure looked like a fortress built of red mud and was decaying and "tumbled-down," with its roof fallen in. He said it disappointed them, especially the general himself. Apparently they were hoping for a more fabulous structure, a grand castle or the remains of a great stone palace like the one Moctezuma had occupied, back in Mexico City.

I was torn apart by all this. Sixty percent of me was thrilled all the vectors were pointing toward our property, and that our land might actually contain a site that had been visited by Marcos de Niza, Estevan, Coronado, and the others. The other forty percent feared the consequences when Mr. Rooney, the press, and the rest of the universe found out about it. I needed to stay a few days ahead of them, to have answers when it all blew up. I kept reading.

Coronado's Chichilti-Calli had never been found. A few archaeologist/historians had argued over its location, but because they couldn't agree on a route, their competing theories had placed it anywhere in a wide area that stretched both south and north of the border. Even if the Coronado route did come close to our property, Chichilti-Calli could have been any of a number of ruins that had been found within fifty miles north, south, and east of us. They were all over the place. They all dated from the 1300s and were already abandoned when Mr. Vázquez came through. Any of them could have been a ruined "red house" in Coronado's day. Today, they were only rubbly mounds, except for the adobe castle of Casa Grande, which still rose three stories high in a national monument northwest of Tucson. To prove which ruin was the original

Chichilti-Calli, you'd have to find artifacts from the Spanish campsite.

I DECIDED I SHOULDN'T GO TOO FAR INTO THE WORLD OF PREHIStoric structures without professional help. I called Dr. Panofsky again, my onetime history professor. "You need someone in the archaeology department," he said. "Smithwick. He knows all about that stuff."

"Who's he?"

"George Smithwick. One of the greats. He's worked on Arizona archaeology for fifty years. His mother was Helen Smithwick-Smythe, one of those feisty lady archaeologists that came out to the Southwest with the first generation of scholars from the East. His father was Francis Smithwick, from the Boston Museum. Well, he was the nominal father. They say Helen was lovers with half the famous archaeologists of the Southwest. It was a great generation! Lots of hanky-panky on moonlit nights in the old cliff dwellings. They say Fewkes came out to visit Helen Smythe when she was working at Chaco, a month before she married Smithwick Senior. Anyway, look at the old photos. Smithwick Junior is the spitting image of Fewkes. Nudge nudge, wink wink. Smithwick was born at Chaco Canyon and has hung out around ruins ever since."

"Who's Fewkes?"

"Oh, never mind."

"Do I want to know all this?"

"Hey, if you want to dabble in scholarship, you gotta know all the sordid details. It's what makes academia bearable. It's not the salaries."

Panofsky was in a weird mood that night.

I called Smithwick at home, and explained my situation. He had a wheezy voice, but he turned out to be sympathetic.

"Ah. Chichilti-Calli. That old story rises to the surface every fifteen years or so. Haury thought it was out near the 76 Ranch, that's not far from your development. But really, there's no evidence."

"But there were a lot of fortresslike ruins in southeast Arizona in 1540. Right?"

"Oh sure. Fort Grant, Eureka Springs, Kuykendall, Goat Hill. Even University Ruin, here in Tucson. The Safford area is best. In the 1800s it was called Pueblo Viejo, or 'ancient town.' Some of the ruins there were three stories high. They were crumbling into mounds by the 1800s, but under the dirt, intact rooms still existed. A Mexican family around 1900 had cleared out a room in one of them and moved in, 500 years after the last occupants left. I always wondered what ghosts troubled their dreams. Most of those ruins were plowed under by Mormon farmers before 1910. My mom and dad worked on some of the remnants. Archaeologists in the early 1900s cataloged most of them, but hardly any were ever excavated properly. They're pueblos, just like in New Mexico. They had stone foundations, but the walls were mostly adobelike material that collapsed over the centuries. They first appeared in southern Arizona in the 1200s. Arizona archaeologists called them the Salado culture. Most Arizona archaeologists think they were local people who picked up new ideas from Anasazi country, farther north. Double mealing bins, for instance. Kivas."

"Did you know that the Coronado chroniclers said the Indians told them that Chichilti-Calli was not built by local people, but by people who moved in from the north?"

"Really? I never heard that."

"It's in Pedro Castañeda's memoir. He said—"

"You can't really trust any of that early Spanish stuff; the historical record is so confused. Besides, Coronado may have been over in New Mexico when he said that. No one knows where he went."

"That's my point. If we could find where their actual route—"

"Like I said, the canonical view is that the Salado culture was just an infusion of new ideas from other regions. Not new people, but just new ideas about architecture, religion, and so on, due to the expanding trade networks around 1100. There was probably a consolidation of regional polities. But actually, I agree with what your

Spaniard said. A lot of these pueblo-style ruins look like they were built by the same people who were building the northern pueblos. Same architecture. I think some of them picked up and moved down here."

"Why?"

"Why? Ah, that's always the big question, isn't it? If you want my theory, the underlying answer is climate change. In those same centuries, from the 1100s to the 1300s, a lot of cultures in North America, from the Mound Builders to the Mexicans, underwent severe social change or collapse. Something larger, something continent-wide, was driving it. Conditions around 1000 had been good, the population had expanded, and the land had reached its carrying capacity, like at Chaco Canyon. Then, came a climate glitch. Droughts. Famines. Population crash. Terrible havoc. It happened all over North America in those centuries. Even the Vikings who came to Newfoundland around 1000, they pulled back by the 1200s. The sagas say the North Atlantic routes began to have more ice—"

"But in Arizona—"

"Neighboring villages fighting over the best agricultural fields. Displaced refugees, turning into marauding nomads, stealing crops from other settlements. That's the way I see it. You can see from the excavations that a lot of villages pulled out of the fertile flood-plains, where they were exposed, and moved up onto defendable ridge tops or back into canyons. Small groups gave up altogether and tried to find new, better areas. Groups of Anasazi pueblo builders moved south into the empty quarter of southeast Arizona in the 1200s, and started building your multistory pueblos, unlike anything else in the area. They only lasted a short while."

"What do you mean?"

"Nobody's sure what happened. They built all these big pueblo settlements, made beautiful Gila polychrome pots, then, *poof!* A century and a half later, they were gone." He sighed, as if it were a matter of personal pain. "Some legends say the locals threw them out after a few generations, before they could integrate and consolidate. Anyway, it all came crashing down around 1390 or 1400. The pueblo buildings were abandoned. A generation later, people were living in little pit house villages. They even stopped making painted pottery."

"How do you know the dates?"

"Tree rings. We have roof beams—lots of construction and repairs up into the 1390s. No new construction after about 1400. There seems to have been a generation or so where people hung around living in the abandoned buildings, but not adding anything new of their own. That's your Polverón stage. Then they left, too. So there were a lot of abandoned ruins in 1540 when your boys came through. There are lots of candidates for Chichilti-Calli. I'm not sure anybody can ever identify it."

"It's an interesting challenge, though."

"Well, yes. To you and me, and maybe half a dozen others. Nobody else cares."

"Don't be too sure about that."

To the natives in the 1500s, the province of Chichilti-Calli must have been an eerie region, dotted with abandoned pueblo towns falling into silent ruin, like a whole county with nothing but ghost towns. The more I learned about it, the harder I realized it would be to prove which Salado ruin was or was not the original Chichilti-Calli. A few miles southeast of us, for example, a big Salado ruin had been used as the site for a cavalry fort in the 1800s. Fort Grant. It was built to protect the new settlers from the Apaches. In our century, it was converted into a medium-security prison, to protect the settlers from all the junior-grade marijuana criminals created by our law-'n'-order state legislature's mandatory sentencing rules. The proximity of the prison to our site was something we didn't mention in our brochures. As Mr. Rooney said, it was hard to find any spot in Arizona that didn't have a prison nearby, or a site where somebody wanted to build one. Both Fort Grant and the earlier Salado pueblo had been built there because of the fine spring-fed stream nearby. In the '60s, model prisoners had been let out on Sundays to have picnics by the stream with their visiting families, and the ruins had been pretty well picked over and obliterated. Parents of marijuana offenders took home many a valuable artifact, which could be sold later. If it wasn't one kind of pot it was another. Maybe the Fort Grant ruin was Coronado's Chichilti-Calli. They could have camped there and gone over Eagle Pass—Chichilti-Calli pass—to the deep and grassy river of the Gila. Or they could have camped at other ruins in the valley foothills. Who could say?

The stories recorded by Pedro Castañeda, about the ruin having been built by northerners, directly confirmed the archaeological deductions that the Salado influence came from the north. The Indians who talked to the Spanish travelers must have told many a story of the old days, handed down from their great-grandparents—the days when the strangers moved in and built the big buildings, painted intricate designs on their pottery, and practiced some foreign religion from the north. What long-lost dramas unfolded between the two cultures? What priceless histories were recited over Coronado's campfires, only to be carried away by the desert winds! But no one cares about the stories of the people they are conquering. That's the definition of conquest, right? If they had cared, it wouldn't have been conquest.

After Coronado went back to Mexico, it was too late to recapture the stories into written history. In the next decades, the Cíbola route was abandoned by the Spanish, and Chichilti-Calli was never heard from again.

I ADDED WHAT I HAD LEARNED TO THE DRAFT OF MY REPORT. I quaked in my shoes about Mr. Rooney's reactions to my conclusion that our development might be sitting right on top of Coronado's campsite. Still, I couldn't change the facts. A good detective—whether policeman or scholar—has to let the chips fall where they may. Political repercussions are always for someone else to work out. Namely, the people with the money.

I handed it in on May 1, Monday. That was about the time Marcos was traversing the Nexpa, near where Phaedra and I dallied, so I thought it was an auspicious date.

In terms of scholarship, I have to set modesty aside and tell you my report was good. I continued to convince myself that it would have a positive effect on the course of events. In spite of any controversy, we would build a rare thing: an American town where inhabitants shared a sense of place that came from real historical roots—not gussied up by chamber of commerce rhetoric, but spelled out plainly through authentic voices of the past.

The report was in two versions, a long version full of footnotes and references, and a shorter executive summary, as Mr. Rooney had requested. There was plenty of time to distribute copies of it, in gold-printed plastic binders, to the supervisors, prior to the upcoming hearing on our rezoning, scheduled for the 24th.

Mr. Rooney asked me to give him his copy in person in his office. He motioned me into a chair while he skimmed the short version. He made a noncommittal "hmmmm" as he read.

Naturally I didn't mention old Steve's helmet, supposedly found just a mile or so to the east of us in the hills. Although it gave me private confidence that ours might be the real site, I hadn't even told Phaedra much about it, just that Steve had some old headpiece that might have been from any time in the Spanish period, even up into the 1700s. She had rolled her eyes when I got to his flying saucer story, and the issue never came up again. Which was okay. Privately, I still thought the helmet was the real thing, but I could see us all being discredited if newspaper reporters converged on Steve's ranch house. Besides, for real proof that you had found Chichilti-Calli, you'd have to discover a ruin with an adjacent campsite strewn with Spanish artifacts from 1540, not a single artifact up in the hills.

So the way I wrote it was that Coronado must have passed nearby, and that our ruin was one of several in the general area that *might* be the one described in the Coronado records. I noted that by preserving it in a park, and adding a colorful interpretive center, we'd be preserving not necessarily the lost Chichilti-Calli itself, but an example of the type, dating from the 1300s. The exhibits would spell it all out: Coronado Estates was located in the broader prehistoric region of Chichilti-Calli. Maps in our heritage center would show the Marcos/Estevan/Coronado route, coming north along the San Pedro Valley to the region of Benson, then turning right, to our valley, and through the pass in the mountains toward Safford. This educational approach, I said in the executive summary, would respond to the preservation issue. In summary, I did my best to turn our potentially contentious liability into a strength.

While Mr. Rooney read, I kept looking for a facial expression, something. There was nothing. Finally, he looked up. "This has some good stuff in it," he said. "This ruin thing . . . it could get ugly. You handled it well. Chichil . . . how do you say that?"

"Chi-CHIL-tee CALL-ee, I think," I said. "That's how Dr. Smithwick said it."

"The only thing we can do is face it head-on. Maybe we could use that name for the clubhouse. Chichilti-Calli Club. Has an in-group ring to it. Exclusive." He waved the report in no specific direction. "We'll get your summary printed up by marketing and hand it out before the hearing. You're absolutely right, by the way. The Coronado ruin coulda been *any* of them. Preserving ours is the key. We'll expand that part of our plan. Good work. I'm giving you a raise. Three percent, effective immediately. Gets you ahead of the cost of living."

Basking in the warmth, I couldn't resist asking him, "Are you worried about the hearing?"

"Nah." I wondered how he could be so cavalier. He seemed less worried than I was. He saw the look on my face. "There'll be a certain amount of grousing, but we've got the votes. There's the lesson for you, Mr. Scott. Never let *anything* come to a vote unless you know it'll go your way. Coronado Estates is too far east of Tucson to become a big political issue. If we had a project this big near the city, it would be different. But only a few extremists give a damn about ranchland so far east of here. So we've got three supes willing to vote our way on this one. That's why we want to get this thing approved *now*. A few years from now, as Tucson spreads east, there'll be too much opposition to pull off something like this."

Mr. Rooney was always thinking ahead.

THE NEXT COUPLE OF DAYS IN THE OFFICE, WE REWORKED THE plan, expanding the park site around our ruin. I found myself listless, staring out the window at the city. Each day I began to find myself less excited about landscapes of concrete. People at desks next to me were talking into phones about cost containment, profit margins, and sales slogans that would attract retired couples. I knew that the economy had to be served, and my officemates had to make payments on their houses and cars and cell phones, but some days I felt my health was being corrupted by breathing secondhand commerce. If I was doing something at Rooney Development to be proud of, it was not what I was paid to do—shilling for Coronado Estates—but rather the fallout, a contribution to the long-term understanding of Southwest history. This troubled me more and more—the idea that the country was organized so that the hackwork got big bucks, while the valuable stuff went unnoticed. Still, I felt good. I felt I was in a period of personal growth. It was one of the last periods in Arizona when I slept soundly, at least when I was not sleeping over at Phaedra's place.

I STOPPED BY THE LIBRARY TO THINK. PHAEDRA WAS STAYING with her sister and Amber that night. She was continuing to resent my visits there. When a man and woman fall in love there have to be all these invisible arrows that flow through space from the man to the woman, like Faraday's magnetic lines of force flowing from the north to the south pole. That year, I learned that for the love affair to work, women need to sense this psychic field. They are quick to detect disruptions in it. Phaedra was seeing my library visits as a disruption, a disturbance in the force. For me, they were an expansion, a communion with my ancient friends, a part of a larger life. The girl with the flute in front of the library was my muse. For Phaedra, the flute player was a temptress I was meeting on campus.

That's the night I realized that my religious conversion to an awareness of history was continuing to give me a new view of everything. I was freed from slavery to the present. My life had the larger context. We all had tiny roles in centuries-old unfolding stories, like the story of the land's morphing from resource to commodity. No longer important to me was the latest 1980s fad, blaring from the TV. Sitting in the library, visiting my virtual friends from past generations made me feel part of a five-hundred-year continuing adventure of civilization that had been going on since the Renaissance.

Looking at the old records that May evening, I had another realization about Marcos—about how the elements of his trip fit together. If he was truthful in saying that he made the side trip toward the coast, it would explain why, according to Coronado, Marcos was disoriented when he led the army up the Señora Valley toward the district of Chichilti-Calli the next year in 1540. Marcos hadn't traveled that part of the route, at least not in the northward direction. In a letter Coronado wrote to Mendoza in 1540 after reaching Cíbola, he claimed that Marcos had indicated "the port of Chichilti-Calli" to be only a day or so from the coast, whereas it had turned out to be ten or fifteen days inland. This was an odd complaint. In the first place, Marcos's *Relación* never specifically mentioned Chichilti-Calli, port or otherwise. For another thing, Marcos tabulated ten to twelve days' travel from the time he left the coastal region until he reached the beginning of the final *despoblado,* where Chichilti-Calli was located. In other words, Marcos's report *agreed* with Coronado's intelligence about travel time from Chichilti-Calli to the coast.

I could see what had happened. Coronado bought into Mendoza's theory that the army could be supplied by sea. In fact, Mendoza and Coronado had sent a captain named Alarcón with a ship full of supplies up the coast in 1540 to find a port and supply the army. In his *Relación*, Marcos had described arriving at the beginning of the *despoblado* only a few lines after describing his foray toward the coast. In the minds of Mendoza and Coronado, Chichilti-Calli had become associated with the region where the ships would be able to deliver their goods. When it turned out not to be so, the blame was assigned to Marcos. Once again, everyone jumped on Marcos without actually listening to what he said.

I felt great. The historical mysteries were yielding to my super sleuthing.

THE MORE I BEGAN TO BELIEVE THAT MARCOS HAD BASICALLY tried to tell the truth, the more I got caught up with another idea I could barely articulate. It was the sincerity issue: the sacrilege of someone's sincere effort being written off by history as a pack of lies. Suppose you lived a tolerably honest life, but realized in middle age that, through some terrible mistake, because of the way events were inexorably unfolding, you would be described as a fraud by the next three generations. Your own grandchildren would believe you were a cheat. Would you start taking steps to rehabilitate your image, or would you just go on, believing in yourself, like Gustav Mahler, who responded to the critics of his symphonies, "My day will come"?

This question haunted me all that week. Is there any personal significance in what the future thinks of you? I'm sure Mr. Rooney didn't think so. Make your millions while you can still enjoy it. Still, we talk about "History's Judgment" as if it were a permanent and important thing. Why do we think people's opinions are better than ours, just because they live in the future? Artists live with this problem all the time. The public and the critics may laugh, but they hope someone, someday, will respond to their work. Mozart had his popularity, then ended up in a pauper's grave. Two centuries later, he was revered as one of the greatest composers in history. And in the twenty-first century? I imagined the next few generations blaming Euro-American culture for bringing on techno-environmental disasters, and reviling white-bread "Western" culture and all its white-bred Mozarts. A century after that, will people revisit outmoded music, and suddenly discover that old Mozart was a goddamn genius? Why worry about the judgment of history, if it's a series of fads and counterfads? Or did some sort of absolute value count in the end?

WEDNESDAY, THE 3RD, I FOUND A LETTER IN MY MAILBOX FROM MY college buddy, Edward. Edward had moved to Alamos, a Mexican town at the south end of Sonora. Alamos was popular with America's two fringes—struggling artists and wealthy expatriates. He told me he had given up on Mexico City. The giant metropolis had a certain decadent excitement, but was a mega-cesspool of pollution, to use his words. The air made his eyes sting. Alamos represented quieter ways and a freer life. Stately old cathedral, cheap restaurants. Edward claimed to be writing a novel about Sonora, a state he called beautiful but forlorn. "People don't realize," he wrote, "Sonora is still undeveloped, like California in the twenties. If Americans knew the beauty of the mountains and rivers," he wrote, "they'd be down here in droves. Sonora would have a world-class tourist economy. It's got everything: deserts, beaches, forests, little towns with plazas and churches. But nobody knows. And now the drug trade is taking over the backcountry. You can't even go out hiking; there are truckloads of guys with guns. The whole society is changing. The old rich families, descended from the conquistadors, are trying to hold on to what they have. The drug economy creates new rich families with ruthless young people who want even more. As for everybody else, they get left behind, poorer than ever."

The letter made me remember of the Edward I used to know, preoccupied with the Big Social Picture. "The problem," he wrote, "is that the quest to get rich gets more nasty every year. The U.S., Mexico, Russia, everywhere. The twenty-first century is when it's going to get really ugly." That was the second person within days who had told me things would get ugly.

Edward said he was going to tell everything in his novel: the cronyism between Arizona business interests and Sonoran officials, the drug trade subverting the farmers, the carefully tuned maintenance of a corrupt police, and the hopeful emergence of a middle class. He said the middle class was so named because they were caught in the middle. He said that seeing America from a third-world country would make anyone hate a lot of things that Americans were doing, but that you have to love what you hate, because if you hate what you hate, it will turn you into a bitter old loner.

He also said I was suffering El Norte burnout, whether I knew it or not, and that I should come down there and reexamine my life from a distance.

I believed what he said about Mexico changing, but I also wondered how eccentric my old buddy had become. It sounded like he was spending a lot of time in the cantinas, taking advantage of the peso exchange rate, and cultivating a writerly air of cynical social criticism. But then, who was I to complain about creeping cynicism?

There was more in the letter. Edward said he had news that might interest me. He described how Alamos, by the 1600s, had become a major stop on the road to the north. All sorts of relics had accumulated in closets down there. He had befriended a young priest in Alamos, and the young priest told him about an old priest in a nearby village who had some books and papers that dated back to the earliest days. Edward theorized that they might shed light on the earliest routes. If I came down there, we could explore the old records together.

In retrospect, Edward's letter was part of a chain of weird linkages. Change one tiny step in my contacts with Edward, and my own future history would have turned out entirely differently. I write to tell Edward about my work. Edward writes back and says he has news that might interest me. Each step seems so innocent. It fitted chaos theory—the science fad *du jour* which was replacing fractals in the magazines. Seemingly insignificant events lead to huge consequences later.

At first I didn't put much stock in his idea that the old churches might yield something. I knew there were boxes of old Spanish records in towns all over Mexico, not to mention the main archives in Mexico City and Seville. Those old Spanish bureaucrats were fanatical about keeping records. Instead of Xerox machines, they had scribes. If you wanted to send an important letter, you dictated it to a scribe. The scribe made one copy to send, a second copy for you, and a third copy that he kept in his scribe book as his own record. Some of those scribe books have come down to us: the minutia of daily life, sales, divorces. But records as early as the 1500s are rare.

I wrote a temporizing letter back to Edward, urging him to tell me more.

ON THURSDAY, MAY 4TH, THE MORNING PAPER HAD ABSORBED MY report, and zeroed in on our ruin and its possible connection with Chichilti-Calli. They loved the idea that somewhere out there was a lost ruin where Coronado slept. Never mind that there were many candidates. They ignored what I said about that. They made our place sound like the Coronado Hotel. The more I read, the unhappier I got.

In the next days, everything went downhill. The romance of a lost ruin consolidated the opposition. It was ironic: our obscure ruin had been in the site files at the Arizona State Museum for years without attracting attention, but now that a political fight was at hand, the environmentalists were suddenly trying to make it into southern Arizona's greatest treasure. The newspaper, seeing an opportunity to create public drama, egged them on with editorials. Preservation began to surface as a battle cry against us. People talked about "historic character." Mr. Rooney felt cheated, since the emphasis on history had been his idea from the start, and now it was coming back to bite him.

My report was suddenly the albatross around Mr. Rooney's neck. I had done my best to lay out the facts impartially, but suddenly I was being quoted by all sides to prove all things.

Mr. Rooney was pissed. He called me in and yelled at me. "How could you hand them this ammunition?"

Tony Beecher, the lawyer, was standing in the corner, a dark presence in his funereal suit, shaking his head sadly. "It's a real problem, Mr. Scott."

"It's a real problem," Mr. Rooney echoed.

"I thought you liked the report! It's what you asked for. You read it. You said—"

"But you and Phaedra were supposed to have your ear to the ground."

I remember thinking: maybe he'd fire me, and I could go rediscover Mexico with Edward. A clean getaway. But Mr. Rooney told me to get back to work on our museum plan.

It didn't help my frame of mind that the newspapers were documenting the simultaneously unfolding surrealism of the Greater World outside our office. Gorbachev had pulled back Russian troops from Europe and was talking about reforming communism, but, amazingly, our secretary of defense was complaining about it. He said it was a Commie trick. Then President Bush disowned the secretary's remarks: no, actually, we would support Gorbachev if he was serious about reform. While the administration struggled over how to respond to Gorbachev's dastardly disarmament, White House aide Oliver North was convicted on three charges of secret gunrunning to fight Commies in Nicaragua. To me, these stories seemed like the rhythms of a dadaist twentieth-century ballet, a joke on the public, playing itself out on some stratospheric political stage, above the heads of the audience.

In the middle of certain nights, I would wake up beside Phaedra and lie awake thinking about how societies work. If the universe is really a bunch of random events, then there might be a kind of quantum sociology, where individual personal acts, like electrons jumping from orbit to orbit, could be represented mathematically as random events, even if they felt like decisions based on free will.

Just as a billion atoms with random movements make a gas that follows predictable laws *en masse,* so a billion citizens' random acts might make a society that also followed predictable patterns, expanding to fill every cultural and economic vacuum. Maybe a society operating under laws of random quantum sociology would make exactly as much sense as our society did.

PHAEDRA SAID NOT TO WORRY ABOUT MR. ROONEY OR PUBLIC criticism, everything was under control. She said he needed me for damage control. At lunch we slipped away to a Mexican restaurant patio where sunlight sparkled through the leaves of tall trees like it did that day when we played in the grove along the Nexpa. Unlike our officemates, who lunched on the run, Phaedra made an art of finding the restaurants with just the right patio to match the weather of the day. She liked to pursue pleasure, at least on the days when the searchlight of her attention swivelled around to me. This was a promising start, but it was one of those days when our conversational connection seemed ill-fated.

Phaedra looked up at the cottonwoods. "You seem kind of distant these days."

Earlier she had fussed about the amount of time I was spending at the library, and now I was distant. Was the relationship souring so soon? "How would you feel if everything you said was being twisted around this way and that? First I've done a great job, and then I'm a jerk."

"You should be happy. You're following in your hero's footsteps."

"My report never said our ruin was the original Chichilti-Calli. I stressed there are a lot of other sites, but the newspaper—"

"Have you been out there to the site? I mean to really look around? Has anyone really looked for artifacts from that period?"

"I've been out to our land, but just with the architects and engineers, not really to look at the ruins. The chance of finding anything would be minuscule. A lot of sediment has washed in from the foothills. Covered things up."

"So there's no real evidence either way. It's all theoretical."

"There are lots of historical threads. They're really fascinating, you know. I'd be happy just to go off and study ruins and manuscripts for a while."

"That's the trouble with men," she said, making another one of her leaps. "You get caught up in abstract stuff. Coronado's campsite, the World Series, car mystique, or the Civil War, you have to have something abstract to argue about. Do you think stuff like that has application to real life, your job, your family?"

"It *is* real life. It's what produced . . . *us*. It's not like trying to market housing developments to county supervisors." I didn't mean to be distant with her. The opposite, in fact.

She smiled with condescension.

I tried to make her see. "I read these guys' letters and it's like I'm right there in the room with them. Sometimes I think I can glimpse Marcos's inner thoughts, but then they are never really exposed. And then there's the question of whether he was trying to hide something. Was he a fake? I try to figure out—why are some people called successes and some are called failures, and does it have anything to do with their real accomplishments?"

"Well you shouldn't wreck your life over it. Just do your work and—"

"Wreck my life? What are you talking about? I'm having fun!"

She said nothing. The conversation was beginning to bother me. For that matter, I realized, I was bothered by her yuppie streak; all that emphasis on job security.

She scanned the tree again, as if looking for rare birds. She looked very beautiful. Finally she spoke up again. "I was thinking about your priest, Marcos, and how people explain things to themselves. My Chicana grandmother, with her shrines to the saints, she thinks God arranged the whole Vietnam War just to send my cousins off to the army to punish them for doing drugs in the sixties. One of them died over there. Anyway, do you think your Marcos really believed it was God's will for the Spanish to subjugate the Indians?"

"I don't know. He was always crusading against the atrocities of the—"

"He probably saw his job as destroying all the other guys' gods. That's what priests do, isn't it? That's their job."

"But he must have wondered about it. Having doubts can be good."

"I hate having doubts."

Those kinds of conversations clarify what the problems are, but they never really solve anything.

THE NEXT DAY IN THE OFFICE, PHAEDRA CALLED ME OVER TO HER desk. "The people in marketing have your report. They're looking for angles. They say that if we are going to call this Coronado Estates, we have to show people why Coronado is sexy. Since you're the resident expert, they want me to ask you, 'Why did you become obsessed with Coronado?'"

"I didn't. I became obsessed with Marcos de Niza. He's the real discoverer. He got there first. The development should be named after him."

"Don't be difficult. Besides, that sounds dumb for a town. Marcos de Niza Estates. Anyway, why did you?"

"I don't know," I said. "I always liked a good adventure. It's like a treasure hunt."

"That's good," she said. "They'll like that."

"Why don't they come and ask me themselves?"

"They say you don't have the right attitude."

"Oh, great."

"It's okay. They'll love 'treasure hunt.'"

I frowned and started to respond, but she interrupted, "Don't say anything more, you'll just mess it up." She was always practical.

Later, in spite of what she said, the Creatures from the Depths of the Marketing Department came to visit me. There were three men and a woman, all younger than I was. When they came into my office they were talking about the graphics on last night's Go-for-the-Gusto Budweiser commercial. Two of them had clothing company logos on their shirts. As soon as we started talking about the development, I noticed that they didn't have a clue about the history of the land, or project itself. They were interested in images for billboards and TV spots.

They couldn't understand how anybody could care about what might have happened long ago, before the last station break. I tried to tell them. They liked what I said, except I could tell I was taking too long to say it. They had attention spans the length of a commercial. I think their brains had been wiped and reformatted in marketing school.

"The more people learn about the mysteries of the place," I insisted, "the more interested they will be."

"No, no, no," they said. Gradually they educated me. "We have to have a single, simple message. Details confuse people." One of them quoted some guru of their field: Marketing deals not with facts but with beauty, and beauty lies not in whether you can back up your claims but in whether people remember them. All this had already been discussed by Mr. Rooney with his lawyers, the Marketeers explained patiently. The point of my report, I learned between the lines, was not its content, but its basic existence. It offered scholarly legitimacy, to show that we had a basis for our claim that our parcels oozed history. The point of scholarship was to support our ad campaign.

I cautioned them that we were in a delicate position: overstressing the history angle was backfiring on us. Also, it was the kind of thing where some professor with an opposing theory could appear and—

"You mean you're not, like, *sure*?"

"At some point you're never, like, sure. You converge on the truth. Each researcher tries to bring new facts to the table—"

They were annoyed. "We were gonna use 'Coronado Slept Here—You Should Too,' but now Tony Beecher says that's out, because they'll crucify us for damaging a historical site. So what d'we do?"

"Let's go back to what you told Phaedra," another one said. " 'Treasure hunt.' That's good."

"They were looking for cities full of gold," said someone else. "We could use that. Everybody's always looking for their own city of gold."

Later that afternoon, one of them came by my office again to announce the central theme of the advertising campaign. They would have a logo of an armor-clad conquistador on a horse, peering out to the horizon. The slogan was "The Adventure Continues: Find Your Own City of Gold at Coronado Estates." She explained why this was beautiful: It tuned into the market they wanted to reach: retiring CEOs and executives, the people who could afford to move to a planned community, who saw themselves as the modern conquerors of the world, who prided themselves on still being young in spirit, and who could see the connection between Coronado challenging the unknown wilderness, and their own challenge on a golf course on the same land.

"Connection?" I said.

But she was already out my door heading back to her office.

I complained to Phaedra about the attitude of the Marketeers, that they were missing the real excitement, and that it was crazy for me to do all this research on my report if they were going to distill it to a slogan. She told me to get a grip on reality.

TENSION WAS MOUNTING ABOUT THE MAKE-OR-BREAK HEARING ON May 24. Mr. Rooney still radiated confidence, but at the same time he lectured us that we should leave nothing to chance, while everyone else in the office helped brief Tony Beecher about the state-of-the-art planning in our community design, so he could convert it into legalese.

At the same time, I was still caught up in the idea that my life paralleled Marcos's. Day by day I was reliving his trip and figuring out what had really happened. I had to keep up with him. He said he entered the final fifteen-day *despoblado* on May 9. Working backwards, that meant that he would have been at the Chichilti-Calli ruin on May 7. I figured I should go out there on that date. It would be Sunday. That Friday I asked Phaedra if she wanted to go out there with me. She said she had something planned that week-end with her sister and her niece. Then she gave me an auspicious look as I went out the door. "Don't forget to come back," she said furtively. "You don't want to miss what I'll have for you." She still made me feel great.

I LEFT EARLY THAT SUNDAY MORNING, WHILE IT WAS STILL DARK and cool, so I could enjoy watching the sun awaken the eastern sky. I stepped out of my apartment thinking about how Arizona dawns taught that there could still be moments of coolness and peace in the world, before kinetic energy took over. Eventually my primal male urge toward speed triumphed over my desire for cosmic peace. As I zoomed along the empty interstate toward Willcox, I loved my car, loved the way it sped across the vast, dark landscape. The enormous, lightening sky seemed ten times bigger than the sky anywhere else on the continent. Didn't Marcos, out there under that sky, pushing forward day after day, feel more alive than any of us city dwellers?

In the dim light, the interstate stretched ahead like a tape measure draped across the swells of the landscape. I thought about how, somewhere along this east-west road, I was crossing the north-south path of Marcos and Coronado's vast army of a thousand men. My car would drive over Coronado's footprints.

I pulled over. High, pale Arizona cirrus hung in the predawn sky like the breath of a god waiting for the day to start. More cars materialized on the interstate, as if by spontaneous generation. The landscape beyond the rushing cars was as quiet as the passage of time, but even in the stillness, the Earth was turning. The heat was waiting in the sunlight beyond the eastern horizon, and the Earth's turning was carrying me there at a speed of ten miles a minute.

Suppose the army crossed where I was parked? So much karma, expended on this spot. Why couldn't I perceive some special vibration as I drove over their footsteps? There must be a twenty-foot stretch of Interstate 10, somewhere between Tucson and Deming, that emitted a special aura. . . . But the chronic, humming white noise of history wiped out the echoes.

My thoughts bounced back off the 1500s onto my own life, like a laser beam reflected off the moon. That's when I realized that sense of place grows from the cumulation of all the events that happened on your own piece of soil, and that the business of the twentieth century has been to stamp it out. We dry up the rivers and hide the mountains with smog. We forget the ancient seas where trilobites wriggled, the projectile points that were chipped from stone, the romances that blossomed in old downtown houses, and the characters who stomped through the dust, searching for golden kingdoms.

AFTER THE SUN CAME UP, I REACHED THE LITTLE TOWN OF WILLcox and stopped at a 24-hour truck stop to get some lunch to take to the site: sandwiches, an apple, some chips, two cold Pepsis—your basic wilderness food. By the cash register was a poster showing the state of Arizona with all the federal, state, and county lands, from national forests to regional parks, shown in pink with a hammer and sickle on each, with some commentary about big government. I wasn't close enough to read the fine print.

On the road again, I turned north to follow the aggravating checkerboard of roads up the Sulfur Springs Valley. I thought about that poster again. I couldn't understand the right-wing redneck philosophy. The land that belonged to all of us, they regarded as belonging to a few oppressive government landlords, and the land that actually belonged to a few landlords, they regarded as belonging to "the people." More surrealism. The valley trended northwest beneath the massive Pinaleño Mountains, but the farm roads were a grid that took you north, then west, then north—never in a straight line toward where you wanted to go. The distant pine-covered tops of the Pinaleños, on the right, were the color of blue slate.

Finally I was there, unlocking the Rooney Development, Inc. NO TRESPASSING gate, and standing on the old ranchland in the grass among the dry cow pies. The land sloped gently up into the moun-

tains. Springs at the base of the range had brought the original settlers, a thousand years ago, up from the dry, grassy valley to live in
these gentle foothills with a panoramic view that seemed to encompass half of southern Arizona. I left the car beside the old dirt ranch
road, and walked through the fields toward the part of the site
where the ruin lay. The sky and the hills and the season and the date
were the same as when Marcos arrived at Chichilti-Calli. I felt I
was as close as I could ever get to the man.

As I walked across the field, I checked the plan map: Here would
be the commercial corner, or "village center" as our plan called it;
already we had bids from Safeway and Costco. And here would be
the parking lot, lined with trees; here would be the street heading
up toward the pricier homes, $400K and up; over there on the flats
would run the golf course. It would be a good-looking town.

In the distance, I could see the low mounds that marked the
ruins. At first you didn't see them; they seemed to be just part of the
rolling terrain. Once you started looking with an educated eye, you
could see there were several of them, marking what must have been
different buildings, now moldering into piles of soil, cobbles, and
pottery sherds. There were no above-ground walls. The walls and
floors of the prehistoric rooms were hidden inside the mounds; you
could see only cross sections of walls, broken off and exposed here
and there on the mound tops.

The ruins were a hundred yards from a stream that gurgled out
of the Pinaleños. I went over and lodged my Pepsis under rocks in
the cold water. I left my lunch there by a tree and went back to
wander around. The highest mound must have originally been a
pueblo at least two stories high, because the worn-down wall tops
were five feet above the surrounding ground level, and a lot of
material had fallen into the rooms to create the mound itself. I
walked around it, getting the feel of its size, tracing the faint rows
of stones two or three abreast. According to what I had read, they
were typical of wall construction in the Salado structures of the
1300s, plastered together with a mixture of lime-based mud mortar,
called puddled adobe. I traced out parts of the grid of room walls,

each room about twelve or fifteen feet square. The walls were thick, capable of blocking summer heat and allowing a small fire to provide winter heat. No air conditioning in those days, no furnaces. I remembered some of the guys at Rooney Development talking cost/benefit ratios on insulation. They argued that electricity would stay cheap for another decade, so no buyer should pay the up-front cost of extra insulation. The meeting ended with a joke. Let the next generation worry about insulation, once we run out of fossil fuels. Everyone laughed. The bottom line in cost/benefit analysis is that the future gets screwed.

I paced out the shape of the plaza and wondered what ancient dances had been held here, what kids sat on the pueblo roofs and watched while their patient aunts taught them the meanings of the ceremonies. I wondered about the lovers who had met in dark corners, and I wondered about all the eternal loves in the history of the world—eternal loves that were not eternal but had died and were buried in time. Did the elders meet in these rooms and debate thirteenth-century climate change? Until their crash came, did their world seem as stable to them as America seems to us?

I had seen photos of mounds like this after excavation, exposing walls and room floors with fire pits. Sometimes, pots were still sitting on the floors, where they had been abandoned centuries ago. Undoubtedly, such treasures still existed below my feet. Sheet wash, rushing out of the mountains every few decades when the storm paths were just right, had swept across the area, eroding the mound edges and filling in the low spots with soil. Entropy was doing its thing.

Our community clubhouse would be there, adjacent to the biggest mound, with the park next to it. Aside from displaying and restoring the main mound, we'd transfer fill dirt to cover much of the rest of the area. Well, okay, the other mounds would be smoothed off a little, but the base of each mound, containing ruin floors, foundations, and lower walls, would be buried and paved over and covered with streets and houses. As Mr. Rooney liked to say, this was better than the fate suffered by most other ruins in the valley, which were being pilfered by local artifact collectors in pickup trucks, not to mention rogue commercial "Indian arts" dealers. Those guys would spend whole weekends digging and stealing pots, both on state land and on private ranches. Mr. Beecher had lined up two archaeologists who would testify that paving a ruin was the best way to preserve it in the long run. If we covered it, people in the twenty-third century could study it with their advanced techniques.

I went back to the stream, got the first of my two cold Pepsis, and ate my lunch sitting on a little rise where I could I gaze across the valley. The distant blue mountains on the southern horizon were in Mexico. The landscape was only a fraction of the vista; most of the view seemed to be sky, with pale cirrus riding high. Over the eastern mountains friendly masses of cumulus were trying to get themselves organized. The sun made the air itself luminous. To the north, I could see the distinctive, lopsided V of Eagle Pass across the Pinaleños, guarded by some crags to the left. It led to the Gila River Valley and the mountainous country beyond. Chichilti-Calli Pass.

As I ate, I remembered an interview I had read with a group of Zunis—the people of Cíbola. On their reservation there were several ruins of the abandoned Seven Cities. The Zunis objected to the Anglo interviewer's question about "abandoned ruins." Instead of answering the question, they objected to the term. They said these weren't "abandoned ruins," but only city sites that weren't being used just now. I loved the way that different cultural traditions made people look at the same facts slightly differently, as if there were all these parallel alternate histories going on in our world at the same time.

Scattered around the place where I sat, fragments of thousand-year-old pots littered the ground. The longer I sat quietly, the more of them I could see. Most of them were earth-brown or earth-red, but some had painted designs. The sherds were dusty but you could see the colors: reds, blacks, whites. Humans, I thought, express their urge toward beauty until the point where they start perverting it with calculations of bottom-line sales. I picked up a stick and started flipping them over aimlessly. When the first sherd flipped, the colors leaped out in the sun, bright as the day the pot had been painted. Probably it was lying here the day Marcos de Niza walked through 450 years ago on this very date, full of hope.

I finished the sandwiches, and wandered around the mounds one more time, just picking up the feel of place, the open air and the old sherds baking in the sun for the hundred-thousandth time. The more you walked, the more you got accustomed to the presence of the past. It was like becoming dark-adapted. At one point, the old dirt ranch road actually crossed the corner of a ruin, and with a start I recognized the spot. In a few more years, a Kwik-E Mart would stand here, contributing to the tax base of the county. Then the land would find its "highest and best use," to use the fifties-era official phrase that drove all land use discussions in Arizona.

It was getting hot. That surprised me because this land of ours was a good bit higher than Tucson. I went back and retrieved my second Pepsi, trying not to get my feet too wet. It was amazing, how nature was able to keep streams babbling for a thousand years without pumps or electricity. I imagined the great pueblo collapsing century by century, stone by stone, and timber by timber. When a house collapses in a *despoblado*, and no one hears it, does it make any sound? Yes. It's the sound of history, ratcheting itself forward by another notch.

After these fields were leveled by bulldozers pushing fill dirt, and this grassland filled with streets and houses, the sky itself would shrink. We could preserve the mound on the clubhouse grounds, but we couldn't preserve the feel of the place, the feel of history.

The wind made a hissing noise in the yuccas that stood around the property. Marcos and Estevan and Coronado and Castañeda had heard the same wind whistle through the bladelike yucca leaves only a generation after Columbus. Not to mention a thousand earlier, Indian traders from other centuries—names lost in time—who trudged along the old trails and tied together the great cultures of Mexico and the Southwest with their pots and their macaw feathers and the Nahuatl words they assigned to geographic features. Soon it would all be swept away so that I could get paid and Phaedra could get paid and a dozen architects could get paid and a new Coronado army of construction workers from Sierra Vista and Tucson could get paid, and a thousand retired folks could be happy in their new houses in the warm sun, Mr. Rooney could have a smile on his face, and the county supervisors could get reelected. Mrs. Rooney would then give big donations to the United Way campaign and the struggling Arizona Theater Company, and she might buy him a new car, to celebrate. The money and the salaries and the smiles and the good deeds would ripple out like the waves from a stone dropped in a pond, and they would disappear, and our generation would die, and when it was all over another town would be here on top of the old one, and a piece of our heritage would be gone.

What would be gone would not be the ruin, but the *experience* of the ruin. Yes, we would make a park here, with much fanfare. But what Americans needed to *feel* was the eerie sense of history radiating from the earth—precisely not what you feel in a goddamn predigested park, with its manicured plants and asphalt walkways. What was needed was not a brass plaque or a visitor center or a lookout point or a gift shop with paperback books of history in bite-size servings, but rather the *absence* of a park.

What allowed the feel of history to seep from the Earth was the emptiness of the landscape, the cleanliness of the soil, the sound of the stream babbling from the ravine, the brightness of the sky and sun, and a night darkness lit only by the moon and stars. The paradox was that the only way for that kind of thing to be part of our public heritage was for nobody to know about it. Otherwise it would be parkified and killed. And I was helping to make that happen.

The breeze stirred again across the grass. It felt good, there in the hot sun. I walked back to the stream and waded in, tennis shoes and all. The cold water around my ankles cooled me off immediately, like a dose of reality. I was still carrying the stick and I threw it into the gurgling water. It made no splash at all and the rushing stream carried it away in an instant.

I DROVE BACK TO TUCSON. WHEN I HIT THE EAST SIDE, I MARVELED at Speedway Boulevard, where masochists in suits imprisoned themselves in metal boxes in the five o'clock sun and sat at traffic lights every afternoon, not knowing anything about sense of place or the people who came before. Their air conditioners struggled gamely with the heat, leaking freon into the atmosphere.

I was feeling more and more like a lemming who was exploring his own little pathway on the hill while the rest of his friends rushed happily toward the cliff.

When I got back to my apartment, the radio was talking about the heat. A record had been broken when the temperature hit 105° that afternoon. Also, there was a story about a Mexico City shootout with a drug-smuggling cult that believed in voodoo and witchcraft. One leader of the cult was a young woman who had once been an honor student in the U.S. Then came a story about water. The radio was promoting the city government's annual summer campaign to get people to cut back on watering lawns, because the Arizona water sources were finite and expensive. On the other hand, the same city government was supporting the Tucson Economic Development Authority, which ran ads in the *Wall Street Journal* trying to attract new industry and new people to the city.

After my day in the open countryside, everything in the city had a strange twist to it. The fact that simultaneous policies of conserving water and bringing in new consumers bothered me should have alerted me that I was headed for trouble in my chosen career.

AFTER I CLEANED UP, I DROVE OVER TO PHAEDRA'S APARTMENT. We had a grand time that night. A strange thing happened later. After I fell asleep in her bed, I had another dream. Through some cosmic accident, I had been born of Jewish parents in Warsaw in 1910; I grew up and lived my life according to the rules. I fell in love, worked hard, saved my money. But at the same time, in my dream, I could look down from the sky like a guardian angel and watch myself. I could see that the Earthbound me was just a cork bobbing on a dark, awe-full tide of history. There was nothing I could do to warn myself of Hitler's rise. Poland was taken over, and in the government office buildings, I could see whole bureau-cracies being set up to deal with the Jewish question. I could watch the black cars fanning out into the streets at 3 A.M. and the zealous men knocking on doors. . . . When frightened citizens answered the doors, the zealous men said, "We're removing you from history." Apparently I cried out in my sleep; Phaedra nudged me and told me to go back to sleep, everything would be all right.

CHAPTER 11

Letters from Marcos

A fter I communed with our ruin, I discovered I couldn't just walk away from the unfinished Marcos story. I had to get to the bottom of the charges against him. The usual complaint was that somewhere around the last populated valley or Chichilti-Calli, he turned back to Mexico and fabricated the rest of his report. So that stretch of the journey was critical to the rest of the story. Was there any way to look at it more carefully? He said he reached that country after his attempt to reach the coast. Where did he make that side trip and how did he get back to the Cíbola trail? I decided to check what the next generations of explorers said about the area.

It turned out that after Coronado's trip, Spaniards didn't return to northern Sonora until the 1690s. By that time, the discoveries by Marcos and the sea captains of Cortés and Mendoza—that the Gulf of California had a northern end, and that California was not an island—had been forgotten. A literate military captain, Juan Manje, who was assigned to assist the Jesuit priest, Eusebio Kino, wrote a memoir about his adventures exploring the area. Manje was the Indiana Jones of the 1690s, pushing forward with Kino from one unknown village to another. Lo and behold, they had the same problem as Marcos: trying to discover the configuration of the coastline, and whether there was a land connection to what we now know as Baja California. Guided by local natives, Manje and Kino made several trips west down the Rio Magdalena to search out the shore.

This was the same problem faced by Marcos, so perhaps Manje's records would shed light on what Marcos might have done!

I soon learned that Manje had written about their 1694 foray in his memoirs. Deep in the library stacks, I found his book, *Luz de Tierra Incognita—Light on the Unknown Land*. His account sounds strikingly like Marcos's *Relación*, but with the missing geographical detail.

> *[Traveling down the Rio Magdalena] we refreshed ourselves with clear, cool water. Then we went on in the same direction, passing through cultivated lands. We found irrigation canals in the settlement of the Indians of Pitiquin, who were away hunting deer. After traveling a few more leagues (about eight miles) west . . . we camped for the night in the town of Caborca, which is surrounded by a grove of trees. The heathen Indians there received us with crosses and arches, and along the swept roads they danced and feasted.*
>
> *We were given lodging in a hut made of poles and mats. Although we counted 160 Indians, we were told that others had gone deer hunting. We concluded that by combining this village and the neighboring settlements, a town of six hundred souls could be formed. We instructed them in knowledge of God, and how he rewards good Christians and punishes the evildoers with the fire of hell. They were terrified by the picture of hell. . . .*
>
> *The place is very suitable for establishing a mission. It has fertile and fruitful lands, all irrigated. The Indians harvest quantities of corn, beans, and squash. If they had hatchets, which they don't, they could cut down the brush and there would be land sufficient for three thousand Indians, who could be gathered here from among the naked peoples to the north and west to the coast. They could build up a good-sized mission, and a flourishing Christian community. The climate is temperate. The area has rich pasture lands, and salt deposits, for raising cattle and horses.*

[In the next few days we traveled west through drier country, trying to reach the coast west of Caborca] On the [first day west of Caborca] the guides informed us that the river sank into the ground and did not run to the sea. Pools had to be dug for drinking water. We continued west over an arid plain with no rocks, and sometimes no grass. . . .

Having walked another six leagues [15–19 miles] we crossed over a mountain, ranging from north to south. . . . We camped in a dry barren and deep ravine and later that afternoon reached the top of the mountains, and from there we could [finally] see the Gulf of California in the distance.

The welcomes under arches, the good villages, and the fact that the locals could describe the coast reinforced my belief that what Marcos wrote down was basically right, even if brief.

I loved to come to Phaedra with my latest discoveries. On the best days, when she didn't accuse me of obsessing too much about it, she'd share my enthusiasm and we'd ruminate about how far official history might be off track. She congratulated me on my discovery of the Manje diary. Meanwhile, she had been adapting her reading to my problem—pursuing popular histories and historical novels. She came up with new input.

"Did you ever hear of Josephine Tey?" she asked me one day.

"No."

"English mystery writer. She did a book called *Daughter of Time*, where her detective hero, Inspector Somebody-or-other—she used him in lots of books—gets laid up in the hospital, and somebody brings him some get-well reading about Richard III. He gets interested in the historical mystery of who killed the two little nephews in the tower. He thinks of it as his latest case, and he solves it. Turns out Richard III got a bum rap from all the historians and also Shakespeare; he wasn't hunchbacked and he didn't do it; the next king did it."

"So . . ."

"He's like Marcos; he got a bum rap, according to you. Ever hear of Tonypandy?"

"No."

"It's Tey's word for this kind of thing. She says it's a village in Wales where there were some demonstrators and riots, so Winston Churchill called out the British troops and they shot a lot of unarmed people in the village. A big massacre. Everyone in Wales knew about it, and it influenced Welsh politics for years. The only thing was . . . it never happened. In reality, Churchill decided not to use troops for fear of just this sort of thing, and he sent in unarmed municipal police, and there was some sort of scuffling. No one was killed. It was distorted into propaganda and the propaganda version is what entered the history books. She calls that Tonypandy. History that everyone knows is true, but isn't. She says the Boston Massacre was the same thing."

"So . . ."

"If you're right, Marcos's story is a case of Tonypandy. Everybody says he lied about Cíbola, but according to you, he didn't." She smiled. "I thought you could use that someday. Maybe you'll write a book about Marcos."

THAT SET ME TO THINKING ABOUT LARGER PARTS OF MY OWN PUZ-zle. In the conspiracy theory advocated by several historians of the '30s and '40s, Viceroy Mendoza had assigned Marcos to bring back a report of a wealthy empire in order to stir up enthusiasm for a northern conquest, regardless of what Marcos actually found. From this conspiracy, the church would gets its chance at mission-ization and Viceroy Mendoza could preempt Cortés from claiming the area, and, hopefully, get rich quick in the process. Win-win. All Marcos had to do was gather a basic minimum of reliable hearsay from the local natives, to establish credibility, then turn around and bring an embellished tall tale back to Mexico.

As I pondered this problem in the next few days, I made a big discovery about conspiracy theories. The way to test one is not to argue over the details of how it worked, but rather assume it is true, and then check the consequences for each player. Marcos's *Relación* claimed he went all the way to Cíbola, and if he blatantly lied about it, where did it leave him? Why would he turn around the next year and lead the army back to the scene of the crime, where he surely would be exposed as a fraud? Any Indian of Chichilti-Calli could have let the cat out of the bag, that Marcos had turned back and only Estevan had gone on ahead. In other words, the conspiracy proposed by Sauer simply wouldn't work. Mendoza and Marcos would know in advance that Marcos would likely be exposed as a liar. Furthermore, Mendoza was the second largest investor in Coronado's expedition. He wouldn't knowingly have put his fortune into a complete scam. No, Mendoza really believed in the gold of Cíbola, and therefore the players could not have been as devious as the historians had claimed.

I WAS HAPPY WITH THAT DISCOVERY, AND I CONTINUED READING Marcos's account of his journey. On the down side, I had to admit that Marcos's description of the journey back from the coast toward the main Cíbola route through Chichilti-Calli is the most garbled part of his account. You can't identify the sequence of valleys, or when he actually reached the Cíbola route again. Was he trying to hide something? Maybe his enthusiasm simply got the better of him and he forgot to record the details. All along, it had a chatty style, instead of giving an impression of careful editing to maximize geographic detail about the route. Here's what he says about the trip back from the coast.

> *[Having established the coastal configuration], I was as grati-*
> *fied as I was with the good news that I had already obtained*
> *about the country of Cíbola. So I returned to continue my jour-*
> *ney toward Cíbola.*
>
> *I traveled in a well populated valley for five days. It is inhab-*
> *ited by splendid people, and so well provided with food that it*
> *could feed more than three hundred horsemen. It is all irrigated*
> *and like a garden. There are compact villages every half*

league or quarter of a league [every mile or so]. In each town of this valley I had a very long account of Cíbola, and they spoke in great detail, because their people go there each year to gain their livelihood.

Here I found a man who was a native of Cíbola, who told me he had fled from the person whom the high chief had appointed in Cíbola. The lord of these seven cities lives in one of the cities called Ahacus, [which is different from the province of Ácus recorded earlier], and in the others he has placed persons who rule for him. This man of Cíbola was of good disposition, somewhat aged, and much better informed than the natives of this valley or the ones I visited before. He wanted to go with me so that I might obtain his pardon.

He told me that Cíbola is a large city, that it has many people and streets and plazas, and that in some parts of the city there are very large houses reaching ten stories. The leaders assemble in these houses on certain days of the year. As described to me before, he said the houses are of stone and lime, with the portals and fronts of the principal houses having turquoises. He told me the other cities were of this same style, and some were larger, but that Ahacus is the most important one. . . . He confirmed what others had said about the clothes they wear in Cíbola, and said that people of that city sleep in beds high above the floor, with bed clothes and with canopies over the beds. . . .

Marcos must have struggled to record phonetically the place names that people applied to the Cíbola region, but he did a good job. The names he recorded are still recognizable, though Marcos seems to have added a *us* Latinized ending. Ahacus was the main town of the province of Cíbola, which today is a ruin spelled as Hawikuh, pronounced HAW-ee-koo. Take off the s from Ahacus and you have A-ha-cu = Haw-i-kuh. The nearby town of Ácus is the famous hilltop pueblo now known as Acoma, down the road a few miles from Zuni. Á-cu = Á-co-ma.

I traveled in [the next?] valley three days, with the natives preparing for me as many fiestas and celebrations as they could. Here in this valley I saw more than two thousand of the hides, extremely well processed. I also saw a much larger quantity of turquoises and turquoise necklaces in this valley than in anywhere I had passed before, and they said that all these came from Cíbola, of which they have as much knowledge as I have of what I hold in my hands. . . .

Even if the routing was murky, the account repeatedly emphasized that the natives of northern Sonora were familiar with Cíbola and that parties of them traveled well-established trade routes in order to work in exchange for material goods. Yet, those who were determined to trash Marcos refused to accept even this basic point. It was a lesson in how history is created. Here is Hallenbeck:

The friar's story of the [Sonoran] Indians journeying to Cíbola and there performing manual labor in exchange for turquoises is a bit of unintentional humor on his part. We can picture those people sweating under the direction of the Zunians about as easily as we can fancy the Roman legionnaires journeying to Cornwall and there laboring for the Britons in exchange for tin.

It's a backward analogy Hallenbeck made. Romans were the rich overlords, and of course would not work for the Cornwall peasants. In the Southwest, the Cíbolans were the rich ones, and it was natural for the country folk of northern Sonora to go work for them to get the precious buffalo hides and other goods.

I REREAD MARCOS'S CHAPTER ABOUT THE LAST STAGES OF HIS TRIP toward Cíbola, after he got back on the main trail. Everything he said about visiting the village in the last populated valley—presumably the Nexpa—projected earnestness. He seemed especially careful and up-front in evaluating the accuracy of the information he was gathering from the natives. He started out talking about Estevan's message, sent back to this village from the final *despoblado*.

> *[Estevan] said that he was very happy because he was growing ever more certain about the grandeur of the country. Estevan also sent word that he had never caught the Indians in any lie, and that up to this point, he always found everything just as they said it would be. Therefore, he predicted that the rest of what we had been told would also turn out to be true.*
>
> *I, too, emphasize this, because from the first day I learned of Cíbola, the Indians told me correctly of each thing I have seen until now, always describing the towns that I would find along the way, their number, and, in the depopulated zones, the places where I could eat and sleep. They never erred on a single point. . . .*
>
> *Here in this [final populated] valley, as in the earlier towns, I placed crosses and performed the proper acts of possession, conforming to the instructions. The townspeople . . . told me that more than three hundred men had gone from this region with Estevan, the black, to accompany him and carry his food. Many also wished to go with me, not only to serve me but also because they expected to return rich with goods. I accepted this favor and I told them to hurry. I was so anxious to see Cíbola that each day seemed like a year.*
>
> *Thus I waited in their village three days without going forward, during which I continually informed myself about Cíbola and the other places. I did nothing but take Indians aside and question them, one at a time. They all agreed in their accounts. They told me about the many people, the arrangement of the streets, the grandeur of the houses, and the style of the porches, just as those before had described them.*
>
> *After the three days had passed, many people had assembled to go with me, and from these I chose thirty chiefs, very well dressed with their necklaces of turquoises, some of which*

had five or six loops. With these chiefs, I took the additional
people necessary to carry the food for everyone, and I was
ready for the road.

One day I realized there were really two mysteries I was trying
to solve. The first one was what I had been concentrating on—
whether Marcos told the truth. More and more I was convinced he
did. The second mystery was separate and deeper—if he had told
the truth, why did so many accuse him of lying?

I went back over the arguments of the historians, trying to avoid
getting caught up in detailed charges against Marcos, and backing
off to look for the big picture, the key charge. It revolved around lack
of time for Marcos to make his journey. He said he left the frontier
outpost of Culiacán on March 7, but when did he get back? That
wasn't exactly known. He was in Mexico City by the end of August,
because he certified some documents there. But the historians Henry
Wagner and Cleve Hallenbeck, and the historian-geographer Carl
Sauer, all seized on the fact that rumors began to circulate in Coronado's headquarters, Compostela, between Culiacán and Mexico
City, by mid-July. The same rumors appeared in Mexico City by late
July, that Marcos had found "a very fine country" to the north. Not a
city full of treasure, mind you, but only "a very fine country." The
source of these rumors was the key to the whole controversy. Critics
used them to claim that Marcos himself had to be back in Compostela by early July to start these stories. If he got back this early, he
did not have time to go all the way to Cíbola and return.

But there was another, more likely scenario: Marcos had been
instructed by Mendoza to send messages back about his progress.
If messages came back to Coronado, describing the good news
Marcos was accumulating on his way north, it would explain
everything. To my mind, it was absolutely confirmed in a letter by
Coronado to Viceroy Mendoza, dated in Culiacán some days or
weeks after Marcos left, and probably written in late March or
early April, 1539. It describes the first few weeks of Marcos's trip.

Friar Marcos, together with Estevan, proceeded beyond the frontier. . . . I left them in the care of more than a hundred Indians from Petatlán and the region from which they had departed. They carried the padre on the palms of their hands, pleasing him in everything they could. It would be impossible to relate or describe his trip better than has been done in every report included in my letters from Compostela; and at San Miguel [Culiacán] I also wrote to you with all the details available. Even if only one-tenth were true, it would be marvelous.

With this letter I enclose one I received from the said padre for your lordship. The Indians tell me they all adore him. I imagine he must have traveled very far inland. He says that he will write to me when he finds good country, and I shan't fail to inform you. I trust in God that, one way or another, we may be able to locate something worthwhile.

There it was. "I enclose a letter I received from Marcos de Niza." Marcos was off the hook.

I ALSO FOUND SOME PROVOCATIVE PHRASES IN A LETTER THAT Coronado wrote to the king on July 15, 1539—a letter I mentioned earlier.

I charged the Indians to take Fray Marcos and the black Moor, Estevan, to the interior of the land. . . . This they did, treating them very well.

After Marcos's party traveled at their normal daily rate, the Lord willed that they should come to a very fine country, as your Majesty will see by the report of Fray Marcos and by what the viceroy is writing to you, and inasmuch as he is doing so I shall not go into details. I hope that God and your Majesty will be well served, not only by the grandeur of the country which Father Marcos tells about, but also by the

planning and activity that the viceroy has displayed in dis-
covering it. . . .

Coronado wrote this from his headquarters in Compostela four months after Marcos left. Marcos was not back yet. This was absolutely clear because Coronado told the king that the Indians treated both Marcos and Estevan very well—a statement that ignored certain fateful disasters late in Marcos's trip. This alone proved that Coronado was not talking to Marcos in person, but was using information sent by Marcos before the disasters happened. He even refers to a "report of Fray Marcos," and he was able to report that Marcos had found "a fine country"—a phrase similar to the phrases Marcos used in his own *Relación* to describe the good valleys and irrigated villages that he was finding in northern Sonora, on his way north. To me, this proved that Coronado was using a letter sent by Marcos from northern Sonora or southern Arizona.

In short, I now knew that by July 15, Marcos had not yet arrived back at Coronado's headquarters, but his messages, written before reaching Cíbola, had.

How could the historians have missed this? After additional reading, I found that not all of them did. A historian named Lansing Bloom had reached the same conclusion, but had been dismissed by Carl Sauer. In an article published in New Mexico in 1940, Bloom emphasized how the "message theory" fits all the available facts:

> *. . . when Coronado was writing on July 15, he did not know [the dramatic outcome of the visit to Cíbola]—therefore, Fray Marcos had not yet returned. How, then, was Coronado able to write as he did about what Fray Marcos had found?*
>
> *If we turn to [Mendoza's] instructions, we read: "Always arrange to send news by the Indians, telling how you fare . . . and what you find. . . ." It would be exceedingly strange if Fray Marcos did not send off . . . reports to both the viceroy and*

*Coronado. . . . [Such] reports . . . can account for anything in
the Compostela letter of July 15, 1539.*

This seemed clear enough, but Carl Sauer, always ready to bash
Marcos, responded in 1941:

*I am completely at a loss to understand the interpretation
[Bloom] has read into this letter.*

Hallenbeck picked up Sauer's cudgel. In his 1949 book, Hallenbeck complains that Marcos deliberately ignored most of Mendoza's instructions. Hallenbeck lists Mendoza's instruction to send
back reports, and then says that Marcos "totally ignored" it, in spite
of Coronado's direct statement that he had received a letter from
Marcos. So Bloom's correct theory was shouted down.

If Marcos's messages back to Coronado and Mendoza explained
the rumors that began to circulate in Mexico by July of 1539, then
that demolished the widespread claim that Marcos had insufficient
time to reach Cíbola and return. I gave old Marcos a mental hand-
shake. In spite of all the conspiracy theories, it looked as if he really
did go beyond Chichilti-Calli and reach Cíbola, instead of turning
back and concocting a lie about the conclusion of his journey.

CHAPTER 12

May 5–May 7, 1539
The House of the Ancient Ones

M*ay 5.* As the sky lightened in the morning, Marcos stepped out of the door of his hut beside the burbling Nexpa stream. This was the day of departure into the countryside. The next populated area he would see would be Cíbola.

The first thing he saw here each morning as he washed in the stream was the panorama of petroglyphs on the rocky cliff across from his sandy glade. The man-lizard figure had bothered him more and more each day. It looked malevolent and demonic. Something needed to be done about it. Marcos dug in his pack and unsheathed the small iron knife that he carried with him. He splashed across the river toward the rocks.

AN HOUR LATER, MARCOS GATHERED ALL THE PEOPLE IN THE TINY village plaza. Men checked their packs; dogs barked; ten-year-old boys argued with their fathers that now they were men, old enough to make their first trip to the great land of Cíbola. The onlookers were excited, and the travelers were keen with anticipation of the impending departure, anxious to catch up with their friends who had already left with Estevan. Tall Man was there, ready to help. With Juan gone on the trail south, Tall Man had jumped to fill the position of first disciple. His smattering of Spanish had improved amazingly during the weeks of the trip.

A delegation of leaders from several local villages chatted animatedly in the plaza. Marcos whispered to Tall Man, "Some of them have come from twenty-five leagues away. Look at their enthusiasm. What an opportunity for making new friends from all over this province!"

It was time for the final ceremonies. Tall Man had erected a tall white cross in the plaza. Marcos was pleased that the natives of the Nexpa valley showed veneration for it, but in the back of his mind there was skepticism about whether they had understood his message about the true religion, or merely regarded the cross as another form of superstition. In front of the cross, Marcos expressed his thanks for the hospitality of the village, and then started reading the proper formulaic words to take possession of the land for the crown and the church. The Indians smiled and nodded among themselves as he plowed on through yet another reading of the *Requerimiento*, explaining how all Indians must pledge loyalty to the crown of Spain.

If you do so, you will do well, and we will receive you in all love and charity, and we will leave you your wives and children and lands, free without servitude, that you may do with them as you think best, freely. The King and Queen will not compel you to become Christian unless you yourselves, when informed of the truth, wish to be converted to our holy Catholic faith, as almost all the inhabitants of the other lands have done. Furthermore, their Highnesses will award you many privileges and benefits. . . .

Marcos read slowly through that section, and the Indians beamed happily and patted each other on the back. Now he speeded up his reading. This was the difficult part:

But if you do not agree to this, or maliciously delay in doing it, I certify that with the help of God we will forcefully enter your country and make war against you in all ways that we can, and subject you to the yoke and obedience of the Church and of their Highnesses. We will take you and your wives and children and make slaves of them, and will sell and dispose of them as their Highnesses may command. Also, we will take away your goods, and do you all the harm and damage that we can, as befits vassals who do not obey, or who refuse to receive their lord, resisting and contradicting him. Further, we state that the deaths and losses that you will suffer from this are your own fault, and not that of their Highnesses, or ours, or any of the soldiers that may come.

Having said this, I am notarizing in writing that I have read this notice and made the acts of possession of the land, and I ask all of you who are present to witness this.

In most villages, the Indians grew very quiet during the translation of this last section, and this village was no exception. In fact, they looked more upset than any Indians he had seen, and as Marcos finished reading, a hubbub broke out in the crowd. The local chief and several others rushed up to him, and remonstrated through the translators. "First you said your lord the king would not make us join your faith; and then you say that he will come and make war against us if we do not. We have always lived with the knowledge that the lords of Cíbola are the greatest lords of our realm. Cíbola is only nineteen days' travel away from us! How can we give allegiance to some other lord in some land far away? Estevan told us you would be our friend, but these are not the words of a friend."

Marcos had a speech ready for this eventuality. "But we *are* your friends. Let me tell you a story to show what I mean. If you find a starving man, he may be sick from lack of food. He may resist eating, but you know that he needs food to live. If he resists, you may have to do what you can to make him take the food. In the same way, we must bring you the Word of Life, and the riches of our society. You will be accepted as citizens under their Highnesses, the king. Let us teach you about this, so that you will agree of your own accord."

"But Estevan said—"

"Forget Estevan, he—"

"Wait Father," broke in Tall Man. He faced the angry chief. "Estevan, whom you admire, is a man like you who was born outside the church and outside the land of the king; but Estevan has submitted to the church and the king, and you can see that now he is a powerful lord and ambassador. I myself want to accept this bargain, and now I am happy and live in a land with many marvels that the Spaniards have brought us. And that is not all. Remember what they say, that those who accept this bargain will not disappear after they die; we will live again with our old friends, in the lands of the gods. These people bring many opportunities. You will see."

Marcos was amazed at the confident words of Tall Man, who had picked all this up from Juan. "We are making no demands on you now," Marcos said to the chief. "You will have much time to ponder these things."

The old chief mumbled in his own language, and returned to the crowd of his people.

Marcos whispered again to Tall Man. "Well done! Now watch. I am going to invite them all down to my campsite at the bend of the river."

The invitation went through the chain of translators, and the crowd moved with Marcos down the slope into the grove of cottonwoods. When they came to the river, a gasp went up from villagers. Marcos saw another frown flicker again across the face of the chief. Suddenly Marcos realized that he might have gone too far, that these rocks might have some sacred significance. But it was too late. The sinister lizard man and the sheep petroglyphs now shared the rock with the ornate Christian cross that Marcos had inscribed.

With his translators, Marcos delivered a final exhortation. "You have told me how this rock contains the symbols of your clans. My friends and I want to express our thanks, in our way, for your most gracious hospitality for these days when I have been a guest in your village. We are brothers now, and I want to add the symbol of my, um, clan, my Christian clan. This is also the symbol of our Father, the God of the Universe, who lives in the outermost sphere of the heavens. May this symbol show our friendship and may it protect your village. And now let me leave another gift for your chief." To the chief he handed a rosary and crucifix, and several strands of small colored blown-glass beads, from a supply that he carried in his own pack for such purposes. Then he added a small knife, and an iron awl, demonstrating how the knife would slice through wood as if by magic, and how the awl could punch through the thickest leather.

Marcos turned to the crowd. "These are gifts that I leave with your chief, to show that we recognize his authority in this district, and that we are friends with all of you." The people pressed forward and murmured, craning to see the gifts. "These are just some of the many things that our people will bring you."

The old man, who had seen Marcos pray with his rosary, was still frowning at the cross on the rock. At the sight of the red, blue, and white beads and the small cross, he brightened a bit. With the knife, and the kind words, and the interest of the crowd, he broke into a smile, which was mirrored throughout the throng as the villagers crowded around to see the beads and marvel at how the knife worked.

There was no time to do more. Cíbola beckoned.

An hour later, with laughter, drums, flashes of blue turquoise, and waves to those left behind, Marcos's party of travelers was on the trail before the sun was two lance-lengths high.

IN THE EVENING, AT A CAMP NEAR A SMALL, FITFUL STREAM, TALL Man came to him. Marcos was startled when he emerged from the shadows cast by Marcos's small fire.

Tall Man said nothing at first. Then he spoke hesitantly. "This northern country is very strange for me. You look at these river valleys and say they are good, but to me the country mostly looks empty. There are not as many trees on the hills as we have, back in the region of Petatlán."

Marcos was not surprised at Tall Man's pensive mood. "I understand. I too, grew up in a different country with more trees and flowers. Each country I have seen is different from the others. It is as if God has many different workshops."

"The world is very big," said Tall Man, "bigger than I imagined. At night I can see that the moon and stars here are the same as in my homeland, but by day, I see that everything else is different. The stars and the emptiness of this country make me want to speak about life—about God and His plans."

Marcos stared into the fire, not meeting Tall Man's eyes. If Tall Man spoke this way, he must be driving at something. Marcos did not want to break the mood. "Yes, go on."

"When I grew up, many things were taught to us by our elders. We learned about our gods, and how the seasons unfolded, and how the world was created. There was a natural order of animals and clans and peoples, and a natural order of those who ruled and those who served. These things had been true among our people for as long as anyone remembered. Now, all those truths have been swept away. The Christian, Guzmán, came and took away many of our people. Former lords among our people now are servants."

"Listen, Tall Man. A great man of the past, named Aristotle, said that some people are naturally servants. Many of our people believe that."

"Do you think that is true?"

"I . . . I don't know. Many things puzzle me, too. I think some of us are called to teach them, or to rule. . . ."

Tall Man reflected on this. "I want to confess something to you."

"Go on."

"The other night, when Juan was telling his story about Mexico, I was out in the shadows, listening. I understand his Spanish now. I could understand how he felt."

"And?"

"Great buildings have been swept away. Moctezuma is gone, and all his court. Then Cortés became ruler. Then Cortés was deposed and the man you call Viceroy is ruler. Only the stars remain the same. I think it is the end of the world. Do you think it is the end of the world?"

"The end of the world will come one day, and when it does, Jesus Christ will come to save us. But that is not for us to worry about today. We must think about how to live. I will teach you more about this. You can be accepted into the church, and—"

Tall Man interrupted. "I talked to Estevan during this trip. He says it was the same for him. He was rooted up like a plant taken from the ground. First he was taken into Spain and later to our world here. His world ended, too. I feel like Estevan is my brother."

Marcos frowned at this. Estevan was not necessarily a good role model.

Tall Man continued. "It seems to me that in our times, the world has gone out of control and even the gods are losing power. It was not this way in the past, when my grandfather was alive. That is why I think the world must be coming to an end in our generation."

"Listen, my son. Even for me the world has changed. Before I was born, none of our people knew about this New World. There was only the Old World. Now there are two worlds." Marcos added a few small sticks to the fire. "Like you, when I grew up, I thought the order of the world was fixed. But now, I see that it changes continuously. A change is not the end of the world, but just the start of something new. I have pondered, what could cause this continuous change? Why is the world not peaceful? I have come to understand it is because of the contest between greed and contentment. This war constantly renews itself. I have seen it happen. If there is too much greed, people will begin to long for contentment, and try to find a calmer way. But when there is too much contentment, the greedy will find fertile fields to sow their own schemes, and take advantage of the others. That creates new inequalities, new rulers, and new slaves. So the world keeps changing in cycles, like the seasons. Some people live in cycles of contentment and some in cycles of greed. God is the spirit Who gives us inner peace to rise above this war, as if we were looking down on it from a mountain."

"You speak of bringing us inner peace, but this reminds me of our story of the snake and the mouse. The snake and the mouse argued about how to live together. The snake told the mouse: 'We must each be content with our lot and then there will be peace.' So the mouse agreed to live with the snake. But when the snake finished proclaiming peace and contentment, the mouse found that he was inside the snake. Only the snake now had inner peace."

Marcos managed a reluctant smile.

They were quiet for a time, looking at the stars. Tall Man jumped visibly when a shooting star sailed quietly across the sky.

"Let me ask the question again in a different way," he said. "What makes your people go to all this trouble to cross the seas and suffer hardships in order to destroy my people? What drives them onward? What makes you, as a man, want to take this long march to Cíbola through this desolate country? Why do you not be calm, live in peace as you say you wish to do, and stay in your church and worship God, and let other people be?"

"Tall Man, my son . . ." Marcos began. This discussion was turning difficult. He was silent for another moment. One thing he liked about these Indian people, they would have their say and then wait patiently while you formulated an answer. They were not like Spaniards, especially Viceroy Mendoza, Bishop Zumárraga, Governor Vázquez de Coronado, and the other officials, who were always interrupting and trying to turn an argument to their advantage. "My son, you have asked difficult questions. Let us ponder these questions and speak of them tomorrow." Secretly, Marcos had been asking himself some of the same questions.

MAY 6. THE TRAIL STRETCHED LIKE A RIBBON OVER THE BARREN brown hills. Prickly-pear cactus dotted the slopes. As they walked along, Marcos reflected that he had been putting off the talk with Tall Man about his questions. Tall Man was as patient as a rock. Sometimes they would exchange glances. Many of the Indians seemed to have an almost supernatural ability to communicate without words; the right glance, with a little nod, would seem to convey the message, "I am still waiting for you to answer my questions."

Tall Man's questions had been almost too personal. How could he answer? Tall Man was on a slippery path of doubt about the world. He seemed to be asking merely academic questions, like the old philosophers, but he was really questioning the divine rights of Rome and Spain to be colonizing the New World. This question had merit, but could lead quickly to mortal sin. An answer was needed that would turn Tall Man away from dangerous doubts, and at the same time give him some glimpse of the honest optimism Marcos felt about the future of these lands.

THAT NIGHT, TALL MAN JOINED MARCOS AT THE FIRE AGAIN, AS IF by agreement.

"Have you come to talk about your questions?"

"Yes, Father."

"I have been thinking about these issues. You know that you have been treated well, ever since I arrived with the viceroy's order to stop the slave raiding and free your people. Isn't that right?"

"Yes."

"These bad things you speak of, the slavery and killing, I have seen them happen in other countries of this New World. My Spanish friends are Christians, but they are also men, and their first instinct is to take whatever will make them rich, and then put the weaker peoples to work for them. That servitude is what you called the end of the world—the end of *your* world. Even if it is wrong, it is not the end of the whole world. We must work to improve the world that is left."

A cold night breeze was descending on them from the hills. Tall Man shuddered involuntarily in the dancing shadows cast by the fire.

"On this trip, our first duty is to the viceroy, who is under the king, who is under God. That is the first answer to your question about why we come to your lands. We must never put our own questions or desires in front of that duty."

Marcos paused, readying his thoughts as the fire faded slowly. "But there is more. We Franciscans have a certain vision of what may come from our efforts. A tree may fall because a man wields an ax. The use of the ax is the first cause for the event. But think further. The man who wields the ax may do so because he wants to build a house. That is the second cause, which is behind the first cause. Do you understand? In public, we speak only of the first cause, since the second cause is hidden in mens' minds."

"Tell me about the second cause. I want to understand."

"You have heard Juan speak of our marquis, Cortés, who conquered Mexico. He wants to conquer these lands. He thinks only of his own glory and is not a true friend of the king. So we must help the viceroy undertake the conquest. You yourself have seen that the viceroy wants the Indians to be free, to give willing submission to the crown and the church. That is why Francisco Vázquez de Coronado, the new governor, freed the Indians of Petatlán from the power of Guzmán. The viceroy will spread freedom and law from Petatlán to Cíbola, and establish fair commerce between our people. He will want the treasures of Cíbola, but not by deceit, as Cortés practiced in Mexico. Or so I believe. He will apply only the minimum force that is necessary, and let us pray that it is none. At the same time, the church will be a partner. Our Bishop Zumárraga, who rules our church in Mexico, has discussed these matters with the viceroy and my churchly brothers. We all seek a way for traders, settlers, priests, and the Indian peoples to exist in harmony. They have read learned books about how to accomplish this.

"There is no way to stop new settlers from arriving. If the king himself made a decree, 'No one shall go north, and there shall be no contact with Cíbola,' there would be a rush of thieves and adventurers who would go just to see what they were missing. So if we do not succeed, bad men, like Cortés, may get here first, and they will bring back the ways of Guzmán. This injustice is what I want to avoid. This is what I called our second cause. But mark me well, there are dangers in speaking too freely about these things, because there are many political intrigues among powerful men in Mexico. It is easy to make enemies there."

Tall Man kept his silence for a long time, as if to show that he understood the last remark. Finally he said, "Perhaps you are right, but I still do not understand what will happen next, or what will come out of all this striving to find treasures in Cíbola." Then Tall Man fell silent.

"Nobody ever knows what will happen next," said Marcos.

They stirred the remains of the fire and watched the last sparks ascend and blow among the stars.

MAY 7. ON THE THIRD DAY OF TRAVEL EASTWARD FROM THE Nexpa, Marcos's party passed among some low, bush-studded hills and entered the west side of a broad, dry valley. In the foothills they found some springs and a little pond with a few trees clustered around, standing like courtiers outside the door of the viceroy's offices. Farther down the weedy slopes were yuccas, as tall as man, crowned by radiating spiky leaves. They turned north up the valley, a shallow plain, lacking a central river or the usual central avenue of tall cottonwoods. Azure, saw-toothed mountains ringed the horizon.

In the last two days they had seen the scraggly smoke of only three campfires in the distant hills. "We have not yet entered the *despoblado*," his guides said. "That comes in another day."

The mountains ahead of them, on the north and east, were higher than the others. The sierra curved west to block their path. As they approached, he could see the forested upper slopes. The guides conferred with the translators. "They say the top of those mountains turn white in winter. At the top is a province of strange spirits. Good people stay away from there."

In the afternoon, the party turned upslope along a drainage into the grassy foothills. Tall Man relayed a speech from the guides. "Now is the time when we will show you a wonder. Long ago, before our grandfathers were born, there were years of strange portents. The rivers ran too deep to cross, and in other years they ran not at all. In those days, the people were restless, and strangers moved into this land from the north, the direction of Cíbola. They had new religions and new ways of building. They did not build simple huts such as you saw in our village, but big houses of mud and timber and stone, impossible to take down and move. These houses were two and three stories high, with thick walls and great plazas. Those buildings were like cousins of the ones in Cíbola, right here in our own land!

"In some areas, the newcomers offered to teach us things, as you did, and they moved into our villages. In other areas, they stayed aloof. But then, in the times of our great-great-grandfathers, these people overstayed their welcome and left our land. Some say their religion was evil, a foreign religion." Marcos eyed the man telling this story, but there seemed to be no hidden implication. "They say our ancestors drove some of them away," the translators went on. "After they left this land, the great houses remained empty. Tonight you will see such a building. The traders who travel on this route call it Chichilti-Calli, the Red House."

Marcos's eyes lit up. At last he would have his first glimpse of the much-heralded architecture of the north.

From the floor of the valley they continued up into the low hills of the pediment, following a little stream that ran out of the mountains. At last, the sinking sun was at their back, casting an amber glow that turned the mountain ahead of them an unearthly, coppery orange. They were coming around a bend in the drainage when the guide said, "Look."

Ahead of them, rising out of the shadows like a mysterious castle beyond the scattered bushes and yuccas, was a huge wall, four times taller than a man, with its top glowing red in the fading sun. Rows of second-floor windows made dark, mysterious apertures. Great *viga* beams stuck out of the sides. Here it was, the house of the ancient strangers, the "people who went before us," as his Indian guides called them—the place where the spirits of the ancient ones could still be felt. Chichilti-Calli. Truly, compared to any of the brush huts and rude plastered mud shrines he had seen in this land, this was a palace, a fortress.

As they got closer, they could see it was in ruins. The main part of the building had risen two stories, possibly three. The roof had fallen in; huge beams had become dislodged where the wood had decayed at one end; the beams angled down to the floor at crazy angles. The walls had been built of ocher adobe and stones, and coated with red plaster. As the sun dropped below the mountaintop behind them, Chichilti-Calli shimmered with an uncanny red light, like glowing blood.

"You see why it is called the Red House," one of the translators said to him, through Tall Man. "It is in the language of the south, where winter never comes."

There was more to the building than he had first thought. The two-storied section ran on for many room-widths. Running at right angles to the main structure was another large wing that had been a block of one-story rooms, so that the whole structure had an L shape that bounded two sides of a plaza. The rest of the plaza was surrounded by a low wall, half as tall as a man, with a few poorer-looking, decaying structures on the inside of the wall here and there. In the distance were several other broken-down structures.

The Indians began putting down their loads at a distance from the walls, and slaking their thirst in the nearby stream. Marcos, who was never allowed to carry anything on the trail, already felt invigorated and refreshed by the sight of this treasure, and without even pausing to drink, he paced off the sides of the building and discovered the main plaza complex was roughly one hundred twenty paces on a side. On all sides, the adobelike plastering of the walls was moldering under the sun and rain, melting around the stones and wooden beams, almost as if made of wax.

At the campsite near the stream, one of the guides told him, "Here is where we have camped for generations. Refresh yourself. Tomorrow we cross through that pass to the north, and reach the beginning of the *despoblado*."

"Why do you not camp inside, out of the wind?"

"To stay in the house would not be respectful to the spirits of the ancient ones. Besides," his informant smiled knowingly, "the walls are not very stable."

Marcos looked through the portals into the dark rooms. He tried to ignore the pagan superstitions, yet the dark, silent interiors suddenly looked more ominous.

His Indian friends unearthed some rolls of reed matting material that had been stashed in storage bins, built by the ancients into the inside walls of some of the outlying rooms. In moments, they had erected a framework of poles and a rude hut for Marcos. "This is where you will sleep. But now, let us eat together, and you can tell us more stories of your kingdom called heaven and the men you call saints."

MARCOS HAD TROUBLE SLEEPING, AND IN THE PREDAWN HOURS HE rose to take a walk around the ancient building. He stayed at a respectful distance. No sense irritating his new traveling companions. It was the dark of the moon, but the sky was ablaze with stars and the crumbling walls were silhouetted against the Milky Way. The windows of the upper stories looked like mysterious eyes, watching him. His initial excitement about the site was now at war with second thoughts, which he tried to fight off. On the one hand, if the people who had come from the northern lands could build massive houses like this, at least two stories tall, which looked so imposing even in their ruination, then there was no telling what grand palaces might exist today in Cíbola itself. He visualized rich castles of stone and timber, with the jewel-encrusted doorways that the Indians had described. But on the other hand, if you really looked at this building objectively . . . The devil whispered in his ear that it was only an old decaying edifice of mud, a far cry from the mighty stone pyramids and bejeweled temples of the Mexica or the Incas.

Having heard that devil's voice, he looked among the scattered debris on the ground for clues about the people who built such buildings. Over a wide area were fragments of fine, polished pottery, brightly painted in red, white, and black, far better than the pottery used by the Indians of these parts. Yet in all the cast-off refuse, he saw not a single metal implement, let alone gold. He searched around the doors and plaza walls, remembering that he had been told how Cíbolans put turquoise or other jewels in their doorways; he found nothing but mud.

The building had a dark, brooding attitude. What events had transpired here? All these fragments. . . . Hundreds of lives. . . . Generations who had lived and dreamed, traded and built. . . . Generations of people without the word of Jesus Christ? It made no sense. According to the Bible, even the Old Testament days had been a part of God's plan, preparing the way for His Son. But there was nothing in the Bible about generations of people living on the other side of the world, completely outside the plan. How did they fit in? Why was the world so much bigger and richer than had been described in the scriptures?

Marcos had an eerie feeling, wrestling with these thoughts. It was as if Satan's agents were hiding behind the building. He breathed a strange prayer, that he had never voiced before: "Oh Lord, let me understand."

There was a noise in the gravel behind him. Marcos whirled around in fright.

It was Tall Man, materializing like a ghost. "Are you all right, Father?"

"I can't sleep."

"It is because this place is haunted by the spirits of the old ones. I've been talking to the people who came with us from the Nexpa villages. They like this place because it is the last place in the warm, level lands before we go across the mountains. But they also say it is a place of many portents."

"Did Estevan stay here?"

"Oh yes. He camped here about eight or ten days ago. They say everyone camps here on the road to Cíbola."

They walked farther around the building in silence.

"Tall Man?"

"Yes, Father."

"Why do the villagers along the way always love Estevan? Why does he exert such power over them?"

"It is because he talks to them as a brother, not as a father," Tall Man said pointedly. "And also—this is what they tell me—the women love him."

"That will be his undoing. It is unseemly."

"But Father, between you and me, you cannot deny the love of women for a strong man, or the other way around. Why do you get so upset about this?"

Marcos harumphed. "God's laws are clear about the relations of men and women."

"Estevan says God's laws are not always what you say they are."

"Estevan grew up as an infidel! He pretends to be Christianized, but his faith is flawed by his background."

"I learned a story about Estevan. On the trail, I was talking to one of the men from the Nexpa Valley."

"Yes? Go on."

"This man had a sister, who became enamored of Estevan when he arrived in the last village. They stayed together several days while he waited for you in the village. Later, she went on the trail with him as far as here because she wanted to be with him."

"You see what I mean? This is unseemly and licentious behavior."

"Why? He says his sister is a beautiful woman!"

Marcos did not deign to reply.

"My friend says that his sister told him many things about Estevan. He did something here that impressed everyone. He had brought a shirt of quilted cotton armor from the south and a Spanish headpiece of iron. He said these could protect him from the blows of any enemy. But when he reached Chichilti-Calli, he made a speech. He said that in all the journey from Mexico, he had encountered only friends, and now as they entered the last *despoblado* to the auspicious land of Cíbola, there could be no disputes or dangers, and he knew the journey would be crowned with success and friendship. So he would not need his defensive armor anymore. And so, even though his headpiece had much magic, he took it and went up into a cave in the hills and made a shrine of rocks, in which he buried the headpiece."

"What was the point of that?"

"This was a gesture to the people. He had come with his protective armor, but now that he met them, he knew he did not need armor anymore. He told no one where he left this material, not even the man's sister. He said he made a holy shrine, and as long as it was undisturbed, our peoples would be friends. I am telling you this story for a reason. Estevan won over the people with this shrine to our friendship. But when you came, you read the *Requerimiento*, and talked about how the king would make war on the people if they did not obey. That was very different from Estevan, who asked nothing but good will. So you see, your attitude is important, and edicts may not be the best way."

"But it is not mere attitudes that are important here. We are talking about the will of God and the rule of law, which must reign regardless of people's feelings."

Tall Man shrugged.

LATER, AS THE SUN ROSE AND THE CAMPERS GEARED UP FOR THE day's march, Marcos paced up and down around the walls of the building, thinking. As the sun gained some height, a glint in the soil caught his eye. He poked with his walking stick, and overturned a small, beautifully shaped bell of copper, the size of his thumbnail. At last—he had his own confirmation that the people who built these buildings had metal. Encouraged, he continued his rounds, eyes always on the ground. In one spot he found a beautifully made pendant of black stone, carved in the form of a bird. In the shadow of the building walls, he found a little pile of turquoise beads, perhaps where a necklace had fallen generations before and the cord decayed. The beautiful beads were more finely shaped than the lumpy nuggets worn by the local villagers. Was this a harbinger of what would be found in the north?

In two weeks he would know the truth about the kingdom of Cíbola.

The sunlight gathered strength. Sunlight, like the light of God, dispelled his doubts.

PART II

CITIES OF INTRIGUE

The Spaniards subjected the great Mexican Empire to the Catholic monarchs of Castilla. . . . God had clearly promised this land to them, through the prophet Isaiah, who said "Make room for thy tent, stretch wide the curtains of thy dwelling places. . . . Right and left shalt thou spread, till thy race dispossesses the heathens and peoples their ruined cities. . . ."

I know no place where these words are so completely fulfilled as in the New World. There, they lead to happiness and redemption among many souls whom the devil had otherwise controlled. What else can be meant by these words, which announce that Christianity must extend not only to walled cities and splendid buildings, but also to nations that live in tents and in the fields?

Andrés Pérez de Ribas
Jesuit Priest, 1645
Rationalizing the European settlement of Sinaloa,
Sonora, and the northern lands.
In History of the Triumphs of our Holy Faith Among the Most Barbarous and Fierce Peoples of the New World, *Ch. VII.*

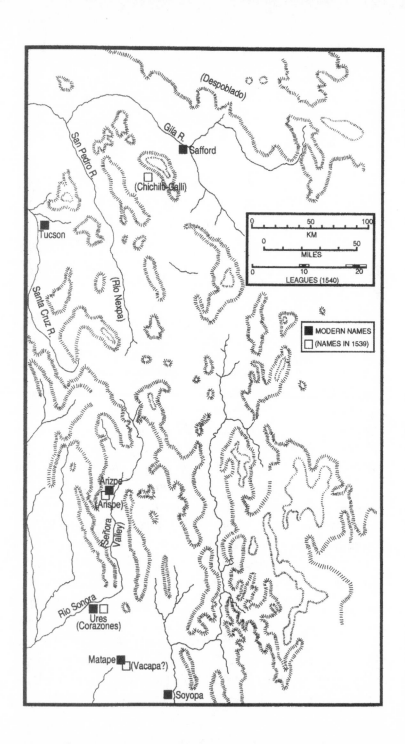

CHAPTER 13

May–June, 1989
Paydirt

May 15. Excitement grew in the office. The board of supervisors' hearing was only a week away. In the letters-to-the-editor page of the newspaper, rhetoric was intensifying on both sides. I had noticed that human passions expand to fill whatever vacuum is available; it's the principle that keeps soap operas and the NFL on the air. But Mr. Rooney had said he had the votes, so where was the suspense? I had great confidence; he always got what he wanted.

In the car on the way to lunch, I was trying to explain to Phaedra why the work on Marcos continued to seem so important. "If I resigned from the company today, somebody else would take my job. But with my Marcos research, it's like I'm the only one doing it."

She stared at me while we pulled into the Casa Molina parking lot. "You're thinking of quitting?"

"No, no. I just mean I'm the only one who's seeing these things in the old records."

"That's 'cause you're the only one who thinks they're interesting."

I ignored that. She meant it as a joke. "Besides, when I was out there at the ruin, it's as if I heard this voice in my ear: We're using up our history the same way we are using up our oil."

"What's that mean?"

"I'm just trying to tell you how it feels, getting into this stuff."

"Well, don't let Mr. Rooney hear you say things like that." She straightened her dress as she got out of the car. "Go publish a history paper if you want to, but don't live in the past." Then she laughed for no particular reason.

Good old Phaedra. For her, the world had dependable rules. Go to work each day. Bring in that paycheck. Help care for Amber. Her life made me realize the fewer people who depend on you, the longer-term view you can afford to have. For me, the world was in flux, according to century-long cycles. According to my newfound theology of history, only a long-term perspective could help you understand what was really happening.

Still, to go from the abstract to the concrete, it was Phaedra's spirit and body that gave me hope. I liked the unpredictable way she reacted to what I said, and the way her laugh lit up her face.

MR. ROONEY CALLED ME IN. "TONY BEECHER WANTS YOU TO HELP him some more with the history. He's gotta be ready to argue *either* side of the argument. On the one hand, we've got a quality plan with a Coronado pedigree; we'll preserve this important ruin and have a historical center, and its good for everybody—local economy, etc. etc. But on the other hand, if the environmentalists start to sell the idea that the site is *too* historic, and we should be denied our zoning, then Tony has to be ready to argue the other side—the real Chichi ruin could have been somewhere else and our ruin isn't unique or important. You're the one who understands the evidence. Work with Tony on it."

I didn't like his idea that there were two alternate sets of historical evidence and I told him so. "The truth is the truth. We got a ruin, we don't know if it's the right one. Period."

"Yeah, well, spin."

"Pardon?"

"Spin is the key to success. Clockwise or counterclockwise. Phaedra tells me you like the library. Go get Tony a list of all the other ruins you can find, especially the ones that have already been excavated—so Tony can argue that we've already got whatever information these places can yield. Add as many references as you can. Every book you breathed on. Make a list. Pile it on. Tony says the more scholarly, the better. He'll know how to use it."

Ordering me back to the library was like throwing Br'er Rabbit into the briar patch.

IF MARCOS'S TRIP BEGAN ON THE DAY OF OUR SOLAR ECLIPSE IN Tucson, it reached its climax during another time of omens. On Wednesday, May 17, Marcos was approaching Cíbola, assuming he told the truth, and Gorbachev was visiting China. Three thousand Chinese students gathered in Beijing to protest Communist Party strictures. Something big was brewing, although it was still in the inner pages of the paper. The front page headline was CONGRESS APPROVES $4.55 WAGE. BUSH READIES INSTANT VETO.

By Friday, May 19, the Beijing demonstration had spread to a million people and the government of China was trying to cajole the students. "Beijing has fallen into a kind of anarchy," a high minister told them. "Think it over. . . . The government can't show restraint forever." This story was still on the inside pages. The front page was about our local war between sprawl and restraint. Rooney Development was fighting this war on the eastern front, but the lead story was about another battle on the northern front, in a sleepy little town called Marana. The headline told the tale: MARANA OKS HIGH DENSITY NEAR SAGUARO NATIONAL MONUMENT. A different group of developers—not Mr. Rooney—had invested in elections in Marana, just north of Tucson. They backed some handpicked candidates for town council and the investment paid off. The council was now packed with progrowth operatives. Fronting for the developers, they promptly annexed huge regions, extending octopuslike arms across the intervening county landscape, into the north edge of Tucson. This was permitted by the Arizona constitution, which conveniently exempted all city land from county zoning ordinances, under the theory that local government is best. Through this ploy, the developers, operating through the Marana

town council, could zone the land as they pleased, without following any of the county restrictions. Cars would soon pour from the
duchy of Marana onto Tucson streets, and the developers wouldn't
have to pay a dime toward maintaining Tucson's infrastructure. It
was a neat scam. It made me uncomfortable. I was one of *them.*

On Saturday, the Beijing demonstrations finally reached the
front page as the Chinese army moved in. But it was a false alarm;
it died down again. Gorbachev, trying to restructure the Russian
economy, offered to reduce Soviet aid to Latin America, but again
U.S. officials dismissed it as some kind of trick. Vice President
Quayle said Gorbachev was "a bit of a phony" for putting forth
such proposals.

By Wednesday the 23rd, the front page was back to normal:
OFFICIAL CAUGHT IN MIDDLE OF HERMOSILLO VOTE-FRAUD SCANDAL
in central Sonora.

WEDNESDAY, MAY 24. THE DAY OF OUR HEARING. MARCOS
should now be reaching Cíbola. The headline said that the Tucson
water utility had shut down three water wells on the east side of
town because the ground water was polluted. Tony Beecher was
afraid someone would drag this out as a new argument against our
development, but the hearing itself was an anticlimax. I watched
from the back row as it unfolded like a well-rehearsed play. Phaedra
sat in the front row, with one of her most killer dresses, on Mr.
Rooney's right hand. The five supervisors, all male, were aware of
her; I think they would have voted for us just to get a smile from
her. The audience included a lot of environmentalists, hikers, and
neighborhood activists. Some of them glared knowingly at Phaedra.

Beecher's eloquent speech made the opposition sound like wild-
eyed fanatics—little old ladies in tennis shoes, housewives, butt-
inskies meddling in the legitimate business of Polvoroso County. A
question should be raised, he implied, about the appropriateness of
these people taking up the time of this busy board; in essence they
had no legal standing in the case, because they had no investment
in or near the area to be developed. The supes listened reverently.

Beecher flirted masterfully with their egos. This was his real job. Zoning, he reminded them, was business to be conducted among elected and appointed officials and community leaders—the viceroy and the aristocratic court officials, so to speak.

When it came time for the audience to speak, a number of them pointed out that, after all, the point of a public hearing was to hear the public. They lambasted our plan with emotional tirades about losing pristine natural desert grasslands—which had its own bizarre twist, since the land in question had been ranched for a century and the pristine grasslands that Marcos saw had long since been consumed by cows. But everyone believes "pristine nature" is whatever they saw when they were kids. The activists' impassioned rhetorical excesses made the supes uncomfortable, and made Tony Beecher sound like an unbiased legal scholar.

Surprisingly, there was little participation in the hearing from the ranching community in the Sulfur Springs Valley itself. Their absence was cited by more than one supervisor as proof that the silent majority favored economic development around the struggling towns of Willcox and Benson. I didn't understand the logic, but that's what they said. After a brief pantomime of profound deliberation, they gave Mr. Rooney the majority vote he already knew he had.

THURSDAY, MAY 25. EVERYBODY CELEBRATED IN THE OFFICE. Champagne corks popped and Mr. Rooney himself went around filling our glasses. Somebody was slapping me on the back; "Good job, Mr. Scott!" It was Mr. Beecher, acting like he was going to make me a partner in the firm.

I tried to get into the spirit of things, because it was a doubly big day for me. "I propose a toast," I said over the merriment. "Marcos de Niza also made it to his goal on this date. Here's to Marcos!"

"*If* he made it," said Mr. Rooney, who had read the whole report.

"Here's to the friar-liar," one of the tipsy marketing department people chimed in. "Author of the best ad campaign in history!"

"Ha, ha." Everybody laughed.

"It's nice to see you having fun," Phaedra said, but I noticed that she spent some time after that drinking with some of Mr. Rooney's junior lawyers. Nonetheless, a bunch of us went out for a big dinner and Phaedra ended up staying with me that night. It was a wonderful night, a Tucson night full of love and the fragrance of the last of the orange blossoms.

AS THE EARTH TURNED, F. SCOTT FITZGERALD'S CURRENTS BORE all of us on ceaselessly past the Rincon Mountains, into the east, toward Chichilti-Calli, night after night. In the last days of May, some of the more tolerant Chinese Party officials began to negotiate with the students. Then the liberal appeasers were arrested by the hardliners. In Moscow, Gorbachev was making troop cuts. The May 28 headline said President Bush was trying to figure out how to respond.

Each day, the sun rose higher into the transparent sky, blazing down on Arizona. Thus began the time of year when, if you stepped outdoors, you could really believe you were less than a hundred million miles from an honest-to-God star, a thermonuclear blast furnace irradiating you with raw photons of infrared, white glare, and hard UV slipping through the no-longer-dependable ozone layer. Rooney Development's air conditioning kept the offices so cold that it actually felt good stepping out into nature's oven to walk to the car. I wondered why Marcos didn't complain about the heat. In the river valleys, he could have walked in cool water, like Phaedra and I did during our hike, but once he left the rivers, he would have been out in the sun and dust all day. Tough bird. Maybe the Great Outdoors seemed more normal in the days before air-conditioning.

WEDNESDAY, MAY 31. PEACE WAS THREATENING THE STATUS quo, in spite of the doubts of U.S. officials. GORBACHEV TAKES UNPRECEDENTED STEP: REVEALS SOVIET DEFENSE SPENDING TO OPEN DIALOG WITH WEST, the headline said. The Cold War was winding down, God was in his Heaven, and all was A-Okay in the province of Chichilti-Calli. Nobody cared anymore about Marcos or ruins, and Coronado was discussed only as a brand name, like Ford, de Soto, Hudson, or Cadillac. We were now consumed with questions of drainage and sales of franchises. But more news from the past was on its way.

A letter arrived from my friend Edward, in Alamos, Sonora. Edward had been asking more questions. The old priest of the town, who had been there as long as anyone could remember, had allowed Edward's friend, Father Antonio, to clean out some dusty storerooms in one of the old churches in a nearby village. Antonio had found chests where some earlier master of the church had stored early records. *Lots* of records, carefully wrapped in leather packets, separated according to different generations and priestly dynasties. Some of the stuff was 1600s and a few pieces went back to the 1500s. Maybe there would be something I'd be interested in. Even if there was nothing as early as Marcos and Coronado, it might have something about the routes used at that time. He thought I should come and have a look. He'd put me up.

I called him at the number he gave. Or rather, I had Phaedra put through the call. It took her half a day of trying to get through. When she succeeded, I took the call in my little office. As soon as I heard him, I recognized his old enthusiasm. "You gotta come. We'll look at that stuff together and we'll sit in bars and talk about it."

"Have you seen the documents?"

"Well, no, but Father Antonio has."

"Why do we have any reason to think there would be stuff about the Coronado period? That was before Alamos was settled. Anything from that period would be in Mexico City, or at Coronado's headquarters in Compostela. Or Culiacán. Not Alamos."

"I only know what they told me. But you gotta understand about Alamos. It was on the main route. People going north used to come through here. Your pal, Marcos, for example."

"Marcos was further over toward the coast. He described islands—"

"Look. You wanna hear about this stuff or not?" He started telling me more about Alamos. It was a bustling Spanish town by the 1600s, a stop on the *Camino Real*, the King's Highway to the north. By the early 1900s, it was nearly abandoned, in ruins. In the 1950s and '60s, Americans looking for contentment bought decaying eighteenth-century Spanish haciendas and began restoring them. "Antonio thinks that when Alamos was being established, the settlers brought copies of the earlier information about the area. But why speculate? Come and look. You're the expert, not me. The old priest is pretty protective of this stuff. But if Antonio puts it to him that an expert from El Norte is coming down here to look at it, he'll open up."

"I'm not an expert. I mean, I don't have any great academic credentials."

"The priests here don't know that. Leave it to me. I'll set up a meeting."

I told Phaedra about it. "You should ask Mr. Rooney to let you go," she said. "He's in a good mood. He's encouraging people to take a few days vacation here and there. Not me, of course. He needs me." She gave me a coquettish smile.

Privately, I knew treasure hunts usually turn out to be wild goose chases, but if Mr. Rooney would spring for it, I was ready for a vacation after that zoning hearing.

THE NEXT DAY MY OPPORTUNITY CAME ON A SILVER PLATTER. Mr. Rooney called me in to tell me what a good job I'd done, preparing things for the hearing. He brought up the vacation himself. I told him about Edward and said I'd thought about going down to Mexico to look at the old papers. Maybe there'd be something about the route to Cíbola. A long shot, yes, but we might find something to confirm that Coronado and the boys passed right across our town.

"Yeah, but it might prove they didn't. Then what?"

"We still know we're in the right general area, and you could get fantastic press coverage for sponsoring original research into the history of the area."

"Hell, if you find evidence they were far away, it might even help us in the long run. This ancient ruin thing almost got out of hand." Rooney pondered for a minute. "It's not a bad idea, Alamos. Nice town. Funky old Spanish architecture. I got a friend with a ranch down there. Actually put some money into our project."

He stared out the window at the mountain for a long time. "I also got a bunch of Arizona investors I wanna keep happy. We could take them for a junket. Hunting. Deer. Get away from home, you know? We get enough of them together, we can get a cheap non-stop flight. Rifles, they can supply on the ranch. All kinds of good hunting down there, know what I mean?"

I wasn't sure I knew what he meant but I didn't want to rock the boat.

"You could all stay on the ranch."

"This guy I know, Edward, he wants to put me up for free."

"Just a couple of days," he told me. "I'm not sponsoring a damn open-ended goose chase. Oh, listen. Phaedra says you're a good photographer. She says you can do anything." He winked. "So bring back a bunch of pictures of the architecture. Sonoran heritage stuff. Facades. Walls. Gardens. Something we can use for ambience in the sales office. And listen. Have some fun when you're down there. Phaedra says you're too serious."

He stopped me just as I was heading out the door. "Oh, you don't have to go hunting with my pals. You don't look like the hunting type. Just look at your old records, or whatever, and get those photos. Phaedra will tell you when we get the flight set up. Hey, Phaedra, come in here!"

IN TUCSON I USED TO LISTEN TO THE NPR STATION WHEN I DROVE home each day. An island of quality in a sea of sell. Congress was trying to close them down because they were supported by tax money. That day, KUAT-FM was playing music by the Mexican composer, Revueltas. I tried to get in the groove for my impending holiday, but the more I listened, the more I heard a disturbing undertone. Revueltas wrote scary music.

* * *

FRIDAY MORNING, JUNE 2. AT THE TUCSON AIRPORT I ARRIVED AT
one of those baby terminals alongside the grown-up terminals. Arizona Sunways ran a flight direct to Ciudad Obregon, at the south
end of Sonora. A counter sold last-minute candy bars and Cokes
that were dangerous, since Arizona Sunways' little flying cigar had
no restroom on its flight of 1 1/2 hours, urinal-to-urinal.

At the terminal, Mr. Rooney's investor cronies showed up,
ready for their weekend trip. I hadn't met them before. They were
mostly upper middle-aged, aging poorly. With them was Freddy
the Fixer and three of Mr. Rooney's staff; salesmen, I think. Freddy
was entertaining the investors but he came over to me just before
we boarded the plane. "I told you you'd like this job," he said.
Three women were also traveling with us. Not middle-aged, if you
get my drift. I suppose there were a dozen in the party.

In the air, I could hear a couple of Mr. Rooney's friends talking
in the next seats. "This thing sure as hell better go through fast.
Rooney talked me into tying up five hundred K in it. I can't afford
to have it drag out."

I tried to follow the route on my Sonora map. The map had
white map syndrome. It been published in Mexico, so Arizona
was white and nearly blank, with only a few town names. Tucson,
and towns I never heard of: Lowell, Charleston, Stein, towns that
died a hundred years ago, but were kept alive in some Mexican
map bureau. Mapmakers, as anal-retentive as accountants, don't
keep up with the news on the other side of their own particular
national border. On the Sonora side, the map was more helpful.
Arizpe, descended from the Indian town mentioned by Coronado's chroniclers, lay ahead, straddling the green ribbon of the
Sonora River.

The drug dealers and the bereaved families of the recent murder
victims were down there somewhere, but you can't see pain from
an airplane. In the eastern distance were the peaks of the Sierra
Madre, dark and formidable. The Spanish route had to lie between
them and the bright, barren coastline to the west. The landscape
below was smiling, open country, cut here and there by rivers bor-

dered with checkerboards of green, fields barely altered from the irrigated plots of the people Marcos met.

By June 2, whatever had happened to Marcos in his quest for Cíbola had already happened. Marcos himself was somewhere down there, heading back home. I looked but I couldn't see him. We were both heading south under our boss's orders. Eventually I spotted the sharp bend in the Sonora River, where it changes from east-west to a north-south valley in a narrow canyon. That gorge was the one that Cabeza de Vaca called the passageway between the inland and the coast, and was also the one that Coronado's soldiers called the gateway to the north. It meant that the lost village of Corazones was somewhere down there in my field of view. Within two hours I was covering a distance that cost Marcos and Coronado weeks of marching.

THE REST OF THE TRIP IS VIVID IN MY MEMORY. WE LANDED IN Ciudad Obregon. At the airport, two customs officers lined up our luggage, and pursued their nineteenth-century ritual of stamping and frowning. I tried to imagine what global chaos would ensue if these little papers weren't stamped and filed.

Beyond the *migración* desk, two chauffeur-driven cars showed up for the mighty hunters. There, behind the chauffeurs, was my old buddy Edward, tall, tan, relaxed, with a shock of unruly blond hair. He looked like a gracefully aging surfer. He greeted me with fanfare, as if I were his own private celebrity. Freddy got the address where I'd be. Edward led me out into the breezy sunshine. I barely had a chance to wave good-bye to Mr. Rooney's hunting friends and promise to rendezvous with them here at the airport at the end of the weekend. Edward and I piled into his big white Pathfinder. "This is the ideal car for this country. It can go any- where," he said, "but in comfort." It was big enough for rough roads, but small enough to move around potholes. "It came with the house," he added, when he saw my surprise at his luxury.

In the congested stretches of the road, other cars seemed to treat the lines painted on the road merely as part of the festive decorations. "Kamikaze drivers," Edward said with a competitive grimace.

The country south of Ciudad Obregon was warm and fertile, full of strange sights. The riverbeds were full of water, flowing peacefully. We crossed the fabled Rio Mayo, one of the rivers Marcos had to cross in the early days of the journey. One hundred feet wide, all water.

The drive to Alamos paralleled the coast at first, maybe twenty miles inland. The middle-distance hills to the east, foreshadowing the Sierra Madre, were as bare and rocky as in Arizona, and had the same purple-red-brown cast. The difference was that here, the foreground was dotted by green trees and green fields with little ramshackle huts. It was wonderful country for walking: flat, moist, fertile. It seemed that Marcos could have made a beeline through here in the first weeks of his trek. But Edward explained that in the old days, before the rivers were controlled, these flatlands were swampy delta country. In the 1600s, when the first records were available, the Spanish *Camino Real* lay inland from here, running through the valleys that wind among the foothills.

Between Ciudad Obregon and the little town of Navajoa, we performed what Edward called the Alamos Maneuver. The Mexican government had built a modern interstatelike toll road the length of Sonora. Each toll booth along the way collects a few dollars. This is a fortune to local drivers. The road is really for the rich upper classes and the Americans. As we drew within sight of the toll gates, Edward explained with a grin that the locals didn't *do* tolls. He swerved off the pavement, across the median, down a muddy dirt road. At a fence, a farmer with a big straw hat watched our approach. The power window went down. A few coins changed hands. Smiles. A jaunty salute. We drove about three-fourths of a mile through the bushes, bumping over dirt clods and mud puddles. At the other end we passed another farmer's field. This guy is actually sitting there with a rope stretched across his "road," but this barrier came down as we drove into view. More smiles. More coins.

"This is crazy," I said to Edward. "What are you paying them?"

"A peso, each end."

"What if the cops see us?"

"Hell, I've done it with the cops sitting there watching. Everybody's happy. The nation gets its dollars, the farmers get their pesos for bypass maintenance, and the local drivers avoid paying for the gringo way of life. Everybody wins."

We passed through the town of Navajoa, and I thought how strange the world was, these merchants, stores, middle-class people in the bustling streets, life going on, alien to Anglo Arizonans, yet no farther away than Flagstaff.

We headed out of the flatlands into the low hills, toward Alamos. The Pathfinder passed a ramshackle cluster of farm cottages descended from the mat houses described by Marcos. Four posts to define the corners, a roof of matted rushes laid across the top, corrugated iron sheeting and salvaged boards, mimicking the reed mats once used to make the sides. Scatters of trash in the yard, mysterious works in progress. Wisps of smoke. We swept through. In our big American vehicle, we were the aristocrats, passing through the eternal peasant village.

Edward turned on the radio. There was music and talk. I couldn't follow the Spanish. "Jesus!" Edward exclaimed presently.

"What?"

"The Chinese students are demonstrating again and the government is sending in the troops against them. It says there are a lot of beatings."

He changed to a station with mariachi music.

IN ALAMOS A HAPPY SYMBIOSIS SEEMED TO EXIST BETWEEN THE two hundred and fifty well-to-do American residents who were buying and restoring the old homes, and the ten thousand Mexican residents who had created a middle class of merchants and artisans doing the restoration work. Little shops catered to tourists, both American and Mexican, who come to see the American colony and the leafy countryside.

Edward took me to dinner at a hotel with a kind of splendor

rarely seen in the U.S. No business-chic foyers, plush carpets, brass, chrome, or sports bars, but rather cascading flowers, tiles, and paintings by local artists who lived down the street. A deep, open porch faced the enclosed patio, and the porch was lined by worn couches and cases of worn books. Edward's friend, the hostess, told us the books are "for reading or taking. People leave their old ones and take home a new one." I browsed. Each book came with a pedigree. The first I picked out was inscribed by someone who bought it in Mexico City; the next had arrived from Iowa.

Over enchiladas and Mexican beer, Edward told me he liked life here. He lived in a cottage on an old estate owned by some Americans. He rented it cheap, he said, in exchange for fixing it up and looking after the main house while they were away, which is all the time. "They're pretty rich," he said. "Maybe they forgot about it."

Researching the history of the area, Edward had met a young priest, Father Antonio, who worked part of the time in the village of ———, down the valley. I don't want to give its name. Who knows what's still there? Father Antonio came from the newly emerging middle class of Mexico, and he saw the country not with the traditional fatalism of the traditional Mexican, but with the optimism of a twentieth-century reformer. Edward saw a story line here. He was fascinated by the land of ancient tragedy, about to enter a new and hopeful era. He saw himself being in the right place at the right time, as happy as Hemingway in Spain.

"What about you?" he asked. "Tell me about your love life."

I told him about Phaedra. "She's smart. She's sexy. She's just . . . interesting, you know? I think I'm in love with her."

"There's trouble."

"It's like she's always . . . there. Whatever I do, I want to tell her about it. I bounce all my ideas off her. She always has some opinion, or some new way to look at things. She makes me think about things, and feel more alive."

"That's good."

"There're different sides to her. I think she's torn between her vision of success and . . . I'm not sure what."

Two of the hunter couples showed up at the next table. The two ladies were practically at my shoulder, attractive, bejeweled, discussing their stay at the hotel.

"Do you have a TV in your room?" said one to the other.

"No. You couldn't get anything but Mexican, anyway."

"You could get CNN. You can get CNN anywhere."

"It would just be a bunch of shootings in China." They made faces.

"In our room, we couldn't get warm last night; it took forever for the fireplace to do any good."

"The bathrooms are kind of tacky. All that bare tile. The water never did get hot."

"You have to let it run for five minutes."

"Well, for what we're paying, they ought to . . ."

Edward leaned over and whispered to me. "Listen to them. People like that travel encased in their own portable hell. Did you know that the average energy consumption of Americans is the equivalent of having a hundred servants?"

We finished eating. Others of the hunters—the ones without lady companions—were at the bar, growing louder and making passes at the *señoritas* who waited the tables. Rooney's three salesmen, whom I knew only slightly, hung out at the end of the bar with Freddy the Fixer, who seemed to be keeping an eye on how things were going. I waved. They nodded amiably, raising glasses of beer at me.

Edward and I wandered over. They were bemused when they found out he was a writer.

"What d'you write?" asked Freddy.

"Books, or rather I try. To survive, I have to write articles, travel articles for airplane magazines and such as that."

"Can you survive on that?"

"I don't need much. Life's pretty cheap here."

"You should come and work for us for a coupla years, like your buddy Kevin. You could do sales, then retire down here and live like a king. Get yourself one of these *señoritas*, or maybe two." They all laughed.

"Where're you doing your hunting?" Edward asked the others.

"Mr. Rooney's got a friend, owns a ranch here. Señor . . . I forget."

"Gonzales," Freddy prompted. "We're staying out there. You ought to come out. It's palatial!"

Edward choked on the last of his beer. "Mmmmph," he said.

"Where are you doing *your* hunting?" Freddy asked. "For the old records, I mean."

"Edward's got a friend in a nearby church," I said.

Edward looked pale and was still gurgling. The conversation seemed to come to an end.

"Have another beer," Freddy offered.

Edward nudged me and said we better be heading out.

"What was that all about?" I said as we cleared the cantina door.

"Jesus," Edward whispered to me as we walked down the narrow street on the high curbed sidewalk. "Gonzales. You go out there and you're about one cousin away from the Mexican Mafia and the drug traffickers. You don't even want to know what they are growing out there. Ranch hands, they run around with AK-47s. I don't want to have anything to do with that outfit. If you're a young American down here, people already think you're after drugs, or making some kind of deal. When drug connections go wrong, they find someone like me to serve as the scapegoat. I go out of my way to avoid that whole scene." We reached the Pathfinder. "Let's get out of here."

Edward's cottage turned out to be palatial, compared to my apartment in Tucson. "See?" said Edward. "Your friend thinks you have to have piles of money to live like a king, but I live like one already."

The plumbing didn't work very well, but why nitpick? Edward reminded me that even King Midas couldn't flush or turn on a hot water tap. Edward had restored the place with love and lots of labor. Tiles, heavy carved furniture, light filtering through louvered windows. Outside, the main house lay across a tiny patio with a fountain and little reflecting pools, and scarlet bougainvillea tumbling over the courtyard walls. We sat there in the languid night and talked until the moonlight faded.

The dirt roads and walls of adobe and even the Mexican beer made me realize that human presence here was an integral, if ephemeral, part of the land, like anthills or clumps of trees. This place seemed only a generation removed from the times of Marcos himself. It felt very different from Arizona; how often did we feel the resilience of soil under our shoes?

EDWARD SAID HIS FRIEND, FATHER ANTONIO, WOULD MEET US OUT at the church in the morning. In the fresh morning air, he drove me through the growth rings of Alamos. We started at the core, on ancient streets paved with old interlocking cobblestones, bordering the plaza and passing between the great old dome-topped church and the gleaming, colonial buildings. A few blocks away from the heart of town, we were on narrow side streets cobbled with rounded stones in front of plastered home fronts and garden walls. A few blocks farther, the streets gave way to dirt roads among crumbling adobe abodes.

The Pathfinder rolled on into the countryside. Tropical plants clutched at the ill-defined edges of the dirt road. Here and there we passed crumbling ruins and overgrown walls. We were traveling through the front lines of the war that is kept secret in the U.S.: humanity's old war, between mankind and entropy.

Meanwhile, there were other wars. Edward turned the radio on again and that's when we heard of the massacre in Tiananmen Square. The reporter said hundreds of students had been shot.

"Jesus," Edward said, for the second time.

I didn't say anything.

*　*　*

I DON'T WANT TO SAY EXACTLY WHICH WAY WE DROVE, BECAUSE there may still be treasures in that valley, where the mountains tower overhead, mantled in green. Suffice it to say we were back in the hills. We stopped at a tiny hidden town, situated on a cheerful little stream. It looked as if it had been there forever.

An old white church, built in the 1600s, stood on the edge of a moldering plaza. An old man rode by on a burro, loaded with fire-wood—fragments of the disappearing forest around the town. The bell tower in the old church was unfinished; three centuries had not been time enough to finish it. It loomed big and square and trun-cated, an unintentional symbol of the conquest of Mexico.

The entrance to the church was a pair of massive wooden doors. The two threshold boards were worn into U-shapes. The boards might have been there since the beginning. I couldn't resist a quicky planner-style calculation. Let's say 10^2 people per week times 5×10^1 weeks/year times 3×10^2 years. I multiplied the num-bers and added up the exponents. It made 15×10^5 people, over a million footsteps, wearing down those thresholds.

We stepped through the door out of the blinding sun of the white plaza and into the middle ages. Cool blackness; then slowly emerg-ing baroque ornateness looming in the dark. Columns, altars, stat-ues of limpid saints, all painted in blues and pinks and whites, and trimmed in silver or gilt with curlicues and gewgaws and tassels in plaster. The silver trim gleamed everywhere, as if spitballs of alu-minum foil had stuck at random. As my eyes grew accustomed to the dark, I was surprised to see another figure in the church. It was an old woman, standing in front of the altar, as still as one of the saints, transfixed apparently. Frozen in time.

"Are we really going to find anything here?" I breathed to Edward.

"You'll see."

The young priest, Father Antonio, friend of my friend, came forth from the medieval shadows. His parents and grandparents had been workers in mines, revolutionaries with modest goals, toilers on ill-fated estates and *ejido* collective farms. He was the first in his line to have that dangerous commodity, education.

Father Antonio grasped Edward warmly by the arm and spoke to me. "Edward tells me you are interested in our treasures. He tells me you care about our history. I say 'our history,' but you know, the history of Sonora is intertwined with the history of what you call your Southwest. These two histories, they are like two vines twined together." He gave me a sly smile and a hearty pat on the back.

"Tell me about the things you've found."

"*Norteños*," he smiled. "Always in a hurry. They do business first, then become friends afterwards. Here, we become friends first. Then we can do business." He waved at the baroque glitter. "These treasures aren't the kind you care about, I suppose. Edward, he tells me that you are a scholar." I gave Edward a dirty look. "For you, the real treasures," Father Antonio was going on, "they are on paper, no? Old texts, maps, ideas. . . ." He ushered us forward, into the gloom.

In the back recesses of the church was a cramped room that was either a storeroom or an office, it was hard to tell. Dim light came through the dirty window of the room. There were old wooden shelves, and wooden boxes.

"I grew up near Mexico City," Father Antonio told us. "To me, Sonora was like your Wild West." He started puttering among the boxes. "Our church, I mean the church in Mexico, is at a strange crossroads in history. When the Spanish first came here some of the priests thought God had given them a chance to throw off the sins of Europe. But, alas, they failed. Look around you. You can see that the families of the first conquerors held onto the land and the money they stole centuries ago. In your country, at least you—how do you say?—pay lip service to equality of opportunity among the classes. But here . . ." He turned to the boxes and started setting some of the smaller ones on the shelves. "I say that today, the church has a chance to act on the side of the people. This is the kind of history that interests me most. We need the history we can learn from these books, to help the people see the pattern of oppression."

Oh, great, I thought. All I needed now was a communist priest, trying to fit Marcos into a Marxist theory of history.

"Don't worry," he said, reading my thoughts. He seemed older than his years. "My interest is in evolutionary change. I don't preach revolution. I merely talk about how we can begin to change the country for the better." He smiled a shy smile. "Of course, my superiors do not approve of my sermons. Father Xavier, for instance, who has been the priest at this church since the stone age. He says I am a hothead with the passions of youth, and that my sermons will lead to trouble. Do you think I am a hothead?"

"You seem very reasonable. These are important issues."

"Ah, you are a good diplomat. All right, let me tell you about how I found these materials." He sat down for a moment on one of the larger boxes, wiped his brow, and told us his story. Since the early churches had offered the only security along the old route to the north, they had become repositories of ancient papers among the town's great families—records of births, property, and marriages. Old priests tended to ignore these materials as they accumulated, generation after generation. Father Xavier had been that way. Antonio had decided to be different. He would make an inventory. It would become part of his mission in Alamos, to preserve the history of the area. If people understood how the present system had evolved, they would be more willing to accept that it could be changed. Even now there was a museum in Alamos, where the old documents could be put on display. To pursue his goal, Father Antonio had started exploring old storerooms, crypts, bell towers. They were apt to yield the most surprising goods. For instance, this chest. . . .

He had finally cleared the space around a modest-sized wooden chest, smaller than a footlocker, maybe twenty inches across. It was darkened by the soot of centuries. There were rotted leather fittings and metal latches that had lost their gleam.

"I can't be sure, but it seems to have been in the Zumárraga family. Zumárraga was a famous bishop of ours, in Mexico City. He is the one who was involved in the story of the Virgin of Guadalupe."

My heart jumped at the mention of Marcos's bishop. As for the miraculous appearance of the Virgin of Guadalupe, it was one of those bizarre Catholic miracle stories. Virgin Mary appears to Indian. Indian brings miraculous poncho to bishop. The problem was that historians had shown that there was no mention of it during Zumárraga's lifetime. The whole thing was mytho-history, which surfaced a century after the alleged fact, manufactured to create an Indian-friendly Catholicism. Now the harmless fable had been transmogrified into a leading symbol of national identity, defended by millions. Religious Tonypandy. Meanwhile, the real Zumárraga . . . he was the one who had invited Marcos to Mexico from Peru in the first place. He actually knew the guy. . . .

"From what I can tell, this material belonged to a cousin of Zumárraga. Family papers, handed down. I looked, but there seems to be nothing about Zumárraga himself. It is as if the personal papers were removed long ago and collected somewhere else. So I think, perhaps for historians like you, my find will be disappointing. Still, as I say, this chest seems to contain things from those early days. I need someone like you, who knows the period, to offer an opinion about their value."

"I'm very interested to see them." I had decided to play the role of the polite academic.

"I'm afraid there is nothing of Coronado here," Father Antonio was saying. "We do have baptismal documents, deeds, wedding documents, that sort of thing. They start in the 1500s and go on to the 1600s, the kinds of things they must have saved over several generations. Then, at the bottom wrapped in an old cloth, there was an old book. I think it is the earliest thing, so I put it in this plastic bag." I noticed that the bag was colorfully printed, marked incongruously with the logo BIMBO, the brand name for the Mexican version of Rainbow bread.

Carefully he opened the BIMBO bag and slid out a worn, leather-bound book, whose stitchings were tattered and frayed.

He opened the cover, propping it against a small Bible so as not to strain the spine of the ancient book. I swear that I stopped breathing when I saw what was on the first page. It was a signature I recognized.

Father Antonio smiled. "You recognize the name? Isn't he the one who was . . . how would you say . . . a black sheep of our church family, for telling lies about something? This seems to be a notebook of some travels, but unfortunately it's before Coronado's trip, and there is no narrative. Just notes, but perhaps, as a historian, you can make sense of them. . . ."

I remember that moment, the light streaming through the window. A jolt of adrenaline hit me. The church room, which had seemed cold and dark, suddenly was hot and stuffy. It had fallen as silent as a lost tomb, or to be more accurate, I had tuned out Father Antonio, who was still talking earnestly. The room was also spinning, and my arms felt like they were made of lead. I felt I should not touch the book, but I did anyway.

It was a small book, about five by seven inches.

I got out my camera and found myself fishing in my pocket for a pen and notepaper, as if merely being in the presence of this thing required documentation.

"You are the first scholar to see these things. I did not want to take them out into the light, even to photograph it. I understand that old inks . . . they fade. Museums keep such documents in dimly lit rooms."

"But we should make some record."

"Of course. But the book should stay inside, in this room. Tell me, is it important?"

"Well . . . it *could* be important. I need to look at it. . . ." Why did I hold back? I had an overpowering feeling that I needed time to assess what was happening.

In that filtered light we turned the delicate pages, my mind racing ahead of the fragmentary notes. I had about half an hour with the book, while Father Antonio and Edward talked. I was no expert at reading the ragged old Spanish script, but the book betrayed an orderly mind, with a heading for each day when something was written. Often there were gaps of several days. Sometimes only a few words were added on a given date. And each date made my heart pound: March 7, 1539, at the beginning, and other dates as far as June. It was a record of Marcos's journey north. There were many entries. During that first look, I could not read coherently. The script was old cursive Spanish and I was too excited. The words I already knew were the ones that jumped off the pages at me: Petatlán, the village of reed mat houses near the Sonora/Sinaloa border. Honorato. A list of strange names, marked "names of islands." Vacapa, dated Easter, April 6. There were other names I did not recognize and cannot remember. There were lists of villages, and sketchy maps. They were hardly maps at all. How do you make a map of a place you have merely walked through? Marcos had no GPS support. He did the logical thing. For each entry, he made a bird's-eye view of his day's travel, for example showing a river course with village names dotted along it, and mountains on either side. Was that the characteristic backward L shape of the Rio San Miguel or Rio Sonora? He had added beautiful sketches of the characteristic mountain profiles and prominent features along the route. Here and there among the pages were sketches of craggy peaks or even characteristic clumps of trees, with scattered notes in spidery handwriting. On one page was a notation "coast turns west" beside a village marked "Ququrpa." It might be the same place as the modern town of Cucurpe.

In my hands, a direct link was forged from the present to the past, from me to Marcos de Niza, person to person, like a long-distance phone call. At first, I thought the notebook was the separate document he referred to in the *Relación*, listing names of islands and towns. Finally, from the nature of the entries, I realized it was more than that. This notebook must have traveled with him, day and night, on the trek to discover Cíbola. It had perhaps been held in Estevan's hands, and perhaps also by marveling chiefs of the long-lost towns—the last prehistoric Americans. Marcos must have delivered the original to Zumárraga. Marcos or Zumárraga probably used it to make a neater list of the names and maps for Viceroy Mendoza. Zumárraga must have kept the original in his archives.

In a daze, I scribbled bits of information, the kind of jottings you take during a quick telephone call, fragmentary and difficult to decipher later. I still have them. Dates, names like Vacapa and Ququrpa, but not a coherent description. I can use the notes to decipher what I saw, but they are worthless in terms of convincing anyone else.

Gently but feverishly I turned the pages, trying to find out what happened at the northern end of the trip. May 3, 4, 5. . . . There it was: a north-trending river marked "Rio Nex-pa" with a village site named . . . I couldn't decipher it. From there, a dotted line led east and then north, and was marked "4 dias." The dotted line led to a site he had marked as "Casa Colorada—Chichilti Calli." Red House. He showed it lying south of a pass through mountains. There was a sketch of the ruin, showing broken roof beams and crumbling walls two stories high, with small upper windows. Near this on the page was a rough sketch, that showed the distinctive V notch in the mountains with some crags on the left side. It was the profile of the pass I had seen north of our ruin. It would have to be checked at the site, but one look convinced me it had been drawn on our land. Our ruin was Chichilti-Calli. A sketchy map on the next page showed the path leading from the red house north and then northeast across the pass, where it hit a large northwest-flowing river with lots more mountains drawn on its north side. That would be the Gila River north of Eagle Pass. Written across the mountains was the word "*despoblado*."

What about Cíbola? I turned more pages. They didn't crack; they were rather stiff but in good condition. The entries for May 21, 22, and 23 were written in dense notation. I didn't try to read them because my attention was grabbed by the entry marked May 25, which was dominated by a sketch, rough but showing the unmistakable shape of a pueblo structure with multiple stories. It seemed to be a view from a distance, with a large mesa behind the pueblo. The caption said "Cíbola." There were more entries after that, but shorter, in a wild scrawl. Marcos had reached Cíbola after all.

That half hour, touching Marcos's book in the dim room in the church in the little town near Alamos, was the high point of my life. As I reached the final pages, I realized that the thread connecting Marcos to me stretched on into the future. I would make this book known, through the proper academic circles. A joint Mexican-American team of scholars would make translations and write important articles. A version would be published in a beautiful edition with facsimiles of Marcos's sketches. He'd be vindicated. Perhaps I would write a preface or a first chapter, telling about the discovery, about this moment. To be truthful, I didn't think about Mr. Rooney and Coronado Estates at all.

OF THE FIVE BILLION PEOPLE ON THE PLANET, ONLY A HALF dozen could have walked into that room and recognized the significance of this book. If anyone else had received an inquiring call from Edward or Father Antonio, events would have worked out differently.

Probably better.

If only I had spent more time reading the text on those pages. If only I had copied more systematically what I saw. I came back down to Earth.

I needed to figure out what to do next.

I tried to talk the good young father into letting me borrow the book, but I was secretly relieved when he would not let it out of his sight, let alone outside for pictures. He let me take a few flash pictures, general shots of the room and the chest and the book sitting on his table. I didn't have a macro lens but I focused as close as I could get, about three feet.

"Is there some way we can get better photos?" I asked Edward.

"Look, I've got a tripod," he said. "And a camera with a macro. We could come back here in an hour and get some closeups if you think it'd be useful."

"No, amigos," said Father Antonio. "I have to go. This evening I have a wedding in the next village, and also there will be a meeting of the farmworkers' committee. You should come back early in the morning, first thing, before Mass. I can let you in. You can take pictures then."

I felt like I wanted to stay the night, sleep next to the thing.

"It's lasted ten thousand nights without you," Edward chided me. "It can last one more. We'll come back while the birds are still singing."

"Okay," I agreed reluctantly. "But let me tell you about what I think we're looking at here." I opened up. I told them about Marcos, and why this was a real find. What they needed, I said, was more historians, specialists. There were several people I could contact. . . . In the end we agreed that I would talk to the Southwest history scholars at the University of Arizona and get somebody down here pronto, and meanwhile, they could call someone at the university in Hermosillo and line up a team there. An international team of scholars would be best. It would have a certain symbolism. I stressed that we should move carefully—not attract the wrong kind of people: collectors or dealers in antiquities. Everything needed to be authenticated.

Father Antonio was carefully placing the book back in its BIMBO bag, and putting it on top of the other documents in the chest. "We'll leave it here. It's safe." He closed the chest. "Tomorrow, first thing," he repeated. I wanted to set a more specific time to meet him, but then I remembered how nobody here referred to time in terms of clocks. It wasn't polite; it was too Anglo.

I was still nervous. "Um, are you sure it is safe?"

"Don't worry," Father Antonio said graciously. "There is a padlock on this door. We've never had a problem."

I could hardly tear myself away, but tomorrow afternoon, Sunday, we were scheduled to leave for the drive to the airport. I needed to call Phaedra and tell her what we had found and let them know I needed more time. I had visions of her explaining to Mr. Rooney how this would really put us on the map, and of my stock going way up in the office.

On the way back to Alamos I noticed the deer-hunters' green truck from the ranch, parked along the road outside the little town. Blasting away up there in the hills, they were. I imagined smugly that they had no idea of what quarry was really to be found here.

I CALLED PHAEDRA FROM EDWARD'S HOUSE.

"Kevin! Where are you?"

"Still in Alamos. I've got news. You'll never guess what we've found. It's fantastic!"

"Well?"

"Paydirt. Marcos's original notebook. The notes he kept on his trip north!"

There was a silence.

"It's unbelievable, Phaedra! I mean, its like finding some original diary kept by Columbus or Leif Eriksson. I've only had a first look. It's got notes about the route and the villages, made along the way. There's a sketch of the Chichilti-Calli area. I'm sure it proves the route came right through our land. I copied some names out of it."

"Do you have it now?"

"No. Edward's friend, Father Antonio, wouldn't let us take it, but tomorrow we're going back to take some closeup photos."

"That's amazing. It's wonderful! It was right there, in Alamos, all this time? Why had no one ever—"

"It's in ———." I named the little village we had visited. "In the church. Old papers, handed down in the family of Zumárraga, Marcos's bishop. Marcos must have left the notes with Zumárraga, and when he died. . . . Nobody had really looked at that stuff until Antonio."

"What do we do next?"

I liked that she said "we." "I want to call Dr. Panofsky, in anthropology at the U. This'll be a big thing. I figure they'll get a team of scholars—"

"You want me to call him?"

"No. Tell Mr. Rooney. He'll get a kick out of this."

"Well . . . maybe not. Listen, we've got news here, too. The day you left, the opposition got a petition out on the streets. A referendum, to overturn the rezoning. Mr. Rooney's livid. The petition people, they're really turning the history thing against us." She explained that the ranchers, environmentalists, and neighborhood no-growth groups had figured all along that Mr. Rooney had the votes, so they bided their time and built grassroots support for a campaign against the project. The petition drive was by the "Committee to Save Historic Sulfur Springs Valley." Worse yet, they were on talk radio quoting my own report. "They make it sound like you proved our ruin is the one. The petition itself is headed 'Save the Coronado Ruin.' Mr. Rooney is upset that people actually read our literature."

I didn't say anything.

"The point is, he isn't going to be happy about what you found. Also, did you hear the news today?"

"What's that?"

"The Chinese soldiers are shooting at those students."

"Yeah, we heard on the radio."

"It's sad, isn't it?"

"Yeah. It's hard to watch from the sidelines. But what can we do?"

It was like any other call home when you're on vacation. It jolted me out of my pleasant unreality. There was only one bit of good news from her end. At the end of the call she said she missed being able to touch me. I said I missed her, too.

I tried to call Dr. Panofsky at the university. Of course he wasn't in. It was after hours. I left him a message describing the notebook and urging him to give some thought about what to do next. I gave him Edward's number in case he wanted to try to reach me, but I also said I would contact him when I got home and show him the pictures. I was feeling full of myself, elated with the thrill of discovery.

I told Edward I ought to call up Mr. Rooney's friends, the mighty hunters, and tell them I might not be coming back on the plane tomorrow. "Later," he said. "Call 'em in the morning, after we know more about what we've got. Right now, I'm taking you to the best bar in Alamos. We're gonna celebrate."

CHAPTER 14

Marcos's Adventures in the Last Despoblado

Marcos said he spent most of that May getting to Cíbola and starting back. In his *Relación*, he described setting out from Chichilti-Calli into the final fifteen-day wilderness north of the Gila. It was more difficult country than he had crossed before.

As for the final journey, I entered the last despoblado on May 9. We traveled as follows. On the first day we went by way of a very wide and much-used road, and arrived for dinner at a water source, where the Indians had erected a sign for me. For our overnight camp, there was another spring, where I found a hut which they had made for me, and another they had built for Estevan to sleep in when he passed this way. There were also old huts and many signs of fires, made by people who had traveled this road to Cíbola.

In this way I moved on for twelve days, always well supplied with food of deer, hares, and partridges, and of the same color and flavor as those of Spain, though not as large.

This seemed straightforward enough, but by now I was sensitized to the way that various researchers had distorted Marcos's words to fit their interpretation. In the sociology of history, everyone had his own agenda, whether in the 1500s or the messy twentieth century. Take Hallenbeck, for example. He couldn't resist turning even Marcos's straightforward mention of shelters into a demand for luxury.

> *The man's energies seem to have been devoted mainly to gathering and embellishing stories of Cíbola, and from the time he first heard of the place until he started home, nearly all of his time was devoted to such puerilities. . . . Next after Cíbola, eating seems to have claimed most of Marcos's attention. [He] sent servants on ahead, not only to prepare the dinner, but to erect a shelter where he could dine in comfort and perhaps take a siesta. This is traveling de luxe. He says nothing of a silver dining service or wine, but I should not be surprised to learn that he had both. . . .*

Marcos stops at a wilderness spring, sees Estevan's hut, eats rabbit stew, and sleeps in a hut the Indians built for him, as had been their practice along the way. Somehow this gets transmuted into luxury travel with lazy naps and fine meals off silver platters. Hallenbeck seemed to be conjuring up more precious metal than Marcos ever did.

Poor old Marcos. While blaming him for reporting impossible rates of "wilderness" travel and touring in too much luxury, his critics seem to have missed what I thought was the real news in these passages—Marcos's clear indication that he was on a well-known and well-used trail to Cíbola, with experienced Indian guides preparing the way, carrying his goods, and making camp. No wonder he was able to cover ground faster than the historians of the 1940s expected.

IN THE VERY NEXT SENTENCE OF MARCOS'S REPORT, AFTER STATing that he had traveled twelve days through the *despoblado*, he begins the climax of Marcos's story—the ill-fated discovery of Cíbola. They were now about three days out from the fabled Seven Cities.

Here we were met by an Indian, who had gone ahead with Estevan. He was the son of one of the chiefs who was accompanying me. He arrived with his face and body covered by sweat, and he was very distressed. . . .

CHAPTER 15

May 10—21, 1539
The Approach to Cíbola

May 10. A day after they left the Chichilti-Calli ruin, Marcos's party reached a broad and grassy river valley. One of the guides pointed ahead of them and said something in his native tongue. Blue ranges ran east-west across the northern horizon. "Those mountains mark the beginning of the *despoblado,*" said the translators. In his trailbook, Marcos jotted down an interesting geographic fact. Until now, the main route had followed north-south river valleys. Here, however, the mountains and rivers turned west. Perhaps this was connected with his discovery that the coast turned west at this same latitude. It confirmed that a major geographic change occurred here. It also meant that instead of traveling along the valleys and ranges, they now had to cross them.

As they crossed the valley toward the mountains, Marcos occasionally caught glimpses of distant ruins, clusters of decaying buildings not unlike Chichilti-Calli itself. The province seemed strangely deserted, like a whole country inhabited only by spirits, with lost cities of ghosts. There were signs of ancient irrigation canals. From one ruin came a thin smoke indicating that someone was living among the tumbled walls.

Tall Man came running up with some of the guides from the Nexpa valley. "They say we will not stop at these villages," he said. "There are people here who chose to live in the ruins of the ancient ones who built Chichilti-Calli, but they say such people are beneath contempt."

"Why is that?" Marcos asked, always interested in new, down-trodden souls who might receive the Word.

There was much discussion. One of the chiefs from the Nexpa Valley was the main spokesman. Finally Tall Man translated, "They are bad people, neither true to our elders' ways, nor to the ways of the northern strangers, because they live in the buildings abandoned by the ancient ones. They are crude people and have no tradition."

MAY 12. TWO DAYS INTO THE DESPOBLADO. TALL MAN CAME TO him again. "I have been learning more stories about Estevan," he said. "We have encountered some of the people from the Nexpa Valley who went part way with him. He is about a week ahead of us. I don't think we can catch him unless he decides to wait before reaching Cíbola." Tall Man scowled. "It seems unlikely. . . . Also, there are more stories about his women friends."

"Ah, that. . . ."

"He sows discord. The women all love him, and it impresses the men, but it makes them jealous. When they were camped at Chichilti-Calli, some of the women got in a fight over him and he set one of his dogs on them. He pretended it was a joke, but one of the women was hurt. That is why he made a big speech the next day about peace, and went off to make a shrine out of that helmet of his. Some of the people say he is a great shaman, but others say he is just a man with too big an opinion of himself. That is why some of these people decided to return home."

This was troubling news. Before, Marcos had been irritated by Estevan's disobedience. But now it was more serious. Was Este-van's legendary ability to charm the natives breaking down? It was outrageous if Estevan created jealousies among their allies. He thought of hauling Estevan before the viceroy when they got back—and yet it would be a bad tactic to admit that anyone in their party had given cause for complaint among the Indians.

"We will have to have a serious talk when we catch up with him," Marcos told Tall Man.

*   *   *

MAY 18. MORE THAN A WEEK HAD PASSED. THE COUNTRY WAS now very different from the sun-blasted grasslands and river valleys to the south. Dark pines closed in on them on all sides, crowding lichen-covered rocks and covering the sky. Would the gloomy forests and craggy slopes never end? The Indian guides from the Nexpa valley said that in a day or so they would come to new grasslands and a shallow river that would lead a few more days upstream to the golden city of Cíbola. The Indians assured him that the area was unpopulated, but Marcos had an uneasy feeling that they could be watched by unseen enemies less than an arrow shot away. Who knew what beasts or demons lurked in the mountains and forests of this New World? He found it hard to sleep, thinking such thoughts. In the daytime, even Tall Man, who rarely showed emotion, kept looking around nervously.

The trail was well-used but difficult. It twisted along hillsides, across streams, along boulder-strewn valleys, and through dense pines. At least there was plenty of water, whereas the previous, shorter *despoblados* had involved day-long treks between meager springs. Best of all, in a few days he would be reunited with Estevan at Cíbola. Marcos predicted to himself that Estevan would renounce his headstrong impetuosity and wait for them, a day's travel from the gates of Cíbola. Then he would smile guilelessly and say, "You see, I waited just as you told me." Marcos smiled at the tongue-lashing he would give the Moor for trotting ahead like a horse too eager for its dinner.

In the evening he had a talk with the young aide who had tried to befriend him. The young man in recent days had fallen to the rear of the group. He called him into camp, with Tall Man. "Do you still say we will find treasures of gold in Cíbola?"

"You will see when we get there. What I say is the truth."

"Two Macaw Feathers says the opposite. He says he lived there."

"Two Macaw Feathers tries to protect the secrets of the priests in Cíbola."

That was all he could get out of him.

*   *   *

MAY 19. ALMOST WITHOUT WARNING, THE TRAIL EMERGED FROM the rugged pine forests into an entirely different country. Gently rolling, golden grasslands stretched before them in a broad expanse. Now they were under a vast sky dotted with puffy, rabbit-tail clouds that looked different from the high, thin wisps of the desert skies south of the *despoblado*. This open country rolled ahead, as far as the eye could see. On the northeast horizon were low mesas of dark blue. They were flat-topped, unlike the toothy peaks that bounded the southern deserts.

One of the chiefs from the Nexpa Valley came to him, smiling, with Tall Man and one of the other interpreters. He stretched out his coppery arm and pointed toward the northeast. "In that direction is Cíbola. Soon you will see."

MAY 21. FOR TWO DAYS THEY HAD BEEN CROSSING THE GRASS-lands. There was no sign of Estevan. The one river they encountered was only a poor winding brook in the broad plain. There were no large trees to punctuate the view, but only occasional scrubby bushes. Nor were the grasslands flat. Here and there, they passed rounded, conical hills, draped in soft robes of yellow grass that gleamed in the sun. Marcos tried not to think about how these unusual hills resembled a woman's breast.

As they came over a rise, the Indians stopped at a cairn of rocks, putting down their packs to rest. One of the chiefs came to him again, pointing. "From this cairn, you can see the smokes of fires in the province of Cíbola, if they are having ceremonies." Marcos squinted. He could see nothing. "Now," the man continued, "it is only three days to the first city."

The natives were throwing their offerings of stones onto the cairn. One of the chiefs took off his strand of turquoises, patiently undid a knot, and slipped off one of the shining blue nuggets, which he carefully threaded onto a feather and placed in the pile, behind a rock. The travelers began picking up their belongings to leave. Only three days, Marcos thought to himself. Exactly at that moment there was a commotion at the front of the group. The guides from the province of Chichilti-Calli were pointing ahead, along the trail.

Marcos moved forward to see what they were looking at.

Far ahead, he could see a lone figure, trotting toward them in the peculiar gait that the Indians used to cover ground in a hurry. His guides were aroused, talking to each other and to Tall Man. Two Macaw Feathers, who had grown more joyful each day anticipating his return to his hometown, now squinted nervously at the distant runner. Marcos could not understand the agitation. "Father, something is wrong!" relayed Tall Man. The loping figure was still too far away for Marcos to see anything amiss, but he had learned not to question the reliability of his guides. It was as if God had given these people some additional sense for detecting each other's emotions at a distance.

When the runner came closer, the cause of concern was more apparent. His eyes were wild, and his body was streaked with sweat and mud. Even before he reached the party, he began crying out to them. He was the son of one of the chiefs in Marcos's party. Some of the guides ran forward, and there was chaos as the Indians began trying to transmit the news from group to group. Marcos's interpreters struggled to listen and talk at the same time.

"Oh, Father, it is a calamity—A disaster has struck them at Cíbola."

"What? What is the matter?"

"Some of our people, killed! The ones who went with Estevan. . . ."

And as the translators tried to explain, Marcos heard random voices crying out around him as the hysterical man came into their circle. Some of the words he could understand; more were fed to him by his translators.

"What?" "What?" "What is this disaster?" "Tell us."

The man had slumped onto the ground, with his elbows on his knees, holding his head.

"Calm yourself. Tell us what happened."

Already the Indians' strange, communal cry of despair was

breaking out among the people from the Rio Nexpa. It was a low moan, rising in volume, like condemned souls' unearthly wail, swelling up from below the Earth. The chiefs clustered around the newcomer.

Eventually the man's story began to emerge in more orderly form, with Marcos's aides relaying it to him.

"We traveled with Estevan. We led him to the accustomed place where we make ourselves known to the people of Cíbola. Their people came out to greet us. We lay down all our weapons before us and gave them the greetings of our chiefs and the people of our towns. We gave them feathers of the best colors, which we brought with us. Then we presented the stranger, the dark man, Estevan. Estevan carried his mace and wore all the feathers and tinkling bells that he had collected from villages in many lands, and he wore painted markings on his face, and he made his dogs run in circles and showed them his magic knife that is stronger even than copper.

"The people from Cíbola wanted to know who he was and where he came from. Estevan told them he came from far in the south, in the warm lands of the sun, where many of his brothers lived with him. He told them that before he lived in the south, he had traveled through many provinces where he got many of the shamanistic somethings that he carried with him, and before that, he had come from a strange land, far beyond the great waters. He said he wanted to come into the city and bring greetings from his brothers and meet their people and talk to them about many wonders. He gave them his magic gourd rattle to show their chief. It had strings of little bells on it and two feathers, white and red. He said he had received this rattle from peoples on distant plains, and that it had magic powers and he had cured many people with it. He would perform cures among them, too."

The audience that gathered around the cairn was now quiet, paying rapt attention. The young man caught his breath and went on.

"They marveled about Estevan and said to us, 'We have never seen a man so dark before. Who is he?' At the same time they asked him, 'Are all your friends so dark, black like you?' And he said to them, 'No, you do not understand. My masters and my friends in the south, they are white men, not like me or any of you. There are thousands of them and you will meet them soon. But first, you must make friends with me.'

"They were astonished at this bold speech. So they turned to us, and said, 'How can this man be black in color and his friends be white in color? This makes no sense!'

"And we told them, 'We do not understand this either, but we can tell you, this man came to our village with people from the southern trade routes, and they say he arrived in their village with another man whose skin was as pale as dust. Pale men and black men both exist. The pale one, they call the man from heaven.'"

"That pale man is here, with us." The chiefs pointed to Marcos.

The mud-caked Indian, now quieter, stared at Marcos with a look that combined sadness, horror, and disgust. Slowly his face became more composed, as if he were finally realizing he was among friends, and he seemed to assess Marcos and the whole situation more critically.

The chiefs pressed around to hear better. "Tell us what happened next."

"Estevan sent his own messengers with these people back to Cíbola with his rattle to announce our presence. And the lord of the city took one look at the rattle, and recognized it as made by people who are enemies of Cíbola. So he said, 'These people must not enter the city, and if they do, they will be killed.' The messengers returned and told Estevan, but he said it was nothing. He said the worse people feared him at first, the better they liked him later. So he pushed ahead to Cíbola.

"People from Cíbola met him outside the city and refused him entry. They took all his goods from him and put us in a large building outside the city, where they gave us no food or water all night. The next morning I was thirsty, so I left the house and went to the little river to get a drink. Just moments later, I heard a tumult and I saw Estevan and my friends, running from the house, pursued by people from the city. There was a fight. I think they killed some of our friends. I saw this only from a distance and I fled up the river, under the cover of the bushes along the stream. I don't know what else happened. I crossed over the hills to the *despoblado* road, where I met you. . . ."

The unearthly wail started again from the crowd and many of the Indians turned toward Marcos with angry expressions.

CHAPTER 16

June—July 1989
Disillusionment

Saturday night in Alamos, after we found Marcos's notebook, we went out celebrating at Edward's favorite cantina. Later, we came back and sat talking one more time in Edward's patio garden. We were too excited and impatient to sleep. The moonlight painted the flowers in a ghostly, silvery color, and I wished Phaedra could be there to share those magic hours. I felt a kind of delirious happiness about the success of my mission. It was the kind of night I didn't want to end, and yet I couldn't wait to get back to the church the next morning. I suppose it was the kind of feeling Marcos had in those last nights as he approached Cíbola, when he still thought his journey was a perfect success.

I was telling Edward the story of what happened at Cíbola.

He reflected on it over his Dos Equis. "If civilization had come out of *our* desert, instead of the deserts of Iraq and Israel, then Cíbola and the Rio Grande pueblos would have figured as the Jerusalems and Babylons of our sacred books. The funny thing is that the Biblical stories happened two or three thousand years ago, but the same stuff was happening on our continent only 500 years ago, and yet we've lost it all. The beginnings of writing; big political battles; the birth of nations. If the Israelites and Arabs hadn't done it all first, we'd be reading scriptures about the leaders of Cíbola and the wild-eyed prophets who came out of the *despoblados*. John the Baptist anointing a future savior in the San Pedro River."

"We all have our own stories," I said finally, "but we forget the ones outside our own ethnic sub-group. Take Estevan, for example. He was the one who first crossed into the present U.S. and first sent back word of Cíbola, so why isn't he famous? He was brave, he was an explorer, he's a perfect symbol of the melting pot. There should be a twelve-foot statue of him at the U.S.–Mexico border, showing how our American and European histories were first linked by a guy from Africa!"

Edward took a swig from his bottle. "You're for it and I'm for it, but how're you gonna get the U.S. public to erect a statue to a black guy who disobeyed orders and botched the job?"

"Hey, that was only the last few weeks of his career. Any good hero should have one or two tragic failings. Look at his spirit! Tracker through the wilderness. Charismatic leader. He's the one who befriend the Indians in each village. He helped free the Indians down here from Guzman's slave raiders. Man of energy and daring. Look at his whole life."

"When has the American public ever been able to deal with a whole life? You only get to be a hero for one big thing. Charles Lindbergh for crossing the Atlantic. Neil Armstrong for having the first picnic on the moon. Babe Ruth for home runs. Estevan had his chance, but he blew the climax of his own story. Besides, you said part of his problem at Cíbola was that he liked s-e-x. Americans are too puritanical to put the official seal of approval on anyone with, um, a cheerfully messy sex life."

I didn't say anything.

"Americans want heroes who are asexual."

I still didn't say anything.

"Did you know there are rumors about Estevan down here, around Alamos?"

"No. What?"

"Among the Mayo Indians, Estevan was a famous guy. There used to be rumors that Estevan had fathered children when he passed through. Certain darker-skinned Mayos were supposed to be his descendants."

"Jeez!"

"We'll probably never know if it's true. It could be just a story. Still, you and I won't live to see a statue to an explorer who came to ruin because he fooled around with Indian women. Asexual nobility, that's what they want. Like a granite statue. No skeletons in the closet."

"Oh, come on. No one know if those stories were true."

"Yeah, and no one knows if JFK slept with Marilyn Monroe, but that doesn't keep the right-wingers from hating him just for the possiblity." He paused. "Conservatives drive me nuts, you know. You go back through history, they've been wrong on every big factual issue. The Earth moving around the sun. Evolution. Race relations. The ozone layer. Acid rain. And now probably global warming. But by definition, they have all the money, which means power, so on the short term we always live under their rules."

We sat for a moment, feeling the cool light of the moon washing over us—the same moon that presided over Estevan and the others. Daylit Mexico might have changed since the days of Coronado, but moonlit Mexico hadn't changed at all. "Coming back to Estevan," I told Edward, "you have to admit life dealt him a pretty interesting hand of cards, as my friend Phaedra would say. The plaque on the statue could just say he was gifted with great vitality."

Edward smiled. "About the Mayo Indians—they live on the Mayo River, not far from here. We ought to check it out. Stay on for a week. We could do it."

"Good idea."

We sat there until the air grew chill and the moon sank behind the tile roof.

"We could write a book about this whole thing," Edward said. "Together."

"Let's do it."

We shook hands on it. It was that simple. In the moonlight, everything is simple.

*   *   *

IDEAS RACED THROUGH MY BRAIN IN THE PREDAWN HOURS, AS I tried to get a few hours of fitful sleep. It no longer mattered what Mr. Rooney wanted to say or not say about the historical importance of the ruin at Coronado Estates. I had the answer and I had a new mission in life: to make the discovery known. Of course, it would take time for the scholars to analyze the document. The best thing I could do was to use leverage in the office to make sure Mr. Rooney built a good park that would preserve what we now knew to be Chichilti-Calli. Do justice to it.

I woke with a start. Outside the window the birds were celebrating the fact that, through some miracle, the sun had risen again, and light was magically streaming down from the sky. It slanted through the wooden louvers of the bedroom Edward had given me. Through the slits, I could see the colors of the rosy sun on the magenta bougainvillea, which had been silvery in the moonlight only hours before. In the distance I could hear a rooster—an unfamiliar sound that made me feel one with the whole world. It was going to be a great day.

Edward knocked on the door. "You up?"

"It's dawn," I called groggily from my bed. "Of course I'm up."

"It's not dawn, it's very early morning. We gotta get over to the church before the joint starts jumpin'. Listen, it's pretty bad news this morning about China. Hundreds of those students got shot, according to the reports. I'm running down to the market. I'll be back with breakfast. The news may be shitty, but I'll make you the best breakfast you've ever had."

HALF AN HOUR LATER WE WERE EATING OUR FRUIT AND BREAD ON Edward's veranda. The Chinese news could not reduce our enjoyment of the morning sounds and the morning flowers. We set out for the village of ———— and its church, Our Lady of Historic Treasures. I felt lucky, just to live in the western hemisphere. The chances were one out of five of being born in Mao's sterile paradise.

When we bounced up the dirt road into Father Antonio's tiny town, it was still early. The plaza was empty. We went around back, expecting to meet Father Antonio at the little back door to his office. I felt out of place, or rather out of time, as Edward nosed the mighty Pathfinder up to the low whitewashed churchyard wall in the dirt plaza behind the church. Edward picked up the cameras and I carried the tripod. The back doors were closed but the front church doors were standing open, and I remember marveling at the very idea of a peaceful village where the church could stand open.

We went in. It was dark and cool and quiet.

We retraced our footsteps of yesterday, toward the back rooms. The door to Father Antonio's room was ajar.

"Hello?"

Edward was in front of me as we went in. He recoiled violently against me. "Jesus! Jesus! Oh, my God!" He said it over and over. He pushed me back and I couldn't see. He was breathing hard.

"What's the matter?" I pushed forward.

"It's Antonio!"

As he said it, I got my first view. I remember Father Antonio lying face up, his eyes half open, staring vacantly at the grimy plaster ceiling. His mouth was a narrow crack, and there was blood on his face and all over the front of his shirt. More blood was pooled on the floor under his head, dark and evil. There had been a burst of automatic weapon fire. A neat row of bullet holes ran across the far wall; the white plaster was chipped by little craters and spattered with blood. There was a piece of cardboard propped against Antonio's body. Edward read the Spanish slogan: DOWN WITH COMMU-NIST PERVERSION OF THE CHURCH!

Edward was kneeling by Antonio. He had been careful not to step in the blood. "Stay back!" he said. "Don't touch anything." I try to remember what I felt at that moment, but it was happening too fast. I was still speechless, and amazed at how Edward had come to grips with the situation, as if he'd spent time planning what to do if something like this happened. "We've got to get out of here."

"What do you mean? We've got to report this."

"You don't know what you're talking about. Forget you ever saw this. This has never happened, as far as we know."

"But the police—"

"You don't know the system in this country. In the first place, the police will hold whoever they find near a crime like this. And likely charge them, just to say they've solved it. It's Napoleonic code, man; if they arrest you, there must be some reason, and you're guilty until you can prove you're innocent. In the second place, some of the police could be in on this; they could be looking for somebody to pin it on. A gringo agitator might fill the bill. You better hope to hell the wrong people didn't see us drive in here this morning."

"This must have happened hours ago, maybe last night. Somebody would have heard the shots; the locals would know we are not involved."

Edward was already pushing me backward, out of the room.

I was trying to force my way into the room. "The notebook!"

"Shhhh! Forget it, man."

"No. It's important. We've got to save it. If we leave now, we may never see it again."

I pushed past him to the chest, where Father Antonio had carefully placed the book the previous night. To Edward's credit, he grabbed a handkerchief to avoid leaving prints, and helped me unlatch the chest and open it. Our hands were shaking.

The lid rose. The book was gone. Everything else in the chest was as we had left it. I started to paw through the stuff. I was hysterical. It had to be here. Edward had to restrain me. We looked carefully around the room. I'm certain we looked carefully and thoroughly. We used the handkerchief to open the drawers of the little table without leaving prints. The book had vanished.

"Come on, man." Edward still had the cameras over his shoulder and grabbed the tripod. He shut the door. "Maybe nobody'll look in here for a while." We started toward the church door. There was still no one in the sanctuary. "Just walk slowly when we get out. In case anybody's out in the plaza, don't act excited. Remember, we never went into the back." He turned and flashed a couple of quick exposures toward the altar. "Insurance. We're just tourists."

I paused. "We should photograph the room, the crime."

"No, no. I don't want anything like that on my film. It would prove we were in there. Anybody stops us, this is what we came for, an early morning picture of the empty church. The light spilling through the doorway. C'mon."

We walked quietly to the car and pulled out, moving slowly at first to avoid making too much commotion. The plaza was still empty, as if the town were waiting for something to happen. After we left town, we drove fast.

WE TORE BACK TO HIS PLACE AND THREW MY STUFF IN THE CAR. IN a daze, I noticed Edward was packing all his stuff, too. He kept telling me to hurry. The next thing I knew, we were speeding out of Alamos for the airport. I felt like he was letting paranoia grow out of a tragedy, but I was still too much in shock to argue.

"What does it mean?"

"It means somebody was getting mad at Antonio's politics. Jesus. It means I'm getting out of here, too. I was too close to him, man."

"But the book. Why did they take the book?"

"How do you know anyone took it? Maybe Antonio carried it home with him."

"No. He put it back in the chest. I saw him."

"I don't know. Nobody stole the book. Nobody even knew about the book. When this blows over, you can come back and ask questions about the book. The church authorities, they'll have gone through Antonio's things. The book will turn up."

We were afraid to hang out in the airport itself, waiting for Mr. Rooney's friends to turn up at noon. We still had a couple hours to wait. We pulled into a parking spot at one end of the parking lot and waited in the car, where we could see what was going on. The sun was hot. There were lots of cars nestled against the curbs, as if it were an ordinary day. I kept expecting a couple of cars full of *Federales* to show up. We kept trying to calculate when someone might show up at the church and find Antonio, and how long it would take to notify the police, and how long it would take to come looking for us.

*   *   *

No cops showed up. Mr. Rooney's friends finally gathered at the airport. They were standing around, talking, smoking. The news of the murder had not yet reached them. We said nothing about it. We tried to act natural. "I'll be all right, man," Edward told me quietly. "I'll contact you. As soon as I get resettled."

I returned to Tucson still in a daze. I hardly remember the flight back. It was the last time I saw Edward.

The papers in Tucson during the next few days were full of news about China, not Mexico. I searched for something about Alamos. They were always reporting murders in Sonora. Nothing. By Wednesday, June 6, the news was that President Bush canceled our arms sales to Beijing. I never figured out why we were selling guns to the Chinese in the first place if we were so gung ho to fight communism. It must have been one of those subtle points of international policy that ordinary citizens could not understand.

I got my pictures developed. They showed that happy moment in the room, and you could see the notebook, but the closeup pictures were fuzzy and none of the pictures were definitive enough to identify anything or read any text. Still, they seemed to me to verify my story.

A day later I found the news from Alamos: a tiny article on page B-2 of the Tucson paper, along with an article about a Sonoran delegation visiting Tucson to promote tourism. Priest killed in church. Anticommunist death squad blamed. Governor of Sonora fears spread of leftist violence from southern Mexican states. Murders of this sort, the article explained, were already common in Chiapas, the south Mexican state where shadowy leftist rebels skirmished with shadowy progovernment factions favoring the established order. "Established order" meaning the landowning families, that is, and the police. Church officials were commonly accused by the government of encouraging leftist revolution. That night I had one of my weird dreams, in which Spanish conquistadors who looked like Mr. Rooney and Freddy the Fixer drove big cars along interstates that stretched north to Cíbola.

Politics wasn't my bag. Still, I felt I should be doing something. Talking to some authorities. But there was no one to talk to. No one on our side of the border had any jurisdiction. I told Phaedra. Phaedra said I should wait. Maybe Edward would call. Meanwhile, she said, I should go sit in some Catholic church, in remembrance of Father Antonio. But it would make no sense. No one would know what my gesture meant, and no god that I could believe in would think much of me sitting around on my duff, either.

I made an appointment to see Dr. Panofsky, my professor in the history department. I'd show him my notes and pictures. He'd know what to do.

What bothered me most was Marcos's book. Why would it disappear? Of course, Edward was right, I couldn't prove anyone stole it. Maybe Father Antonio came back that night and moved it to some place of safekeeping until we were to come on Sunday morning. Yes, he would have probably wanted to look at it more carefully, after I spelled out its importance.

When I went to see Dr. Panofsky, he had called several colleagues to hear what I had to say. They dragged chairs into his little office, and sat expectantly. I showed them my scribbled notes on Antonio's cheap paper, and the fuzzy photographs of a notebook lying open on top of a chest. Father Antonio's hand was in the picture, still alive, holding the notebook open, oh so carefully.

They laughed at me. Not to my face, but in effect. They had seen this kind of stuff before. Not-quite-focused pictures. Unverifiable notes. Apocryphal finds. Hearsay. Rumor. Tales of lost gold mines. To them I was a treasure-seeking amateur. They politely told me thanks for coming by. After the others left, Panofsky said, "I believe you, but what can I do? There's nothing here you could publish in a serious journal. If you get something more, be sure to let me know."

I couldn't blame them. In terms of hard evidence, I had nothing.

* * *

I talked to Phaedra about my visit to Panofsky. I waited for Phaedra's special talent to kick in, her uncanny ability to absorb the situation, and come up with new ideas. This time she listened and then told me what I already knew. "There's nothing you can do."

"But I can't just forget it."

"You can't jump into the middle of a political killing in another country. I'm just glad you got out of there okay." She gazed at me intently and took my hand.

"That book wouldn't have just disappeared. . . . Someone took it."

"You don't know that. Maybe it will turn up. No one would destroy something like that."

"I was so close. I had the key to this thing in my hand. Now—"

"You've got your life. You've got a good job. The notebook will turn up. Life has to go on."

It was nice for life to go on, but I started looking for a private detective. I didn't want to talk to anybody else about it. It seemed too crazy. There was a guy I had heard about once. "Investigations in Mexico," his ad said. That was good enough for me. I called. "Does it cost me to talk to you?"

"Take me to lunch at Magritte's," he said. It was a yuppie bistro on Congress, near my office. Carillo was his name. He was a debonair guy, muscular, in his forties, with a big black mustache and short black hair. He looked like he knew what he was doing. He said he had walked over from his office, but somehow he didn't even look sweaty. We sat on the tiny upstairs balcony, and I told him the story. I found I was telling it in hushed tones. The tables seemed too close together.

"There's nothing much you can do when the Mexican police are involved," he said. "Not through official channels, anyway. Meet me at my office, let's say 5:15, after you get off."

He had a grubby office on West Congress, across our dried-out river from downtown. It was nearby and I thought I ought to walk to get my exercise. I started in that direction but my route went right past my parking garage and it was so damn hot on the streets that I ducked into the garage and picked up my car. It made me feel guilty.

CARILLO INVESTIGATIONS, the sign said on the door. The main decoration inside was a calendar with a busty Aztec maiden holding a dead Aztec warrior. "The way you tell it," he said, "I can't just go in and say we want a notebook you saw there. But in terms of poking around, I've got friends down there. I called one of them. He's got cousins who've got friends who've got more cousins. Also, I know Alamos. I go there on business. Lots of wealthy American husbands and wives on the lam, usually shacked up with the party of the third part. I could fly down there, ask some questions, find out which police were there, who the suspects might be. Let's talk money. There's expenses. I don't just mean plane fare and hotels. To get good info, there are certain kinds of fees, if you get my drift."

I told him about my ludicrous checking account.

"That'll cover it. Why don't you write me a check for half of that? That'll get me down there. If I find the notebook, you double it. If I don't, you give me another check for half the amount of the first one. What d'ya say? I'm sure you got a savings account you're not telling me about. Ask around. People will tell you, I'm pretty honest when it comes to prices."

I wrote him the check and signed the one-page contract he pushed across the table.

"Give me a couple of weeks. A month, tops."

AROUND JULY 1 WE BROKE HEAT RECORDS THREE DAYS IN A ROW, with temperatures in the 110–112° range. Scientists talked global warming. President Bush's people still denied it. Republican congressmen assured the public it was "junk science."

Life was going on as usual.

In shopping malls throughout Polvoroso County, the petitions to restrict our development were being circulated. If enough petitions were signed, a public referendum on the rezoning would occur in

November. If it overturned the supervisors' rezoning vote, Mr. Rooney would have to start over and submit a new rezoning plan at lower density, with more attention to the ruin. Archaeology was the opening wedge of the opposition's attack, but land preservation was the main goal. Lower-density zoning would make the whole development much less profitable for Mr. Rooney.

I waited to see what instructions he would give me next.

A few days after I got back, he called me in and told me to bring my photos from Alamos. Mr. Beecher was sitting in the corner again, looking grim. He had a copy of my report on his knee. Mr. Rooney started through the whole thing one more time. "You make it sound like our site is a goddamn *Jamestown* or something. I went out there and looked at it when you were gone. It's just a bunch of rock foundations made by people who couldn't build as good as we do. Jesus, they didn't even shape the stones. So, anyway, you've got no way to prove whether our ruin really is Coronado's Chichi, right?"

"I told you, I think the notebook I found proves that Chichilti-Calli was our ruin."

"But you came back with nothing!"

I didn't say anything.

"Well, isn't that right?"

"Just my notes and photos."

"Show us the photos," Mr. Beecher said from the corner.

I handed over the prints. The negs were hidden at home. "They show the notebook, but not sharp enough to read anything. I couldn't get close enough with that camera."

Mr. Beecher scowled at them. "These are laughable," he said. He handed them back.

"So you've got nothing. Nothing that will stand up," Mr. Rooney said.

"I guess you could say that."

"You didn't tear out a page or something? Even a little scrap for a souvenir? It could be dated. Radiocarbon."

"God, no."

"Of course, to the agitators, the facts don't matter," Mr. Rooney said. "Those people don't care about the *actual* ruin; they just want to rally public opinion."

"By the way," Mr. Rooney added as I left, "don't say anything in public about your supposed notebook. We look bad enough as it is."

"There's not much I *can* say."

FOR THE NEXT FEW WEEKS, MR. ROONEY DIDN'T SHARE MANY thoughts with the staff, but sometimes I could hear him shouting angrily behind the doors of his office. During those awkward moments, Phaedra would roll her eyes. She was very good about keeping her job separate from her ordinary life, and did not pass on much privileged information about what was going on. Word around the office was that Mr. Rooney had commissioned a poll, which revealed the electorate was 71 percent against the development. Seasoned pols said the petition passers could easily get the twenty-five thousand signatures they needed to call the special election, which meant we would lose our zoning.

The TV news covered the opposition passing the little pink petitions at shopping centers, banks, car washes, everywhere. SAVE THE CORONADO RUIN. It was ironic that they had no proof that it was Coronado's ruin. I had gone all the way to Mexico and found the proof, but couldn't back it up, and they had less than I did. Just a theory. My theory. The pure, romantic possibility, unsullied by fact, made everyone want to save it. From us.

Everyone in our office was angry every day. All the upper echelons, Mr. Rooney, Mr. Beecher, and their aides believed not only that there must be a way to win this, but that we had a right to win it. To them, wealth was the material manifestation of moral superiority.

Everywhere I went, life seemed to get more surreal. In the U.S. it was the surrealism of wealth standing in the sunlight in the public square and declaring itself to be virtue. In Mexico, it was the surrealism of wealth hiding in the shadows, pretending not to exist, like death behind the cheerful crosses and flowers in the town cemetery, and like the sinister presence hidden in the music of Revueltas.

* * *

JULY 15. THIS WAS THE DATE WHEN CORONADO HAD WRITTEN TO the king from his frontier post in Compostela to say that he had heard of Marcos's discovery of a "very fine country" to the north and that the Indians were treating Marcos and Estevan well. As usual, my mental clock was ticking off the events of Marcos's summer. I was still Chief Inspector Scott, Detective of Time.

I kept watching the paper for news about Alamos, and the mail for a letter from Edward. Nothing. Where was he?

JULY WORE ON. YOU HAVE NO IDEA HOW WEARING SUMMER CAN BE in Tucson, the tenth and then the twentieth day with afternoons hovering around 100 degrees or 110 degrees. The annual summer thunderstorms were finally starting in the southeast corner of the state, as the seasonal mass of moist air worked its way up from the Gulf of Mexico; but Tucson wouldn't get its first cooling rain until that air mass reached us. Lightning touched off grass fires not far from our property. The fires didn't matter around our office; we were planning to remove the vegetation anyway.

A few days later, the great summer thunderheads of moisture finally marched on our city from the east, rising up in massive phalanxes over the Rincons. Armies of clouds encircled the city each afternoon, and lightning flashed in the evening darkness. This happened day after day, but it took many days before the rains finally started.

Phaedra was growing more changeable, too. Some days she'd meet me with warm sunshine, but other days she was a wall of clouds. She'd say Mr. Rooney was getting more uptight, the job was getting harder, and she didn't want to talk about it. Women always ask for communication from men, but I'm sure they use the phrase "I don't want to talk about it" more than we do.

After the first heavy rains, the Santa Cruz River came to life. It gurgled through Tucson in short-lived happiness, and carried off debris such as construction materials, tree limbs, and an occasional Volkswagen. When I was in high school, I knew a Mexican kid who said his grandfather could remember when the river ran most of the year and they used to go swimming in it every summer afternoon.

On the rainy days we finally got our afternoon respite from the heat with the temperature dropping from the 90s to 70 in half an hour. On other days it would stay over a hundred all afternoon. Still, once the monsoon season arrived, the psychology of summer had an element of hope for the first time.

On the streets, the people passing the pink petitions were getting more signatures every day.

DURING THE WEEK OF THE FIRST RAINSTORMS, CARILLO CALLED and asked me to come over.

"I had a nice vacation in Alamos," he said when I got there.

"I don't want to know about *vacations*. I want to know about the *notebook*." I was beginning to talk like Mr. Rooney.

"Yeah, well. I'm afraid there was more vacation than notebook. But I gave it the old college try and I learned a few things for you. There were three *Federales* called out to that church that Sunday morning after the killing was reported. Later, the same three worked on the so-called investigation. I know somebody who knows somebody and I got to talk to one of them. He had a distinct impression from their bosses that this was a job where, you know, nobody wanted too many questions asked around town. In a political killing, if the killers are locally powerful people, sometimes it's better not to know, see? So when the police announce that this killing was a political statement against church policy by unknown terrorists, it makes a convenient nonsolution. No locals want to come forward in a situation like that. But my guy was pretty straight with me. He said there was no sign of anything having been disturbed in the church office. They're sure it wasn't a robbery thing. There was money in the desk and in the victim's pocket. Also, there were no rumors about missing notebooks or papers or anything like that, either among the police or around town."

"So what was it all about?"

"Maybe just what they said. A hit from the powers that be. There's a lot of wealthy ranchers and mine owners down there, want to nip land reform in the bud. They don't want another Chiapas uprising. If you're sitting on land your family has occupied for six generations, you don't like any talk of the government coming in and carving it into *ejido* farms for the peasants. You want to preserve the system. Especially if you're growing marijuana or something lucrative like that." Carillo wiped his hands together, as if he had finished a meal. He looked around his office. "Anyway, you've got a pretty cold trail. A dead end. Except for one thing."

"What's that?"

"I hung around town. There were rumors. I tracked down this old guy. He claimed he had seen a green Pathfinder driving into the village at three in the morning. That's unusual in a little town like that. Three or four guys in it."

"Green."

"Yeah. A new-looking one."

"Three A.M."

"Yeah. Your late-model Pathfinders, they are a sign of the upper classes. Ranch owners for example. Your friends stayed out on the Gonzales ranch, right?"

"Yeah."

"The thing is, I learned Gonzales has two or three green Pathfinders out there. Ranch cars. Local scuttlebutt is that he's connected to the drug trade. Doesn't prove anything. Nobody got a license number, anything like that. Coulda been from anywhere. Still . . . like I said, about preserving the system."

"That's it?"

"I did the best I could. I got pretty damn close to it, in fact. Closer than I'd like. Nobody could do any better. Like I said, my guess is that somebody wanted the priest out of the way. Maybe Gonzales or maybe somebody else."

"You left out one thing. Why was the notebook missing?"

"I talked to the church officials. They went through Father Antonio's things. They agree there were lots of old records in the room, and they recognized your description of the chest. But they say there was no old notebook, no BIMBO bag. Are you sure you didn't make all that up?"

I didn't say anything. He studied me intently. "No. Well," he said, "I just wondered. I mean, you seem so interested in that old Spanish stuff, I was trying to figure what's in it for you. You come back from Mexico, telling the other *aficionados* you've seen this historic notebook, it sorta puts you on the map. It's like those Lost Dutchman mine stories, where somebody claims to have seen a map—"

"I saw it."

"Maybe your priest friend hid it somewhere. Or maybe he was looking at it when they came for him. Somebody saw that it was old and took it home as a souvenir. I don't know. . . ."

That was the end of the story. I quit for the day and went for a lonely beer in the Old Adobe Patio, a venerable downtown patio-restaurant that was about to be put out of business by some renovation to create office space.

THE SCUTTLEBUTT IN OUR OFFICE WAS THAT BEFORE THE REFERendum could occur, Mr. Rooney would have Tony Beecher contest everything they could think of about the petition. Arizona law, with its slant toward veiled plutocracy, provided a smorgasbord of ways to shoot down public referendums. The lawyers would find signatures where people forgot to add their zip code, or neglected the middle initial they had used on their voter registration form, or gave a different address than the one they listed when they had registered. By the logic of the election process, these lapses meant they were incompetent to vote or have an opinion on Polvoroso County issues.

The counterscuttlebutt on the streets was that the petition passers were marching ahead, and would easily gather twice the number of signatures they actually needed—enough excess to insure an election even after Tony Beecher's minions had combed the petitions for signatures to reject over legal trivialities.

The counter-counterscuttlebutt in our office was that with the kind of money Mr. Rooney had raised for this project, spending a few hundred thousand to tie up the referendum in court would be chicken feed. The citizens' groups would find it hard to raise this kind of money to fight back.

Sometimes I thought about how I could publicly tell my story about the lost Marcos notebook, contrary to Mr. Rooney's advice. At least that would establish the facts of the route, and then the controversy could proceed from there. Maybe I could write it up in some kind of scholarly article, as part of an account of my research on Marcos. But I kept coming back to the fact that I had nothing to back up my claims.

In the end I said nothing in public. I felt like one of those minor gods up on Mt. Olympus, knowing important truths and watching foolish mortals struggle, but having little power over the outcome.

CHAPTER 17

Marcos Reports on Cíbola

Marcos's life and my life had turned upside down. I had made a quest to Mexico and ended up on the fringes of a murder; Marcos had made a quest to Cíbola and the same thing happened to him. Marcos told about his own disaster in his *Relación*. After he met the first bloodied refugee, the chief's son who had fled up the river and reported a skirmish, the Indians in his own party, the ones from the Nexpa Valley, began to turn against him.

After we received the ruinous news of the events at Cíbola from the first Indian who had escaped, I feared all would be lost. It was not so much losing my life that I feared, but being unable to return with information about the greatness of the country, where God, Our Lord, could be so well served, and the royal patrimony of His Majesty could be enlarged. In spite of everything, I consoled my Indian companions as best I could, and told them they should not necessarily believe everything the fugitive said. But they told me, through tears, that he wouldn't have described anything he hadn't seen.

So I withdrew to ask Our Lord to preside over this matter according to His will, and to enlighten my heart. Having done this, I returned to the others. With a knife I cut the cords of the bundles of clothing and trade goods that I had been carrying. Until then I had not opened these bundles, nor given anything

from them to anyone, but now I distributed them among all the
chiefs, and told them not to fear, that they should go along with
me. And they did.

Marcos now pushed on for a day or two toward Cíbola, and
reached a point one *jornada* from the first city—the same area
from which Estevan had sent his messengers to Cíbola. At this
point, he found two more survivors from the group who had gone
with Estevan.

They came covered with blood and with many wounds, and
upon their arrival, they and those with me began such weeping
that it made me cry, too, from both compassion and fear. There
was so much commotion and outcry I was not able to learn
anything about Estevan, or what his group had suffered. I
urged them to calm down, so we could learn what happened.

"How can we be silent," they replied, "when hundreds may
be dead among our fathers, sons, and brothers who were with
Estevan? We have always gone to Cíbola, but now we can
never dare to go there again!"

I tried to pacify them as best I could, and rid them of fear,
though I was not without needing someone to rid me of it
myself! I asked the wounded Indians about Estevan and what
had happened. At first, they wouldn't speak to me, standing
and weeping with their friends from their own towns. Finally,
they told me how Estevan arrived at the place one jornada
from Cíbola, and how he sent his messengers with his talisman
gourd rattle (the one with the bells and red and white feathers)
to the chief of Cíbola, to make it known that he was coming in
peace, and to perform cures.

Marcos went on to describe how these Indians confirmed the
story of the first one, that the governor of Cíbola concluded from
the style of the rattle that Estevan's party consisted of enemies, and

angrily refused them entry. From their account, Marcos put together a more detailed account of the disaster.

The messengers returned to Estevan very upset, fearing to tell him what happened. When they finally did tell him, he said not to worry, it was nothing. . . . He was sure that even though the lords of Cíbola had answered angrily, they would receive him well. So he traveled on, arriving at the city of Cíbola just before sunset, along with all the people who had gone with him, who must have numbered more than three hundred men, not counting many women who had gone with them.

The Cíbolans wouldn't let Estevan enter the city, but put his party into a large building with good apartments, outside the city. They personally confiscated everything that Estevan carried, telling him that their chief had ordered this. This included his trade articles and the turquoises and other things he had received from villagers along the road.

The escapees reported to me, "All that night they gave us nothing to eat or drink. Next day, when the sun was a lance-length high, Estevan went from the building with some of our chiefs. At once, many people came out of the city, and when he saw them, he began to flee, and we with him. Immediately, they inflicted these arrow wounds and gashes on us. We fell down and other men fell on top of us, dead. So we remained until night, without daring to move. We heard loud voices in the city, and saw many men and women watching from the terraces of the city. We saw no more of Estevan, but we think they shot him with arrows as they did the rest. No one escaped but us."

In view of all this, and the terrible prospects for the rest of the journey, all I could think about was their loss and mine. God knows how much I wished for someone to give me good council and assistance, for I confess that I felt at fault.

I told them Our Lord would punish Cíbola, and that when the Emperor learned what had happened, he would send many

Christians to chastise them. But they didn't believe me, because they believe no one can withstand the might of Cíbola. I begged them to feel better and stop weeping, and I consoled them with the best words I could find—too many to repeat here.

After this, I withdrew a stone's throw or two, for an hour and a half, to commend myself to God. When I came back, I found one of my Indians, Marcos, crying. He was one of those I had brought with me from Mexico. He told me, "Father, these people have plotted to kill you, because they say it is your fault that Estevan and their kin are dead. They believe that no one, man or woman, is likely to survive this trip."

I proceeded to distribute what I had left of the garments and trade articles, to calm them, and I urged them to realize that even if they killed me, they could really not harm me because I would die a Christian, and would go to heaven. But those who killed me would suffer, because more Christians would come to search for me and kill all of them, even though such a thing would be against my own wishes. These words and my other speeches appeased them, though they still felt great resentment over the people who had been killed.

I proposed that some of them should go on with me to Cíbola, to see if anyone had escaped, and to learn what we could about Estevan, but got nowhere with this plan. At last, two of the chiefs, seeing me determined to go on, said they would go with me.

With these and my own Indians and interpreters, I pursued my journey until within sight of Cíbola. It is situated on a plain at the skirt of a round hill. It has the appearance of a very beautiful town, the best I have seen in these parts. The houses are of the style that the Indians had described, all of stone, with stories and terraces, as well as I could see from a hill where I could view it. The city is bigger than Mexico City. At times, I was tempted to go on to the city itself, because I knew I risked only my life, which I had offered to God on the day I started the journey. But, in the end, I was afraid to try it. I real-

ized I was in danger and that if I died, I would not be able to make a report on this country, which to me appears the greatest and best of the discoveries we made.

When I remarked to the chiefs about how beautiful this city was, they replied that this one was the least of the Seven Cities. Furthermore, Totonteac, the kingdom beyond Cíbola, is even better than these seven. They said it has so many houses and people that it has no end.

Viewing the geographic setting of the city, I thought it appropriate to name this country the new kingdom of Saint Francis. There, with the aid of the Indians, I made a great heap of stones, and on top of it I placed a cross, small and light because I lacked the equipment to make it larger. I announced that I was erecting this cross and monument in the name of Don Antonio de Mendoza, Viceroy of New Spain, for our lord the Emperor, in token of possession and conforming to the instructions. I proclaimed that in this act of possession I was taking all of the Seven Cities, plus the kingdoms of Totonteac and Ácus and Marata beyond, and that the reason I didn't proceed onward to them was to return and give account of what I did and what I saw.

And so I turned back, more full of fear than food. With the greatest haste, I rushed to overtake the people I had left behind. I overtook them after two days of travel, and went with them all the way until the end of the fifteen-day despoblado. Here, they did not give me as good a reception as before, because the men, as well as the women, were making a great lament for their friends killed at Cíbola.

Still fearful, I hurried immediately from the people of that valley, and went ten leagues the first day, then eight, then ten, [about 20 to 31 miles per day] without stopping until past the second despoblado.

Whenever I read this account, I was overwhelmed by the sad irony of it. Here, then, was the climax of all Marcos's efforts. In a few fateful hours, the bluster of self-confident Estevan had created a disaster. In a single day the natives of southern Arizona, who had cheered Marcos's and Estevan's arrival, became fearful antagonists to the Spanish cause. Moreover, while all the information Marcos recorded about Cíbola was essentially true and could be confirmed in modern Zuni—the multistory buildings, the stone construction, the turquoises in doorways, the broad community of towns full of intelligent people—Marcos lost his chance to confirm the exact nature of the cities. Instead of returning in triumph, he was now fleeing without having set foot in the city and without any certain knowledge of what had happened to Estevan.

As with many of Marcos's other details, the story of how Estevan was detained outside Cíbola was supported by later historical evidence. In 1896, the twenty-five-year-old historian George Winship, fresh out of Harvard, published a crucial study of the Coronado documents, noting in a footnote that Estevan's detention in a house outside of Cíbola "is precisely the method pursued by the Zunis today against any Mexican who may be found in their vicinity during the performance of an outdoor ceremonial." Some scholars believe that Estevan, arriving in the latter part of May, might have unknowingly violated some taboos associated with springtime ceremonies. In any case, was Estevan really dead, as the Indians had suggested? Marcos could not be sure.

MEANWHILE, IN MEXICO CITY, OTHER EVENTS WERE UNFOLDING in that summer of 1539. I was confident of my reconstruction of what was happening there during June and July, while Marcos was still hastening back to the south. The cheerful messages he had sent back on his way north began to filter into the ecclesiastical and court circles. Since Marcos knew how far it was to Cíbola, he was also able to send Mendoza a prediction that he could be back in Mexico City in August with firsthand reports of the Seven Cities. Viceroy Mendoza had wanted Marcos's reports to be secret, but among the power brokers, gossip was spreading about the populous and prosperous lands beyond the northern frontier—lands ripe for picking. Cortés, who must have had his spies everywhere, was one of the first to respond. With disingenuous innocence, he wrote to the viceroy on July 26, 1539, claiming that he was already sure of such a country's existence, and offering to take over the exploration with his own ships—no doubt the last thing Mendoza wanted to hear. The wording absolutely confirms that news of Marcos's discoveries arrived before Marcos himself did.

> *I am infinitely pleased . . . with the news about Fray Marcos because although I was certain that a good country would be found, I did not think it was so near. My ships will find out what may be beyond, which I am sure must be something great. God desires that we shouldn't be idle, but act otherwise, because he placed us here for each to use his own talents. As Fray Marcos will return so soon, he will give more news. I beg your worship to order that the details be sent to me, especially about the location where it is, for I firmly believe he will have marked it down.*

The first few lines seem to confirm that the July rumors dealt only with "the good country" that Marcos had found in Sonora, but not the ultimate goal, which lay "beyond" and might be found to "be something great."

The Spanish archives contain another letter from Cortés to the viceroy, written nearly two weeks later on August 6 from Cuernavaca, about seventy miles south of Mexico City. This letter shows again that good news from Marcos was circulating, and that Viceroy Mendoza had sent Cortés some confirmation of the discovery of good northern lands, based on Marcos's messages.

> *Distinguished Sir:*
> *Today I received great favor and much happiness, when your lordship sent the letter concerning news of Friar Marcos. I had been wishing to receive this news on account of what is being said around here about that country. I hadn't given credence to*

it until I saw your letter, since your lordship had written to me that you would have me informed of whatever Friar Marcos might say.

It's worth rendering praise to God . . . that in our very own times He is pleased to reveal to us this knowledge that has so long lain hidden. We may succeed in giving Him thanks for so great a boon by making proper use of it.

If anyone is going to be successful in this affair, surely it is God himself. It was God who wished to reveal this, not by expenditures for huge fleets by sea and large armies by land, but through a single, barefoot friar, so that we may better understand . . . that to Him alone the glory is due, and nothing can be attributed to man.

By August, all Mexico City was abuzz with rumors of Marcos's good discoveries, and everyone awaited his joyous return. No one yet knew about the debacle in the supposedly golden empire, or the nature of its cities.

CHAPTER 18

May—October, 1539
The Man from Heaven Returns to
Mexico City

M*ay 26*. Around and around went the thought in Marcos's head as he fled down the trail south from Cíbola. Was he a coward for turning back? Twenty-four hours earlier, he had stood on a ridge above the mouth of a canyon, gazing north upon the legendary province. With his own eyes, he had seen the evidence that the stories were true. The canyon mouth, to which his nervous guides had led him stealthily through the scrubby forest, opened out of hills due south of the city. Crouching out of sight behind some large rocks, he had a view across a broad, flat plain toward a large, craggy, round mesa. The mesa had sheer, castlelike rock walls at the top and a hilly slope slanting two-thirds of the way up the sides. An impressive city climbed up the lower slopes in clusters of buildings. There was no doubt about the architecture; in the main part of the city, he could see tiers of room blocks rising at least four stories high as they stepped up the slope. It was no dream; his own sketch showed the terraced buildings he had recorded in those fevered moments. Outlying structures of one and two stories were scattered around the base of the hill, and on the plain. The plain was a broad, flat river valley, divided by a line of low bushes marking an inconspicuous river course or canal. Irregularly shaped farm fields, green and golden, checkered the plain. Little brush structures dotted the fields, apparently for the farmworkers. The whole scene gave off a sense of fertility and prosperity, like a well-ordered agricultural town in Spain, France, or Italy.

Two Macaw Feathers was one of those who had crept with Marcos through the backcountry to this canyon. "This isn't my city of Ahacu," he whispered into Marcos's ear as if the people of the distant city would hear them. It is down the valley, to the left." He pointed west. "Ahacu is the town Estevan would have approached. It is the best town. This valley runs on both downstream and upstream, where there are other cities. The province of Cíbola is very large and has many people."

Marcos could see the cultivated fields stretching in both directions along the valley. If there were six more cities, the province was large indeed, covering more area than the island-bound city of Tenochtitlán that Cortés conquered.

"Will you go on to Ahacu, then, to your own city?" Marcos asked him.

"After the news about Estevan and his party, it is a bad time. I will lead you back out of this canyon, away from Cíbola, and wait for a better time to come back."

IF THE STORIES BROUGHT BY THE INDIANS WERE TRUE, MEMBERS of the party from the Nexpa had been killed on the river plain somewhere near Ahacu, west of the town he had seen. And Estevan too? Or were he and other Nexpa natives being held captive in some dungeons of Ahacu or one of the other cities?

To turn back from a point so close to his goal had seemed madness. How much more might he have learned about life in the cities themselves? Yet, if he had gone any closer, it would have risked everything he had worked for, everything he had learned. The last message the viceroy would receive would be only the message of good news that he had sent back from the village on the Nexpa. If the people of Cíbola were as hostile and unfriendly as the recent disaster indicated, the viceroy should be warned before sending another party into the jaws of danger. If there were six other towns of the size he had seen, and perhaps smaller satellite villages, it might take an army to subdue the whole province and bring it the

light of the church. Prudence—or was it fear?—won the debate in
Marcos's mind. With one last look over his shoulder, he had begun
his retreat. "Hurry, hurry," Tall Man kept saying. "If Estevan told
them that more Spaniards were on the way, they will be looking for
us. We can rest at sunset, but the moon will rise a couple of hours
later and we can walk for a few more hours before sleeping." They
traveled as fast as they could, with Tall Man and the other Mexican
warriors posted at the front and back of the party.

MAY 28. AFTER TWO DAYS OF FORCED MARCH ACROSS THE GRASS-
lands, Marcos struggled into the forested hills. His mind was growing dazed with lack of sleep, lack of food, and the hypnotic
repetition of footsteps on the trail. Every hour had been a hour of
doubt. They hiked into the night, and started again before dawn,
covering as much as ten leagues per day instead of the more usual
six or seven that marked a good *jornada*.

Marcos could not help but reflect that only a few days before,
when he had traversed this fifteen-day *despoblado* in the other
direction, he had been full of cheer, satisfaction, and optimism.
Now, the hourglass of fate had been inverted, and the sands ran
from good to bad. Why had the Lord turned this grand voyage of
exploration into a debacle? Why was he suddenly being punished?
God had led him forward into new lands, each more pleasing than
the last—land crying out for missionization, like a lost sheep looking for a shepherd. And now, this! All the hopes, all the accomplishments seemed snatched from him in an hour, in a minute, in
the twinkling of an eye. How could fortunes change so fast?

With each step, Marcos gnawed at the problem like a dog
wrestling with a bone. It was all because of the willfulness of Estevan. If the Moor had just followed orders. . . . If only Estevan had
not run ahead on the trail. . . . If only he had heeded the Cíbola governor's order not to approach the city. . . . They could have camped
together, somewhere across the valley from the first town, and
parleyed until the people of Cíbola understood their peaceful intentions. In all Estevan's years wandering in this new world, he had

seen only the poor villages of the eastern prairies and the valleys of New Spain. He had no experience with the sophistication of a kingdom as mighty as Cíbola.

What was the fatal moment that destroyed all their dreams? Wasn't the whole disaster set in motion much earlier, in Vacapa, when Marcos decided to send Estevan a few days on ahead? Was it his own fault, then? But he had given Estevan such clear instructions. . . .

Suddenly there were voices ahead. Dozens of figures were up there, on the trail. It was the chiefs and their followers who had come north with them from Chichilti-Calli, but who had refused to go on toward Cíbola when the bad news arrived. Marcos's party had caught up with them. Marcos felt a wave of relief with his party reunited, but it was short-lived. Tall Man came running back from the front of the party. "You better wait here," he said. Then he and Two Macaw Feathers returned to the knot of people who were gathering on the trail ahead, like wolves gathering in a pack.

Marcos was weary. He hardly dared to sit down to rest, because it would be too hard to get up again. He leaned on his staff and said a prayer instead, asking for resolve to go on, in the face of danger and dashed hopes.

Finally, Tall Man came back to join him. "It is not good. The men who came with us from the Nexpa Valley, they say that you are no longer welcome among them. One of the chiefs sends you this message: 'You and Estevan came to them from the south saying you brought good news. But you have brought only sorrow. Our friends are dead and you have made enemies of the people of Cíbola, with whom we used to trade.' Some of them want to slay you as a gesture to reestablish friendship with Cíbola. Other voices were raised on your behalf. They said, 'He is a good man, he did not mean harm to us. He brought us gifts, and he has many brothers to the south who would harm us if we do harm to him.' Finally, they all agreed that it is better for you to live and go home to your people. They will not attack you. But you are not welcome to travel among them."

Marcos was too weary to protest or invent some new strategy. "What should we do?"

"We have to follow them on the trail at a distance. They don't want to talk to you. They will move very fast to get out of this country and back to their people."

"But they were my friends."

"Not anymore."

Marcos could see the chiefs up ahead, carefully turned away from him. When he caught the eye of any of them, it was only a cold and hostile glare.

JUNE 6. ALREADY THEY WERE IN THE PROVINCE OF CHICHILTI-Calli, having flown through the wilderness of mountains like a bird going south for the winter. It was as if the Indians had deliberately been testing his endurance. Marcos was exhausted. He had been hoping for rest and safety, once they reached these first villages south of the long *despoblado*. But the travelers from the Nexpa had retained their aloof antagonism during the whole trip. And there was little succor to be had now that they reached the towns. In the first village, when news spread, women had come forth to scream at him and shake their fists. Many of them had been told their sons might be dead on the plains in front of Cíbola. Two Macaw Feathers, as well as the young guide who had been trying to impress Marcos, said they would remain at this village. Marcos, along with his guides and translators from Mexico, had been forced to sleep without a brush hut amid the cottonwoods outside the village, with Tall Man keeping watch. Even Tall Man seemed to eye him strangely, as if making some evaluation. Marcos tried to find something to thank God for; all he could find was that he was alive, on a cool river, and that although the days were now hot on the trail, the nights were pleasant.

In the remaining villages along the Nexpa, people glared silently at him from the huts and ramadas. Word of the events at Cíbola had spread ahead of them along the trail. The villagers' faces were like stone. Marcos's party was told not to stop within the towns. No additional word from Cíbola had caught up with them, which was only to be expected because they were fleeing south so fast. Rumors trickled out from the villages. Everyone was terrified that warriors from Cíbola would arrive with some fearful ultimatum. Was it possible that Cíbola would try to make war on them for sending Estevan and Marcos north?

Marcos and his remaining party pressed on into the second *despoblado*, south of the Nexpa headwaters.

JUNE 14. IN THE FIRST VALLEY SOUTH OF THE NEXPA, THEY finally encountered Indians who smiled and shared food more willingly. At last Marcos began to lose his fear. The villagers built brush huts for him and he could rest at last. Yet he could not afford to make long stops, as he had done coming north. Hostile messengers might come from Cíbola or the Nexpa villages to stir up trouble against him, and in any case he must try to reach Culiacán and Compostela, where he could report to Governor Vázquez de Coronado, and send word of his discoveries on to the viceroy. What would he report to the viceroy? His brief view of Cíbola across the valley revealed much less than Mendoza would want to know. Marcos would have to emphasize the details he had learned from the Indians on the way north. How much time had he actually spent in sight of Cíbola? Probably less than a quarter part of an hour! Pitiful.

ALONG THE TRAIL HE TALKED TO TALL MAN, THE ONLY ONE LEFT who would listen to him. Tall Man remained quiet, as if using the opportunity to soak up more Spanish before reaching Culiacán. "Everything has a purpose," said Marcos. "Cíbola has done ill to us, and the viceroy will have to send many soldiers to protect the next expedition. Perhaps this is God's way of bringing enough Christians into this northern world to settle it and set up a new branch of His kingdom on Earth. Anyway, when we go back to Cíbola, God will reveal his own plan."

"We?"

"I meant the Christians in general, but who knows? Maybe you and I will be among them. Yes, I would go back. Perhaps my calling is to find out what happened to Estevan, and set right his death."

"Avenge it?" Tall Man looked excited.

"No . . . Unless they continue to show violence toward us. We must try to establish good dealings with them, not start many generations of hostilities. Meanwhile, do you remember that when we came north along the coast, people told us of towns where there might be gold or other metal to the east, in the mountains? As we go south, we will stay to the east, and inquire about gold in the inland mountains. Perhaps, as far as gold is concerned, we can still find something more definite to report to the viceroy."

JULY 8, LATE AFTERNOON. AFTER WEEKS OF TRAVAIL, MARCOS finally sat at the rude wooden table in what the soldiers laughingly called "the Governor's Palace" in the rustic town of San Miguel de Culiacán. Outside, the heat of the day was dissipating. How good, at last, to be back in civilization, with a glass of wine in his hand! Two giggling Indian servant girls were about to bring him a supper of beans and mutton stew. He could hardly believe he was safe at last. He and his party had encountered foraging Spanish soldiers north of Petatlán. In the interests of getting his message to the governor, he had forgone his custom of walking—and had accepted a horse to ride the last thirty leagues. He was almost afraid of this luxury, for he did not want to lose the toughness of the trail. His journey was not over. Another forty days of travel, more or less, were needed to reach Mexico.

The frontier province around Culiacán was in peace, God be praised. Governor Vázquez de Coronado was not to be found there. He had gone on his own expedition toward a land called "Topira," in the mountains to the north and east to investigate rumors that gold was used there. On the return journey, Marcos, too, had stayed to the east and had attempted to penetrate the mountain gorge where gold had been mentioned, but the country was very rough. After confirming stories that the Indians there had only earrings and small implements of gold, he had decided to press on to Culi-acán. He hoped Vázquez had had better success. The soldiers said he was planning to return to the provincial headquarters in Com-postela, twelve *jornadas* to the southeast, on the road to Mexico City. After a day of rest, Marcos would have to leave for Com-postela in hopes of finding the governor there. In his zeal to carry his news as quickly as possible to the governor and the viceroy, he would continue to allow himself the luxury of travel by horse and wagon.

JULY 22. AS THE MIDDAY SUN SHONE DOWN FROM NEARLY OVER-head, Marcos rode into Compostela with an advance group of horsemen that had left the pack train two days back. Twenty-nine-year-old Francisco Vázquez de Coronado strode across the bright cobblestones and greeted Marcos heartily, shaking his hand and giving him a mock Roman salute: "Hail the conquering hero!" The soldiers laughed and shared in the cordiality.

Almost before Marcos had a chance to gather his breath, the jovial governor started reviewing the situation as they walked across the bright plaza in front of the town's little church. "I myself just returned to Compostela only nine days ago from Topira. What a waste of time! We found some mineralization in the mountains and a few small trinkets, but there is no golden treasure there. Not like Tenochtitlán. I was very disappointed, but then I got your letter when I arrived here, your letter about . . ."—he lowered his voice—"the rich lands you have found. By order of the viceroy I have not talked about these things publicly." Marcos noticed one or two of the soldiers straining to overhear these tidbits.

"Already on the sixteenth," Vázquez continued, "I sent messen-gers with your letter to Mendoza, and I also sent a letter to the king with the same messengers, to inform him of your good news, the grandeur of the lands you found, and the good treatment the Indi-ans gave you and Estevan. This is a wonderful day. You are safe and we are together again."

"Wait . . ." Marcos said, as they entered the cool shade of the governor's quarters. "There is other news . . ." He had been dreading this moment.

Vázquez hustled Marcos inside. "No, no. We must not talk here," the governor said, glancing around furtively. "You must clean up first. Miguel here will show you the rooms I have set aside for you here in my own house. Wash away the dust and then we will talk further. Here are my private chambers, where no one can hear us. A plate of tortillas and beans, and a pitcher of wine will await us in half an hour."

Marcos marveled at Vázquez de Coronado's self-possession. "I must tell you," he whispered, "the news is not all good."

THEY MET AGAIN IN THE GOVERNOR'S ROOM, BEHIND A MASSIVE door. They sat where the room opened onto a breezy enclosed porch on one side, out of earshot of the soldiers. Cascades of bougainvillea fell from pots in the garden. Marcos began pouring out his story in hushed tones, even before the wine arrived. At first, Vázquez betrayed a flash of anger when he learned of the debacle in Cíbola. Then silence. As Marcos finished his plate of beans, the governor's smiles and vigor returned, like one of those strange Indian balls of rubber, that bounced from the floor back into the hand. "Listen, you are right that some of this news is not as good as we hoped. But we must look at the whole melon, not just the seeds that stick in our craw."

And at once Vázquez began to outline a strategy. "Your trip, after all, has been a success in terms of the viceroy's original orders. Cíbola and other northern empires have passed from rumor to reality, thanks to you. And we know there is a road to get there. If we are ever to have a conquest of the north, that is what people must hear in Mexico City. Yours was a successful mission of discovery, in spite of the unpleasantness with that fellow Estevan. After all, he was only a servant, and an unruly one at that. You were brilliant in the face of a difficult task. You got information about the coast, you sent back messages, you reached this place called Cíbola, and you confirmed both from Indians and from your own eyesight that it is a populous and good land. This is a record we can be proud of."

Marcos flushed with pleasure and noticed the governor's "we" with an inward smile. Now it had become partly *his* discovery. Governors were all cut from the same cloth!

"You seem uncertain about the riches of Cíbola." Vázquez continued after a sip of wine. "Give me a more candid opinion. What about gold?"

"I looked for gold, I asked about gold, but as I did not get into the city, I could not confirm gold." The governor looked distressed. "There is lots of turquoise," Marcos added hastily. "They say it is even in the doorways."

"Based on everything you heard, what is your bet? Gold or no gold?"

"I am not a betting man, your lordship. But it seems easier to believe that such a city would have gold than to believe it does not."

"Hmmmm. I see you are a good politician." Vázquez smiled conspiratorially. "That leaves it something of a problem, how to organize a conquest. But we do not lack for those willing to gamble."

"The lands themselves would be a valuable addition to the king's domain."

"Lands are valuable but they are slow to return the profit needed to finance the venture. If the viceroy is to raise an expedition, he will need something more . . . tangible. And he must act soon. Your confirmation of a rich kingdom will only inflame those who want to organize their own expeditions."

"So, what do you want to do next?"

"We need to go back to Mexico City as soon as possible. We must send a messenger on ahead, to the minister provicial in your order and to the viceroy, reporting your return. Also, I have ordered three of my best scribes to be available; you must start writing a *Relación* of your journey. The scribes can take it down and make copies. We must have a report ready to give the viceroy as soon as we get back. The scribes are trustworthy and can keep secrets, but if I may say so, Father, mind whose ears may be behind the corners and doorways. Remember that we are to report first and only to your minister provincial and the viceroy, in secret." Vázquez de Coronado pulled at his thick brown beard. "If the news of your discoveries circulates among the common citizens in the street, the viceroy will be displeased with us, and you and I will have no advantage in court for discussing these matters with His Lordship."

"Yes, yes, I understand."

"As for the bad feelings in those provinces over the death of Estevan and a few Indians," Vázquez continued after a sip of wine, "surely this can be remedied one way or another. Did not Cortés and other conquerors face worse situations? I will ponder about this."

JULY 23. MARCOS FOUND HIMSELF IN A SMALL UPPER ROOM WITH the three scribes the governor had given him. Already he and the governor had sent a messenger with a short letter to the minister provincial, Father Antonio de Ciudad-Rodrigo, informing him of the imminent return, and asking that instructions be prepared about what he should do next. If Marcos and Vázquez left for Mexico City promptly, as planned, the messenger might get there only a few days before them, but at least it would give them some warning.

Now, the scribes sat together at a long table, quills poised, while Marcos sat by a window where he could sample the breezes, as if they were blowing him images of his trip. He talked about the trip starting at the beginning, but sometimes he would get onto a tangent about details, personalities, or speculations and almost forget the scribblers. The chief scribe would interrupt to get him back on track, and the three quills would resume their three simultaneous copies. Marcos's memory was aided by the presence of his leather-bound trailbook. As Marcos chatted about the journey, the chief scribe repeated each statement in a more concise form, which he and the other two copied down, word by word.

For an hour last evening and several hours this morning he had been paging through the trailbook, using it to prompt him about the various episodes of his *Relación*, day by day, page by page. At the moment, he was recounting how he had sent scouts to the coast from Vacapa. "This is why I deferred departing from Vacapa in pursuit of Estevan Dorantes, don't you see, because I was waiting for those scouts from the coast, and besides, I thought Estevan would wait for me as I ordered him to. Did you get that down? I had arranged this with Estevan, very clearly."

Suddenly there was a knock on the door, which opened without further ado. The governor stepped inside, an imposing presence. He shut the door as the scribes bent to their work with renewed vigor. "How fares the new Homer?" Vázquez asked.

"I am almost to the point where I first learned about Cíbola," said Marcos.

"Take no notice of me. I will just listen."

"Well," said Marcos clearing his throat, "as I was saying, the messengers I sent to the coast finally came back to Vacapa on Easter Sunday, along with some people from the coastal islands. As I said before, those islands are very poor in food, although people do live there. These people from the coast were an interesting lot. They wore shells on their foreheads for decoration, and they told me that shellfish of that type do contain pearls. They told me there were as many as thirty-four islands there, close to each other along the coast, and I have the names here, written down as best I could get them." He waved the trailbook. "Here, you can copy them down." Marcos reached for his wine.

"A moment," said the governor. "Be careful not to write down too many names and directions in the official *Relación*. It will be circulated at court. Cortés and the others will comb through it for details to support their own expeditions, but the viceroy must control the conquest. The details of the route and the village names must be kept in a separate document for the viceroy's eyes only. Put just enough in the *Relación* to authenticate that you were there."

"I understand, Governor. Oh, by the way, do you suppose we

could send someone down for another jug of wine? It gets dry up here in a hot room, talking like this. I haven't talked so much since I left New Spain! My throat is not used to it."

Vázquez smiled. "You shall have it. Just keep dictating."

"Anyway, as I was saying . . ."

Marcos was thoroughly enjoying telling his adventures. This was the best part of the trip.

JULY 26. MARCOS LEFT COMPOSTELA WITH VÁZQUEZ DE CORON-ado, embarking on the trail to Mexico City. Marcos had been surprised when Vázquez had come to him the day before, with the announcement that they would leave at once. He had not even finished the *Relación*. He had expected to have a few more of these enjoyable days in Compostela. But Vázquez had concluded that the viceroy would need to act quickly on the news of the north, and it was essential for both of them to be there to advise him. Normally the trip took four weeks, but they hoped to shave a few days off that.

So Marcos found himself bouncing along the rough road on horseback. Sometimes groups of soldiers would ride up to him, following alongside, flattering him, fishing for some tidbit about his discoveries. It was a game with them to see if they could needle him into some admission of colorful information that they could share at their campfires.

"Father, they say that you have discovered great lands to the north."

"My son, you know that the news of what I have discovered is a great secret, meant only for His Lordship's ears."

"Father, is it true as they say in the old stories, that in the north there is a Queen Califia who rules over a tribe of Amazon women?"

"There are many great wonders in the north."

"Then I want to be the first in the army to go conquer these women. I will be the one to conquer the queen herself." The soldiers all laughed.

Sometimes a lone soldier would ride close to him. "Father, I know the discoveries you made must be reported first to the viceroy, but I have a brother who was a sailor for the ships of the marquis Cortés, and he says that the marquis also believes in rich cities in the north. People say he plans to reach them by sea. Now, I don't want you to tell secrets, but if there is to be a conquest of the north, either by land or sea, I want to be ready. I will need to buy equipment. . . . Can't you give me some clue if a conquest is likely? I will dedicate myself to the work of the Virgin in this new land. . . ."

"My son, you have a good heart. I cannot say the great things I saw, nor can I predict what the viceroy, in his wisdom, will see fit to do, but between you and me, I think you should be ready for great things to happen."

At night, a guard was posted at a distance of thirty feet around a tent erected for Marcos, and at sundown he would get out the trailbook, consult his notes, and then in hushed tones, continue his dictation to the scribes.

". . . And in this valley, they brought me one of their hides to examine. It was like the hide of a cow, half again as large as one of our large cows. It had a kind of woolly hair on it, as long as a finger. I tried to find out what kind of animals these are. I think they were trying to say it has just one large horn, on the forehead, but I cannot understand how this could be. Anyway, they say that this horn curves toward the chest, and then turns out in a point, and it is so strong that nothing, no matter how hard, can withstand being broken by a blow from it. And they say that these animals have a great hump on their back, like a camel. I think they may be related to camels, since camels like deserts. Although, I must say, I also saw a drawing of the animal that showed a profile more like an elephant. So maybe these animals are related to elephants. They say that there are countless numbers of these animals in the kingdoms of the plains, beyond Cíbola.

"In that same valley I received messengers from Estevan, saying that, from his point of view, he was very happy because he continued to grow more confident of the grandeur of the northern country. He had already entered the final *despoblado*. . . ."

* * *

WEDNESDAY, AUGUST 20. AS THE SOFT, HUMID AIR DARKENED into evening, the procession led by Vázquez de Coronado and Marcos clattered over the causeways across the marshy lake into Mexico City. Ahead he could see the broken silhouettes of two of the ancient Mexican pyramids, whose summit temples had been ripped apart, and whose paving stones and upper terraces were still being dismantled to provide blocks for the ever-expanding community of Spanish buildings. Even in the ten months he had been gone, it seemed the pyramids had shrunk. Marcos approved. The pagan past must be destroyed, for the Mexicans' own good. Yet, after talking with Juan on the trail and hearing the Mexican view of the conquest, a small voice in him asked questions about the misery inflicted by the wholesale destruction of a society. Was this the only way to bring the glories of Christian civilization to these people? Was there some other way? If Christians had the true Word of God, they could hardly express tolerance for other peoples' ways of living, but didn't that mean endless conflict and destruction? As he entered the familiar streets at last, he resolved to dedicate himself to solving this question.

A smoky veil hung above the city, and the most memorable moment for him was not the sight of the city, but its odors. Marcos could smell the aromas of a hundred cooking fires, refuse heaps, and slop buckets as well. Tapping his nose, he joked with Vázquez, "Civilization at last, eh?"

As they crossed the causeway, he could not help but remember the scene recounted by Juan: Over these very causeways, Cortés and his soldiers had tried to fight off the pursuing Mexican warriors as the army tried to escape the island city of Tenochtitlán during *La Noche Triste*. He could not help glancing down to try to catch a glimmer of the gold that had been lost in these murky waters.

As they penetrated down the streets toward the city center, Marcos was taken aback when merchants, servants, drunkards, and loiterers called to them, "Is it true what they say about the north country?" "Is it true there are rich lands and towns?"

So his journey was a matter of street gossip already? "There are many discoveries," he stammered. "They will be revealed soon enough."

THURSDAY, AUGUST 21. MARCOS SPENT THE MORNING OF HIS first day learning the news of Mexico City. His own first messages about the existence of Cíbola had started arriving in July with Honorato. Honorato had done a good job of trying to keep things quiet, but word had begun to leak out. The final message, sent with Juan from the province of Chichilti-Calli, had arrived some weeks later and Juan had not been so successful in keeping the secrets. Tongues wagged. Soon everyone had heard of Juan Olmedo, and people in the streets were gossiping that a rich city had been found by him. Others said it was the priest Honorato who had first reported it. Others said Marcos de Niza was somehow involved, but no one knew where he was. Already, letters had flown back and forth between the viceroy and the marquis Cortés about how to conquer the northern lands. Everyone said the viceroy would have to act fast to beat out the marquis. Rumors among Marcos's fellow Franciscans said the wise viceroy would see that the expedition included many missionaries to assure an orderly conquest.

Marcos ran headlong into these rumors at midday, when he prepared for a meeting with the bishop. His first stop was his favorite barber, Carlos Anguita, who operated a small shop with his barber's chair in a shaded patio only a stone's throw from where the mighty Moctezuma himself used to hold court. Anguita embraced the friar when he entered. "I've been waiting for you since Juan Olmedo arrived! Naturally, he came to me for a shave. I knew you could not be far behind! Lupita, bring a cup of wine for the father. Let's celebrate." As Marcos was enthroned in the worn chair, several of the barber's friends settled on crude wooden benches and old building stones, pried from the ancient Mexican temples.

"Tell us about your adventures!" They wasted no time.

"I can say little until I report to the viceroy."

"But everyone knows you went to the north and found great lands! You can tell us about that!"

"It was a long trip with many strange sights." Soon Marcos found himself elaborating. The viceroy could hardly hold it against him if he talked about findings that had already leaked out. Besides, it was a difficult penance to ask a traveler not to tell his story. Still, he tried to choose his words judiciously. "I saw many fine lands on my way, fertile green valleys that run between the mountains, and have broad irrigated fields. You should see the people there, with their many strands of turquoise jewels around their necks, and turquoise on their noses and ears!"

"And women, too, eh, Father?"

"Women, too. There would hardly be many people in those populous lands if there were no women."

There was much laughter. Marcos knew how to ingratiate himself with these men.

"Women and jewels, what could be better!"

"I saw some little temples or shrines, with jeweled idols of turquoise or emerald, as Cabeza de Vaca also told about. And some Indians along the way told me of a valley where they use gold for plates and implements. But I tell you to think about the greater riches, the many good sites for farms and Christian settlements. These Indians are intelligent. They can be Christianized."

"But what about the cities, the ones that Dorantes and Cabeza de Vaca heard about?"

Marcos hesitated as the lather was applied.

"I told you, I'm not allowed to say much yet. But I can say that I learned the whereabouts of that land. It's a great trading center; I even saw it with my own eyes."

"What is it like? Tell us? Does it have jewels, too, and gold? Is it as rich as the city we took from Moctezuma?"

"My sons, you realize these are secret matters which I must report to the bishop himself this very afternoon, and to the viceroy tomorrow. You must make me look very presentable, Carlos!"

"But you can tell us!"

"They did not, um, let me into this city. It has walls like a palace. . . . So you can see there is a reason I can't tell you too much." Marcos smiled but the men looked crestfallen. To cheer them up, he added, "I did hear many tales—how that city is the most important place in that part of the world."

"Then they have gold?"

"As I said, they did not let me in. I will tell you one secret, but keep it behind your vest. Several Indians told me they have turquoise jewels set in the doorways of their houses."

One of the men lounging in the courtyard spoke up. "They must have gold. Two, maybe three years ago, Andrés Dorantes showed me a copper bell that he said had come from that country. Anyone who can work copper can work gold."

WHEN MARCOS RETURNED FROM THE BARBER, A SCRIBE DELIV-ered one of the clean drafts of the *Relación*, filling nine sheets of fine paper. "Governor Vázquez now has a copy and Minister Provincial Ciudad-Rodrigo has the other. Ciudad-Rodrigo wants to see you as soon as you are ready. The meeting with Bishop Zumár-raga is set, as soon as you can get there."

Things were moving quickly.

IN THE AFTERNOON HEAT, WHEN MOST SPANIARDS SOUGHT A REST in the cool shade, Marcos and the head of the Franciscan order, Father Antonio de Ciudad-Rodrigo, hurried across the ancient plaza of Mexico City to the quarters of their bishop. The elderly bishop welcomed them warmly. He seemed to have aged during the months Marcos was gone, but his mind was lively. "The news is very exciting, Father Marcos. You are to be congratulated for your great venture—and your courage. Sit down, sit down." They arranged themselves around the viceroy's ornate table. "Father Antonio here sent your last letter over to me, carried by Juan Olmedo himself—your Juan. A remarkable young man. And now I have read your draft report, brought to me by Vázquez himself.

You say there are cities with multistory buildings in these new lands? You saw such buildings?"

"Four stories tall at least, I saw them across the valley with my own eyes. Some of the Indians told me there were even greater buildings and larger towns in that valley. It is a very big valley, with many fertile fields."

"They must have massive timbers, good for building."

"Yes, it is a land of many resources. They use large timber crossbeams. On my journey, I passed one of the large houses, in ruins. The roof had fallen in and I could see the posts and the timbers that ran from supported wall to wall to support the upper floors. They use stonework for the walls. They are good builders."

"Then they are cultured people, these people of Cíbola. What are the prospects of Christianizing them?"

"They have their own gods, so there is much work to be done. No one in those lands has heard of Christianity. If the bishops' Seven Cities of Antilia exist, they are not in those lands. But the Indians there are great prospects. I talked to people who had lived in Cíbola. In Cíbola they dress well, with cotton garments and well-finished leathers, like our cowhides, and they have a wool-like fabric, too. They trade these materials with additional kingdoms farther on. They have well-ordered fields—I saw them. People say they are modest and have but one wife. They also have priests who measure the seasons and make ceremonies to honor the sun and moon and the rains. We may have trouble with their priests. They say the priests are secretive and meet in hidden chambers called *kivas*. But I believe the people are well-suited to receive the word of God from our brothers. We need to find a way to send priests there, and get them into the city."

"Ah, but preaching to them and truly converting them are two different things, as we are sadly learning here. While you were gone, there was a troubling case. It's still dragging. We had a Christianized Indian, Carlos, well-known, a leader in his village. We had given him responsibilities in town. Now it turns out he was secretly keeping the old idols in his very home. It's an outrage.

He's the son of one of the noble families of the Mexica and served as a young man in the house of Cortés himself. Yet we have witnesses who say he not only keeps alive his superstitions, but is guilty of dogmatizing against the church, and making fun of the priests. It is an outrage. I will have to make an example of him."

They fell silent a moment, pondering the challenges of the New World.

Marcos, ever restless, picked up the thread of the conversation again. "It's not only in Cíbola that we have potential converts. The people I met along the way, between here and Cíbola are eager to learn. They met me with arches of flowers, listened to my lessons, and respected the crosses I left in their villages. On the way back, some of them even came out to meet me with new crosses they had made themselves."

"But Vázquez tells me the people of those valleys are angry at us now because of what happened at Cíbola because of the unfortunate business with Estevan."

"Ah, well, that is farther north, in the province of Chichilti-Calli, where the people fear the wrath of Cíbola. They are afraid to show friendship with us, but I am sure that if we send priests—"

Ciudad-Rodrigo broke in. "If I send brothers of our order there, they could be killed like Estevan was killed. Cíbola must be subdued first."

The bishop continued the thought. "Which means the viceroy must send soldiers north, to protect out efforts to convert the country. He can be convinced to do that, because he wants to ensure that he reaches the country before the marquis Cortés. I'm sure you understand the realities of court politics. And I'm sure you realize that it is in the church's interest that the viceroy wins the race, because Cortés is like a loose cannon rolling on a tossing ship." The bishop paused. Age had not dimmed the calculating gleam in his eye. "You see, two years ago, when Mendoza talked to Andrés Dorantes about organizing an exploration of the north—the trip you have just taken, Marcos—he told me the king had ordered him not to take any money from the royal treasury to finance a conquest because it might turn out to be a disappointment. Mendoza's strength with the royal court lies in being able to prove that he is financially prudent, and will add to the royal coffers, instead of depleting them as so many administrators do in this land. To organize a conquest, he will have to be able to motivate men to invest their own fortunes. And the only thing that will motivate these men is the chance to get a fast return on their investment."

Father Ciudad-Rodrigo picked up the thread. "They will make the effort to subdue Cíbola only if they believe Cíbola is another Tenochtitlán. Yet you say that you were unable to confirm gold in Cíbola. That leaves us with a problem."

There was silence in the room.

Marcos stared at the table, feeling shame. This was the embarrassing truth. All his efforts—the epic journey, the discovery of new lands, the elucidation of *tierra incognita* on the maps, and the reconnaissance of mighty Cíbola—had not brought back the answer to the only question that everyone else really cared about. How could he have drifted so far from the concerns of everyone else? Was it his sin of pride, or had he just been away too long? Perhaps some day, when the history of this land came to be written, people would recognize what he had— He realized his silence was getting awkward.

"It's a lingering puzzle for me, this question of gold," he answered finally. "On the one hand, I believe it is not the most important thing about that land. The peoples of the north, waiting in darkness to receive the light of our Lord—"

"Well, of course," said the bishop.

"On the other hand, I lie awake at night thinking about it. It should be there, gold. And when I talked to the Indians about it, well, I tell you frankly, my lord, it was frustrating. I could not get a clear picture. As I say in the draft, I think they work in some metals, but not for tools as we do. It seemed to be more for ceremonial objects, like the bell given to Dorantes. Remember, it was the same among the Mexica. They had rooms full of gold, but their swords were edged with obsidian flakes. If the Cíbolan goldwork is for religious purposes, perhaps there was some reticence to tell me about it. Also, these people like to tell you what they think you want to hear. Some of them talked of gold treasures among the priests, but I was not sure I could trust them. They were trying to curry favor. . . . Surely we all agree that if Cíbola does not have gold, we will be surprised."

"Our agreement does not make it so," said the bishop. "Still, you say that parrot feathers and other goods are traded to Cíbola from the south. So I imagine that knowledge of gold working has been transmitted from Mexico to the north?"

All three of them were nodding in agreement.

The bishop leaned forward conspiratorially. "Listen, my son. The viceroy is aware of all these arguments. When it comes to this question of gold, he does not want a report full of theories or a ponderous analysis, or even a lot of detail. I'm not proposing that you distort anything. I would say, just don't write about the evidence for gold in Cíbola, one way or the other. Tell him your ideas in private. To get to the point, I have marked a few passages. . . . A minor cut here, a small change of emphasis there. I know what the viceroy wants to see. . . ."

Marcos's mind was whirling. All he wanted to do was tell his story! Why wouldn't they let— This was no time to argue. Besides, the strongest urge of an administrator was to alter any report from his staff. Marcos mustered a small smile of acquiescence.

"Remember," the bishop was saying, "it is the hope for gold and jewels and such kinds of wealth that will drive the conquest, which in turn will allow the Holy Church to begin the conversion of the people." He nodded toward the window. "The people out there in the streets already believe there is gold in Cíbola, based on their rumormongering. Denying it hurts our cause. As for promoting it, we cannot claim things that you did not truly confirm. And if others want to speculate about gold, then let them do so. Everyone will understand that it is a bit of a gamble. If the viceroy is to succeed in his noble objectives of claiming the northern land for God and the

king, then it can only help him if the commoners believe they will
find something worthwhile in the Seven Cities. I'm sure you understand."

"Yes, my lord, I think so."

"Tonight, you will work with the scribes to prepare the final
draft of your *Relación* and we will send it over to the viceroy.
Tomorrow you will have your meeting with him."

FRIDAY, AUGUST 22. IN THE STONE PALACE AT THE HEART OF
Mexico City, Marcos found himself complimenting the viceroy on
the marvelous wine he served as they began their talks.

"Nothing is too good to celebrate your safe return," Antonio
Mendoza laughed through his black beard. "Both the wine and the
crystal glasses were imported from Seville—a gift of the king himself." Mendoza reminded Marcos of Governor Vázquez; they both
had a striking presence and fiery black eyes that radiated a desire
toward action. "But let us talk. Of course, I have enjoyed your
account of your adventures and I have read the draft report that
Ciudad-Rodrigo's messengers sent over this morning. And I talked
to Vázquez yesterday, too.

"I must say," he continued, "that although we are all pleased to
see you, we are disappointed about one thing." Marcos knew what
was coming, and he could not help notice that the viceroy had
switched to a royal-sounding 'we.' "You say very little about the
riches that may be inside Cíbola. We must talk of this, man to man.
It is the crux of the matter."

"I tried to report only what I knew, my lord. It is what I understood you wanted."

"Yes, yes, but you misunderstand. It was good to keep the report
brief, and as the bishop no doubt told you, it is best not to put more
in it than we need in order to authenticate your journey and the rituals of possession. But let us put parchment aside for the moment.
No one wishes to embarrass you or your order—or the bishop—
since you have all served us so well, but are you really telling us

that after we sent you all that way to learn if there is a wealthy empire in the north, and after you got within sight of it, you cannot tell me if it has gold?"

Marcos felt his position grow more preposterous by the day. He would never be able to explain it. "I gave you evidence that the Indians did talk of gold in some of those northern valleys, that people in those valleys have many jewels in the form of turquoise, and there is absolutely no doubt that the people of Cíbola have culture. As for the gold of Cíbola, one can infer what one can infer."

Mendoza was growing more agitated. "Oh yes, infer. Turquoises are pretty baubles. And then there is the talk of copper and . . . babble, babble, babble. The sound of the wind in the trees brings me as much information as that. Come now, give me something solid. The bishop talks of how these lands could be settled, and how a prosperous country could be built with the aid of converted Indian people, but you've left the Indians up in arms. Tell me, how am I going to get gentlemen to risk their fortunes to travel north and subdue these lands for the king unless I have something shiny to show them?"

"I would put it to them the other way, my lord. Knowing what we know so far, how can anyone afford to miss out on this opportunity?"

A faint smile began to flicker across Mendoza's face. "Hmmmm. That's good," he said.

Marcos sipped his wine and then coughed modestly. "Of course, it is not for me to tell you what to say."

"No, I tell you, that's a good approach. The soldiers already want to believe in gold there—as if that would make it true. And if we want soldiers to sign up for an expedition, we should not deny it because, well, after all, your information is damnably equivocal. Better that we should not throw cold water on these hopes, either in your report or in the streets. Then, as you say, how can anyone afford not to sign up?" Mendoza nodded to himself and took another sip of his wine. "We have another problem, though. I believe you and the bishop are on my side in wanting to coordinate the conquest of that new land with me, but you must remember that

Hernán de Soto, from Cuba, has been given a royal charter that gives him control of all the gold and riches that he may find in the lands of Florida and beyond, to the west. He gets to share them between himself, his army, and the royal treasury—and the charter includes gold in tombs as well as revenues received for capturing and ransoming local chiefs, as they did in Peru. You, of all people, understand the possibilities for outrages.

"Now, here's the rub. My messengers tell me that in May, while you were gone, Soto actually set out from Cuba to Florida with his army. He's well-prepared. They say he even interviewed Cabeza de Vaca when he went back to Spain a year or so ago. Already, he may be marching toward the lands you found. No one knows how far west it is from Florida to Cíbola; mapmakers argue about these east-west distances. Your claim to the lands is good, but it will not help us if Soto plants his flag in Cíbola before we can get there."

"Well, I—"

"Wait, there is more. Pedro de Alvarado, who conquered the lands of Guatemala, has been moving equipment to build ships on our southwest coast, just like Cortés. Alvarado, too, has a grant from the king to explore north. Alvarado—the same one who ordered the massacre here in Tenochtitlán, during the conquest! Do you want him subduing the natives in Chichilti-Calli or being the first to reach Cíbola? With him, it would be a slaughter."

"It's a disaster to be avoided. I—"

"Wait, it gets worse. You may not know this, but Cortés, this very summer while you were coming back, sent one of his captains, Ulloa by name, north with three ships along the same coast you traveled. They will try to counter your claim. My people say he will try to take your information and combine it with what his captains found, to make his own claim on the northern lands. They say he has spies everywhere, and certainly in my court, trying to find out what you learned. I already have pretty letters from him, offering to collaborate in a conquest, and also stating that your discoveries are really no different from what he had already learned during his earlier coastal explorations! He is a brash man, that one! He's even approached Francisco Vázquez about making an alliance with him. Imagine the impertinence! All of this is getting out of hand. That's why your information is so important to us, and yet also it is why we must be careful what we say."

"Yes."

"Now, pay attention. There is something we must discuss in this report of yours. The final draft will be in your own words, of course. I do not want to influence you. It must be your report of what you saw. Still, it is very important what you say about the coastal route. In the draft, you say that in one of the most northern valleys, before the final *despoblado*, you turned west and tried to reach the coast."

"Yes, along a river that ran west to the sea."

"You say that you went downstream on that river, but it dried up, and then you say that by talking with the Indians you confirmed that the seacoast turned west a little beyond. But you also state in the draft that you did not actually get to the coast or see it."

"The land toward the sea grew very bad, my lord. A coastal desert. Very little food or water. And, at my back, Estevan was still moving on to Cíbola. I was torn between going forward to the sea and going back to catch Estevan. Everything the Indians had told me so far had proved reliable, and I felt that their information was the best I could get without endangering the expedition. So I turned back toward Cíbola. You see, I still hoped to catch Estevan. And if I had caught him, things might have turned out differently."

"Ah, yes, well, there are always many treasures beyond the word 'if.' Now, listen and understand me, man to man. Think of Cortés. In your draft, you make it too clear that your estimate of the coastal configuration is just that—an estimate. Cortés will take this draft and say, 'Marcos de Niza never set foot on the northern coast. My sailors were the first to reach it. It is mine.' As for me, Father Marcos, I trust your observations. Everything you report seems consistent. Cortés has no army and since you indicate that Cíbola must be inland from any port, I have little fear that Cortés will reach Cíbola itself. Clearly we have the best claim to Cíbola. But as for the coastal province, and establishment of a port of supply, we have a problem. We don't want to give Cortés the chance to claim the coastal route as his domain. If there is a hearing, the Council of the Indies could side with him. . . ."

Mendoza paused, as if looking carefully for his words. "Now as I said, I do not want to influence what you say. But why do you have to make it so clear that you are reporting on the coast without actually having reached the coast? It could ruin our chances of an apostolic claim to these lands under my legal authority as representative of the king. Just remember that the best interests of you and your friend, the bishop, lie with me. Your report would be just as valuable, and just as true, if it merely stated you made an excursion west toward the coast and learned the coastal configuration. I marked a sentence or two that could be removed. Then, if a question comes up of exactly where you were, or what land you claimed, we could let the lawyers in Spain argue over what you meant. By the time they finish, we will have established our presence in Cíbola. Take a few days, no more, and look at the report in that light. Then you can send me a final copy. Of course, the words in the report must be yours, in the service of truth and our Lord. All my comments are just suggestions. I'm sure you understand."

"Yes, my lord."

EATING HIS EVENING MEAL, MARCOS FELT THAT, ALL IN ALL, THE interview with the viceroy went well. He knew that if a great lord deigns to change some wording in one's report, then it has become *his* report, and he has accepted it. Events continued to move fast in the next few days. On Saturday and Sunday Marcos closeted himself with a draft of the report, taking out a few words here, changing a few words there, and testing the effect on Father Ciudad-Rodrigo. Marcos was not surprised that on the same day the viceroy issued a proclamation forbidding anyone from leaving the country by sea or by land in search of the northern lands, except by his own permission. On Monday morning, August 25, scribes were set to work copying the final draft of the *Relación* into good, clean copies. On the 26th, these copies were signed by Marcos and certified by Ciudad-Rodrigo. Ciudad-Rodrigo arranged for messengers to deliver a final, formal copy to the viceroy. The earlier drafts were destroyed, to prevent them from leaking out with wording to which the viceroy objected.

Tuesday, September 2, was a big day; Marcos was invited to attend a formal court assembly in the presence of Viceroy Mendoza, the pompous Juan Baeza de Herrera, secretary of the royal *audiencia,* and other notables. Everyone was dressed in his finest attire, and the final copies of the *Relación,* along with Marcos's original instructions from the viceroy and the certification by Ciudad-Rodrigo, were spread out on a great oak table with pomp and ceremony. Marcos was announced formally with his title of vice commissary for the Franciscan order in Mexico. Then he was asked to stand, humbly, before the board, and to recite a declaration that the contents of the *Relación* were true, depicting accurately what had transpired on his journey. The secretaries of the royal *audiencia* then signed the documents with a flourish, attesting the truth of the contents. Everyone breathed a quiet sigh of relief and went home. Marcos's journey was officially over.

ONCE THE *RELACIÓN* WAS CERTIFIED AND SUBMITTED, RUMORS spread faster than ever in Mexico City. People stopped him on street and pressed him for information. He adopted his own cautious catechism, which he found himself repeating daily: "With my own eyes, I saw one of the prosperous cities of the north. From what we know so far, it is not unreasonable to conclude that there may be gold there." Let people make of that what they would.

A SURPRISE CAME IN EARLY OCTOBER. MARCOS LEARNED THAT Mendoza had sent orders to Vázquez de Coronado to have a party of horsemen ride quietly north under one of Coronado's captains, a capable veteran named Melchior Díaz. They had specific orders to explore the route to Cíbola and try to gather more information. What was this? Did the viceroy not believe him? Why should he send someone else to check his story? After all this, would the discovery of Cíbola be credited to Melchior Díaz, and not Marcos de Niza?

After a prayer to absolve himself of jealousy, and after a brief discussion with the viceroy himself at church one Sunday, Marcos felt better. "After all," the viceroy said, "since you did not enter Cíbola, we are naturally curious to get news of wealth and the attitude of the people. This is why Díaz was sent. No disrespect toward you, Father. Such a great discovery as yours naturally requires swift elucidation." After all, Marcos told himself, Mendoza was a prudent politician and manager. Maybe Díaz would learn something new.

Just after Christmas, word came that Díaz had set out from Culiacán on November 19 with a small group of horsemen, on Marcos's own route. Meanwhile, Marcos resolved that he himself would return to Cíbola with the first expedition of conquest, to insure that his name and God's will, as best he could understand it, would continue to play a role in the final triumph.

PART III

THE CONQUEST OF CÍBOLA
AND THE FATE OF CHICHILTI-CALLI

There is much evil to be uprooted here.

JUAN NENTVIG, JESUIT PRIEST,
writing about Arizona and the modern-
day border region, in 1764.

CHAPTER 19

August–September, 1989
Real Men Don't Cry at Football
Games

The more the opponents talked about Coronado and history, the more the local business establishment rallied to Mr. Rooney's defense. Jobs. Economic growth. The petition campaign heated up. The newspaper reported local banks denying permission to pass the petition in front of their branch offices. You can't pass petitions on private property without the property owner's okay. That includes banks' front walks and parking lots. Arizona State Law.

There were no specific new directives to me from Mr. Rooney. Our work on the development went on from day to day, meeting after meeting, as if governed by a liturgical calendar. Like Marcos, I was back home, reporting to my monastic cubicle each morning, following the appropriate rites, and realizing that even the best rituals don't guarantee you control over your own life.

I KEPT WAITING FOR A LETTER FROM EDWARD. NONE CAME.

PHAEDRA WAS COLLECTING ALL THE LITERATURE SHE COULD FIND from the opposition. She couldn't go to their meetings anymore; the reception was too unfriendly. But she collected the op-ed pieces written against us, and sometimes she'd go out, incognito, find a mall or a post office, and chat up the petition passers to delve into their thinking.

Eventually, the referendum organizers announced that if they succeeded in getting the zoning rescinded, they would then try to get the ruin purchased by the Archaeological Conservancy for eventual candidacy as a national monument. It wasn't a bad idea.

I tried looking at all this from my new, grand historical perspective. History was full of short-term political skirmishes, battles we never hear about, passionate causes that never mattered in the long run. Wasn't this just another one? I wanted to believe it but I couldn't.

In my *corazon de corazones*, I admitted that the idea of public, protected status for the ruin—as opposed to private management in the middle of a housing development—made sense to me. Sure I was conflicted, but what else is new? We're burning through everything as if there're no future generations, and it's hard not to be conflicted if you're paying attention.

If I really believed in preserving the site, why not quit and go over to the other side? I kept taking refuge in my role as a scholar: My main function was to uncover the historic information and get it out to the public. Other people could debate its use. No one person could do everything. Maybe as an insider in Mr. Rooney's organization, I could do some good.

FINALLY MR. ROONEY CALLED ME IN AND GAVE ME A NEW DIREC-tive. "As long as we have a park there, we should take *advantage* of it. We're going to lose some revenue if we lose lots to preserve the ruin. But if we have a little museum, maybe there could be admission fees for non-residents, and a line of souvenirs. Chichi cups. Chichi T-shirts." He had a merry smile. "You know about the kinds of pictures that should be on them. Coronado on his horse, something like that. Give me some sample designs, a business plan."

"Why should we charge people to get in there? Wouldn't we attract more people to the development if we—"

"Because, goddammit, I told you, this whole thing is costing us time and money."

"But you'll get a lot of ill will. People are used to national parks and monuments. They don't want to pay to experience their own history."

"The hell they don't. Don't you read the papers? Now that we're cutting taxes and getting the feds off our backs, you're gonna see user fees to get into all those places. The people who care about that stuff, *they* should pay for it. It's more fair that way, if you wanna get into that. Anyway, your job, Mr. History, is to make it interesting enough for people to want to come in. Not just displays, but games or a ride for kids. Or a weekly chuck wagon cookout."

"But then the whole place would lose its sense of—"

"Get on it."

Great. Now I was huckstering tourist curios.

THAT EVENING, A FRIDAY, I ASKED PHAEDRA OUT FOR A WALK. I was mulling over an idea I wanted to discuss with her. "It'll be an urban hike," I said.

"That's an interesting idea." I wasn't sure if she was being sarcastic, but she agreed. We still liked to spend time together.

We parked my car in a shopping "plaza" and walked west on the north side of the street, near the Showcase, our maintenance-challenged theater that specialized in literate films. It was screening two films, one French and one Italian. Looking at the pictures of beautiful foreign actresses on the poster display made me feel good, like I was a citizen of the world.

Neon signs and flashing beacons stretched in both directions for miles. The colored lights had an urban sort of beauty. I tried to enjoy the *Bladerunner* ambience, but I was still weighed down by the inexorable flow of events. The better my intentions, the more I seemed to be presiding over the prostitution of history. I remembered a Russian joke Edward had told me in Mexico: "Things are getting better. Well, maybe not as good as yesterday, but definitely better than tomorrow."

Phaedra laughed when I told her the joke, and said it was funny, but it was the kind of reaction that, in her, implied the real conversation hadn't started. We walked along quietly for a block. Walking nowhere in particular, it seemed like we had plenty of time to talk.

Summer evenings in Tucson are balmy once the sun kisses the horizon. I should have felt great. This was the lavender moment: the day's photon overload ends, and the mountains briefly turn an unearthly violet in the mixed glow of the pink sunset and the high, blue sky. I wanted to watch the lavender moment unfold, but it was being swamped by the glare of the streetlights, headlights, shop signs. The best sunset we saw was on a Marlboro billboard.

Speedway Boulevard was the spiritual heart of the city. Cars crammed its length. The economic heart, the so-called downtown where I worked, was actually crowded against the western edge of the metropolis, along the Santa Cruz riverbed, where the Spanish settlers in the 1700s had built their riverside fort, atop an ancient Hohokam town site dating from A.D. 800. After the U.S. bought southern Arizona from Mexico in the 1850s, like a slab of ham, Tucson's American settlers started tearing adobe bricks out of the old fort's walls to build their own settlement amid the old Mexican buildings. The U.S. Army built a new fort on a tributary creek east of town, to protect the area from Apache attacks, and the city grew toward it along Speedway, as if attracted by a magnetic force. The business center remained on the old Spanish site, where clumps of tall glassy buildings eventually grew in our century, like quartz masses growing by some petrologic process. With the daylight came the lawyers, bankers, and developers—my kind of people?—and at night emerged the transients and our city's young *graffitistas* with their cans of spray paint. Speedway was the road that connected the emptiness of downtown with the melancholia of eastside suburbia.

Sorry for being so gloomy; as I said, I was feeling pessimistic that evening.

To be more objective about Speedway, it was the most commercial and noisy of the city's commercial strips. It achieved its fifteen minutes of national fame when a local Romeo lured his girlfriend into the desert and killed her with a rock in the 1960s, attracting

Life magazine to our town to cover the trial. Should it have been called *Death* magazine? Entranced by our strange metropolis, they published a famous telephoto view looking down Speedway Boulevard through the confused mess of cars, ads, electrical wires, telephone poles, and cheesy storefronts and dubbed it the ugliest street in America. In short, it was strip development at its laissez-faire height. The traffic noise was deafening.

Coronado Estates would avoid all this. Right?

Phaedra watched me like a hawk. She had a sixth sense about relationships; I knew she was trying to figure out what was bugging me.

The sidewalk stretched in front of us, but a few feet from my elbow, cars and trucks and buses roared by in a frenzy to reach the next traffic light, leaving a blast of sound and exhaust fumes. Red taillights blazed past us in long streaks, like ghostly red lines in an urban time-exposure photo.

"Speedway was never designed for walking," she shouted.

"That's what makes this walk interesting," I shouted back.

"I wasn't complaining. I'm having fun." Phaedra's infrared detectors had deciphered my melancholy, even though I hadn't raised what was really on my mind. I could tell she was going to try to cheer me up.

"Do you think I should quit?" I shouted at her.

"What?"

"I've begun to think about quitting. Giving Mr. Rooney a big speech and walking out."

"Quit?"

"Quit the job."

She stared at me in horror, like I had just contracted some horrible disease.

"People are misusing my report everywhere and Mr. Rooney's mad at me, and now he's got me planning gift shops and tourist trinkets. . . . I'm stuck right in the middle. Quitting's the only way I see out of this mess."

"What mess?"

"When I started out, I thought something really good could

come out of all this. Now, thanks to me, they're going to screw up a unique historic treasure. That day I went out to the site and just stood there, it had a kind of . . . spiritual beauty, you know? That's how people should experience it."

"Well, you know it can't sit that way forever."

We walked another block without talking.

The traffic was thinning out a little. I tried again to explain. "In the seventies, when I was in junior high, a slate of green-leaning candidates won control of the Tucson city council. Briefly. It's a classic in the urban planning textbooks. Did you ever hear that story?"

"Tell me."

"They changed the water rate structure to give everybody a low base rate for basic needs, and a higher rate for higher consumption. For instance, they put in an energy charge for pumping water uphill to fill swimming pools in the foothills. The big consumers saw their bills rise by a factor of two or three. People screamed.

"Turns out, a lot of the price hike was just due to timing. It was a textbook example of political stupidity for the environmentalists to raise the rates just when summer was coming in, when people used more water anyway. But the business community saw their chance and organized a recall election. Their issue was the big increase in water rates, but the actual goal was to defeat the slow-growth movement. Anyway, they won. Threw out the greenies. Later, their stooges on the new council pointed out that higher rates would be needed, after all. To accommodate the projected growth, they needed to drill new wells in the next valley. So they left the general water-rate increase intact, except, of course, they reduced the energy surcharge to the wealthier half of town."

"The point being . . . ?"

"Elections are never about what the ads say anymore. Any public debate evolves up to a point, but when the money machine kicks in, the whole discussion mutates. Historical facts get distorted into political fodder—factoids, to decorate the campaign, like ornaments on a Christmas tree. It's like that tonypastry thing you told me about."

"Tonypandy."

"Everything I worked for is being subverted. Our site is just a symbol for bigger forces."

"You can't quit. What would you do?"

"I can always find something else. Get out of the corporate manipulation scene. Go work for a city that's willing to look toward the future, like Portland or Boulder."

"And make half as much money. That's dumb."

"I oughta be doing something I believe in."

"What good would it do to quit? Besides," she said, stopping for a moment to formulate one of her great postulates: "History's most ignored gestures are resignations over principle."

We walked a little farther. We came to the place where some new crosswalks had been installed, and median dividers with mosaic tile murals. We took a moment to enjoy them for the first time at close range, on foot. Fledgling trees rose from the median strip into the evening sky, hoping not to be vandalized before they were big enough to withstand initials gashed into their trunks.

"Look," she said. "Trees. Public art. See? That green city council of yours, it left a legacy. You have to keep doing your part and hope it adds up."

We came to a red light.

"Mr. Rooney's figured out people want to buy fantasies, not reality," I said. "He's using me to provide his own private reservoir of images that he can tap. Put a smile on the citizens' faces as they pay up."

"They're buying lots and houses. Good houses. What's the matter with you?"

I could see it all from Mr. Rooney's point of view now. Who cared whether Marcos had told a colossal lie, or where Coronado slept? That stuff was all romantic foolishness, with no relevance to these rushing cars and their rushing drivers, who had someplace important to go and were not such deadbeats that they had time to walk along Speedway.

She put her hand on my arm. "Kevin, you're such a nice guy, but can't you stop being such an idealist? I don't want you to . . . get hurt. There's a lot of stuff in the world we have to ignore, just to stay sane."

"What do you mean?"

"It's just. . . . Your view of things is so narrow."

"*My* view? *My* view? The further into history I get, the wider my view is. I feel like a camera that just changed to a wide-angle lens. Hey, you're the one defending the corporate party line."

She glared at me.

When the traffic light turned green, we crossed to the south side of the street and kept walking west, toward the Tucson Mountains, nature's skyline somewhere beyond the end of Speedway. On this side of the street, white headlights rushed toward us. My pupils couldn't keep up with the alternation of glare and darkness. Because it was Friday night, kids in cars were coming out like vampires. The traffic was growing again. Mating rituals were in progress. As with frogs, manhood had something to do with how much bass you could crank out of your speaker system. The cars and trucks blasted interchangeable thumping bass lines to interchangeable songs.

"You know," I told her, "Mr. Rooney looked over my report with those steely eyes and that little smile, and then he said, 'This has some good stuff.' I was just handing him the 'stuff' he needed to sound educated and caring. When they stick a TV camera in his face, he'll use my 'stuff' and come out looking like the one with the great sense of history."

"You're jealous!" She exclaimed at me as if she had solved a puzzle. "You're jealous of Mr. Rooney! You're worried that he understands how to turn the past into the future better than you do."

"That's ludicrous."

We came to the big Methodist church. Could Marcos have ever imagined that his new land would see Protestant and Catholic churches in the same town? He would have heard about Luther's heresies; Luther had nailed his theses to the door in 1517 and been excommunicated in 1520. Then he insulted the established order even further by translating the New Testament into German by 1522. What would Marcos have thought if he had been told that his new land would be founded on the idea of tolerance for other people's beliefs, and that Catholics, Lutherans, Jews, and Muslims all would coexist—or try to—not to mention the newfangled Methodists, Baptists, Presbyterians, Mormons, Jehovah's Witnesses, and Unitarians?

We paused and looked at the bubbling fountain in the grassy yard out in front of the church. It was quieter than the sidewalk. Phaedra wet her fingers in the tiled pool and sprayed me with cold water. "You need to cool off," she teased.

We played tag around the pool.

"Methodists make nice fountains and green lawns," she observed, "but they don't have the sense of mystery that you can see down at San Xavier." San Xavier was Tucson's old mission church, built in the 1700s. It was south of town on the Indian reservation, stark and dusty on the outside, full of baroque decorations on the inside, with no green lawns. "My sister and I were raised Catholic," she said. "Did you know that? Not that I practice much now."

"When I see people with their saints and their shrines I think, 'Those poor people are living back in the 1500s.' "

We sat down on the fountain.

"But it's a free country," I added.

"Why do you like Marcos if you don't like saints and shrines?"

"He was an interesting guy. He must have had to face doubts." I looked up at the steeple. "I used go to a church like this, with my parents," I continued. "I stopped in college. Later I went back to a Christmas Eve service with some friends who wanted to sing carols. The preacher was reading scriptures and for the first time I really listened to what they said. I mean, having been away, I could hear it fresh, from a cosmic perspective. It was such a medieval view of the universe. Angels come down to proclaim the end of the old world order. A new king will impose justice and set up a new empire where only the children of God are welcome—the ones who accept the new faith. I looked around and I couldn't understand how all these pious families could pride themselves on American democracy and then listen to this stuff. Then there was the part about how the true believers will trample the unworthy sinners under the soles of their feet! It sounded like Germany in 1930 or the Soviets in the 1950s."

"You're too literal."

"My motto comes from the writer, Nathaniel West: 'Forget the crucifixion; remember the Renaissance.' " We dangled our fingers in the fountain, looking at the rippling reflections. "Can you imagine what it must have been like for Marcos and those guys? A whole new world, complete with aliens. They argued over whether the Indians were human beings. A few decades later, Galileo discovered satellites moving around Jupiter instead of the Earth, and your friendly church arrested him for heresy. And they burned Giordano Bruno for speculating that there might be other worlds like ours. History's biggest lesson is that the true believers always think the world revolves around themselves, and everybody else has to be either reeducated or stamped out. It's the same with all zealots. Conquistadors, communists, fundamentalists. . . . Now its us, saying we have a God-given right to develop our property, regardless of what anyone else thinks, regardless of the past or future, regardless of the rest of the community, because it belongs to Mr. Rooney and he can do whatever the hell he wants with it. All because of our economic dogma."

The water in the fountain made a pretty sound. It was nice, sitting there. Phaedra radiated patience. "My, my," she said. She still looked as if I had a disease and needed special care.

"We're living in the middle of a five hundred–year revolution," I said. I was on a roll. "We all need to back off to see it. Look around. Men on the moon, but we've still got decent people all around us talking to saints, reading astrology columns, legislating against evolution, claiming that Indians are the lost tribes of Israel. Ever since Marcos's day, it's one cult after another denying the knowledge that's out there."

To shut me up, Phaedra pointed across the street. On the corner was the 31 Flavors where my school buddies and I always went for ice cream cones. It was an ancient landmark; I assumed it had been here since Hohokam times. We went in and ordered two double-scoop chocolate mint cones. It was quiet inside. Generations of local high school and college kids had worked there, all fresh and full of fun. There were only a few tables inside, and a college couple was sitting at one of them, like generations before them, holding hands and talking intensely. Phaedra whispered, "I feel like we're intruding if we stand here." We took our cones out the door, into the roar.

Outside, an earnest college student with a crew cut was distributing the petition. The pink form was beginning to look familiar. SAVE THE CORONADO RUIN! Under the pretense of being ready to sign, I borrowed the clipboard and noticed that already tonight he had picked up twenty-four numbered signatures. I began to read.

Then came my second greatest shock that summer, after the death of Father Antonio. The petition started with some rhetoric about saving an important historic site. The next paragraph, I discovered, stated that the signer was *in favor* of our development and our wonderful plan for a park. The petition actually supported the zoning that had been passed in June.

"What is this?" I asked the kid. "I thought this petition was against the rezoning!"

"That's the *other* petition," he said, with a sly grin. "The one the ecoliberals are circulating." This one is a countermeasure.

"But . . . that's dishonest!"

"Oh, man, lighten up! You gotta read what you sign." His grin was really annoying.

I thrust the clipboard into Phaedra's hands. "Look at this! Look at what they've done!"

"I don't want to talk about it," she said.

That's when I knew she was in on it. I called her a couple of times that weekend, but she said she was busy. True to her word, she didn't want to talk about the petitions.

*   *   *

TWO DAYS LATER THE MEDIA CAUGHT UP WITH THE SCAM. THE
paper announced that a second pink petition, in favor of the development, was being circulated. This petition made no pretense of
being legit. Unlike the "real" petition, it was not even registered
with the county elections board. But its existence meant that people
who thought they had signed the real petition now didn't know if
they had signed the real one or the fake one. If they now sought out
the real one to sign, they might be signing twice, risking an
increase of the percentage of signatures that would be invalidated,
and a rejection of the whole effort.

On Monday, Phaedra spent hours closeted in meetings with Mr.
Rooney and his staff. Tuesday she invited me to lunch. I agreed. I
wanted to see what she'd say.

"Look," she said when two beers had been served. "About those
fake petitions, it wasn't actually us," she said. "Our office, I mean."
She was very grim. "I want you to know I wasn't involved in it. But
I confess I knew something was in the works. I heard Mr. Rooney
and Mr. Beecher talking about it. The false petition was put out by
an ad agency that we work with. Mr. Beecher's daughter-in-law
runs it. They're the ones who put it on the street. They paid the cir-
culators. I don't know if the money came from Mr. Rooney or
somebody else."

"Jesus! How can you . . ."

I was going to ask her how she could stand to work with these
people. But after all, I was still working for the same outfit.
Besides, I knew her answer. Like everybody, she needed to pay the
rent; there might never be a better job for her than this one; she had
to keep Amber in mind.

"You should have heard them," she continued. "They thought it
was some kind of joke. They call it 'dirty tricks.' "

"That's what the White House plumbers called it."

"What?"

"Never mind. We should quit. Both of us should quit."

"Damn it! Don't say that." She scowled at me and tried lamely to turn it into a male/female thing. "You're lucky. What'd Descartes say about male senior staff? You think, therefore you are paid. Me, I just have to do what they say."

We stayed together that night, but I could feel this drift, as if different tidal currents were tugging us in different directions.

AFTER A WEEK, IT BEGAN TO BE CLEAR THAT THE FALSE PETITION was backfiring. People were incensed. They began seeking out the real petition and signing in droves. After the paper reported the number of signatures would be enough to require a referendum, Mr. Rooney played his next card. He had Tony Beecher file a suit in the Arizona courts to throw out the petition altogether. It seemed that its wording was too vague. Furthermore, many early copies had been circulated without the full text of the supervisor's zoning decision attached to them, before the opposition realized that was required by law. Worse yet, careful measurement showed that when the opposition tried to rectify this by cramming the text of the decision onto the petition form, it had been printed in a type size one point smaller than specified by law. *Et cetera, et cetera. . . .*

WRITING ABOUT IT YEARS LATER, I'D LIKE TO BE ABLE TO SAY I HAD some flaming argument with Mr. Rooney, where I stood up to him about the lawsuit and the petition. I'd like to say I made a brilliant speech about what was happening, convincing Phaedra and all the rest of the office to change our tack. It would make a better ending to the story.

The closest I came was the day Mr. Beecher stopped by my office. He was tall and handsome, and had the calmness of self-assurance. He had lawyer eyes. They radiated the sense that no one else understood how the world *really* worked. He paused at my door and asked me, "So, do you still think Coronado really slept on our property?" His tone of voice implied that his lawsuit had changed the answer.

I didn't even respond to his question. I said, "How can you live with what you did about that petition? I mean, that was interfering with the electoral process! It's unconstitutional."

He smiled a Cheshire-cat smile. "That's an interesting argument. But there's such a thing as free speech. You should lighten up. Politics is just another form of give and take. It's a game. Why do you think it has to be so solemn and boring?" He left.

"Because the future is where our children live," I called down the hall after him. I'm sure he heard me. It's the only respectable thing I said while I was working for Mr. Rooney. But as Phaedra would have told me, it probably had no consequence.

JULY 20 WAS THE TWENTIETH ANNIVERSARY OF THE FIRST LANDing on the moon. Our species' first steps onto another world and the anniversary only made page two in the paper. It was being forgotten. Americans had given up their new lands in the sky and gone back home. Viceroy Mendoza and governor Vázquez didn't know it yet, but the Spanish were destined to do the same thing with their discovery, too. What is it about exploration, that the adrenaline stops pumping as soon as you reach the goal?

ON THE SURFACE, THE GREAT OUTER WORLD OF AUGUST, 1989, looked normal, but underground, it was seething with unrest, like a volcano getting ready to explode. Spurred by Gorbachev's reforms and the anticommunist riots in China, the Soviet Union was struggling toward the end of the twentieth century's most dramatic and tragic social experiment—the failed seventy-year demonstration project called communism. They had tried to build a system on ideas that Edward would have approved: greed was bad, and you should help your neighbor. What a disaster. It was collapsing around them in a shambles of self-serving bureaucracy. A Russian worker's comment was quoted in the paper. "Under your system, you work and you get paid. Under our system, we pretend to work and they pretend to pay us." The joke made American readers feel good.

The global changes were too slow for the media to see, and so that momentous August was considered a slow news month. I still watched the papers for news from Alamos. Nothing. On August 7, our secretary of state was in Mexico, and the newspaper (page four) said he was "calling for a new U.S.–Mexican era." There was a total lunar eclipse on August 11, signifying nothing. Behind the scenes, legal wheels were turning; Mr. Beecher's lawsuit was working its way through the system.

I watched for a letter from Edward. Still nothing there, either.

People in Tucson talked about the heat. On the last day of August, the afternoon temperature surpassed 100° for the 78th day, tying the previous year's record.

Meanwhile, I tried to heed Phaedra's advice, keeping my nose to the grindstone, reviewing our street layout and traffic flow plan, attending meetings about the proposed park, pricing souvenir mugs, struggling to get back into the swing of things. Phaedra approved, but watched me warily. I was still reading Captain Manje's 1721 book for fun, and I tried not to think too seriously about things. I had a relapse when I came upon this passage describing Tucson as it was in 1716, written by Father Luis Velarde and reported by Manje:

> *The land is level, although scattered mountains and sierras beautify it. On the banks of the rivers are elms, willows, tamaracks, and walnuts. There is no question but that these lands contain many valuable minerals, yet no one seeks them. Vegetable crops include corn and a small bean. Since the priests came, the Indians harvest wheat as well as beans, lentils, squash, and melons. At the missions they raise abundant fruits such as grapes, peaches, figs, pears, and sugarcane, just as in any other country. The Indians plant cotton and weave cloth to dress themselves. In this region, nothing is lacking.*

After I read that, I'd drive by the dry riverbeds and the cottonwood stumps, and wonder what we had done to Tucson on our watch, during our century of progress.

*   *   *

THE TUCSON SUMMER BEGAN BURNING ITS WAY INTO SEPTEMBER, the month when hyper-summer turns back into normal summer. Everyone in Arizona had gone a little crazy with the heat, and on September 1, the Arizona courts agreed with Mr. Beecher and his lawsuit. The petition against Coronado Estates was thrown out, the referendum was cancelled, and Mr. Beecher got a nice pat on the back to go along with his half-million-dollar salary. At the same time it gave a sound thrashing to the addled environmentalists and neighborhood associations who dared to oppose manifest destiny.

That Friday was a day of good cheer in our office. In the afternoon, Mr. Rooney personally brought several bouquets of California flowers to the office and put one big arrangement on Phaedra's desk. He was all smiles, and would nudge people with his patrician elbow and say, "That false petition—it was the cleverest political joke I've heard in *years*."

Phaedra's pacification program had been keeping me calm for days, but Mr. Rooney's attitude made me lose my cool. "Doesn't it bother you that the polls were against us?" I asked him. "This 'joke' overruled—"

"Popular opinion?" said Mr. Rooney. "Popular opinion is what the man in the street has absorbed from TV. It's just gossip. It doesn't have any bearing on what's *right*."

"Yeah? Well, that's probably what Coronado said when the Indians complained."

Mr. Rooney scowled at first, then let it pass. "Hey, that's a good one. Ha, ha. Well, that's what history is all about. The people with the better ideas win. It's the way things are supposed to be. When you and your planners start to meddle with that, you're trying to hold back the natural order of things. Look at the Rooskies."

Phaedra was standing beyond Mr. Rooney, chatting with one of Mr. Beecher's tie-wearing aides, and glaring at me.

No one ever owned up to the possibility that our company had anything to do with the electoral shenanigans.

I saw now that my belief in the future of city planning was as naive as Marcos's belief in happy little Indian hamlets dotted through pastoral fields, administered by benevolent Spaniards. Neither Marcos nor I had reckoned on the power of an economic system that extolled goldlust as the wellspring of light and happiness.

SATURDAY, SEPTEMBER 2, WAS A BANNER DAY FOR ME; MARCOS went before a formal assembly of Viceroy Mendoza and the lords of his court, and handed in his *Relación*. I studied the papers to see how far we had come in 450 years. The inner pages said evangelist Jim Bakker was judged competent to stand trial for embezzling $4 million from his religious ministry to finance his lifestyle. Also, Colombian officials rejected U.S. advisors as a way to deal with their drug lords; they responded that the U.S., as the biggest drug consumer, might look into its own heart about why it was creating this market in the first place.

IN THE WEEK AFTER OUR COURT VICTORY, PEOPLE STOPPED TALKing about Coronado's campsite. Everyone lost interest: the public, the media, the people around our office. Chichilti-Calli had had its fifteen minutes of fame. Time to move on to the next issue.

Mr. Rooney called me. He was cheery. "Now that we have our approval, we can firm up the design for the park. The plan you were working on was the fallback, in case we had to appeal the court decision. But now, we don't have to be quite so, um, *extravagant* in giving up space."

He unrolled a set of drawings. "This version is based on my original conception." He had gotten somebody else in planning work it up for him. "Here's the big mound, the main ruin. That'll be the focus. We'll have a loop walk from the clubhouse, here, that goes out around the ruin on one side and back across the top of the mound, so a visitor can get a feel for the size of it. The foundations will be outlined in stone and cement, and there will be one or two places where we cut away the mound and stabilize the walls so people can see the wall construction. It'll be great! The display area will have pottery and stuff from the other mounds, where we've had to do some grading."

As he chattered, I could see what had happened. The clubhouse had grown since the last iteration, and the park had shrunk. The enlarged gift shop and restaurant took up part of the open space I had built into the old plan. A new golf and tennis pro shop nicked one corner of the mound. The rest of the park had contracted, encroached upon by the swimming pool and the walk to the golf course. The park would encompass only the core of the main mound. The second largest mound was now the site of a cabana in the swimming pool complex. The other mounds and the rest of the area would be leveled by grading to create the roads and house pads and a commercial space designated on the plan as CONVE-NIENCE MART.

"The museum will display the most interesting artifacts, and explain them. Your job will be to write up the signs for the exhibits."

I studied the plans. "There is no museum!"

"Well, it's more like a display area, in the clubhouse lobby, and it includes the decor in the restaurant. It'll be a *theme* restaurant, see? I'm working with some interested parties. They want wall displays made up of pottery sherds. And if we find whole pots, they'll be in the cases in the lobby. It'll be beautiful. And a big interpretive display, here, in this corner. Have the text for the displays ready for me next week."

THAT'S WHEN THINGS FINALLY CAME TO A HEAD FOR PHAEDRA and me. It was one of Tucson's September Saturdays, when the sunlight on the pavement begins to lose its summer glare, and the afternoon temperatures drop back into the nineties. During that season, masses of midday clouds would cluster like cauliflowers over the Catalinas and the Rincons. Eventually they would thicken and spread across the sky and block the sun by four P.M., but by September, the summer gods had begun to lose interest in their duties, and the clouds would merely offer a farewell to summer with a sigh of thunder. Another generation of kids had come to town for their first semester of college. Phaedra and I had a date to go to the first football game.

The stadium was filling up. At the Great Desert University, the games came not in the afternoon, as God intended football, but in the evening, as if there were something to hide. Hopeful fans donned red shirts and blue pants, or worse yet, vice versa, and parked as close to the university as they could get and ate picnics off the backs of their pickup trucks and then headed for the stadium to promote sportsmanship, leaving dumpsters and occasional front yards full of aluminum beer cans.

Phaedra and I were in the stands but I was still in shock about the collapse of the interpretive center, and I was seeing the game and the whole world as if I were an alien from Alpha Centauri. I couldn't get my game spirit to kick in. When the action started, players came running out on the field as if they were looking for a parade to join, and everyone cheered, and the announcer said things in ultra–low-fi sound that no one could hear anyway because of the shouting. Then they started playing football, getting dirty and sweaty, trying to get the ball to one end of the field or the other. I had this aerial perspective in my mind about the appearance of the stadium, like a big cereal bowl of Wheaties, and we were the flakes.

It was one of those days where you can't be sure whether you remember the original thing, or only the substitute memory/dream that has stuck in your head from replaying the mental tapes too often. My whole life had been feeling like a strange and twisted dream from that moment when I saw Antonio's body in back of that church in Sonora.

The game was more Phaedra's thing than mine, anyway. She wanted to be there to celebrate the arrival of fall, and just to belong to the crowd. Fans cheered. And here I was, trying to cover my attitude by making cynical jokes about everything. "I've analyzed this game," I said. "The goal is to get the ball to the other end of the stadium, right? Couldn't they do it better by cooperating? If the two teams would cooperate, they could get it back and forth dozens of times."

"Jesus, Kevin, it's just a game."

"It's not a game, its some sort of tribal ritual to prove *our* young men are better than *their* young men."

I thought I was being mordantly amusing, but that was the point where she blew up at me. She turned to face me, meeting my eyes. "Kevin, it's *over* between us. I like you, and you're a decent guy, but I can't go on like this."

"What?" Actually I didn't hear her very well because of the screaming fans next to us.

"You're withdrawing into your own little world. I can't go there. I have to be realistic."

I tried to psych out what she was saying. She was facing me. I was surprised to see, in the middle of the game, she had tears in her eyes. We had hardly said anything yet. "I want a normal life," she said. "I want to be part of things. With an ordinary job in an ordinary office with ordinary people."

"But you can see how crazy everything is. You said so yourself. You're the one person I know who has a sense of what's really going on."

"Yes, but that doesn't mean I want to become a hermit or live in some intellectual bullshit counterworld. I want to live in the real world, with a house and a TV and a salary and a nice car. Maybe it's not all perfect and honest and idealistic, like your make-believe world, but at least I can fit in. With you, it's like you've got this complete disconnect. Listen to yourself! I mean, I like history too, but like Mr. Rooney says, you shouldn't let it affect your life."

"So now Mr. Rooney is your *coach*?"

"I don't want to talk about it." She was getting more tearful, more angry. Finally, she got up and left and told me not to come after her.

* * *

I STARTED AFTER HER ANYWAY BUT SHE LOST ME IN THE CROWD before I could collect my senses. After she left, I was alone with thirty thousand fans, who were all screaming at the players. I went into an altered state, a state I can remember only from strange images, as if in some sort of vision. The players clashing, and all these guys in the stands, working off their testosterone by yelling at the players and the refs. The women in red jackets who had come with them were yelling, too, but it seemed more forced with them. Great waves of sound washed across the stadium, threatening to drown the players. The players grunted and played harder, as they were supposed to do. I saw the people in the stadium—players and fans—as pawns of the town's huzza-ing tribal boosters, though it was all handled by middlemen known as the university athletic department, who laundered the money.

The cheerleaders jumped around a lot. The skimpy outfits they wore were faintly ridiculous, like bathing suits in the middle of a desert. Why weren't those outfits as sexy as the heavy sweaters cheerleaders wore at the eastern universities? It was another of life's eternal mysteries.

The band played whenever the time seemed right.

In my daze, it was the band I focused on, and I saw one kid, a clarinet player in the third row. I flashed on this vision of his life. I don't know where it came from, but it was very strong, very vivid. In high school he had practiced on an old, dented, silver clarinet. But when he went to college, his grandfather had given him a beautiful, expensive, shining clarinet. His grandfather had been in a touring band, and this very clarinet had been picked up and played once by Benny Goodman. "Treat it with respect," the grandfather said. "Remember, Benny Goodman once played this clarinet." It was a Stradivarius clarinet, so to speak.

During practice, the Stradivarius clarinet usually stayed safely locked away in the kid's locker in the music building—much safer than his dorm room. It came out during the games, when the kid sat out in the stadium, feeling omnipotent, with the clarinet that Benny Goodman had played. The huge array of brilliant stadium lights turned night into day and reflected off the instrument. The golden full moon, rising during the game, seemed obscured by the lights and even by the noise of the people cheering and screaming.

What the kid did not know is that, within a mile of his stadium, a thousand years earlier, smaller crowds had sat on an earthen oval embankment and watched a similar struggle for possession of a rubber ball, brought up along the prehistoric trade route from central Mexico. I seemed to be the only one who knew about the ancient game. I wanted to tell the kid. The crowds of a thousand years ago cheered and screamed just as loudly. Emotion expands to fill whatever vacuum is available. The prehistoric fans screamed and cried and tried to establish their preeminence, but today no one knows their names and only a few archaeologists know of their existence. The silent ball courts and prehistoric pit house foundations and pottery sherds lie under parking lots. That's what I wanted to tell the kid, because he didn't know it and I wasn't sure he would ever have the chance to find out.

The kid was thinking of how terrific the overture from *Star Wars* had sounded when John Williams conducted it in the film, and how awful it sounded when a hundred bands played it in a hundred half-time shows every weekend. Like me, the kid was in an introspective and rebellious mood. When the band director ordered them to play "Bear Down Arizona" for the thousandth time, he played something else. Sitting in the middle of the band with martial strains of the music rising around him—strains which themselves were blanketed by the cheers of the crowd and went almost unheard—sitting in the middle of all this he played little riffs and tunes, like Benny might have played in 1939.

No one heard him, of course. What he was doing was totally disconnected from the hubbub, and no one paid the slightest attention. Charles Ives would have been proud of him. How many musicians could get away with this before someone noticed that what was being played is not what they thought they heard? Two of them could do it. Three? The director might notice. The crowd wouldn't care. The crowd heard the noise but didn't listen.

I found myself wandering out of the stadium, on the high concrete ramps that led from the stands down to the streets. The streets and houses made a great sea of starry lights, stretching out in all directions toward the foothills of the Rincon Mountains and the Catalinas. Red corpuscles of light flowed down the arteries of the city. The entire scene could be wiped out in a flash. The crumbling Soviet government might go postal and use their nukes. We had a huge air force base at the south edge of town, where the Santa Cruz Valley opens into a broad, flat plain. We had all grown up here knowing that Our air base was on Their target list.

Or we could get totaled by the random crash of an asteroid—just as the dinosaurs were brought to extinction sixty-five million years ago—and then there would be nothing left to worry about. It would take only one of the tiniest bits of cosmic flotsam to do the job. One of the astronomers at the university had been quoted in the paper as saying there were dozens of the little buggers that often passed by the Earth closer than the moon.

But suppose the Soviets didn't strike and an asteroid didn't crash into the scene. What would happen then?

I imagined that the clarinet player, with his independence, had stumbled onto a road to intelligence and strength. "Is it possible to employ intelligence and strength?" Andre Gide asked in *The Immoralist*, "or must they be altogether outlawed?" It was a strange line, one that had stuck in my mind since a literature course in college. Every time I was about to forget it, some new stupidity would occur in the world that would bring it to mind. The kid would emerge from the stadium and from the university into the dangerous sea of twentieth-century lights that spread across the entire world, the global county fair that knew nothing of prehistoric ball courts or Coronado's long march. Would he be able to use intelligence and strength at the same time? The billboards and TVs—BUY NOW! OWN NOW!—would be much louder than the obscure messages seeping out of the soil. Being a citizen of a rich and prosperous land, as Marcos called it, he would be able to afford to pick and choose. He could draw from the society just as much as he needed, but it would be hard to be stop there. He would feel a kind of guilt that Marcos could not even have understood. As early as 1949, in *The Man with the Golden Arm*, forgotten novelist Nelson Algren called it "the great, secret and special American guilt of owning nothing . . . in a land where ownership and virtue are one." All through this kid's life, he would face the "guilt that lay crouched behind every billboard. . . ." Oh yes, he would be a free citizen of a global economy, but as Monsieur Gide said, "To know how to free yourself is nothing. The arduous thing is to know what to do with one's freedom."

I KNEW WHAT TO DO WITH MY FREEDOM. I CALLED IN SICK ON Monday morning. I had to think.

CHAPTER 20

1539
Testimony from Mexico City

I was in a daze. All current phases of my life seemed to be headed toward an end: Phaedra, Mr. Rooney, Coronado Estates. I kept thinking about Phaedra, how she had been seduced by the dark side of the economic force. I could have ended my Marcos work, too, but I had lived with Marcos too long. His story had become my touchstone for relating to the rest of the world. It was the one thing that gave me some continuity and purpose in those days after the football game. If our lives were really parallel, I needed to follow his, all the way. Maybe it would help me understand why some people fit in their culture and some people don't.

There were three levels to his mystery, I realized, and I had dealt only with the first two. The first level was Mr. Rooney's level—the mystery of the route and whether he had really come north through our land and gone all the way to Cíbola, and I had solved that to my satisfaction. The second level, the question of why scholars thought he had lied, I thought I understood from the fact that they had mistakenly denied the possibility of messages sent by Marcos from the north. The third level was a still deeper underlying meta-level. How does the official version of history get written? How does Tonypandy get started? How did Marcos get the blame for the failure of a later expedition? When Lansing Bloom pointed out in 1940 that Marcos might have sent messages, why didn't that "take?" Why didn't it rebut the earlier historical theories and end the calumny against Marcos? What maintains false paradigms? How do they start? In many ways, the culture I was seeing all around me seemed based on false paradigms. What propped it up? Could I learn something about my own disenchantment?

In the collapsing Soviet Union, they had whole armies of propagandists, rewriting history into its official version, airbrushing old news photos in order to literally remove from history Marcoslike figures who had fallen out of favor. But why did things go so wrong in the absence of an organized effort?

To understand the third level, I needed to understand how the case against him got started in the first place. Was there something back at the beginning that started people calling him a liar? Something I had missed? It all meant I couldn't just drop Marcos, I had to follow his story through. What was he was saying when he got back to Mexico? After all, the main charge against the guy was that he trumpeted lies from the pulpits and street corners, claiming that Cíbola was full of treasure just waiting to be carried off by conquistadorial entrepreneurs. In this version, the whole motivation for Coronado's army was that Marcos conned them by promising gold. I needed to move beyond the journey itself, and look at the subsequent weeks and months, after Marcos got back to Mexico.

The first weekend after the game, in a haze of therapeutic beer, I spread out my books and Xeroxes on my apartment floor. Between unanswered calls to Phaedra, I started a chronological file of all the events after Marcos got back. Judging from my notes, by some miracle I actually did some good work, even if I can't remember doing much of it.

As I said before, no one knows the exact date of Marcos's final return to Mexico City, but there were clues. On his way back from Cíbola, Marcos met Coronado at Compostela, and then they traveled on together to the capital. The linkup at Compostela had to be after July 15, because Coronado's letter from Compostela on that date indicated Marcos had not arrived there yet. The two of them were probably in Mexico City by August 23, because Bishop Zumárraga wrote a letter that day that seems to come from conversation with Marcos, suggesting the explorer had arrived a few days before that. He had to be in Mexico City by August 26 because his formal *Relación* was certified there on that date by the head of his order, Antonio Ciudad-Rodrigo. There was an obvious rush to certify Marcos's *Relación* in Mexico City after August 26, which also implies that he arrived not too many days before that.

Those dates carried implications. The distance from Compostela to Mexico City is about 520 road miles, and so, if Marcos and Coronado traveled 20 miles per day in haste to reach Mendoza, they would have taken twenty-six days from Compostela to Mexico City. That means they could have left Compostela around July 26, to arrive in Mexico City around August 21. Everything checked. Thus, Marcos didn't have to be in Compostela by late June or early July, as the historians demanded, based on their no-message theory. Hallenbeck, for example, insisted that Marcos had to be in Compostela by about June 20–25, and others said early July. Compared to Hallenbeck, my reconstruction gave Marcos a whole extra month to get back from Cíbola, and all the grousing about Marcos not having time to make his journey was nonsense.

The remaining Big Question was what Marcos said in Mexico when he got back. The first thing I noticed was that even Pedro Castañeda, the soldier-chronicler who usually blamed Marcos for misleading everybody, admitted that Marcos tried to follow Mendoza's orders of secrecy on his way back from Compostela to Mexico City.

He made things seem all the more important by not talking about them to anyone but his own friends, under the promise of secrecy, until after he had reached Mexico City and seen Antonio de Mendoza.

No evidence there to claim that Marcos was starting rumors of gold.

So where did those rumors come from? As I studied books about that period, I found the smoking gun that explained how part of the story got distorted. Various scholars pointed out that publishers in

Europe at that time cheerfully added lurid passages to explorers' books about the New World, because it was good business. Gold, monsters, cannibalism, and beautiful women wearing jewels—they all made books more sexy and sold more copies. So, when Marcos's *Relación* was published in Europe a few years after he gave it to Mendoza, the publishers added flamboyant passages, putting words in Marcos's mouth. The most notorious example came just after Marcos says he spotted the city. In the original notarized copies, Marcos simply said:

The houses are of the style that the Indians had described, all of stone, with stories and terraces, as well as I could see from a hill where I could view it. The city is bigger than Mexico City. At times, I was tempted to go on to the city itself. . . .

However, a popular book about American adventures, published in Venice in 1556 and edited by an Italian named Ramusio, had various inserts from an extraneous hand, possibly Ramusio's himself. The published text at this point says:

The houses are of the style that the Indians had described, all of stone, with stories and terraces, as well as I could see from a hill where I could view it. The city is bigger than Mexico City, which has more than 20,000 houses. The people are almost white. . . . They possess many emeralds and other jewels, though they prize none as much as turquoises. These they use to decorate the walls and doorways of their homes, as well as their clothes and vases, and they use them as money throughout that country. They wear cotton clothes and cattle skins, and the latter are considered more valuable. Because they possess no other metals, they utilize vessels of gold and silver. They make great use of it and there is a greater abundance of it than in Peru. They buy it with turquoises in the province of the painted Indians [which Marcos reported to the south], where it is said that many mines are found. I was not able to obtain as detailed information about the other kingdoms [beyond Cíbola]. At times, I was tempted to go on to the city itself. . . .

The embellishments do not appear in either of the two original copies signed by Marcos himself, notarized before Viceroy Mendoza, and preserved in Spain, nor in a third early copy preserved in Vienna. Bits and pieces, like the cotton clothes and buffalo skins may have been cribbed from other parts of Marcos's report or from his messages or from other people's recollections, but the vessels of gold and silver were clearly not part of any official report. To the European publishers, fact-checking was not the primary concern. They had discovered marketing.

You can trace a whole lineage of other authors, from the 1600s onward, who used various translations of Ramusio's version, and passed on the misquotes of poor Marcos. Here, then, was the explanation of why generations of writers blithely claimed Marcos talked about gold.

But identifying fake embellishments does not prove that Marcos himself didn't make similar off-the-record exaggerations, as charged, after he got to Mexico City. The young bucks in Mexico City clearly believed that Cíbola was full of gold; they got the idea from somewhere. Was there any contemporary record about what Marcos actually said?

I went through all my documents, looking for letters and quotes, and arranging them in chronological sequence. The next thing I could find was the letter I mentioned earlier, written by Bishop Zumárraga on August 23, 1539, to an unknown correspondent. Excitedly, he wrote,

. . . Fray Marcos has discovered another much larger country, 400 leagues beyond where Nuño de Guzmán went, and near the island where the marquis Cortés was. Many people are moving to go there. The marquis pretends that its conquest belongs to him, but the viceroy is taking it for the Emperor, and wants to send friars ahead without arms. He wishes the con-

quest to be a Christian and apostolic one, not a butchery.

The people are very cultured, in their wooden edifices of many stories and in their dress. They have no idols, but worship the sun and moon. They have only one wife and if she dies, they do not marry another. There are partridges and cows, which the father says he saw, and he also heard a story of camels and dromedaries and other cites larger than this one of Mexico. . . .

I figured Zumárraga was basing this on face-to-face conversations just after the friar returned, because it contains details that he could not have found in Marcos's *Relación*, and at the same time it contains some errors he would not have made if he were quoting from Marcos's written reports, lying on a desk in front of him. For example, Zumárraga said that the Cíbola buildings were made of wood, whereas Marcos consistently wrote about stone construction. So the elderly bishop must have been misremembering some conversation, not copying a report.

In any case, there's not a word about gold and jewels in this letter. If Marcos had been ranting about gold in his private conversations, wouldn't Zumárraga have mentioned it? As for other large cities and camels, Marcos's *Relación* makes it clear that the Indians told him about the other Pueblo districts along the Rio Grande and among the Hopis, and about the hump-backed beasts of the plains—the buffalo.

MARCOS'S DISCOVERY WAS THE BIG NEWS OF THE DAY IN MEXICO City. Things moved fast. The certification of Marcos's *Relación*, by the head of his religious order, came only three days later and Ciudad-Rodrigo took pains to certify that the report was true and sober. This certification may have been part of Mendoza's campaign to build up legal documentation for his claim against Cortés.

I, Fray Antonio de Ciudad-Rodrigo, friar of the order of the Minorities and Minister Provincial . . . affirm that I sent out Fray Marcos de Niza, a priest, friar, and ecclesiastic. In all matters of virtue and religion he is esteemed by me and my brethren of the governing deputies. . . . He was approved for this journey of discovery because of these qualities, and because he is learned, not only in theology, but also in cosmography and the art of navigation. . . . He went with another lay brother, Fray Honorato, by the command of the lord Don Antonio de Mendoza, viceroy of this New Spain. His Excellency gave him all the equipment and supplies needed. His instructions, which I saw and which His Excellency communicated to me . . . were given to Fray Marcos by the hand of Francisco Vázquez de Coronado. He received them willingly and executed them faithfully, as in fact has appeared. As the above is the truth and there is no falsehood in it, I have written this testimony and signed it with my name. Dated in Mexico [City], the 26th day of August, in the year 1539.

Fra. Antonio de Ciudad-Rodrigo, Minister Provincial

No indication here of any suspicion that Marcos was concocting a fraud!

A FEW DAYS AFTER THAT, ON SEPTEMBER 2, 1539, THE OFFICIAL *Relación* of Marcos's trip was notarized by several secretaries in front of Mendoza and his court.

In the great city of Temixtitlan, part of Mexico City in New Spain, on the second of September, in the year of our lord Jesus Christ, 1539, the very reverend father, Fray Marcos de Niza, vice-commissary of the order of St. Francis in these parts of the Indies, appeared before the very illustrious lord, Don Antonio de Mendoza, viceroy and governor for His Majesty in this New Spain, and before other very magnificent lords. Fray Marcos presented these writings: his instructions from the viceroy, as well as his own Relación of his journey, signed with his name and sealed with the general seal of the Indies. These documents

consist of nine sheets counting this one, on which go our signa-
tures. He stated and affirmed and certified that the contents of
the said instructions and Relación are true, and that what is
stated therein did occur. All this was done so that His Majesty
may be informed of the truth of that which is described. . . .
Their lordships ordered us, the secretaries, to sign with our sig-
natures, because the above has been presented and declared to
be true, and so we attest the same and declare it to be the
truth. [Various witnesses are named.]

Juan Baeza de Herrera (Chief Secretary)
Antonio de Turcios (Secretary)

Here was the certification of a report that contains not one
word about gold in Cíbola, yet Hallenbeck and Wagner portrayed
these flamboyant certifications as desperate attempts to put a
veneer of legitimacy on outrageous fraudulent claims of discovery. It seemed more likely to me that these notarizations were
orchestrated by Mendoza to legalize his claims against Cortés,
who was moving to challenge Mendoza for rights to the northern
conquest.

BUT WHAT DID MARCOS SAY IN THE NEXT WEEKS, ONCE HIS
report was certified? Was he ranting from the pulpits about gold in
Cíbola, as charged by later historians, or perhaps slyly cornering
soldiers in the streets to con them into joining an expedition of conquest? Amazingly, as I assembled scattered references in chronological order, I found a number of documents giving a picture of
what was happening. The next relevant one was a letter buried in a
1934 paper by the historian Henry Wagner. It was written by a little known friar, Gerónimo Ximenez de San Esteban, dated October
9, 1539—giving us a view of information circulating in Mexico
City six weeks after Marcos's return. Ximenez refers directly to a
conversation with Marcos, and, like Zumárraga, he reports some
details about Cíbola that are not in the official *Relación*.

In the month of September last year a friar of the San Francis-
can order, French of nationality, left the city of Mexico in search
of a country about which the governors of these parts had heard,
but had not been able to find. He traveled over 500 leagues
through inhabited territory, and then through a despoblado for
more than sixty leagues, at the end of which he came to a very
well settled country. That country had people of much culture,
who had walled cities with great houses. They wear shoes and
little boots of leather and many wear silk-like clothing down to
their feet. I say nothing of the richness of this country, because it
is reputed to be so great that it does not seem possible. The friar
himself told me that he saw a temple of their idols, the walls of
which, inside and outside, were covered with precious stones. I
think he said they were emeralds. They also say that in the coun-
try beyond that land, there are camels and elephants.

To Wagner, of course, the rich country and the jewel-encrusted
temple were direct examples of Marcos's notorious exaggerations.
But a careful reading did not convince me. The first claim, of an
unbelievably rich country, is not attributed to Marcos himself, but
to rumor. Many phrases like "a rich country" were correctly used by
Marcos on his way north to describe the good lands he found. They
were likely in his messages, and now they were being used in the
streets to discuss Marcos's discovery. The next sentence is specifically attributed to Marcos, and claims jewel-encrusted temples! At
first, even I thought it was a deathblow to Marcos's veracity! But
then I realized that Marcos could not have been telling Father
Gerónimo that the jewel-encrusted temple was in Cíbola, because
he was already on record as never having set foot inside the city. He
wouldn't hand in a certified report saying he had never entered the
city, and then turn around and tell Father Gerónimo, "Oh, by the
way, when I was in Cíbola, I saw this temple full of jewels." In fact,
Gerónimo's letter never said the temple was in Cíbola, but only
somewhere in the northern country. I recalled to myself that the

Spaniards in Mexico had no mental map of Sonora, Arizona, and New Mexico; to them, anything Marcos saw beyond Petatlán was in the "rich and prosperous new lands" that Marcos had discovered. Obviously, Marcos was telling his fellow ecclesiastic about a temple he saw not in the city of Cíbola, but somewhere along the way, probably in one of the villages of northern Sonora or southern Arizona.

This fits other historic records, which say that these villages had small shrines decorated in various ways. Castañeda described seeing a war shrine there whose walls were decorated with arrows. Cabeza de Vaca reported having been given "emerald" arrowheads—which were probably turquoise. And Cushing, of course, confirmed that in Zuni, the people set turquoises in some of their building walls—probably a widespread tradition. Modern archeological excavations of villages along the Rio Sonora reveal special platform mounds with what the archaeologists called "public architecture." There seemed no reason to doubt that Marcos had seen a shrine decorated with turquoise, which he described as a blue-green stone like emerald. Father Gerónimo was relaying something of this sort. The main thing was that in spite of Father Gerónimo's enthusiasm, he makes not a single mention of gold—not a hint to support the claim that Marcos was raving about precious metals. Marcos's basic descriptions seem to have been true, and merely misinterpreted by both hearers and historians.

WHAT WAS BEING SAID ABOUT CÍBOLA BY THE ROUGH SOLDIERS in the streets? In the scholarly books, I discovered, incredibly, a list of eyewitness statements about what was being said in the streets of Mexico City. In November of 1539, legal inquiries were made about the arguments between Cortés and Mendoza over the incipient conquest of the north. In Havana, testimony was taken from seven passengers on a ship from Mexico, who were asked to report what they had heard about the discoveries of lands to the north.

In the town of San Cristóbal, of Havana, on the island Fernandina of the Indies of the Ocean Sea: 12th of November, 1539, witnesses testified as follows before the noble sir, Juan de Rojas, Lt. Gov. of this town, appointed by the illustrious and magnificent Don Hernán de Soto, Governor.

(1.) Witness Núñez testifies: I swear that in Mexico City, maybe three months ago more or less [mid August], I heard the following public discussion. A Franciscan friar—that is to say Fray Marcos—had come from the land of the interior. He said he discovered a very rich and populous land, and that it was 400 leagues from Mexico. They say that one can get there for certain by means of the Rio de Palmas, and that the marquis, Hernán Cortés, sent ships of discovery in that direction. It's been heard that there is an argument between the marquis and the viceroy over the conquest of the said land and that the viceroy has ordered that no other ship go here. I believe this is the case, because no announcements have come from the land. That is the truth.

(2.) Witness Francisco Serrano testifies: I think it was a month and a half ago [late September] I heard that a Franciscan friar came from a newly discovered country 400 leagues from Mexico, by way of the road from Jalisco. They say it is very rich and populated with great walled cities, and that the people there are regarded as kings or lords, and that the houses are excessively large, and the people are of good character, that they speak Mexican. They say the viceroy will send people there, and that they are Captain Francisco Vázquez de Coronado and other captains. The viceroy puts much faith in them.

(3.) Witness Sanchez, the Dyer, testifies: More or less a month and a half ago [late September], I heard it said publicly that a friar has come from a new land that is very rich and very populated with cities and towns. People said that it is 400–450 leagues by the road from Jalisco. It is said to be inland, toward the middle of the new land. The viceroy has armed people and captains to go to the new land.

(4) Witness Francisco de Leyba (in Veracruz) swears: I heard it said that a friar has come from a new very rich and very populated land of cities and towns, 400 leagues from the frontier. And I heard it said publicly that the viceroy has appointed armed captains to go to the said land. . . . This is the truth.

(5.) Witness Hernán de Sotomayor testifies: In the town of Los Angeles it was said in public that the houses of the new land are substantial and of stone, and there are walled cities and consequential people, and this is the part of the land where Dorantes and Cabeza de Vaca traveled. . . .

(6.) Witness Garcia Navarro testifies: I heard it said in public that about a month or a month and a half ago [late September to early October] a friar arrived from a newly discovered land. They say it is about 500 leagues from Mexico, in the land of Florida [a term used for the North American mainland north and east of Mexico], and is toward the north part of that land. It is a rich land of gold and silver and other valuable commodities, as well as large towns. They say the houses are of stone and earth, in the manner of those in Mexico, and have substantial size and bulk. Cultured people live there; they don't marry more than once and they wear burnooses, and ride animals but the types of animals are unknown.

(7.) Witness Andrés Garcia testifies: I had a son-in-law who was a barber who shaved Marcos de Niza after the friar returned to Mexico City. My son-in-law told me that the Friar told him the following things. After he crossed the mountainous area, there was a river, and many settlements were there, in both cities and towns. The cities were surrounded by walls, with their gates guarded, and were very wealthy, having silversmiths. The women wore strings of gold beads and the men wore belts of gold and white woolen clothes. They had sheep and cows and partridges and slaughterhouses, iron forges, and other substantial things. He said to me that I should stay [in Mexico, rather than leaving on the ship to Cuba, because] of the discovery of this new land.

How to summarize? In terms of the charges against Marcos, was this glass half full or half empty? Between August and October, people on the streets were talking about Marcos's discoveries, but five out of seven of those witnesses said nothing at all about metal. Witness Navarro mentioned rumors of gold and silver, but he might have been relaying news about ores, in which case the statement was true. For example, in 1736 abundant loose silver was discovered on the surface at Arizonac, near the border south of Tucson, and this was what led—at last—to the settlement of the "Arizonac" territory. Perhaps Marcos picked up reports of such mineralization. Only the last report out of the seven says anything about gold jewelry in Cíbola, and that one was a third-hand report of a witness who talked to a barber who talked to Marcos.

To me, it was getting clearer and clearer: no prosecuting attorney could have nailed Marcos for trumpeting gross exaggerations about fabulous golden treasures in Cíbola, based on such eyewitness testimony! If you add up Marcos's *Relación*, the letter of Bishop Zumárraga, the letter of Fray Gerónimo Ximenez, and the seven witnesses from the ship in Havana, then you have ten "eyewitness" records of what Marcos reported when he came back. Eight out of ten say not a word about use of gold in Cíbola, but give only sober, essentially correct information about newly discovered lands with their well-populated towns, the high culture of the people, their leatherworking, their large buildings, and the buffalo—yet Marcos went down in history as the notorious lying monk.

Even the Spanish historians of the next generation who reported on the episode did not accuse Marcos of lying about gold, but only halfheartedly claimed he exaggerated the wonders of Cíbola. Here is material from one of the first histories of the period, written about forty years later by a Mexican historian, Suarez de Peralta, born about 1535–40. Peralta was an infant when Coronado came back in 1542, but he may have gathered these recollections from eyewitnesses or participants in the Coronado expedition.

The country was so stirred up by the news the friar had brought from the Seven Cities that no one thought about anything else. He said the city of Cíbola was big enough to contain two Sevilles and more, and that the other places were not much smaller. He said the houses were very fine buildings, four stories high. Also that in that country there were many of what they call wild cows, as well as sheep and goats and rich treasures. He exaggerated things so much that everyone was for going there and leaving Mexico depopulated.

The news from the Seven Cities inspired so eager a desire in everyone that not only the viceroy and the marquis [Cortés] made ready to start north, but also the whole country. Everyone wanted to follow them so much that they traded for the licenses which permitted them to go as soldiers. People sold these as a favor, and whoever obtained one thought it was at least as good as a title of nobility.

All this excitement arose because the friar who had come from there exaggerated and said it was the best place in the world, that the people in that country were very prosperous, with all the Indians wearing clothes and possessing many cattle. The mountains were said to be like those of Spain, and the climate the same. For wood they burned large walnut trees, which bear quantities of walnuts better than those of Spain. They must have many mountain grapes, which are very good eating, plus chestnuts and filberts. According to the way he painted it, this should have been the terrestrial paradise. For game, there were partridges, geese, cranes, and all other winged creatures—it was marvelous what was there.

Actually, he did tell the truth in all this, because there are mountains in that country, as he said, and herds, especially of cow-like beasts, and there are grapes and game without doubt, and a climate like that of Spain.

All these claims of exaggeration may sound bad for Marcos, yet he is charged only with exaggerating the prosperity of Cíbola.

Once again, he is not charged with claiming gold *per se*, and even the phrase "rich treasures" comes only after the buffalo, sheep, and goats. Speaking of sheep, I was amused that even though Suarez de Peralta accused Marcos of exaggerating, he then sheepishly admitted that, well, actually, the things Marcos said were basically true.

So why did they all rush off convinced they would get rich off the gold in Cíbola? From the documentary record, it appears not so much that Marcos publicly claimed discovery of gold, but rather that the Spaniards of Mexico simply *assumed* that Cíbola was a gold-filled kingdom, based on their experience with Mexico and Peru. Gold in the north was their own preconception—a dream from inside their own heads—not a claim by Marcos!

To me, this was a stunning new conclusion. If Marcos did not promote gold in Cíbola, then the whole Coronado expedition was history's greatest example of the game of telephone: he said that she said that her cousin heard that the viceroy believes that . . . Preconception ran roughshod over truth. Even if Marcos told reasonably sober stories about Cíbola, all the citizens of Mexico were psychically primed to translate this news into a tale of Tenochtitlánlike treasures. Over and over, the words actually attributed to Marcos are about a prosperous land, multistory buildings, a city named after the trade in buffalo products, and cultured people with good clothes—but with the help of expectation and a few money-grubbing publishers in sixteenth-century Europe, he goes down in history as claiming discovery of a golden city. It's good old quirky human behavior: "We all know what's true, so let's not get side-tracked with the details of what the guy actually said."

SO THE WHEELS WERE SET IN MOTION FOR CORONADO'S GRAND army of conquest. And here, then, was part of the answer to my third-level question, a revelation of the true nature of the world. Marcos had not been a purposeful liar or agent of a carefully constructed Machiavellian conspiracy, but yet another fallible guy trying to do his best and getting run over by the culture around him. In other words, I saw my own predicament.

Thus climaxed my education about grand human affairs. The greatest army the New World had ever seen was launched to conquer a preconceived empire of Golden Cities which had never even been reported by its own reconnaissance team!

I COULD NOT HELP CHECKING THE REST OF THE OLD SPANISH DOCuments to follow the story of how it all played out to its grand climax in front of the gates of Cíbola. The beginning of Coronado's vast expedition was recorded by the soldier, Pedro Castañeda. Castañeda said that as soon as Coronado and Marcos arrived back Mexico City and talked to Mendoza,

> ... it began to be announced that they really had found the Seven Cities, and a start was made in gathering an army to go conquer them. The noble viceroy arranged with the Franciscan friars that Marcos be made father provincial, as a result of which the Franciscan pulpits were filled with such accounts of marvels and wonders that more than 300 Spaniards and about 800 natives collected in a few days.

Mendoza proceeded to organize a giant military expedition. In the scenario of Wagner, Sauer, and Hallenbeck, Marcos's promotion was a cynical payoff for exaggerating reports of gold. But if Mendoza knew it was a scam, why did he invest large amounts of his own fortune? In my scenario, the promotion of Marcos was a more sincere reward and Mendoza really believed the conquest would net easy wealth.

A later Mexican historian named Mota Padilla, who wrote around 1742, also recorded the start of the expedition. He used various old sources, including documents he said he found in Culiacán, written by participants in the expeditions, but now lost. He reported that Mendoza

> ... determined to avail himself of the many noblemen who were in Mexico, bobbing up and down like corks in water with-

out having anything to busy themselves with, depending on the
viceroy to do them favors and maintaining themselves at the
tables of various citizens of Mexico. . . . It was easy to enlist
more than three hundred men. . . . He gave them thirty pesos
each and promised them grants in the land that would be set-
tled, and more once it was ascertained that there were hills
containing silver and other deposits.

Again, I thought it was interesting that the payoff was described
not so much in gold to be plundered from Cíbola but in land and
mining options.

The stakes were high and Mendoza was no fool. He must have
harbored private reservations about the fact that Marcos had not
been able to enter Cíbola or see its wealth for himself. He must
also have wanted to know more about its defenses, and the hostility which Marcos had documented. Thus, only two months after
Marcos returned, Mendoza quietly made one more attempt to clarify what was in the north. He sent a party of horsemen under one
of Coronado's captains, Melchior Díaz, to get more information
about the Seven Cities, the fate of Estevan, and the mood of the
people.

Meanwhile, Cortés still wanted to be lord of the sea. In the summer of 1539, within days of when the first positive messages came
back from Marcos, Cortés had sent ships off to explore the northern
coasts. No word was expected from them for many months, but
Cortés insisted on his right to northern conquest. Mendoza and
Cortés argued about this until Cortés packed off to Spain to press
his claims at court.

In early 1540, the giant expedition was ready. At the last minute,
the viceroy decided not to go in person. On January 6, he conferred
the leadership of the expedition upon his close friend, the governor
of the northwestern frontier, Francisco Vázquez de Coronado. The
viceroy also issued instructions. Prudently, he decided the army
should not march *en masse* from Mexico City to the northwest
frontier, fearing the undisciplined troops might stir unrest in the

country in-between. Instead, soldiers set out in small groups to Coronado's headquarters in Compostela, to be assembled there on February 22, 1540. The governor held a review and tabulated the results, listing 270 mounted men with lances, swords and other hand weapons, some with coats of chain mail. There were an additional 70 infantrymen, and more than a thousand horses, not counting pack animals, livestock, and six field guns with powder and shot. The army was not primarily Spanish. It also contained more than 900 Indian fighting men and servants, along with horse-handlers, cowboys, and shepherds. The total force was more than 1200 men and a few women. The next day, February 23, 1540, the army departed for Cíbola, taking Fray Marcos de Niza and other fathers to lead the way.

MEANWHILE, DÍAZ AND HIS HORSEMEN HAD REACHED Chichilti-Calli, where his progress was blocked by winter snows in the mountains north of the Gila River—the last *despoblado*. Frustrated, Díaz spent a number of weeks in the province of Chichilti-Calli gathering information. Like Marcos, he sent back a report, which reached the viceroy only in March, after Coronado's army had left. The report exists today only in a summary, found in a letter from Mendoza to the king, dated April 17, 1540. Mendoza said:

> *Some days ago I wrote to Your Majesty that I had ordered Melchior Díaz . . . to take some horsemen and see if the account given by Friar Marcos agreed with what he could discover. He set out from Culiacán with fifteen horsemen on last November 17. On March 20, I received a letter from him, sent by four of his horsemen.*
>
> *He says that after he left Culiacán and crossed the river at Petatlán, he was received very well by the Indians along the way. He would send a cross to the place where he was going*

to stop, because the Indians venerated this sign ever since the days when Marcos passed through and freed them from the slave raiders. The Indians would make a house out of mats, to house the cross, and somewhat away from this they would make a lodging for the Spaniards, drive stakes to tie the horses, and supply fodder for them and an abundance of corn wherever they had it. In many places, the Indians said they were suffering from hunger because it had been a bad year. . . .

Díaz also says that the people whom he found along the way do not have any [permanent] settlements, except in one valley 150 leagues from Culiacán, which is well settled and has houses with lofts.

I remember rushing to check the map when I first read this. The distance of 150 leagues would be about 375 to 465 miles. The modern road distance from Culiacán to the Sonora River Valley is about 430 miles. So Díaz was reporting the settlements along the Sonora River valley, which contained Corazones and other towns that the Spaniards regarded as the best along the route. Everything checked with what Marcos had said. The report continues to agree with Marcos, but gets less encouraging.

After going 100 leagues from Culiacán, he began to find the country growing cold, with severe frosts, and the further he went, the colder it became, until he reached a point where some of the Indians who went with him were frozen, and two of the Spaniards were in great danger. . . . They decided not to go any further, and to send back an account of what he had learned, which is as follows, taken literally from his letter:

"Seeing that it is impossible to cross the despoblado from here to Cíbola because of the heavy snows and the cold, I will give your lordship an account of what I learned about Cíbola, which I determined by asking many people who have been

*there as long as fifteen or twenty years. I got this information in
different ways, interviewing some Indians together and others
separately. They all agree in what they say."*

A long description of the lifestyle in Cíbola follows, including
the following passages quoted from Díaz, and giving more emphasis to military intelligence than Brother Marcos provided.

*"There are seven towns, being a short day's march from one to
another, all of which together are called Cíbola. The houses are
of stone and mud, coarsely worked, with three and four stories.
They utilize the low ones but they live in the highest ones. In the
lowest, they have some loopholes, as in the fortresses of Spain.
The Indians say that when the Cíbolans are attacked, they station themselves in the houses and fight from there. When they
make war, they carry shields and wear leather jackets made of
cows' hides, painted, and they fight with arrows and stone
mauls and other weapons. . . .*

*"They have many turquoises. . . . The clothing of the men is
a cloak over which is the skin of one of their cows, like the one
that Cabeza de Vaca and Dorantes brought, which Your Lordship saw. . . .*

*"My informants were unable to tell me about any metal, nor
did they say that they had it. They do have turquoises in quantity, though not so many as Father Provincial Marcos said.
They have some little stone crystals, like this one which I
enclose, of which Your Lordship has seen many in New
Spain. . . . The men spin and weave cotton.*

*"They have dances and songs, with some flutes that have
holes on which to put the fingers. . . . They sing in unison with
those who play, and those who sing clap their hands in our own
fashion. One of the Indians who accompanied Estevan the
black to Cíbola, an Indian who had been a captive in Cíbola,
watched them practicing their playing and singing.*

"The region of Cíbola is famous, on account of having these

houses and an abundance of food and turquoises. I haven't been able to learn any more than what I related, even though, as I said, I have talked to Indians who lived there fifteen and twenty years.

"The death of Estevan the black happened in the way that Friar Marcos described it . . . and so I do not make a detailed report here, except to say that the people of Cíbola sent word to the people in this village and its neighborhood that if any Christians should arrive, they should not be considered invincible or supernatural. Instead, the messages from Cíbola said that the people of this region should rise up and destroy the Christians forthwith, because they are mortal and can be killed. They said they confirmed this by keeping the bones of the one who had come there. The Cíbolans also said that if the people in this area did not dare to do it, then they should send word to Cíbola so that the Cíbolans themselves could come and do it.

"I can very easily believe that there has been some communication between these places, and that this advice has been received, because of the coolness with which these Indians have received us and the sour faces they have shown us."

It was not so different from what Marcos said, but with a different tone. Díaz judged that Marcos overestimated the importance of turquoise, but stunningly, in spite of his direct questioning, he hadn't been able to find about any more about gold than Marcos did. His words were measured and frustrating. "Nor did they say they had gold!" I wondered what Mendoza thought about his investments as he read Díaz's report.

CHAPTER 21

1540
Marching Toward Cíbola

M*arch, 1540*. At last the great Christian army was on the road leading north. They had left Vázquez de Coronado's capital in Compostela, and were marching under fair skies toward the coastal outpost of Culiacán, and to Cíbola beyond. Marcos de Niza walked in the vanguard with the other five priests who had been assigned to the expedition. Ahead of them runners sped forward to reassure Indians in the local villages that they had only peaceful intent.

Behind, the expedition stretched in ragtag order. First came Coronado, with his officers and guard and black servants, his page, his campaign tent, and personal goods. Then came the 350 horse-men and foot soldiers, the horse loads of supplies for the army, the lumbering cattle and sheep. Stretching behind there were the Indian allies assembled from the valley of Mexico and the pacified provinces around Compostela. Overhead, the sky was a sheet of clouds. The desert under a leaden sky seemed to Marcos like the sea under an overcast: expansive, muted, pensive, waiting for something to happen.

The end of 1539 had been a joyous time for Marcos. Viceroy Mendoza had wasted no time in exercising his authority. After for-bidding unauthorized expeditions, he organized the historic con-quest under his own command. The Mendoza expedition would approach Cíbola by Marcos's land route, but with separate naval support. Mendoza and Coronado—the blackbeard and the brown-beard, as the men called them—had both put much of their own fortunes into the venture. This alone insured a serious and success-ful effort. Confidence rose among the young hellions of Mexico City. The days of glory were not over! People bought shares in the new expedition. Young men pawned their belongings for a sword, a crossbow, a scrap of chain mail—anything that might be useful in conquering the great walled cities of Cíbola. In the cantinas, they placed bets on whether Cíbola would yield more gold than Cortés found in Tenochtitlán.

In the midst of the excitement, the Franciscan order, with the blessing of the bishop and the encouragement of the viceroy him-self, elevated Marcos to the post of father provincial of the Francis-cans in New Spain. This had given him new credibility. He had been able to preach sermons in packed churches about how God had chosen Spain to set an example in the New World, and how God had confirmed this by revealing the wonders of the northern lands not to ruthless soldiers (his listeners would understand he meant Guzmán and Cortés), but rather to a humble, lone explorer—an unarmed friar. Let this be a harbinger, he said, of how the north could be conquered with friendship.

Marcos had no illusions. He recognized that no matter what he said about fine lands, the intelligent Indians, and the glories of a missionizing effort, the men in his audience heard only unspoken words about yellow metal. In answering their questions, he always fell back on his politically and morally prudent phrases: anyone could reasonably infer from the available information, etc., etc.

Such was the adulation heaped upon "Marcos de Niza, the explorer-priest" that whispers constantly reached him: He was being touted as a candidate to become bishop when old Zumárraga died. Visions of a soft life in the bishop's palace constantly assailed him during his lonely nights; he tried to put them out of his mind by praying for the gift of modesty. His place should be not amidst the trappings of luxury, but on the frontier, opening up the New World. He noticed that he actually felt happier, on the trail, under the blue sky, than in the smoky halls of Mexico City.

At the same time, the whisperers gossiped about Viceroy Mendoza. Why had he quit the expedition? Had he lost faith in the quest? No, he had left all his investment in place. Vázquez de Coronado had a huge personal stake too. According to Marcos's informants, most of the governor's funds had come from his wealthy young wife, Doña Beatriz, who had inherited wealth from her father, the deceased treasurer of New Spain. They had mortgaged property to finance the expedition. It meant that Coronado would allow nothing to stand in the way of success.

MELCHIOR DÍAZ, THE CAPTAIN SENT NORTH TO REEXPLORE MARcos's route, had not yet returned, but a letter from him had come back down the Cíbola road. Coronado had read it and had copies made before forwarding it back to Mexico City. Marcos had not seen the letter, but he heard rumors about it. People said Díaz had not yet reached Cíbola when the letter was written. Rumors flew among the soldiers. Díaz had seen bells of gold traded from Cíbola. No, said others, Díaz had learned there was no gold. No, it was just that he had learned nothing new. The guides had been instructed continually to seek news of Díaz's party, which they might expect to meet any time, returning from the north.

More important to Marcos was the relationship between Cíbola and the Spanish. He had left the frontier in turmoil, with the apparent death of Estevan and the Nexpa Indians. Marcos prayed desperately for friendship, but the holy spirit whispered in his ear: the foundations for the future peace had to be firm. The Indians of Cíbola could not be allowed to kill Spanish emissaries who came in peace, or Christian authority would be undermined throughout the new lands. Coronado would agree with him. As Bishop Zumárraga once quipped, Indians were good-hearted, but if you allowed them to steal your hat, on the next day you would find that you had no shoes. If Cíbola did not renounce its violence, then punishment would have to follow before peaceful relations could begin.

AT EACH VILLAGE BETWEEN COMPOSTELA AND CULIACÁN, THE natives met Marcos and his vanguard with arches, garlands, and shouts of joy. One day, when the army reached a point a few days south of Culiacán, an Indian guide spotted horsemen in the distance. Melchoir Díaz and his party materialized, riding south along the road. Marcos ran forward as the affable Díaz leaped from his horse, and the two men embraced like long-lost brothers. Foot soldiers from Coronado's army came running forward and crowded around them. Marcos and the soldiers shouted a hundred questions at once. "What is the news from the north?" "Tell us about Cíbola!"

Díaz merely smiled. "Ah," he murmured, "you know we can say nothing. We are under strictest orders to report only to the governor." Ominously, Marcos saw some of the soldiers in Díaz's group slyly shaking their heads at the foot soldiers in a way that was less than enthusiastic.

"He is not just the governor anymore," one of the army soldiers said, "now he is our general."

"I will go to give my report to my general," called back Díaz.

THAT AFTERNOON, VÁZQUEZ DE CORONADO ORDERED THE ARMY to make camp early, and Marcos found himself called before the general himself. He waited outside the awning of the general's giant, circular field tent, pitched on a rise at one end of the camp. Its red and gold banners fluttered in the wind while Marcos cooled his heels. Finally, he was called in. Díaz was already standing inside with one of his aides, while the general sat behind a small wooden table, a scowl on his face.

"I have heard the report of Don Melchior," Coronado said in a carefully controlled voice, "and I am sorry to say that although he endured many hardships, he learned little more than you did, and little more than was in his letter. Like you, he was unable to get into Cíbola; he never did get beyond Chichilti-Calli because of the severe winter. Now listen to me. While I count both of you as my friends, I am disappointed in you, and this is why I want to talk to you together."

Marcos felt a certain satisfaction that the great Díaz had learned no more than he himself. It had been an insult, after all, that Mendoza had sent a captain to check on his results, as if he couldn't be trusted! Yet Díaz and his tough soldiers had been stopped by a little snow in the mountainous *despoblado*! Marcos fought to stop his gloating. If he thought about it more closely, surely he felt genuine distress that Díaz and his party had not reached Cíbola, because they would have confirmed and improved on what he learned.

Coronado was still talking. "You both spent time among Indians whom you say have been to Cíbola, but neither of you is able to confirm how much gold is there. This is outrageous! We come all this way with this huge army, and yet still, at this late date, we do not really understand what is inside the walls of that damned city. Díaz says that he showed metal samples to the Indians who had lived there, and they recognized it, but he says they speak only about a few trinkets traded from the south. Where is the treasure? I ask you that!" Coronado glared at them.

"Absence of proof does not prove absence of gold," Marcos said. "The Indians in Chichilti-Calli province were angry at us when I left. Perhaps they do not want to give true testimony now."

"That is so," Díaz chimed in. "When we saw them, they did not wear the turquoises and the finery that Father Marcos described; they showed us only poor villages and frowns. It was hard to get them to talk. They said the people of Cíbola ordered them to attack us when we came through! We had to be on guard all the time, and we mollified them only a little with our presents. We told them *we* were their true friends and liberators, not the people of Cíbola. We told them how we were bringing priests who would give them wonderful news from the heavens above. But they wouldn't listen.

Truly, as much as I tried, I could not get any proof of treasure. They did talk about turquoises, but if you want my candid opinion, well, I think that a disappointment at Cíbola is not excluded."

"What about you, then?" the general turned to Marcos. "You said they were friendly to you when you were on your way north. If you understand them so well, why couldn't you learn more from them?"

"They definitely recognized copper, and—"

"But copper is not gold, Father. You said there was gold there."

"No, I did not." Suddenly Marcos's anger was growing. For months, people had been exaggerating his report. "All I said is that it is reasonable to assume that they have gold. How can they have such sophisticated cities and no gold? Why would they have copper and not gold? Maybe they keep it secret—that's what one Indian told me. That would explain why they would not let Estevan into the city. Other Indians told me this story was false—but maybe they were the ones trying to hide the truth."

"Damn it, you're trying to have it both ways! Sometimes you say it is reasonable to expect wealth there, and then you deny predicting it."

Marcos paused. "I have a theory. You know that Indian news travels fast over these trade routes. Perhaps the Indians in Cíbola heard rumors about us—people in the south that are interested in gold. They are afraid of our intentions. No wonder they try to keep it quiet."

"Talk, talk, talk! You are being too cunning with your pretty logic, Father." Coronado snorted with ill-disguised contempt. "Who can tell with you priests whether you are really interested in honest wealth, or just manipulating us with lies, to open up new lands so you can get at the souls there?" He caught himself. "I'm sorry, Father. I know your interests are not of small account. But you know we organized this conquest expecting to find the treasure we need to pay our expenses subduing that land for the king. If it's there, why don't you have more positive reports? What do you have to say for yourselves?"

At first, neither Díaz nor Marcos responded.

"I can tell you only what I saw with my own eyes," Díaz stated calmly at last.

"What did you learn about the sea? Do you think there is a

chance for the ships to reach the army up there? The viceroy has sent ships up the coast under Hernán de Alarcón, to meet us in Culiacán and follow us."

"In Chichilti-Calli, there is a wide river that flows west. But the Indians say it is many days from there to the coast, and the river level changes with the seasons."

"Ah," said Coronado, "the so-called port of Chichilti-Calli. The viceroy has great hopes for that one. The problem is, this whole expedition is being built on hopes. And what is your assessment, Captain, of the Indians of Chichilti-Calli? Will they still be angry when we arrive there? Are they a threat?"

"Along much of the way, the Indians are friendly, as Father Marcos described. But along the Nexpa and all through Chichilti-Calli they are bitter because of the deaths of their kin at Cíbola. I think not as many were killed as the Indians told Father Marcos, but still they are hostile to us because the people of Cíbola are angry at them. I talked to a man who had been a prisoner there after Estevan died. So we must be on guard when we pass through that region."

"Ah!" said Marcos. "If fewer men died than I was told, then perhaps we have a better chance to rally them to our side."

"You have nice theories," the general said. "We will find out if they are correct."

WITHIN DAYS, MARCOS LEARNED THAT RUMORS HAD SPREAD through the whole camp. Behind his back, everyone was whispering: "Díaz could not even get across the snowy mountains to Cíbola. That's how difficult the road is." "They say Díaz talked to the Indians but he could learn nothing about any gold in Cíbola." "I heard that there was no great city, such as Marcos said he saw, but only ruins of cities." "They say Marcos got it all wrong; the way is not smooth, but rough, and the Indians ahead are not friendly, but incited against us." "This march is no better than chasing after a wisp of smoke." "Yes, but if there is smoke, there must be fire."

Years later, in 1545, when Marcos was spending time trying to understand how his life had gone wrong, he was to see testimony given by one of the soldiers, Diego Lopez, in an official court review of the expedition.

From the day the expedition met Melchior Díaz, I had no hope of finding anything in Cíbola. From Díaz, the army learned of the ruins that were found in the lands ahead, and that there was nothing in that land. Because of this, it was common knowledge and widely believed in the camp that Friar Marcos had not seen what he had previously described.

After he left Coronado's tent, and late into that night, Marcos argued with his fellow priests about Díaz's report and the rumors circulating in camp. "No one has any right to get discouraged," he reasoned. "Díaz didn't even reach Cíbola! Has he reported anything different from what I reported? Basically, no! So why the change in attitude in this camp?"

"The men have high expectations. You yourself said it seemed likely that wealth would be found, but Díaz came back empty-handed."

"Why do they treat him as the master scout, and rail against a poor friar who got there first and brought back the same answers?"

"He's a hardheaded soldier, like they are. They think all of us priests are dreamers."

Marcos took the opportunity on the next Sunday to give a stirring sermon to the disgruntled, ragtag troops.

"You are on an apostolic mission, a mission for the faith and for the king! If you comport yourselves well, your place in heaven is assured. It is the Devil who tries to plant doubt in your minds! No one knows what the road ahead will disclose. Because of the deviltry of Estevan, and the winter snows that stopped Captain Díaz, there simply is not enough information to allow predictions. You must hold back your opinions, just as a careful rider reins in his horse on an unknown road. You should not be discouraged simply because Díaz brought back no grand news. After all, our friend, Díaz, did not even reach Cíbola as I have done. I have seen the multistoried city and its fair valley! Every single bit of information, including my own eyewitness view, promises a wealthy kingdom in a rich land, with fair rivers, forests, and fields of corn, beans, cotton, turquoise, and who knows what metals—a land we can conquer and pass on to our heirs in the name of the viceroy and the king. Do you really want to let Satan discourage you before you even reach it—before we even get as far as Culiacán? Do you want to give up and straggle back to Mexico City to be laughed at as quitters who gave up before even leaving our lands of New Spain or encountering your first hardship? Do you want to assure the loss of the funds you've invested in the expedition?

"God would not have sent me all the way to Cíbola and back without a purpose. The purpose is for the Christians to enter that land and claim it for God and king! That is God's will! If you press on, your hearts and hands and pockets will be filled with the riches of that land!" From the troops came murmurs of approval.

APRIL, *1540.* ONCE THE ARMY REACHED THE CITY OF CULIACÁN, Coronado assembled the army on the dusty plaza and read new orders, exhorting them to glory in the loudest voice he could muster. Finally he got to practical details. "We are carrying too much baggage. It will slow us down in the unknown lands ahead. Set aside all but what you absolutely need. Viceroy Mendoza has ordered ships to sail up the coast under my captain, Hernán de Alarcón. Alarcón's ships will pick up our baggage here and transport it north. There are reports of large rivers in the lands to the north, including the land of Chichilti-Calli, just before the fifteen-day, final *despoblado* through the mountains. We hope to establish a port, where we will get the supplies back, to improve our comfort in the northern country.

"Also, you must remember always that the viceroy and Bishop Zumárraga command that the northern Indians not be mistreated on this expedition. No Indians may be drafted or forced into carrying the packs and gear of you Spaniards, as had happened in other armies. You must strip down to what you can carry for yourself in packs, or on your horse or burro if you have one."

During the next days, piles of carefully labeled goods accumulated in the rude plaza and were loaded onto burros and carts to go down the road to the loading docks.

WHILE THE ARMY PREPARED TO LEAVE CULIACÁN, A STRANGE thing happened. One day a young soldier named Truxillo reported having a salacious vision while bathing in the river. When the story got out, he found himself dragged with much embarrassment before the general himself, in the presence of Marcos. "Out with it, Truxillo!" the guards told him. "Confess the story that you've been telling around camp."

"It was the Devil, your lordship. As Father Marcos tells us, the Devil wants to stop our expedition. It was not my own voice, but Satan's voice in my ear."

"Well . . . ? What?"

Truxillo mumbled into the ground. "The voice said that if—"

"Speak up, man!"

"It said that if I were to assassinate you, I could—please forgive me, it was not my thought—I could marry your wife, Doña Beatriz, and have your fortune. But it was not my idea. I report only what the Devil said to me. It was like a dream, not a daytime thought."

Perhaps it was the presence of Marcos himself that kept the outraged general from ordering an immediate and severe punishment. As it was, the General ordered Truxillo to be banished from the expedition and to stay behind in Culiacán.

Marcos saw his chance in this, and preached another sermon in Culiacán, pointing out that this was proof of the Devil's terrible determination to disrupt the expedition, which in turn proved logically that the expedition must be doing God's work. Satan was their enemy, whispering in young men's ears and trying to break the brotherhood of the army! The army must redouble its commitment. The soldiers must keep their thoughts pure. The men must not lose their faith in the journey's goals, no matter what malicious news was whispered on the way.

It was a stirring sermon.

A week after the sermon, he learned the truth from the men. Truxillo had simply become discouraged by the news from Díaz and wanted out. He had brazenly made up the whole thing in order to get Francisco Vázquez to order him to stay behind.

SHORTLY BEFORE THEY WERE TO LEAVE CULIACÁN, THE GENERAL called for an assembly in the plaza, at dawn, before the sun grew too warm. Here, he would announce another important decision.

As the sun climbed into the sky, Coronado, Melchior Díaz, Marcos, the other friars, and other officers stood on a hastily built platform in front of the assembled troops. "This army," the general shouted at the top of his lungs, "will occupy the Seven Cities and pacify that land. However, any army is a sluggish beast, and it will take much effort and time to cross the plains, rivers, and mountains that are reported along our route. Because the going will be slow, and because Melchior Díaz has been unable to reach Cíbola, I have decided to take a smaller vanguard and move ahead rapidly and see what we can learn. The advance party will include the priests as pathfinders, seventy-five horsemen, another twenty-five foot soldiers, and one hundred fifty Indian allies as support. If passions have calmed in Cíbola, perhaps I can make the initial contact. Perhaps we can better befriend the people of Cíbola with a smaller party, and prepare the way for a peaceful arrival of the whole army. The rest of the army will follow, with the animals. You must march as fast as possible. When the whole army arrives, we will investigate all the Seven Cities and explore the northern provinces."

Coronado, speaking forcefully, went on to remind the men that he would tolerate no ill treatment of the Indians in the villages along the way. The army was always to camp outside of Indian towns, not in the towns. Guards would be posted to assure that the men made no molestations of the natives, who at all costs must remain friends and allies of the Christians. Marcos nodded in agreement with these words. The two or three wives who had come along on the expedition, and the Indian women traveling with the native allies from the region of Mexico City, would travel with the main army. Coronado went on to remind the soldiers how important it was to promote friendship with Indians along the way. After all, the army might be weary with the treasure they would carry back, and they should not leave vengeful villagers along the way who might make plans to attack them during their return. They would avoid the fate of Cortés's men who lost *their* gold at the last minute, during *La Noche Triste*. The men cheered at the image of themselves carrying the melted-down gold ingots and coins of Cíbola, back to Mexico.

MAY, 1540. MARCOS TRAVELED IN THE GENERAL'S ADVANCE party. Along the main trade route, they came to the town that Estevan had described, Corazones, where Dorantes and the party of castaways had been fed a banquet of deer hearts. When the Indians of Corazones understood who they were, they grew excited and asked to touch Marcos's robe. They said they had heard rumors about how their old friend Estevan had angered the governor of Cíbola and that now, even a year after his death, people in the province of Chichilti-Calli as well as in Cíbola were in turmoil about what had happened. Marcos noted that the people of Corazones called Estevan their brother. He tried to explain that Estevan had suffered from the sin of pride, and God willed everything—even Estevan's suffering and apparent death at Cíbola. Perhaps it was Estevan's punishment.

In the next few days, the army followed the river upstream through a gorge in the mountains into a broad, fertile valley called So-no-ra, which the Spaniards rendered as Senora, or Señora, in honor of the Virgin. In the northern part of the valley, Marcos recognized villages he had passed on his way south. The people were quiet and somber as the army marched by in good order. Marcos never failed to point out to the soldiers that these little temples were decorated with carved turquoise ornaments, both on the inside and outside. "And if these poor villages have temples with such jewels," Marcos proclaimed, "think what must lie ahead in the four-storied cities of Cíbola!"

EARLY JUNE, 1540. CORONADO'S ADVANCE PARTY CONTINUED upstream past the village of Arispa, one of the major towns of the

Señora Valley. The stream thinned to a trickle, and they entered a four-day *despoblado* across pleasant but dry grasslands and low hills. Marcos was apprehensive. Next would come the headwaters of the Nexpa where the villagers had lost some of their young men in Estevan's disaster at Cíbola. The soldiers grew nervous but Coronado reminded them that Cortés had defeated forces ten times the size of his own. Yet Coronado himself grew quiet as they rode downhill toward the distant line of green cottonwoods that marked the Nexpa.

Marcos and the others scanned the trees for signs of smoke from village campfires or Indians hidden in the brush. They saw nothing.

To Marcos's amazement, the valley of the Nexpa was nearly deserted. The village could hardly be recognized as the ones who had greeted Marcos with arches of flowers and music of flutes only a year earlier. So much had changed! Gone were the smiling villagers and chiefs with their many strands of turquoise. Instead, they were greeted by nearly empty village sites, the domed brush huts standing mute as if in a ghost town, or falling into disrepair. A few morose and scrawny elders stared mutely at them from the outskirts of the second village as they approached.

"FRAY MARCOS," CORONADO THUNDERED THAT NIGHT IN A DESERTED town. "You said these Nexpa villages were some of the best you saw, but they are the poorest towns we've seen in this whole trek!"

"The Indians have taken their goods and deserted the towns. They are afraid of us. They knew we were coming. Ask Captain Díaz! He can tell you about the villages here!"

"It's a trick," one of the officers muttered.

"You mean a trick by the Indians?" said another officer. "Or by our friend, Father Marcos?"

SOME OF THE VILLAGES HAD BEEN PARTIALLY BURNED. THEY COULD see charred remains of brush houses here and there. Other houses were occupied by stragglers, usually old men and women who showed no emotion as the priests and horsemen passed by. It was as if Marcos were in a different valley from the Nexpa he had known before. Only when they came around a bend in the river and he saw the cross that he had carved on the rocks could he reassure himself that this had been the valley of turquoise-bedecked, smiling chiefs who had urged him to wait so that they could go with him on the Cíbola trail. There were a few of the older people left in this village.

Coronado pulled Marcos and the other priests aside. "You got us into this mess, Father," Coronado told him. "Now you can get us out. Tell them we mean no harm, but we will not tolerate any interference." Marcos went forward with his interpreters to parley with the few elders.

"Our people heard you were coming," the old men said. "They do not care for you anymore. They have gone away. Do not seek them because they have banded together and are hiding in very strong places. The people of Cíbola wanted them to attack you when you came here, but some of them believe you meant them no harm, so they decided to go away, instead. But if you go after them, they will attack you."

"But we are friendly toward you!" Marcos said. "Don't you remember what I read to you, that we bring you salvation and the protection of our king? We can help you and you can help us. If you do not, these soldiers may become very angry."

"We who stayed behind *are* your friends. But the young men, they want to kill you all. We tell you as friends, you should turn away and go back where you came from and leave us alone. We are telling you this not only for ourselves, but also in the name of the lords of mighty Cíbola. The lords of Cíbola say they do not want to see you. If you go to Cíbola, it will be between you and the lords of Cíbola; it has nothing do with us. You must tell them we did nothing to help you."

Some of the old women bartered some large baskets of cornmeal for beads and some metal awls, but this food was inadequate.

MID-JUNE, 1540. "THIS IS A HOUSE OF MUD, A DUMP GROUND!" The general knocked plaster from the red walls of the ruined castle of Chichilti-Calli, and kicked pottery sherds aside with barely suppressed rage. He ordered Marcos brought forward and the two of them walked around and around the great, ruined, red house and then out among the outlying ruined buildings, with their fallen roof timbers sticking out at crazy angles, and their walls sagging.

"But why are you angry?" Marcos asked, trying to revive Coronado's spirits. "Both Melchior Díaz and I told you that Chichilti-Calli was an ancient building, falling into disrepair. But think about what it implies. It was a mighty fortress when it was built. Parts of it rose two stories. The Indians here said it was built years ago by people who came from the northern lands where we are going. It proves that the northerners can build grand palaces."

"There is a big difference between a palace of jewels and a palace of mud. This is a palace of mud, you idiot! I'm sorry, Father, but all along the way we've heard stories from the Indians about the wonders of Chichilti-Calli. If this is the best they can do—"

"Imagine a whole hillside of buildings three times this big. That is what I saw with my own eyes."

"The men were expecting Chichilti-Calli to be a ruined castle, like the walled city of Avila. They were expecting to find the castoffs of rich kings and nobles. You give us this . . . this dirtpile! And broken pots of painted clay. There is nothing here to buoy up the spirits of the men. And another thing: Where is the river?"

"The big river is over the pass ahead, in the valley on the other side."

"You said we could make a port in Chichilti-Calli, where the ships of Alarcón could find us. You said it was near the sea! But my guides tell me we have moved inland, twelve or fifteen *jornadas* from the sea!"

This infuriated Marcos. "No, your Lordship, I beg your pardon. It was Díaz and the viceroy who talked about a port at Chichilti-Calli. I said the river was big enough to send boats with supplies, but I never said that it was close to the sea. And if you read my report, I tabulated that it was ten or twelve days from the coastal province to here, just as your guides told you. I have a copy; I will show you if you like."

"I don't want to see your dammed report! I want to see something I can show the men! They've been muttering against you all the way from Culiacán. Where you said there were good roads they found only rocky trails. Where you said we would find villages with men wearing necklaces and nose plugs of turquoise, we find only poor old men living in hovels!"

Both of them were shouting now. A few of the men lurked at a distance, fearful. They had seen the governor-general order executions when he was in this mood. "Look, everything I said was true! The road was a good foot-road for me and my companions. I wasn't talking about a thousand men and their animals. Obviously, the natives who are here are putting on their poor face and the rest are hiding. If you don't like the route and the province of Chichilti-Calli, why do you blame me? Your man Melchior Díaz is the one who traveled the route by horse, and spent many weeks here. Did you get so much better information from him? I tell you about trade in cowhides and the resting spot of the ancient red house, and you convert it like an alchemist into commerce in gold bullion and a soft bed in a ruined palace!"

"That's enough. This is an outrage!" The general picked up some bits of colored pottery and hurled them into the nearest mud-crumbled ruin. "Clay pottery! Listen, Father Marcos. Don't try to attack my officers or drive a wedge between me and my men. Melchior Díaz is one of the best I've got. If these lands fail to meet our expectations, it is your fault. You were the one who painted the pretty picture! I won't let you blame him. I can say nothing to my troops now; I must retain my silence and optimism in front of them. But I'm warning you, if this whole thing is a failure, you are the one who will take the blame."

Marcos got little sleep that night on his blanket across the little stream from the main army. The moon took forever sinking behind the dark bulk of the ancient building. The journey wasn't supposed to turn out like this. He could only hope that all the squabbling would be forgotten when the army marched into the plazas of the Seven Cities to behold their wonders.

CHAPTER 22

September, 1989
Conflagration

Monday night, after I had called in sick, I got an unusual call from Mr. Rooney himself. He was still in his cheerful mode. Actually, he was always in his cheerful mode. He was calling from home. I couldn't believe it.

"Sorry you were out today. You okay?"

"Yeah, I was . . . Well, I'm better now."

"Great! Phaedra tells me you're still worried about the history of our place, and the old Spanish records. Let's have a talk about that. Why don't you come up here to my place and have a drink with me? Celebrate the court ruling. You did good work, you know."

I winced at Phaedra's name. Was Mr. Rooney now going to offer paternal counciling about the breakup of my romance?

I'd never been to Mr. Rooney's house in the foothills.

"Don't worry, I'll send somebody by your place. Pick you up."

THE DRIVER, OF COURSE, WAS FREDDY THE FIXER. "YOU'LL LIKE MR. Rooney's place," he told me. Other than that, he was tight-lipped.

"But what does he want from me?" I asked.

"You'll see," he said. "Sometimes he tells me what he's thinking, sometimes he doesn't," he added, as if that explained something.

We paused at the gatehouse, where a uniformed attendant approved our entry into Mr. Rooney's subdivision, where the streets were quiet and there were no billboards. The house was extravagant, as I expected. It made up for the spartan office. It sat on a ridge at the foot of the Catalinas, on the boundary of the national forest, overlooking the city. The living room was as big as a dance hall and had a huge window on the city side, where distant lights twinkled through a thin haze layer. Paintings on the walls depicted old ranches and the Grand Canyon. There was an original Maynard Dixon. Dixon used to live at the intersection of Tucson Boulevard and Prince Road, back in the '30s, when that was out in the country. Now it was considered "central city,"—an expendible neighborhood that needed to be cut in half by a freeway to service the new neighborhoods Mr. Rooney had built on the east side.

Another huge window opened on the mountain-facing side, which must have given a fabulous view of crags and canyons in the daytime. There was a small fire crackling in the fireplace, the warmth pleasantly tempered by the air conditioning. The nice thing about the American dream is that when you succeed you can move out of the smoggy valley, up, up and away, into the foothills, away from the traffic and the mess you've made in the city, earning your money. Freddy just stood there by the door to the living room, like one of those heavies in a gangster movie, when Mr. Big is having an Important Conversation.

Mr. Rooney was expansive, glad to see me. Wanted to know what I'd drink. I settled for a rum and Coke.

Mr. Rooney settled back in his chair. "You know, your case interests me."

So now I was a case?

"You're a bright young man. You could have the world at your feet if you had the right . . . I don't know what to call it. Mind-set?"

"Mind-set?"

"To you, the future is somehow related to the *past*. I mean, you thought what we did with the property should depend on its history. That's why you were so concerned about that journal by that Marcos fellow."

"Well, it's priceless, isn't it?"

"To some people more than others." He smiled, as if to show we were still friends.

"It contained the names of the towns, the route, the evidence that he made it to Cíbola. . . . If I could have studied it . . . I mean, it would have been a treasure for scholars in any case, but if it established where he went in southern Arizona, well, then we would have known. . . ."

"Known what?"

"That Chichilti-Calli was on our property. I'm sure I could have proved it, from what I saw on one of the pages. That book could have been the core of the historical center on our property. Big pages of it, blown up on one wall. His own handwriting. With translations. Also, if it proved that Marcos actually got to Cíbola, it would salvage his reputation."

"So?" he coaxed.

I didn't know what to say. There didn't seem to be any point in arguing with him.

"I'm curious about how your sort is always so interested in some *academic* truth. Me, I think there's two kinds of truth, academic and practical. Historical truth falls in the academic category. Did Oswald shoot JFK? Did Washington ever tell a lie? Did Shakespeare write Shakespeare? Who knows? It's all a matter of interpretation. Even with an old notebook or an old map, there would always be a matter of interpretation. Tony Beecher taught me something. For every Ph.D. there's an equal and opposite Ph.D. In a court of law, he could pull in a dozen experts to contest any claim ever made, no matter how many old books you had. That's academic truth for you—it's malleable. Practical truth is the only thing that affects *real* life, Kevin. That's what's beautiful about the law, it establishes practical truth. Tidies things up so you can move forward.

"If you want to talk about the past versus the future, well, the only thing that counts is the future, and the only thing that determines the future is practical truth. It has nothing to do with history. It has do to with our own *vitality*. You've done good planning work for us, I'll give you credit for that. But our main need for you was to legitimize the history of the site, the connection to Coronado. Like I told you at the beginning, I talked to some of your profs at the university before I hired you. I knew all about your interest in Coronado and Marcos. You did what you were supposed to do—sprinkle holy water on our plan. Frankly, I didn't realize you'd get so obsessed with it. You went overboard. You can see that, can't you?"

"A lot of it was on my own time." I hesitated. What was he after? "Am I supposed to apologize?"

He got up and walked to an ornate desk. "There you go, misunderstanding my motives. I don't care about your apology. Like I said, you're a promising young guy. I'm taking my time here, trying to *teach* you something. That's why I need to promote you into some area of work where you can use your talents better. Some day after I'm retired, you could be one of the movers and shakers, if you play your cards right. But not here. You'll understand all this better after you mature a little bit, and you'll thank me."

"Understand all what better?"

He fished in a drawer. "As for now, you'll probably be very upset. You see, after Phaedra told me about your call from Alamos, my friends down there were able to locate something. . . ." He pulled out the book from the church in Alamos, Marcos's notebook.

"My God! Where did you . . . ?" I had started to get up.

"Sit down. Sit down!"

"But—"

"When Phaedra told me about the notebook, I realized it might be important." He hesitated. "Listen, I want you to know, I don't always approve of the politics and activities of my friends down there. It's a different culture and things can get out of hand. Sometimes you have to accept that people in another country have their own way of *doing* things. . . ." He paused. He had been waving the book around like a stage prop that helped him dramatize his points. I was terrified the fragile thing would fall apart. "We better leave it at that," he added.

He sat down again, calmly. My eyes tracked only on the ancient book in his hand. My heart was now beating wildly. I couldn't breathe. I sat very still, as if my own motion could damage Marcos's legacy. I knew I had to get my hands on it, one way or another. As soon as I could look at it, translate it, get another look at the sketch maps of river valleys . . .

He set the book down in front of him. I cringed as he opened it, but he treated it gently. "You think I'm *afraid* of what this book says?"

"Be careful," I said.

"I'm not afraid of it. Suppose it really does say our ruin is the one on the route to Cíbola. There would be another hullabaloo. The ultimate test would be in court, but Tony could find some experts to question its authenticity, question the interpretation, discredit what it says. If that didn't work, maybe we might get forced to go for a larger park or museum. Really I'm not afraid so much of giving up some of the land; I'm more afraid of the *time* it would cost us. Time, we can't afford. Time is the biggest *cost* in our business. You realize how much the investors have tied up in this project? How much interest they could be earning every day on that money? We have to make that back, and more, and soon, or they go somewhere else and we get killed. You're a smart guy. You understand how the economy works. We can't afford to get tied up in court over some stupid argument about routes in the 1500s. And my God, what if the feds decided they wanted to take the land for a national monument? We'd get something out of it, of course, but there would be endless arguments about how much land we should set aside and whether there is money in the park service budget to make an offer—and God knows what.

"I had to hang onto this book to see which way the wind was blowing. But now, you see, it's all over. Without this book, our site becomes just another development, and that ruin becomes just one more of a hundred ruins, just another pile of dirt. The future marches on."

He tore out the first page, and threw it in the fire.

"No!" I screamed and lunged. Freddy rushed from the door with amazing speed and pushed me down into the chair, holding my shoulders. He had the strength of a horse. I was twisting and turning. And managed to kick him in the balls, not hard enough. It hardly phased him, but he loosed his grip enough that I was able to lunge for Mr. Rooney. I actually had my hand on the book for an instant as he recoiled and pulled it away. A scrap of the leather cover came off in my hand.

Just then, Freddy grabbed me from behind. He had a half nelson on me and dragged me back to the chair. I struggled but I was powerless in his grip.

"Don't hurt him," Mr. Rooney said.

I could feel that Freddy was being careful not to really hurt me. I still had the fragment of leather in my hand. I kept it balled up in my fist.

"That was unseemly, Mr. Scott," Rooney said. "This isn't a bar. We're having a civilized discussion here."

Mr. Rooney tore out the pages one at a time. I remember that they burned with a faint crackling sound.

I screamed again. "Let me look! You bastard, at least let me look."

It wasn't a thick book. He had already burned a quarter of the pages, but now he started holding them up for me to see. I strained forward, against Freddy the Fixer's grip. I remember trying to memorize everything, fitting each page into the framework that I knew about the trip. I must have been in some state of shock where, strangely, some details stuck in my mind and others were lost forever. There were sketches, a view of a valley with a bend to the left, or a rocky domelike peak on the right. There were village names: "Ququrpa," the name I had copied when I saw the notebook in Alamos, along with "Tu-apo" and "Aquitoa," all near the page where Marcos had written that the coast turned west. Later I was able to link all three names with old village names on the Rio San Miguel and Rio Magdalena, showing that Marcos did veer west toward the sea. A few pages later, I saw "Nex-pa, Chichilti-Calli," and the sketch of the pass near our property. Into the fire. More pages. Random phrases. ". . . the towns in that province are scattered a league apart. . . ." ". . . the souls of the Indians. . . ." "The beginning of the dry season. . . ." Four pages about *sierras* and *rios*, and the fifteen-day *despoblado*. Finally, I caught a glimpse of the key sketch of Cíbola, with little houses piled on houses with the profile of a mesa behind it. That priceless drawing, into the fire.

"I didn't have to show you this, you know. But I'm not heartless."

He told me that someday when I was older, I'd see that history wasn't as precious and romantic as I thought. He said we make our own future. He threw the rest of the book into the fire. The fire lapped it up with a rosy smile. There was nothing I could do, but I managed to stick the dry leather scrap in my hand into my shirt pocket without them noticing.

"Well, Kevin," he said, "it's been educational, on both sides. I don't think you're in a position to cause any more trouble about historic sites. I'd advise you not even to *try*." Freddy gave me a gentle shake to emphasize the point. "I don't suppose you're anxious to keep working for me. It's regrettable. You're a good man, even if you have a few funny ideas. I think I was like you, once. . . ." He looked almost wistful, staring into the fire. "Anyway, I'm serious. You've done good work. I want to promote you on out of here, to something *new*, where you can make a fresh start. A different city would be good, you understand? There'll be a bonus in your severance check. And a letter of recommendation in case you can use it."

Freddy drove me home. "Nothing personal," he said as we came back down Campbell Avenue into the city. He had complete self-control. "You're a nice guy. Mr. Rooney says you're really smart but you have a lot to learn."

I NEVER WENT BACK TO THE OFFICE. I WAS IN DAZE. MY FINAL paycheck arrived the next morning, hand delivered to my apartment by Freddy the Fixer, nice guy that he was. He had eased me into Mr. Rooney's domain, now he was easing me out. Mr. Rooney, bighearted boss, had included a $3000 severance bonus check. Also inside the envelope, cozy with the check, was the letter of recommendation. Pretty amazing stuff: all about what a fine job I had done on both the planning and the historical research. "Mr. Rooney's sorry to see you go. He's already sent the recommendation letter to some builders he knows in L.A., just to show that we parted on friendly terms. Understand?"

Freddy the Fixer asked me to sign a termination paper, somehow implying it was seriously in my best interest.

I said, "What if I don't?"

Freddy gave me a steely look, then broke into his schmoozy smile and patted me on the back. The last pat was the hardest. "Aw, c'mon Kevin. You're a good guy. I like you. Okay?" He was as calm and neat as ever, in his sport coat and tie. Today he looked like an assistant coach. Jesus, I thought, these guys killed a priest in Mexico. Or did they?

I signed the paper, but I did my best to give my signature a different slant from normal. Freddy didn't seem to notice.

"It's really not a good idea for you to hang around Tucson, Kevin," Freddy said. "Go someplace else. Everybody'll be happier."

"Just tell me," I said. "What happened to Edward?"

"Edward who?"

"Never mind." I decided I'd better not press it.

Freddy shrugged and left. I breathed a sigh of relief.

ALONG WITH THE CHECK THERE WAS A TERSE NOTE FROM PHAE-dra: "Sorry it didn't work out. You're a wonderful person, but I can see now that our paradigms are different." Who else but Phaedra would write a Dear John letter with the word "paradigms" in it? And she said *I* was the intellectual one!

I spent a lot of time thinking about that note. It was one thing for me to tell myself that it was over between us, but something else for her to say it. Nobody wants to be the dumpee. The real question for me was, what did she really know about Rooney? How close had she been to him, anyway? My God; had she slept with him? How much did she know about Alamos? Or the pleasant fireside chat? Had she been stringing me along the whole time, just to keep abreast of what I was uncovering? No, it didn't make sense. It was another conspiracy theory. Maybe the answer was simpler. The guy sees a relationship as a pleasant status quo, the woman sees it as a pervading question: Where is it going? She saw before I did that it wasn't going anywhere she wanted to go.

The trouble with a breakup is that you never have a chance to get the rest of the story. Every "final conversation" simply leads to more questions. I concluded she didn't know what Rooney had done in his living room Monday night. I wanted to go tell her about it, about the cultural criminal she was working for. I wanted to justify myself. There was no point in it; it wasn't going to make her want me, even if she and Freddy and Mr. Rooney did all keep telling me what a fine fellow I was.

I tried to call her again. When I phoned the office, they said she had gone away on a trip. I wanted to hang around for a week to let it blow over, then try to talk to her. But I couldn't be sure if Rooney's goons would come looking for me. Was I paranoid? I kept seeing Antonio's body sprawled on that floor. I wanted to believe his murder really was a political killing, that Rooney's rancher friend was behind it, and that Marcos's notebook finding its way to Rooney through these contacts was an opportune by-product. But an inner voice, as well as Freddy's, told me I had to get out of there.

Also in the envelope was an airline voucher good one-way, anywhere in the world, which is what allowed me eventually to escape that reality into my own reality. An enclosed note, typed, was clipped to the ticket: USE THIS!

WHY STAY? WHAT DEFENSE DID I HAVE? NONE. THE BONUS CHECK and the letter of recommendation proved our friendship, even if my signature on the receipt was a bit funky. I couldn't go to the police because there was nothing I could accuse him of. "Murder in Alamos?" I could hear Tony Beecher talking. "What murder? That political killing? The poor young man must be mad! We did our best for him when he left, but . . ."

And I couldn't take revenge. In the first place, I didn't believe in wasting my time that way. It made your own karma as bad as the bad guy's karma. In the second place, if I took a potshot at Rooney, or smashed his car window, the law would come after me. I would become that pathetic figure of countless newspaper stories: the disgruntled former employee. He, on the other hand, was the model citizen. When I, the bookish loner, tried to defend myself with talk of the continuity of civilization, or Rooney's crimes against History, with a capital H, no one would understand what I was talking about. He had worked it out beautifully. Nobody ever accused Mr. Rooney of not being in control of things.

I thought about the little scrap of leather. It wasn't much bigger than a postage stamp. I had fantasies of using it to bring down Mr. Rooney and his evil empire. I'd take it to some lab, and a radiocarbon date would prove that it originated in 1530 plus or minus ten years, which would prove it was authentic and then . . . what? The disgruntled and deranged former employee had managed to get a piece of sixteenth-century leather. So what? As usual, I had nothing. I put the piece of leather in a small plastic case, so I could look at it. The last bit of Marcos's book. I still have it on my desk, here in France.

The more I thought about it, the more I realized I *wanted* to leave. I wanted to escape from all the sun-blasted, air-conditioned, twentieth-century conquistador madness. There wasn't a lot to pack: some clothes, my box of books and papers about Marcos.

Where would I go? Someplace far away, where Mr. Rooney wouldn't hear of me again, and I wouldn't hear of him.

That's when I realized I had to drive to Cíbola, to see it for myself. Zuni, New Mexico; it wasn't so far. The search for Cíbola was what got me into this mess in the first place, and now I had to follow through with it.

In a daze, I followed my plan: I took Mr. Rooney's check, packed the car, didn't stop at the office, and set out on a drive up to Zuni, to see the place where everything climaxed back in 1540. I thought if I stood on the ground where Marcos and Francisco Vázquez experienced *their* epiphany, it would help me put my own life in perspective. I didn't tell anyone where I was going. I didn't want anyone from the office coming after me, even Phaedra. As usual, I was following Marcos: after I saw Cíbola, I would decide what to do next.

THE MODERN ROAD WENT NORTH UP THE SAN PEDRO TO THE GILA River and then through the fifteen day *despoblado* between the Gila and Cíbola—I mean Zuni. It's still a depopulated zone, but now it's reduced to a five-hour *despoblado*.

At dawn I found myself passing Oracle, north of Tucson, dropping down into the valley of the Nexpa, a.k.a. Rio San Pedro. St. Peter's River. Those old Spaniards had a limited repertoire of names. The valley stretched across my windshield. I could look down like God on the sleepy valley, the town of San Manuel, and its giant smokestack rising from the middle of the valley. Here, I thought, they mined copper to feed history's climactic aberration, the twentieth century. A giant new pit mine was yawning in the dawn light, on the hill toward the next tiny town, which was named Mammoth. The Galiuro Mountains to the east beyond the San Pedro were a deep blue wall, but I knew they would soon be bleached by the blinding silver light. I had to keep going, to get up into the high country of the *despoblado* before the sun rose too far.

Now I was down in the valley itself, driving through the cluster of shops that defined urban Mammoth.

ELEVATION 2348 FEET

FOUNDED 1876

That was about the time of the Anglo invasion into the province of Chichilti-Calli, twenty years after our great-grandparents bought southern Arizona from Mexico. Maybe that's where Arizona's property rights obsession had come from, the fact that the place had never really been explored and settled by our own pioneers, but had simply been *bought*. It established the mentality that everything was for sale. All the mineral wealth that Marcos and Coronado were looking for came into the possession of the ultimate conquistadors, was finally pulled from the Earth, and was shipped back to the glittering capitals of the world to make trinkets for the noble families. Capitalism has many glories, and its greatest is extracting resources.

Mammoth was still sleepy. A pickup truck was parked in front of the 7-Eleven, and a guy with a cowboy hat was coming out with something in a brown paper bag. That homely scene brought me back to Earth, and reminded me that most folks didn't care about developers or Coronado or Marcos de Niza. Like Phaedra, they were more interested in getting by.

Exiting Mammoth on the other side of the 7-Eleven store, I crossed the river on the two-lane country road and admired the cultivated fields. The Anglo settlers put their ranches and farms in the same fields cultivated by the people that Marcos met. The fields eventually gave out into thickets of mesquite and cottonwood. I drove along with the windows open, hearing the cicadas buzz. I was leaving Chichilti-Calli forever.

I felt a pang of longing for this brown countryside, so barren by the standards of Easterners. Missouri Congressman Thomas Hart Benton railed against the idea of buying it in 1853, calling it "utterly desolate, desert, and God-forsaken." I had friends from the East who said they hated it at first, but ended up loving the clean skies and the openness. Later, when they went back East they said they felt claustrophobic. In college I had a friend from Baltimore who said he liked Arizona because he could drive half an hour out of town and scream as loud as he liked without anyone hearing him.

Along the Nexpa and throughout the province of Chichilti-Calli, Anglo town names were replacing the ancient Mexican and Hohokam names. There was a kind of free verse poetry to them, a poetry of history. Reddington, Hereford, Benson. Pomerene, Dragoon, Mammoth. Winkleman, Christmas, Eden. In some of the towns, the mines were playing out and the downtowns had boarded-up shops.

* * *

PASSING THROUGH THE LITTLE TOWNS, I WEAKENED. I TRIED TO phone Phaedra again. Finally I reached her sister. She confirmed that Phaedra had gone. No, she wouldn't tell me where.

For the next fifty miles I tried to calm down. The empty landscape allowed me to refocus on the big picture. Across the mountains in Phoenix and Tucson, Arizona's passion for progress was playing itself out, generating the thin brown blanket of haze I could see on the horizon to the left. Upstream, behind me, lay the city of Sierra Vista, which, as Phaedra had pointed out during our happier hours, had just become the third-largest city in the state, thanks to its perpetually prospering military base, Fort Huachuca. Because Sierra Vista was following the economic trail blazed by Phoenix and Tucson, the old Nexpa river was dying, and the cottonwoods and farm fields around me would be gone within a few decades. Calling the developers land-rapists was not inappropriate. They used the land to slake their own desires as fast as possible, and they left the rivers dry and unhappy.

Every time I slacked off the gas pedal, a pickup truck roared around me. I wondered: was I the only one driving this road who perceived this century not as a time interval, but as an explosion, uprooting us all?

Somewhere up ahead were the Seven Cities of Cíbola, lost in the midst of the twentieth century's chaos.

CHAPTER 23

July 7, 1540
Eyewitness Testimony: The Battle of Cíbola

As I sped toward Cíbola thirty times faster than Coronado could move, my mind slipped back through poorly lit tunnels of time. I thought about his army's anticipation as they traversed these same hills and plains. I had assembled a complete set of letters and later testimonies by participants in the final approach to Cíbola. Cut and pasted into sequence, the writings gave a graphic picture of the march north and what happened when the army arrived at the goal of their dreams.

One of the first accounts was by Coronado himself, writing to Viceroy Mendoza on August 3, 1540, shortly after arriving at Cíbola. He told about reaching the village of Hearts and then marching north into the upper part of the Rio Sonora valley—the segment they named the Senora—and on to Chichilti-Calli.

I reached the Valley of Corazones on May 26. I rested there a number of days. . . . In this valley we found more people than in any earlier part of the country, and a great extent of culti-vated land. There was little corn for food, but I heard there was some in another valley called Senora. I didn't want to take it by force, so I sent Melchior Díaz with barter goods. By Our Lord's favor, he obtained some corn by this trading, which sustained our Indian allies and some of the Spanish. Ten or twelve of our horses had died from carrying heavy burdens combined with

*lack of food. Some of our blacks and some of the Indian allies
also died here, which was no slight loss.*

*The people there told me that Corazones is five days from the
western sea. I sent messengers to summon coastal Indians who
could give me information. I waited four days in Corazones,
resting the horses, and then came coastal Indians who told me
of seven or eight islands directly off the coast at that area.*

*Eventually I set out from Corazones and kept near the sea-
coast as well as I could judge, but in fact I found myself continually farther off. By the time I reached Chichilti-Calli, I was
fifteen days from the sea, although the Father Provincial had
said it was only five leagues distant and he had seen it. We all
became very distrustful, and felt great anxiety and dismay to
see that everything was the reverse of what he told Your Lordship.*

*The Indians of Chichilti-Calli say that when they cross the
country to the sea for fish or anything else they need, it takes
them ten days, and this information, which I gathered, appears
to me to be true. As for the coastal orientation, the sea turns
west directly opposite Corazones for ten or twelve leagues,
where I learned that Your Lordship's ships had been seen.
These must be the ships that had been sent to search for the
port of Chichilti-Calli, which the Father said was at 35 degrees
latitude. God knows what I've suffered for fear the ships may
have met with some mishap. . . .*

*I rested for two days at Chichilti-Calli. There was good rea-
son for staying longer, because we found the horses were
becoming so tired; but there was no chance to rest because our
food was giving out. I entered the edge of the final despoblado
on Saint John's Eve. . . .*

It was peculiar, Coronado's claim that Marcos thought Chichilti-
Calli was a mere one-day journey of five leagues inland from the
sea. This was the claim that puzzled me earlier, since Marcos's
official *Relación* clearly described a journey of one to two weeks
from the sea to the beginning of the *despoblado* at Chichilti-Calli,

perfectly agreeing with Coronado's information. Was the disgruntled governor grasping at every straw to set up Marcos as the scapegoat?

THE SOLDIER, PEDRO CASTAÑEDA, ALSO DESCRIBED THE ARMY'S march through the Rio Sonora Valley to Chichilti-Calli, and then on to the outskirts of Cíbola. On this part of the march, Castañeda was with the main army, lagging some days behind Coronado's advance guard, but in several different chapters of his memoir he described events involving the two parties. By combining these accounts, I produced some good scenes of life in the up-till-then-prehistoric villages.

> *Senora is a river valley thickly populated by able-bodied people. The women wear petticoats of tanned deerskin. . . . The chiefs of the villages go up like public criers onto some little heights they have made for this purpose, and make proclamations for the space of an hour, regulating the things that the people have to do. They have some little huts for shrines, all over the outside of which they stick many arrows, like a porcupine. They do this when they are getting ready for war. . . .*
>
> *The people further along are the same as those in Senora and have the same dress, language, habits, and customs—all the way to the desert of Chichilti-Calli. The women paint their chins and eyes like the Moorish women of Barbary. These people are great sodomites. They drink wine made of the pitahaya, which is a fruit of a large thistle that opens like a pomegranate. The wine makes them foolish. . . . There are native melons so large that a person can carry only one. They cut these into slices and dry them in the sun. They are good to eat, delicious and sweet, tasting like figs. They are better than dried meat, and they keep for a whole year when prepared this way. . . .*
>
> *When the general and his advance party crossed this inhabited region and came to Chichilti-Calli, where the wilderness*

begins, he found nothing favorable there. He could not help feeling downhearted. Although the reports were still encouraging about Cíbola, there was no one along who had actually seen the place except the Indians who went with Estevan, and already these had been caught in some lies. Furthermore, the general was much affected by seeing that the fame of Chichilti-Calli was summed up in one tumbledown building without any roof, though it appeared to have been a strong place at some former time when it was inhabited. Plainly, it had been built by a civilized and warlike race of strangers who had come from a distance.

Meanwhile, the soldiers of the main army were following some days or weeks behind Coronado's vanguard. In a province called Vacapan [close to Marco's Vacapa?] there was a large quantity of prickly pears, of which the natives made preserves. They gave these away freely, and so many soldiers in the main army ate too much of them, falling sick with a headache and fever. The natives might have done them much harm if they had wished.

After this, the main army continued its march till they, too, reached Chichilti-Calli. The building was large and appeared to us to have been a fortress. It must have been destroyed by the local people of the district, who are the most barbarous people that have yet been seen. They live in separate huts, and not in settlements. They live by hunting. . . . The men in General Coronado's advance guard saw a flock of sheep one day after leaving this place. . . .

At Chichilti-Calli the country changes character and the spiky vegetation ceases. The rest of the country toward Cíbola is all wilderness, covered with pine forests. The reason the character changes is that the gulf reaches up as far as this latitude, and the mountains change direction, turning west to parallel the coast. Thus, the army had to cross and pass through the mountains here, in order to get into the level country where Cíbola is located.

Coronado's advance guard saw their first Indians from the country of Cíbola at a river eight leagues [about 20–25 miles] out from Cíbola. There were two of them, and they ran away to report us.

A soldier named Garcia Lopez de Cardenas, who would soon save Coronado's life, was in the advance party, and in testimony recorded in 1546, he gave eyewitness recollections of the first contacts with the people of Cíbola. The testimony was taken during a trial against Cardenas for cruelties to the Indians during the expedition. Cardenas was convicted and sentenced to serve in the army for thirty more months, and pay a fine of eight-hundred gold ducats to be used to finance religious and charitable works.

The expedition came to a point within three or four leagues [10–12 miles] of Cíbola, without having any skirmishes with the Indians. When we reached that position, I was ahead with eight or ten horsemen and noticed some Indians on a hilltop. I advanced alone, making signs of peace and offering presents of things I carried to trade. With this, some of them came down and took the articles that I offered. I shook hands with them and remained calm, giving them a cross and telling them by signs to go to their town and tell their people that the expedition was coming peacefully and wanted to be their friends. They returned to Cíbola, and I remained there to await Francisco Vázquez and the others.

At this very place, the soldiers camped for their last night before reaching Cíbola. I went ahead with a few men to guard a bad pass, so that if the Indians should approach with hostile intent, we could block them. At midnight many Indians attacked us at this pass. Because of the Indians' cries and shouting and arrows, the horses became frightened and ran away. . . . Had it not been for two mounted guards, the Indians would have killed me and my ten companions.

Casteñeda added an amusing vignette of that last night before Cíbola:

The Indians from Cíbola, hiding in a safe place, set up a yelling that startled the men so much that they leaped up from their sleep, ready for anything. Some of them got so excited they put their saddles on backwards, but these were the new fellows. When the older veterans mounted up and rode around the camp, the Indians fled. None of them could be caught because they knew the country.

Cardenas picked up the story.

The next morning Francisco Vázquez arrived with the rest of the men, and learned what happened. From there we all set out together in order and marched toward Cíbola. About a league from the city, the army spotted four or five Indians. Upon seeing them, I again stopped my men, and went ahead of the others, alone, to talk to them, making signs and demonstrations of peace. They didn't wait for me, but left.

So we Spaniards marched in the same order as before until we came close to Cíbola. All the Indians of Cíbola along with people from other nearby places . . . had gathered there to oppose us.

An account labeled *Tralado de las Nuevas*, by an anonymous member of the army, emphasized the dire condition of Coronado's troops at this point. They had lost several more men and run out of food while crossing the final fifteen-day *despoblado*.

His grace reached the province on Wednesday, July 7, with all the men except for one who died from hunger four days earlier and several blacks and Indians who also died of hunger and thirst. . . . The army did not approach the city as well as it should have, because they were all very tired from the difficult journey. Yet there was not one man in the army who would not have done his best. . . .

Pedro Castañeda also described the arrival. When Castañeda refers to "Cíbola" in this passage, he means the first village the army encountered. This was the multitiered pueblo Marcos recorded as Ahacu, the first town approached on the trade route from the south, across a rolling grassy plain. Today it is the ruin called *Hawikuh*. The army drew itself up on the plain in front of the hillside city. This was the soldiers' first look at their long-imagined destination.

When Coronado and the army saw the first village, which was Cíbola, such were the curses that some hurled at Friar Marcos that I pray God protects him from them. It was only a little, crowded village, looking as if it had been all crumpled into one spot. There are haciendas in New Spain that look better at a distance. Cíbola is a village of about 200 warriors. It is three and four stories high, with the houses being small and having only a few rooms, and without their own courtyards. A single courtyard serves for each section.

The people of the whole district had assembled there. There are seven villages in the province, and some of the other six villages are even larger and stronger. All these people waited for the army, drawn up in divisions in front of the villages.

Coronado himself described what happened next, writing in his August 3 letter to Viceroy Mendoza about four weeks after the event. He also gave a similar account at his trial in 1544, when he was exonerated of charges of mistreatment of the Indians. A combination of details from the two accounts gives a clear picture:

When I arrived within view of Cíbola, I noticed many smokes rising in different places around it, and I saw some Indians in warlike array, blowing a horn. I sent Don García Lopez de Cardenas and two of the friars, Daniel and Luis, plus the notary,

Hernando Bermijo, and some horsemen a short distance ahead to read them the Requerimiento, as prescribed by his majesty. This was to tell them that we were coming not to do them any harm, but to defend them in the name of our lord, the Emperor.

About three hundred Indians approached with bows, arrows, and shields. Although our side summoned the Indians to peace three times through the interpreter and explained the object of our coming, these Indians never consented to submit to either the Pope or the King. Being proud people, they weren't affected by the reading. Because we were few in number, they thought they would have no trouble defeating us. They advanced and started shooting arrows and even pierced Friar Luis' gown with an arrow, which, blessed be God, didn't harm him.

As they advanced, I decided I wanted to be present. Taking a few mounted men and some trade articles, and ordering the army to follow, I joined the advance party. I arrived with all the horsemen and footmen, and was observing the large body of Indians arrayed in front of the city, as they began to shoot their arrows. In obedience to Your Lordship's orders and those of the King, I did not let my army attack them, even though the men were begging to begin the attack. I told them they ought not to offend these people, that what they were doing to us was nothing.

But when the Indians saw that we did not move, they grew bolder, coming up almost to the heels of our horses to shoot their arrows. They wouldn't stop shooting arrows at us. Seeing that the Indians were wounding the horses and had pierced Friar Luis' gown, I knew there was no time to hesitate. As the priests approved of the action, I ordered an attack on them. The Indians turned their backs and ran to the pueblos, where they fortified themselves.

García Lopez de Cardenas was with the advance group that read the *Requerimiento*, and he described the same events and continued the story at his trial in 1546.

The Indians rushed our group, shooting many arrows. They pierced the friar's habit with an arrow, and lodged another in the clothing and armor of the notary.

When Francisco Vázquez saw this he came up with all the rest of the army to help. Upon his arrival, but before any more hostilities could begin, Vázquez again summoned them to peace, but they would not submit. Then he ordered an attack because the Indians rejected the offers of peace. In that skirmish, they killed about ten or twelve Indians, but the others fled toward the Pueblo of Cíbola.

After the Indians had taken refuge in the pueblo, Francisco Vázquez again urged them to accept peace. While this was happening, Father de Niza, the Franciscan friar who was guiding the army, arrived. Francisco Vázquez explained what had happened and when the friar heard it and saw that the Indians were fortified, he said, "Take your shields and go after them." So Francisco Vázquez and some of the others did so, and began the main attack upon Cíbola.

I was intrigued that, according to Cardenas, the priest who approved the main attack on the city was none other than Marcos de Niza. What was his state of mind? Thirst to avenge the death of Estevan? Fear? Or was he trying to ingratiate himself with the soldiers? Or did both Coronado and Cardenas exaggerate the enthusiasm of the priests for the attack, in an effort to absolve themselves of the charges that they had used too much force?

CORONADO HIMSELF DID NOT IMPLICATE MARCOS IN THE ORDER TO attack the city, but took the responsibility himself.

When the Indians retreated to the city, I ordered that they be summoned anew, asking them to submit peacefully, and giving them assurances that no harm would be done to them, and that they would be well treated. Seeing that they would not agree and that they continued shooting arrows from above, and considering that the army was suffering from hunger, I ordered that the city itself be attacked.

A similar description comes from the anonymous author of *Tralado de las Nuevas.*

[After they pierced the gown of Friar Luis] the army took Sant Iago [Saint James] as their protector, and the General rushed them with the whole force, which he had kept in good order. The Indians turned and tried to reach their city, but they were overtaken and many of them killed before they could escape. The Indians killed three horses and wounded seven or eight of them.

When my lord, the General, reached the city, he saw that it was surrounded by stone walls and high buildings, four, five, and even six stories high, with flat roofs and balconies. The Indians had secured themselves within it, and would not let any of us near without shooting arrows at us. But since we could get nothing to eat without capturing the city, his grace decided to enter the city on foot, while surrounding it by horsemen, so that those inside could not get away. Because he stood out from the rest in his gilded armor, with a plume on his headpiece, all the Indians aimed at him, and they knocked him to the ground twice by stones thrown from the flat roofs, stunning him in spite of his headpiece. . . . Besides knocking him down, they hit him many times with stones on his head, shoulders, and legs, and he received two small facial wounds plus an arrow wound in the right foot. Praised be Our Lord that he came out on his own two feet!

Coronado himself describes the events of the attack on the city in his August 3 letter and in his 1544 testimony, which combine into a clear account.

I assembled my whole army and divided it as seemed best for an attack on the city, surrounding it. The hunger which we suffered would not permit any delay. So I dismounted with some of these gentlemen and the soldiers. I ordered the musketeers and crossbowmen to begin the attack and drive back the enemy from their defenses along on the roofs, so they couldn't injure us. But the crossbowmen broke all their strings and the musketeers could do nothing because they had arrived so weak that they could scarcely stand on their feet. Therefore, the Indians up above were not impeded at all from defending themselves and doing injury to us.

As for me, as I tried to enter through a narrow street of the pueblo. The people threw countless great stones from above, knocking me to the ground twice. If I hadn't been protected by the good headpiece I wore, I think the outcome would have been bad for me! My comrades picked me up from the ground, however, with two small wounds on my face and an arrow in my foot, along with many bruises on my arms and legs. In this condition I retired from the battle, very weak, as if dead. I think that if Don García Lopez had not come to my help, like a good cavalier, throwing his own body atop mine the second time they knocked me to the ground, I would have been in much greater danger. . . .

When I regained consciousness they told me that the Indians had surrendered, and the city was taken. This was through God's will, and inside the city we found a sufficient supply of corn to relieve our necessities.

As for our injuries, army-master García Lopez, Pedro de Tovar, Hernando de Alvarado, and Pablo de Melgosa the infantry captain, also sustained some bruises. Agoniez Quarz was hit in the arm by an arrow, and a soldier named Torres . . . was hit in the face by another. Two other foot soldiers received slight arrow wounds. It was because my armor was gilded and glittered that the Indians directed their attack mostly against me. That is why I was hurt more than the rest and not because I had done more or was farther to the front than the others. Two or three more soldiers were hurt in the battle on the plain, three horses killed, and seven or eight horses injured. . . . All the gentlemen and the soldiers bore themselves well, as was expected. . . .

Pedro Castañeda said that the battle lasted about an hour, and another account indicates that the battle ended in the afternoon. At Coronado's trial in 1544, he was asked about whether any cruelties were inflicted on the men and women of Cíbola, after the surrender.

No, we did not inflict any cruelties. On the contrary, I ordered that all of the people be well treated, especially the women and children of the area, and I forbade anyone to touch them under severe penalties. I sent for some of the chiefs and explained through the interpreter that they had done wrong in not coming to render obedience peacefully, as they had been asked, but that I would forgive them if they would now comply. If any of them wished to stay there with their women and children, they would be accorded good treatment, and I would leave their belongings and houses undisturbed, and the wounded would be cared for.

They replied that they realized they had done wrong, and that they wanted to go to the nearby pueblo of Masaque in order to return from there with other neighbors to render obedience, because the community of Cíbola included people from all those pueblos.

Next day, or within two days, the chieftain of Masaque and those of the other pueblos came with presents of deer and cattle skins, yucca fiber blankets, and some turquoises, and a few bows and arrows. I gave them some of the barter articles that we had. They went away very pleased, after rendering obedience to his Majesty and saying that they wanted to serve him and become Christians. . . .

Later three or four Indians came from a more distant pueblo

and told us they had heard about us, the strange new people,
bold men who punished those who resisted them, but gave good
treatment to those who submitted. They too had come to make
their acquaintance and be our friends.

García Lopez Cardenas, during his trial in 1546, reaffirmed in-
dependently that the Indians left peacefully after the battle, and no
other cruelties were inflicted. This seems to have been true, but I
wondered how much these gentlemen sweetened their accounts for
the purposes of the court inquiry. Coronado's letter of August 3,
written only about three weeks after the events, reaffirmed that
there were no atrocities, but gave a somewhat pithier account of the
Zunis' reaction in the days after the battle.

Three days after I captured the city, some of the Indians who
live here came with an offer of peace. They brought me some
turquoises and poor blankets, and I received them in the King's
name, with as good a speech as I could. I tried to make them
understand the purpose of my coming, which is, in His
Majesty's name and by the commands of Your Lordship, that
they and all others in this province should become Christians
and should know the true God as their Lord, and His Majesty
as their King on earth.

After this, they returned to their houses, and suddenly, the
next day, packed up all their goods and fled to the hills! They
left their towns deserted, with only a few people remaining in
them.

In the first hours after the battle, the near-starving Spaniards
occupied the city and requisitioned corn and other food supplies. In
those same hours they realized that they had conquered a modest
agricultural town with no gold or substantial metalworking. Their
dreams of instant wealth dissipated in an instant cloud of dust.
Another of the anonymous accounts, called the *Relación del Suceso*,
describes the Spaniards' gradual understanding of Cíbola.

When the Indians . . . left their buildings, we made ourselves at home. Friar Marcos understood, or at least gave us the impression, that the area which contains seven villages was a single community which he called Cíbola, but actually it is the whole settled region of seven separate towns that is called Cíbola. The towns each have from 150 to 200 or 300 houses; in most towns the dwellings are joined in one large structure, but in others they are divided into two or three compounds.

This commentary gave an answer to the various historians who ridiculed Marcos for exaggerating the size of Cíbola. There had been some confusion about whether the term Cíbola referred to a single town or the whole region of the Seven Cities. Marcos's *Relación* compared Cíbola to Mexico City, and the early historian Peralta quoted Marcos as saying Cíbola was the size of two Sevilles, but if Marcos thought of the whole settled area as one coherent community, his conception of the size was justifiable.

ABOUT A WEEK AFTER THE BATTLE, CORONADO WAS ABLE TO GET out into the province and take a look around. According to the *Tralado de las Nuevas:*

Despite two small facial wounds plus the arrow wound in the right foot, his grace recovered, and on July 19th he was able to make an eight league [20–25 mile] round trip to see a high rock where the Indians of that province had fortified themselves.

This was the great mesa which the Zunis call *Toyolana,* some miles east of Ahacu. Anglos later called it Thunder Mountain. An imposing edifice, it is more than a mile across and rises hundreds of feet above the plain, just east of the modern town of Zuni. Even in later centuries, Zunis retreated and barricaded themselves at its top in times of stress. A ruined pueblo at its southern foot faces some hills across the cultivated valley, and it may be the town Marcos saw when he crept through those hills on his stealthy approach.

In his letter of August 3, Coronado tells more about his first few weeks' attempts to unravel the secrets of Cíbola, which he spelled "Cevola"—each Spaniard making his own attempt to transliterate the native words.

The Seven Cities are seven little villages, each with the kind of houses that have been described. The are within a radius of 5 leagues [12 to 15 miles]. Together they are called the kingdom of Cevola. Each has its own name and no single one is called Cevola. . . . The Indians say that the kingdom of Totonteac, which Father Provincial Marcos praised so much and said was something marvelous and of great size, is only a hot lake, on the edge of which are a mere five or six buildings. . . .

Coronado was in a bad mood—a mood to debunk everything that Marcos said. His letter was not just an official report to the government, but a grim quarterly report to his business partner and coinvestor, Mendoza. His mood led him to be too pessimistic. Some of the "facts" he reported in this letter proved incorrect, such as his claim that Marcos had erred in reporting big cities beyond Cíbola, like Totonteac. Only a few weeks after the above letter was written, a party sent out by Coronado discovered the large Hopi pueblo towns in Northern Arizona. The 1940's historian Herbert Bolton thought they were Totonteac. Hallenbeck thought Totonteac was the even larger group of pueblo towns on the Rio Grande near Albuquerque. Either way, Marcos's report was actually correct. Coronado also confirmed that Marcos had correctly reported a nearby town called *Ácus*, which turned out to be the pueblo of Acoma, still thriving on a mesa top not far beyond Cíbola/Zuni. A few months later, Coronado's whole army traveled farther east to the Rio Grande, and discovered the large pueblo communities who traded directly with the buffalo hunters of the plains. Coronado's glum but fascinating letter continued:

When I recovered from my wounds, eight or ten days later, I went to a town [in the province of Cíbola], that was larger than the first one. I found a few of the Indians there, and told them they shouldn't be afraid. I asked them to summon their lord or governor. From what I can see, none of these towns seems to have a single chief, because I haven't seen any principal house by which any superiority of one over others could be shown.

Later, an old man, who said he was their governor, came wearing a mantle or blanket of many pieces; I argued with him as long as he stayed with me. He said he'd come back with the rest of the chiefs in three days, to arrange the terms that would exist among us. He did so, and they brought some small ragged blankets and turquoises. I said they should come down from their hilltop strongholds and return to their houses with their wives and children, and become Christians, and recognize the King. But they still remain in their strongholds with their wives and all their property.

I ordered them to have a cloth painted for me with all the animals in that country. Although they are poor painters, they soon painted two for me, one with animals and the other with the birds and fishes. They say they will bring their children so that our priests may instruct them, and that they want to know our laws. They say it was foretold among them more than fifty years ago that people like us would come, and from what direction, and that the whole country would be conquered.

As far as I can tell, these Indians worship water, because it makes the corn grow and sustains their life, and the only other reason they have for it is that their ancestors did so.

I was amused by the condescending comment that the only reason for the Zuni religion was that their ancestors had handed it down. As if the cross-waving Spanish had different justification for their own beliefs! Coronado continued his report to his partner. The quarterly profit report for this venture was not encouraging. . . .

I send you the two painted cloths and a buffalo skin, some turquoises, two earrings of the same, fifteen Indian combs, some plates decorated with turquoise, two baskets, and coils that the women wear on their heads to carry jars of water. With one of these coils, a woman can carry a jar of water on her head up a ladder without touching the jar with her hands. . . .

As far as I can judge, there is little chance of getting gold or silver, but I trust in God that if there is any, we will get our share of it. . . . Some gold and silver has been found in this place, and those who know minerals say it is not bad. But I have not yet been able to learn from these people where they get it. I perceive they don't tell me the truth in everything, because they anticipate I will depart soon, as I have told them. . . .

I can't give Your Lordship any certain information about the dress of the women, because the Indians keep them guarded so carefully that I have not seen any, except two old women. . . .

Around 1560, Bartolomé de Las Casas recorded more information on the lifestyles and religious practices of the people at Cíbola, compiled from accounts generated during the Coronado expedition. These are similar to practices recorded at Zuni centuries later, in the 1800s. Who among us, I thought, would be able to collect better information on an alien culture?

The province of Cíbola is the nation which we found worshiping the sun and sources of water. When they worship toward the sun, they raise their hands and rub their faces and the rest of their bodies. In the case of the water sources, they bring many feathers of various colored birds and place them around the water sources, close to the water. They also sprinkle ground cornmeal and other yellow powders.

They made the same offerings and the same ceremonies to the cross, after seeing that our Christian people venerated it. They touched it with their hands, and then they rubbed their faces and their entire bodies. After that, they made offerings to it, including many vessels, such as bowls of cornmeal.

Coronado reserved the bitterest words in his August 3 letter for Marcos de Niza. In his disappointment, Coronado surrendered to the human impulse to blame someone else for the fact that he and Mendoza had sunk their fortune into conquering only a quiet community of contemplative people, pursuing their age-old agricultural practices and nature worship.

Now it remains for me to tell about this city and kingdom, of which the Father Provincial gave Your Lordship an account. In brief, I can assure you that in reality Friar Marcos has not told a single truth in what he said, and everything is the reverse— except about the name of the city and the large stone houses. Although they are not decorated with turquoises, nor made of lime or good bricks, nevertheless they are very good houses, with three, four, and five stories, where there are very good apartments . . . and some very good rooms underground, paved, which are made for winter and have something like hot baths.

The people are of ordinary size, and intelligent, although I don't see how they can have the judgment and intelligence to build these houses, for most of them are naked except for the coverings of their private parts. . . . Cotton thread was found in their houses. . . . I think they have a quantity of turquoises, which they had removed with the rest of their goods . . . when I arrived. Two points of emerald and some broken garnet-like stones were found in a paper, along with other stone crystals, which I gave to one of my servants to keep until they could be sent to Your Lordship. He lost them, or so he tells me.

CHAPTER 24

1540—1543
Fate

During the first days in Cíbola, Marcos spent most of his time alone, in one of the white-plastered upper rooms at one end of the pueblo of Ahacu. The residents of Ahacu had retreated up the broad valley to their isolated mountain fastness a few leagues away. A pall of defeat hung even over the victors, scrounging for corn meal in the storage bins of their deserted, dusty prize. His room was not unlike a monastic cell. The soldiers shunned him and sent scowls his way when he showed up for his meager rations of tortillas and a few beans. The saving grave was that everyone's attention was focused outward, on the surrounding towns and the resources of the countryside, so there was little time for the soldiers to harass him.

Publicly, he kept pointing out that the reality of the Cíbola province, with its multiple towns, multistory stone-walled buildings, fields, turquoises, cotton garments, fine cowskins traded from the east, forested hills, good rivers, and intelligent townspeople was not so far from what either he or Captain Díaz had reported. Not a word in his *Relación* had been proved incorrect, yet every dream between the lines was grotesquely wrong. To himself, he had to admit that after seeing Peru and Mexico, he had expected more within the cities themselves, and had let this expectation slip through in his speech. God knew he had tried to separate fact from speculation—a distinction that did not seem to impress most mortals.

There were no exotic temples, no jewel-encrusted walls, no treasure rooms of gold. Here and there were turquoises mounted in wooden door frames for good luck, or a gold earring that had been brought by a trader from Mexico. But the subterranean *kivas*, or sanctuaries, of these people held not gold treasures, but looms for weaving, carved wooden dolls that served as idols, and other useless religious paraphernalia used by the men of the village in their ceremonies.

There was one last, great irony that the members of the expedition were only beginning to admit to themselves. The seemingly indisputable copper-bell argument for foundries and advanced metalworking in the north, advanced by everyone from Dorantes to Mendoza, seemed to have been false. There was not nearly as much worked metal in Cíbola as in Mexico. After collecting samples of copper bells and a few other copper and gold items from the pueblos and interviewing the inhabitants, Marcos and the others were beginning to draw the conclusion that most of these materials had been received in trade from Mexico. The army had marched five hundred leagues in order to track down items that had been manufactured in Michoacán and other provinces only a few days west of Mexico City!

At the end of July Marcos heard the report that the rest of the army was approaching, catching up with the vanguard that had captured the Seven Cities. Hidden in one of the turret-like upper rooftops of Ahacu, he scanned the horizon to catch sight of them. Below him were the terraced apartments, fire pits, plazas, and kivas of a busy agricultural town. Finally he caught sight of the army. Hardly manifesting military order, they straggled across the bloodied plain in front of the now-conquered town. With them were the supplies and remaining livestock. Marcos could see from their gestures that they were as shocked by the appearance of the city as the general's vanguard had been. He prepared for another onslaught of scorn. The grand army had conquered seven pueblos of corn meal and dust.

Should he fight back against the slander that was being directed at him? The list of conquistadors' complaints against him seemed so exaggerated that there was no place even to begin a rebuttal. He had promised a wide, level road for the horses, they claimed. He had promised a port for Alarcón's ships. He had promised metal-working in gold, silver, copper, and iron. He had promised pagan cathedrals where a fortune in gemstones could be pried from the walls and idols in a few moments. Marcos always challenged his attackers to show where he had promised these things, but by the time he uttered the words, his critics had turned away in contempt. The moment was not right to try to begin defending himself. Perhaps, he thought, he was simply being tested, like Job of old.

In his lonely upper room, he spun options and rationalizations by the hour. Ever the optimist, he looked for a new beginning. How would he present all this when he arrived back in Mendoza's court? All right; Cíbola was not as rich as Tenochtitlán. But who knew what lay in the cities beyond? There were many stories of more large cities, both to the west and to the east along a wide river. And as for the land around Cíbola, were there not indications of metal deposits in the hills? What about the people themselves? They were even more interesting and intelligent than he had guessed. Their society, with its elaborate priesthoods, ceremonies, and building skills, was far more sophisticated that of the Indians near Culiacán or on the way north. Cíbola cried out for missions, which in turn would open opportunities to search for the sure-to-be-found mines. There were the agricultural fields and resources of timber and nuts and wild game in the hills. These lands, just as he had described, could support large communities of Spanish settlers. A new Mexico could be built here. The opportunity must not be lost! The men merely needed to change their perspective. The riches to be gained would involve wholesome years of sustained effort, not a greedy plan to reap huge profits in one year and then retire in luxury. Having reached Cíbola, the army sat in the middle of a glorious new world if only they could see it from a long-term perspective. How could he make the men realize that a happy, prosperous life is the patient work of a lifetime—not something you acquire by a get-rich-quick scheme?

In his darkest moments, in the moonless hours before dawn when the last stars gleamed through his stone window, Marcos despaired. No one would listen to him. The general himself was as hostile toward Marcos as the common soldiers. "You'll be the one to pay for this," Vázquez had repeated in one of his many tirades. As everyone blamed him, his own colorful career and all his dreams had passed their zenith and now were plunging inexorably toward some unforeseeable nadir. How could anyone's reputation and authority collapse so fast?

Sometimes in his private moments—which was now most of the time—Marcos marveled at Cíbola's combination of sophistication and simplicity. He occupied many hours by writing notes about the province, which he could deliver to his Franciscan brothers. The people had an intricate system of clans and priests who charted the sun's annual movements from one of these rooms, and studied the amount of rainfall in the different seasons, the habits of the animals, and other natural phenomena. On the other hand, the province was less technically advanced than he had thought from the descriptions of the Indians to the south. Oh, their words had been correct, but the images conjured by the words were misleading. The cities were massive, with terraced stories rising one over another. But they were not walled cities, built to protect treasures like those of southern France, as he had thought from a distance. Rather, the thick base walls supported the upper floors and formed the defensive shell to protect the apartments and storage bins from nomadic enemies. The buildings were closed to the outside but opened into spacious interior plazas where ceremonies could be watched from the walls. Only narrow, elbow-angled entryways admitted visitors to the interior of each pueblo. Defensively, they were brilliant. Vázquez de Coronado had been easily knocked senseless by missiles from above when he tried to fight his way into Ahacu.

Truth to tell, Marcos was amazed how far these people had progressed *without* large-scale metalworking, horses, or wheeled vehicles. Cíbola was a low-rent version of Tenochtitlán, without the gold. The Franciscan order must find some way to use this kind of information when missionaries were sent back. Marcos could only hope that a blessed culmination of his work would occur within a year or two, after the public realized the opportunity.

ON THE FIRST OF AUGUST, THE GENERAL DELEGATED HIS FAITHFUL captain, Melchior Díaz, to take a group of soldiers back to the base camp at Corazones. The general was rumored to be writing a long letter to the viceroy, to be sent back with them. Only God knew what abuse he would heap on Marcos in that epistle.

ON AUGUST 5, THE SMALL RETURN PARTY GATHERED AT THE gates of Ahacu, ready to march back across the plain where the battle had been fought a few weeks before. Puffy clouds of pure white dotted the blue sky like fluffballs of cotton. The plan was that Díaz would deliver the group to Corazones. From there a party could be sent to Mexico to report to the viceroy. Meanwhile, Díaz himself would lead a side trip west from Corazones to the coast, in search of the ships of Alarcón, which were carrying the army's supplies.

Marcos had agreed with the general's demand that he "volunteer" to go back with the group to Mexico. Vázquez de Coronado himself bade farewell to the group, and gave a speech about how they should inform everyone to the south that the conquest was only beginning, and that soon the army would search for other wealthy cities that were said to exist beyond the province of Cíbola. As they marched out across the plain, Marcos heard some of the soldiers grumbling.

"The general is whistling in the wind."

"No, the gold may be in the pueblos to the east. It's unfair for him to send us back to Corazones. We are missing a chance for riches and glory."

"I say good riddance to this place."

*   *   *

FOR THE NEXT FIFTEEN DAYS, MARCOS WAS IGNORED BY EVERYONE
in the party during the march through the *despoblado*. It was
Marco's second disastrous retreat from Cíbola. When they reached
Chichilti-Calli, a handful of Indians camped around the ruin
frowned and melted away into the underbrush of the foothills. The
army camped around the base of the ruin that night, but in the
morning, Díaz ordered Marcos to the front of the party, and told
him that it would be up to him to calm any of the now-hostile Indians they might meet. He should remind them, Díaz said, not only of
the love of Jesus Christ for them, but also of the stern justice
administered to anyone who would dare attack His Majesty's
troops. Díaz was a capable fellow. The soldiers liked him.

The villages along the Nexpa were still nearly deserted. Marcos
led the way south along the river, recognizing that if a poison arrow
from behind some bush or rock brought him down, there would be
those among the rough soldiers who would say he got what he
deserved.

The soldiers themselves watched the trail anxiously as they
headed south into the Rio Senora valley. Marcos traveled with his
thoughts turned inward. Occasionally he waded in the cool waters
of the stream or stopped to gaze at the hills that bounded the valley,
and he had a premonition that he, the discoverer of these lands,
would never come this way again.

His reception was no better at the garrison in Corazones. The
scruffy-looking and malnourished troops there had expected
returnees from the north would bring pouches of gold and horse-
loads of cornmeal for each of them. When the soldiers heard the
dismal news, Marcos found himself with a new title: Traitor of
Cíbola. He was happy to leave for Mexico City with the first party
sent south by Díaz. Díaz stayed behind, to seek news of the army's
supply ships.

EVEN IN MEXICO CITY, MARCOS COULD NOT ESCAPE POINTED
fingers. The capital needed a scapegoat to explain why a thousand

men marched north only to capture a town of mud and stone. Marcos turned to his mentor, the bishop. The bishop's appraisal was frank.

"Privately, you are my friend," Zumárraga told him. "But publicly, you understand, I cannot defend you. The church itself would be discredited. You must not stir things up by fighting this. Instead, you must turn the other cheek. Your service to the church now is that you must be meek. That is to say, you should not be too visible."

The church circulated the story that Marcos's health was broken by the travels to Cíbola. And indeed it was—or was it his spirit? He was shunned in the streets as the man who had made up stories about gold. Doña Beatriz, the wife of Francisco Vázquez, sent a courier to Bishop Zumárraga with an angry message stating that if the reports of the army were true—if Cíbola was barren of gold— then her investment had been lost and she was almost ruined financially. It was all the fault of Friar Marcos, and the church should censure him and provide some reimbursement for her.

The bishop responded by calling in the Franciscan hierarchy. Marcos was becoming an embarrassment for everyone. The announcement was made that Marcos would move to the monastery in the old gardens of the Mexica, on the south side of the lake, at Xochimilco, effectively removing him from public life in the central city.

DURING THE NEXT YEAR, FROM BEHIND HIS MONASTERY WALLS, Marcos kept his ears open for further news of the army. The bare, monasticlike adobe rooms, the plain wooden benches, and the contented people he had seen in Cíbola had convinced him more than ever that the greatest treasures of the northern lands must be spiritual. He listened to the birds sing and watched the splendor of the tropical flowers, and he came to believe that real riches had nothing to do with conventional ideas of wealth. Maybe that was the message he was called to teach. Such treasures are all around us and take years to be discovered.

As for gold, he still hoped it would be found in kingdoms such as Totonteac or Marata or Ácus, which he had been first to report. Perhaps the army would come marching home one day, all smiles, with gold from Totonteac or beyond, and his reputation would be restored. Month after month he asked about news, but he learned only that Coronado had ordered his men to explore further inland.

Occasionally Marcos met with the bishop and other old friends. He was included in theological discussions about the possible settlement of the distant lands, but the discussions were now only academic. Everyone knew that unless Vázquez de Coronado found gold somewhere in the plains far beyond Cíbola, settlement was out of the question in their lifetimes. The chance to experiment with Bartolomé de las Casas's ideas about building a perfect society in the New World had been lost.

THE ARMY FINALLY STRAGGLED IN, A FEW SOLDIERS AT A TIME, during the fall of 1542. An air of failure marked their every step. They had been defeated not by an enemy, but by the evaporation of their dreams. Like Marcos, Vázquez was a changed man, grayer and slower in his movements. Rumors said that the army's failure to find either gold or glory weighed heavily on his soul. Soon after returning to Mexico, the once-great general resigned his governorship and retired to his estates, trying to prosper at least on a small scale and to cast off the dark mantle of humiliation. Few people saw him, though his wife was seen at church, holding her head high and looking neither to the left nor the right.

With the would-be conquistadors back in town, Marcos, for his part, had to cloister himself even further from public view. The expedition had become the New World's greatest disaster. There were those who said Marcos's life was in danger from disgruntled soldiers—that he had better not walk the streets after dark.

Month after month, by talking to young monks who had talked to soldiers, Marcos pieced together the story of the army's adventures. At first, Coronado had refused to give up. Like Marcos, he had concluded that there would be a rich empire someplace beyond the horizon of Cíbola. He sent out parties to the west, who discovered the great mesa-top pueblos of Totonteac and a great canyon beyond. Totonteac was even more populous than Cíbola, but to the soldiers it was just another dust heap. Then the whole army moved east from Cíbola a few days to an even more populous land of many pueblo towns along a great river—a land called Ti-huish. They occupied several towns for the winter, but found no gold or treasure.

In Ti-huish, the general learned more about the nomadic peoples who lived on the plains and hunted the great cowlike beasts whose hides figured so prominently in the trade with Cíbola. Those people traded with the pueblos, and they told of still another trading center, called Quivira, somewhere further northeast across the prairie. Some of the Indians said it was very wealthy. From April to June 1541 Coronado took the army out there for a journey of many weeks, across fearfully empty plains. In these featureless plains, some of the soldiers who were sent out on hunting expeditions lost their way because of the lack of landmarks in the sea of grass, and never returned. Across these plains, Coronado traveled north with a small, brave band, hoping that Quivira would have riches. But Quivira turned out to be an even poorer collection of villages than had been seen at Cíbola. They returned and joined the main army at Ti-huish empty-handed.

After this, Coronado's dreams of gold died. The soldiers told the story about how, one day, the general fell off his horse, and was never the same thereafter. It was if something had broken in his mind. If he was dispirited after Cíbola, he was more so after that accident. He began to dream not of opportunity, but only of home and his wife. A debate raged for many weeks among the officers and troops. Should they continue exploring in hopes of finding rich ore deposits, and starting mines of gold or silver, or should they give up and go home before still more disasters befell them? Many said that God had cursed the expedition. Everyone realized that if they turned back to Mexico, they would return as paupers, having gambled away their fortunes on the Cíbola dream. Marcos was heartened to learn that sixty of the soldiers said they wanted to stay and establish a settlement in the area—an option which might have led to yearly trade caravans between Cíbola and Mexico. But in the end, Vázquez de Coronado overruled those who wanted to stay, and announced that the entire expedition would return home.

The disgruntled soldiers, facing failure, packed up and returned through Cíbola toward Mexico. Meanwhile, a Spanish relief army had been heading north. The two armies met within a couple of days of Chichilti-Calli. They camped together for a few days at the famous ruin. The northbound army, full of enthusiasm for the new lands, tried to convince Coronado to allow a contingent to occupy the north. Coronado again talked them out of any plan to resume the conquest. Adding injury to insult, the returning army found that the garrison at Corazones had argued continuously with the once-friendly natives, and had eventually been gutted by an Indian attack.

Meanwhile, Alarcón's ships had sailed up the barren coast, seen no sign of the army, and returned home. Díaz, leading a search party west from Corazones, had managed to find messages buried under a beachside tree by Alarcón, but had then been mortally wounded in a bizarre accident. Mounted on his horse, Díaz had been impaled in the groin when his own spear stuck in the ground and he overrode it. He lived for some days, and the soldiers tried to carry him back on a litter, but he died and was buried along the trail.

From various parts of Sonora, the army divisions straggled back to the ruins of Corazones and then back to Mexico. The dream of the north was dead.

To Marcos the whole adventure had been a preposterous mistake, a mad dream. If the men hadn't let their expectations rise so high, they would have seen the land differently. What seemed a land of poverty might have been seen truly, as Marcos saw it, as a land of potential glory. Yet one of God's strangest laws seemed to say that great dreams get only one chance. The ideas of someone like Bartolomé de Las Casas, the political backing of the viceroy, the blessing of the bishop, the enthusiasm of the soldiers, all had to be carefully stage-managed and coordinated into one grand, all-or-nothing climax. If an orchard could not be planted, fertilized, and watered with just the right timing, the fruit would never be harvested. Listening to the tales of discouragement, Marcos realized that for his generation, it was too late. Looking beyond the disgruntlement of the short-sighted men, he saw that the dream would have to wait until a new generation could take it up.

Meanwhile, the soldiers cultivated their own theory of what had happened, and it soon got back to Marcos, in spite of his seclusion. "Tell Friar Marcos," a soldier said to one of Marcos's priestly friends, "that this is what the general told us in his speech at Chichilti-Calli when he ordered us home. He said, 'Thanks to that bastard Marcos, we have all lost everything. But let us hold up our heads and start over again in the lands of Mexico. We have done our best and we have proven that there is nothing worth having in these northern provinces. The fault lies with Friar Marcos and his lies, not with us.' Those are the general's exact words. That was the final truth we learned through all of our efforts. Let Friar Marcos sleep with that on his conscience, if he can."

CHAPTER 25

September, 1989
Cíbola

Idrove north across the Gila River at Winkleman and headed into the fifteen-day *despoblado*. Just as Pedro de Castañeda said, I found myself leaving the "spiky vegetation" behind. Outside the car, a bird perched on one of the last saguaros, singing an ancient song.

For me it was a five-hour *despoblado*. Pine forests soon replaced sagebrush-strewn scrublands, just as Castañeda predicted. Then I came out of the forest onto vast grassy plains, and the Zuni River. The final march to Cíbola. Somewhere around here, in this dry flatland, Marcos encountered the bloody natives who had witnessed the death of Estevan. This piece of the road, ominously named Route 666, crossed the shallow, mud-banked stream of the Zuni River and continued north. Somewhere near here, Coronado's army encountered the first natives of Cíbola. There were no markers to commemorate these incidents. You had to know the secrets from the old books to feel the excitement of what had happened in this landscape.

Soon I took a right onto Route 61, heading east across the state line. Somewhere, a few miles ahead was the kingdom of Cíbola, with its scattered "Seven Cities," goal of all those dreams back in the 1500s. It had been a long drive, and I was dealing with some defeats, but it was costing me a lot less than it cost Marcos de Niza and Francisco Vázquez de Coronado.

* * *

I KEPT WONDERING WHAT IT WOULD BE LIKE AT CÍBOLA ITSELF, at the site of the battle that marked the end of prehistory and innocence in the West?

Funny how things work out. I drove into the town of Zuni, with its trading posts and little tribal museum, its gas stations and a couple of roadside restaurants, scattered along both sides of the highway. In the mighty kingdom of Cíbola, little kids were riding around on bikes and older kids were hanging out in front of the stores with packs of Marlboros. The pueblo itself was back a few blocks off the highway. Marcos de Niza and Francisco Vázquez de Coronado weren't exactly daily concerns, even though this was the scene of the Grand Denouement.

The town of Zuni was the only survivor among the famous Seven Cities, once known as far south as mid-Sonora. All the other towns were abandoned ruins, scattered in the plains and foothills nearby. There was a marvelous link to the past, visible even along the street: the multistory stone architecture described by Marcos was still everywhere to be seen in Zuni; stone walls of cobbles, laid one on another.

Tourists ignore Zuni, but that makes the town more real and down-to-earth than the pueblos around Albuquerque, Santa Fe, and Taos. I pulled into a little restaurant, the Zuni Kitchen. No one but a few locals, wearing down-home jeans. I sat at a table and ordered what the menu called an Indian taco. No one looked twice at me. Here I was, in the heart of the northern empire. Coronado himself probably ate at this same restaurant. I wanted to flash a badge, like a cop, ask them what they knew about this fellow called Marco and his pal, Frank Vázquez.

There was a museum in town. I couldn't resist. I headed over there after I ate. It featured some cartoon drawings by a Zuni artist, poking fun at Cushing, the ethnologist who had lived with the Zunis in the 1880s and recorded the ancient custom of embedding good-luck turquoises in doorways. To the Zunis, it was the gawky Cushing who was the ethnic curiosity from another culture. The drawings spoofed his strange Anglo habits, and raised an image of

Zuni anthropologists studying the peculiar rituals of the European-Americans. It was a great display; it taught that we could all laugh together at each other's foibles.

The museum made me conscious of another story waiting to be told here. How did all this history seem from the Zunis' point of view? In the summer of 1539 appeared a black man, dressed as a native shaman, telling wild tales of a thousand white brothers. A year later, came Coronado and his army. The Zunis retreated and began their five hundred–year battle with the Spanish and later with the Anglos' Bureau of Indian Affairs, radio, and television, culminating with the MTV virus. Where is the young Zuni writer who will tell this story as seen through Zuni eyes?

IT WAS TIME TO GO LOOK FOR ANCIENT AHACU. I GOT INTO MY CAR, which had heated up in the bright sun. In those days you could drive around freely on the reservation. Nowadays, I understand you need a permit. Still, they are not quite as strict as in Estevan's day.

I studied my maps. Scattered around modern Zuni, the other six cities of Cíbola were now prehistoric ruins. Several of them lay to the east, where the valley is dominated by the imposing, flat-topped circular mesa Toyolana. That's where the Ahacu natives fled after Coronado's attack. A major ruin in that direction, named Kiakima, lay on the slope at foot of the mesa, and it may have been the town Marcos saw from the hills across the valley.

In the other direction from Zuni, to the southwest, lay the ruin called Hawikuh. That was my goal. It was Estevan's destiny, Marcos's A-ha-cu, Coronado's despair.

Navigating by guesswork, I drove through Zuni, looking for a road down the river to the southwest. I tried several dusty roads out of town until I hit the right one, paralleling the shallow grassy valley. The valley stretched for several miles and the road angled away from the river, passing low rises.

There, on the brow of one of the low hills, lay the ruins. You had to poke around to find them. Centuries ago, the roofs that sheltered

Coronado had collapsed, and the wind had blown soil into the rooms until the whole thing formed merely a mound on the side of the low hill, not unlike the mound at Coronado Estates, but bigger. On the surface of the ground I could see the stone outlines of the tops of walls, a two-dimensional slice through the building. On the slopes of the hill, some faces of stonework walls were exposed.

After Coronado stormed Hawikuh in 1540 and then moved on, the town had its ups and downs. In 1630, the Franciscans, spiritual heirs of Marcos de Niza, established a church there. Its ruins lay at the base of the hill, perhaps on the spot where Estevan was housed for his last, fateful night. Finally, when the Pueblos revolted against the Spanish in 1680, the town was destroyed and abandoned. The ruins lay quietly for two centuries until the northern Europeans arrived with their characteristic curiosity. The traveler/explorer, Victor Mendeleff, mapped them as an archaeological site in 1886. In 1917 they were excavated professionally by a Smithsonian expedition under Frederick Webb Hodge and a team of associates. They laid bare the walls and room floors, collected artifacts, and then, to preserve the site, pushed the dirt back into the excavated rooms when they finished. So Hawikuh cannot be called pristine. Still, pottery sherds were strewn everywhere.

Did Hodge find evidence of Estevan, or an old cross left by Coronado, or Spanish armor, or evidence of the battle? Amazingly, he did not talk much about this. He was studying the prehistory of the Zunis, not the Spanish conquest. So he wrote up an analysis of Zuni prehistory and shipped the excavated material back east to a museum in New York for storage. A review of this material during the 1990s, I learned later, turned up copper points of crossbow arrows, the very points fired by Coronado's army during the forgotten battle. Certain points were indistinguishable from those being found at that time in Coronado army campsites near Albuquerque and in the Texas panhandle. One researcher who studied all three locations said he could identify points made by the same individual craftsmen—individual anonymous soldiers who rode with Coronado from Mexico City to Cíbola and back. Astoundingly, Hodge and his team had missed the historic significance of these relics, noting them only as "Spanish material." That's the Achilles' heel for all of us: We see only what we seek. My geology professor at the university used to joke about how much easier it was to see geologic features after they had been explained to you: "If I hadn't believed it, I never would have seen it."

Near the foot of the hill I could see the foundation of the old Spanish mission church, built less than a century after Coronado and Marcos. The symbols of both Native and the European culture had fallen into ruin, side by side. Would our cities look like this some day? Or the whole world, when little green people from Arcturus stand on hilltops and wonder about the rubble?

As I walked along the brow of the hill, a dry wind swept over the grassy plain. Above were the big, cotton-puff cumulus clouds beloved of the northern New Mexico painters—clouds completely different from the bluish cirrus wisps over Tucson and Chichilti-Calli, on the other side of the fifteen-day *despoblado*. I looked across the quiet plain. There's where Estevan walked up to the city walls. There's where Marcos's Indian allies were bloodied and fled down the river valley. Was Estevan killed just below where I stood, or was the old Zuni legend true, that he had been taken to Kiakima, one of the other towns, and killed by the large rock in the gorge there? Had Marcos crept along those hills to the south, to catch a glimpse of Cíbola? There, across the grassy plain was the place where Coronado's two hundred–man advance party appeared on July 7, 1540, tired and hungry, lining up, reading their proclamation, issuing their veiled challenge.

Damn, this was one of the pivotal sites in the history of North America. This very spot, a four hundred–yard circle around me. Where was the brass plaque? Where were the parents, teaching their children? There was nothing. The wind raised a little eddy of dust on the empty dirt road. How could we—the Euro-Americans, the Native Americans, the Afro-Americans—ignore this spot where all our destinies had first converged?

I tried to listen for the shouts of the men that had crossed that empty and historic field. In the rocks around me, the molecules vibrated; didn't they retain some aural fossil record of the "Saint Iago" battle calls and the war cries of the Zunis? For a moment I thought I could hear some other echoes, still ringing off the rocks. "Such were the curses that some hurled at Friar Marcos that I pray God protects him. . . ." Well, things had gone to hell for both Marcos and me. We had underestimated goldlust and made the mistake of assuming that people would find truths interesting for their own sake. We learned that words are poor weapons against preconceptions.

This trip was supposed to inspire me. I had fantasized sitting on these ruins, coming to some calming realization that it was over with Phaedra, that it was also over with Mr. Rooney and his crew, and that my Marcos de Niza phase had ended and my life could move on. In my fantasy, I would realize what I was supposed to do next. Here I was, but where was the great revelation?

I sat on the wall and tried to get in a receptive frame of mind. I heard the echo again. No, it was an old pickup coming down the dirt road. It contained four kids from Zuni, and a very loud tape deck that made a thudding sound. I strained to hear the words, thinking they might symbolize something in this sacred place. It was rap music and the words were about fucking bitches.

The truck drove on by, and the kids didn't see me. The *boom boom boom* of the Zuni kids' distant stereo, like an ancient drum, receded until everything was quiet again. I got back into my own car. The windows were rolled down against the heat. The breeze blew through the front seat.

As at Chichilti-Calli, the very lack of a monument was what preserved the sense of place. Yet as soon as we realize something's interesting, we destroy it, like little boys toppling someone else's sand castle in the sandbox. The only answer I could come up with was that we all needed more sense of *sanctity*.

This was an insight, but it wasn't the revelation I needed about what I should do with my life. I decided to keep driving, to follow Coronado's tracks eastward.

CHAPTER 26

Epitaphs

After I left the Cíbola battlefield, I drove to Albuquerque. I stayed several months and got a forgettable job in a state agency. It took me back and forth to the capital in Santa Fe. I saw my old Albuquerque friends, and set up a post office box. The box was a buffer against Rooney's prying minions. It also probably meant that Edward could not find me, if he was still out there somewhere. I thought a lot about how to reestablish contact with him. I mailed off some letters to his old addresses. As for Mr. Rooney, I still didn't know far he might go, but I hoped he'd leave me alone if I made no trouble for him.

Rooney might have unsavory friends in Mexico, but after I calmed down, I couldn't imagine him plotting anything serious against me. I continued to develop my theory that whatever happened in Alamos, the murder was not directly the plan of people I knew. I visualized Phaedra telling Rooney about the book, and Rooney telling Freddy to get his hands on it, and Freddy telling their rancher friend, and the rancher sending his heavy-handed goons to get the book, using this as an opportunity to get rid of a left-wing priest. Or, better yet, it was probably one of the investors, one of the gun-toting hunters who felt his easy profit was threatened when Freddy mentioned that I had found something that might pin down Coronado's ruin. They made a deal with the rancher, picked up the notebook on the fly, and gave it to Freddy as a gift. Maybe Freddy himself was all the way back in Arizona before he realized what happened to Father Antonio. Rooney never ordered an actual killing. I didn't believe in American businessmen planning murders. It was too Hollywood.

In New Mexico I had a simple lifestyle because my acquisition hormones were at low ebb. I saved up piles of money that came in handy later. That was one of the good things about America, you could get rich enough to have a good life if you just resisted the urge to buy. The trouble is, you have to isolate yourself from the American mythos. Then the TV programs, malls, and gas-guzzling cars start to look more and more bizarre, and you start to be apart from everyone, like Marcos.

A few months later I still missed Phaedra. I sent her an e-mail from an aol account, just to say hello. She wrote back, saying things were moving along with Coronado Estates. Construction had started. By the way, she was engaged to a lawyer who worked for the firm and she was very happy, and even little Amber liked the guy.

So much for that. It sounded like she had found what she wanted. Jesus, a lawyer! I sent another e-mail saying I was glad if she was happy. . . . I also drank too many beers in the next few weeks.

I was still waiting for a revelation about what to do—the revelation that hadn't come at Cíbola. I knew that Albuquerque couldn't be permanent. I didn't want to run into Freddy the Fixer, who also hung around the corridors of power in New Mexico. Meanwhile, most of the letters I had sent to old addresses of Edward in Mexico had come back. Edward seemed to be gone for good. I missed him. I wished I had brought something of his back from Alamos to keep along with my fragment of Marcos' notebook.

In the absence of a revelation, I spent that first year in Albuquerque plugging away at the loose ends. I felt that if I could close the book on Marcos and the other guys, then I could wrap up the story of my own sojourn in the land of Chichilti-Calli, and move on. I tried to work through the characters, one by one, to see what happens to people who, in spite of reality, are perceived to have failed.

Coronado came home with only knowledge instead of gold—a flaw that Americans have never been able to abide, like winning second place in the Olympics. Suarez de Peralta, the historian, described the return he had witnessed as a boy.

> *[Coronado] was very sad and weary, completely worn out and shamefaced. . . . When he came to kiss the hand of the viceroy, he got a poorer reception then he would have liked since the viceroy was upset. As the army came straggling in, the country that had been joyous in 1539, when the discovery of the Seven Cities of Cíbola had been announced, had become a country of gloom.*

In 1544, two years after his return from Cíbola, he had to face a review of his conduct as governor and expedition leader. In those days, reviews of royal officials' behavior were routine, but the trial must have seemed a bitter irony. Historians are divided on his actual conduct of the expedition. Some paint him as one of the most benign of the conquistadors. Others suspect he was guilty of more oppression than was ever officially admitted, and that the trial was a whitewash.

> *Charge: Having established a Spanish settlement in the valley of Corazones, Vázquez de Coronado should have picked some able and reliable person to administer and pacify that province. Because he was remiss in not choosing a competent governor, and because of the ill treatment shown to natives by the soldiers he left there, the natives rebelled and killed many Spaniards and the original town was abandoned, and even the neighboring people revolted.*
>
> *Response: Vázquez de Coronado said he had appointed Melchior Díaz to go back from Cíbola to Corazones and settle there and bring the natives to obedience of his Majesty and into knowledge of God. Díaz followed these instructions, and then followed further instructions to search for Alarcón's ships*

on the coast. When Díaz left Corazones, it was peaceful. The revolts of the Indians came later, when Diego de Alcaraz took over after Díaz left.

Vázquez de Coronado also said that in all the towns through which he passed between Culiacán and Cíbola, he always arranged for some men to go ahead of the main army, carrying a cross as a sign of peace, and to assure the natives that no harm would be done. He himself gave the Indians trade articles that the viceroy had supplied, and this pleased them. He said he did not know of any person in the army committing any cruelty or ill treatment to the natives, because he kept the army so disciplined that no one dared disobey him. Whenever any of the Indians from Mexico City entered the natives' fields, he punished them harshly in the presence of the natives. Because of his edicts, no Spaniard or Indian ally dared enter the natives' houses. The army always camped outside the towns, in order to avoid the kind of trouble that soldiers can cause.

Charge: When the army reached Cíbola, the natives of the main town came out to meet them peaceably, furnishing them the needed food and provisions. Yet Vázquez de Coronado and his captains, without legitimate cause, waged war and burned the pueblo and killed many people. It was for this reason that a large portion of the province took up arms.

Response: Coronado gave his account of the approach and battle at Cíbola, supported by other testimony, as already mentioned.

The trial also involved accusations about the conduct of his governorship. Additional charges and responses were made, but Coronado answered successfully and escaped heavy penalties. The official who signed off on the sentencing was an old friend. . . .

Sentencing of Coronado on charges regarding his conduct of the expedition, on February 19, 1546: In the criminal suit, we find that the royal prosecutor did not prove the accusations and charges against Francisco Vázquez de Coronado for the offenses claimed in the newly discovered land. We pronounce these charges not proved. Therefore we absolve Francisco Vázquez of all that he has been charged with in this case, and we order the prosecutor to perpetual future silence in these matters.

Don Antonio de Mendoza [Viceroy]

Coronado had to undergo still another trial in 1547, but it was inconsequential. Nonetheless, his health declined, and he took numerous vacations from his various duties. Finally he died in November of 1554. He was buried in a convent that had been founded by his father-in-law and supported by his wife, Doña Beatriz, whose fortune had supported his expedition.

FROM CORONADO'S STORY, I LEARNED THAT GREAT DEEDS ARE NO guarantees of a glorious old age. The same lesson applied to my friend, Marcos. He continued to sink into obscurity. I could find surprisingly little about him during the postexpedition period. Scholars had lost his trail, except for one poignant letter from Marcos to Bishop Zumárraga, written in 1546, six years after his return from Cíbola, and the same year Coronado was being exonerated in his first trial. Marcos was proabably around fifty years old, and the two trips to Cíbola, along with the psychological stress, had taken a toll:

With all due reverence and devotion I kiss the feet and hands of your reverence. . . . You will know that on account of having left the warm country, my health has become very bad. On this account the Father Provincial orders me to return to the warm countryside at Xochimilco. As an orphan, I have no father and mother, nor have I a friend nor refuge except your lordship; you've been more than a father in all my necessities without my meriting it. I beg your lordship through your great charity to make me for a few months a donation of a little wine. I am in great need of it, because my illness is a lack of blood and natural heat.

I will receive this as the greatest charity. If you can do this, write me for how many months and how much each month your lordship wishes to give, so I can send an Indian to get it at the proper time.

Praying that the Lord God will guard and save your reverent person, from this your house, today, Friday, your lowest servant and chaplain,

Fray Marcos de Niza

The seventy-eight-year-old bishop replied.

To this I say, father of mine and servant of God, that during the months and years that I live, while your sickness and necessity last, every month an arroba of wine shall be given to you. Starting now, I send it to you, and order Martin de Aranguren to give you the best there is, from my account. The hospital overseer, Lucas, or his companion, will give it to the Indian who comes for it if I should be away from the city. February 27, 1546.

P. S. If more should be needed, it will be given with good will.

Using the scant information available, historian Henry Wagner, writing in 1934, traced Marcos's life to its end.

I do not read the subsequent history of [Marcos], so far as known, as anything but a tragedy. All of the early chroniclers of his order are silent on the subject. Gerónimo Mendieta alone mentions him. He says that on his way home from Spain in 1554, he passed through Jalapa, where he found Niza crippled from the hardships through which he had passed. Because he thought that the hour of his death was drawing near, Niza was taken to Mexico City to be interred with the ancient holy ones and there he finished his life's journey. In the Menologica Franciscana of Fr. Augustin de Vetancourt it is stated that he died in Mexico City on March 25, 1558. . . .

What about Mendoza? In spite of sponsoring the disastrous expedition, he was regarded as a competent viceroy. Surely he recovered from the situation. Suarez de Peralta wrote about it forty-seven years later. . . .

Many people had lost friends and fortunes because they had entered into partnerships with those who went, mortgaging their estates and property in order to get a share of the profits. They had drawn up papers so that soldiers on the expedition could claim possession of mines in the new land, in the name of those who stayed behind. Many had sent their slaves on the expedition, also, since there were abundant slaves in the country at that time. Thus, the loss and grief were widespread. But the viceroy felt it most of all, for two reasons: first, it was the outcome of something that he thought would make him more powerful than the greatest noble in Spain; and second, his estates were ruined, because he had spent so much of his time and fortune in organizing the expedition.

In the end, as such things happen, the viceroy succeeded in putting it behind him, and devoted himself to the government, and in this he became known as the best of governors, being trusted by the King and loved by all his subjects.

More or less a happy ending there. Mendoza served Mexico well, and a decade later, in 1551, he was offered the viceroyalty of the still richer province of Peru—an offer that was considered a promotion. By then he was in poor health, but he loyally accepted the new responsibility. He moved to Lima and died there on July 21, 1552.

*   *   *

CORTÉS, THE GREAT RIVAL OF MENDOZA, TRIED FOR YEARS TO GET the king to grant him titles to the northern lands, but in the end he must have felt glad to have escaped the curse of conquering Cíbola. He died at age sixty-three, in 1547. For a ruthless man, he had been oddly philosophical. In his last will and testament, he mused on the debate about the Spanish dealings with the Indians. The conqueror who had destroyed the Aztecs and kept Indian slaves throughout the rest of his life now related his concern about the question of the Indians' humanity.

> *It has long been a question, whether one can, in good conscience, hold Indian slaves as property. Since the answer to this point has not yet been determined, I enjoin it on my son Martín and his heirs that they spare no pains to come to an exact knowledge of the truth, as a matter that deeply concerns the conscience of each of them, no less than mine.*

And then there was the enigmatic Estevan, whose personality had precipitated much of the story. What if Estevan had followed Marcos's orders and waited for him? How different would history have been if Estevan had stayed out of Cíbola? Could Marcos and Estevan have pacified the governor of Cíbola, leading to a friendly contact, and a completely different history with the Spaniards?

What was the real cause of Estevan's debacle? Several documents revealed further insight into what happened. Astoundingly, news of Estevan's arrival at Cíbola spread within months through the native trade network over distances of hundreds of miles, and was collected by Captain Hernando de Alarcón about a year later, in 1540, when he sailed into the mouth of the Colorado River, in his ill-fated effort to supply Coronado's army. Several days up the Colorado River, somewhere near present day Yuma, Alarcón recorded this scene.

An old Indian man was telling his friends grand things about me, and pointed to me with his finger, saying "This is our master, a child of the sun." They made me comb out my beard and they straightened up the clothes I was wearing. Their faith in me was so great that they told me about their past and present troubles and their attitudes toward one another. I asked them why they told me all this, and the old man replied, "You are the lord, and nothing must be concealed from the lord."

So I asked him about Cíbola, and whether he knew if people there had seen anyone like us. He said no, except a black man who wore things that tinkled on his arms and feet. Your Lordship will remember how the Moor who went with Father Marcos wore bells and feathers on his ankles and arms, and carried plates of various colors. He arrived at Cíbola a little more than a year ago.

I asked why the people of Cíbola had killed the Moor. He replied that the governor of Cíbola had asked the black if he had any brothers, and he had answered that he had an infinite number, that they had numerous weapons, and that they were not very far away from there. When the governor heard this, he assembled many of the leaders of that province and they decided to kill him, so he would not reveal their location to his brothers. Therefore, they not only killed him but also tore his body into many pieces, which were distributed among them all so that everyone would know that he was dead. He had a dog with him, like mine, and the governor had that dog killed a long time later.

Other accounts of the death of Estevan were collected by the Coronado expedition itself in Cíbola. Pedro Castañeda, who published his memoir decades later, recorded more clues about what happened. In spite of the fact that they spent three months marching to Cíbola together in Coronado's army, Castañeda apparently did not talk much with Marcos, because he repeatedly described how "three friars" originally went with Marcos, and how "friars" had discovered Chichilti-Calli and made the trip to Cíbola, whereas in reality Marcos was the only friar on that trip after Honorato dropped out. So I corrected Castañeda's "friars" back to the singular when I excerpted his account. I liked the way that Castañeda fleshed out the personalities of Estevan and the others, more than any other author of the time, but I realized that when you have gossip from only one source, you have no test of its accuracy.

It seems that after the friar and the black started their journey, the black didn't get along well with the friar because he took the women that were given to him and also because he collected turquoises and accumulated a hoard of goods. Furthermore, the Indians along the route got along with the black better than with Marcos, because they had seen him before. That's why Estevan was sent ahead to open the way and pacify the Indians, so that when the rest of Marcos's party came along they would have nothing to do but record the discoveries.

After Estevan left the friar, he thought he could get all the fame and glory for himself, and that if he alone could discover the reputed cities, with their multistory houses, he would be considered bold and courageous. So he pushed onward with the people who had followed him, and crossed the despoblado between the southern country and Cíbola. Estevan was so far ahead of the friar that when Marcos reached Chichilti-Calli, on the edge of the despoblado, Estevan was already at Cíbola. . . . Estevan reached Cíbola loaded with turquoises and beautiful women, who came along and were given to him by the Indians who followed him and carried his things. These people had joined him from all the settlements he had passed, believing that under his protection they could traverse the whole world without any danger.

But the people of the province Cíbola were more sophisticated than those who traveled with Estevan. They lodged him in a small structure outside the town, and the older men and governors listened to his story, taking steps to find out why he had come to their country. For three days they inquired about him and held a council. The black told them about the white man who was following him, who was sent by a great lord and who knew about the things in the sky, and about how he was coming to instruct them in divine matters. From this account they concluded that Estevan must be a spy or a guide for some nations who wished to come and conquer them. They were also suspicious as to why he would say the people in the country where he came from were white, when he himself was black. Furthermore, they felt it was wrong for him to ask for turquoises and women. So they decided to kill him.

They did this, but they did not kill any of his followers [contrary to the initial story given to Marcos by the overly excited Indians who escaped from the skirmish]. They kept some of the young lads, and let the others, about sixty persons, return to their own country. The ones who fled were badly frightened. They came upon the friar in the wilderness sixty leagues from Cíbola, and told him the bad news, and this frightened Marcos's party so much that they would not even trust the ones who had been with the black. So the friar opened the packs they were carrying and gave away everything he had except for the holy vestments for saying mass. They returned from there by double marches, prepared for anything, without learning any more about the country than what the Indians told them.

Coronado himself described the fate of Estevan in the letter he wrote from Cíbola on August 3, 1540, based on information obtained directly from the people. The Cíbolan version of the story, perhaps understandably, shifts some of the blame from themselves to the people from Chichilti-Calli.

The death of the black is perfectly certain because many things he wore have been found. The Indians say they killed him here because the Indians of Chichilti-Calli said he was a bad man, not like the Christians, since the Christians never kill women,

and yet he did. It was also because he assaulted their women,
whom the Indians love better than themselves. That is why they
determined to kill him. But they didn't do it in the way Marcos
thought; they did not kill any of the others who came with him,
nor the lad from the province of Petatlán, whom I was able to
recover after arguing with them for two or three days.

It was intriguing and faintly voyeuristic to notice how the question
of Estevan's relations with women kept cropping up. Were jealous
Spaniards exaggerating? Or was his sexual life really so extraordi-
nary? The allegation that Estevan had pursued, assaulted, or even
killed women—a claim allegedly made by the Nexpa/Chichilti-Calli
Indians, relayed by the Zunis, and then repeated by Coronado—is
the only charge that Estevan harmed women or anybody else on the
way. Was it true? Who knows? Perhaps some of Marcos's notes in
his trailbook would have provided the answer.

Frank Cushing, the anthropologist who lived with the Zunis
from 1879 to 1884, recorded a legend handed down among them,
probably describing the death of Estevan.

It is to be believed that a long time ago, when roofs lay over the
walls of Hawikuh, when smoke hung over the house-tops, and
the ladders were still unbroken at Kiakima, then the Black
Mexicans came from their abodes in the land of everlasting
summer. . . . At that time, one of the Black Mexicans, a large
man with chile lips, was killed by our ancients, right where the
stone stands down by the arroyo of Kiakima. The rest ran
away, chased by our grandfathers, and went back toward their
country in the land of everlasting summer.

I continue to be obsessed by the third level of the Marcos mystery—how deeds get transformed into history, or rather mistrans-
formed. It wasn't enough to follow Marcos and his generation of
compatriots to their deaths; I needed to understand how Marcos
was carried forward through time, because there were so many

strange and inconsistent interpretations of what he had done. I found that the whole story of Marcos was lost to the next genera-tions of Mexican Spaniards in a strange and ironic way. I spent many months in Albuquerque piecing this together, and after I got to France, I met a scholar in Nice, who was writing a biography of Nice's forgotten son, and I learned more from him. Working with an obscure American researcher, he had written a paper on the his-tory of Marcos's reputation. He gave me a copy, which I devoured. It led me to review the texts of the Mexican historians who wrote about Marcos's journey.

In early 1540, just after Marcos returned from the north but before Coronado's expedition returned in failure, a friar in Mexico, known as Motolinía, was writing a *History of the Indians of New Spain*. He retold the story of Marcos and Coronado leaving Mexico City in 1538 to explore the northwest.

> *In the year 1538 provincial Fray Ciudad-Rodrigo sent two fri-ars and a captain north to make discoveries. Having crossed the land already conquered, they took two well open trails. The captain chose to turn right, toward the interior [into the] diffi-cult mountains. As for the two friars, one fell ill and the other, with interpreters, took the path to the left, following the coast.*

Motolinía was correctly reporting how Marcos, Honorato, and Coronado left Mexico City in 1538 and split up at Culiacán, with Marcos going northwest and Coronado going east into the moun-tains. The curious thing is that he doesn't mention their names.

> *After a few days [the friar] arrived in a land of poor people who called him a messenger of Heaven and kissed his robe. . . . Nearly everywhere on the road he heard of a well-populated land where people wore clothes and had houses with flat roofs and many stories. . . . Cloth of cotton and wool, and turquoises, are found among the poor people whom the friar contacted. They obtain them from the large towns. . . .*

Up to this point in his account, Motolinía does not indicate that Marcos had either reached those towns or come back to Mexico City, and his text sounds like it may have been put together from the messages that had come back from Marcos. Next, Motolinía mentions that competing armed groups had already tried to learn about the north by land and sea [referring to Guzmán and Cortés, but again not by name], but that God let them be discovered by a barefoot friar. Everyone, said Motolinía wanted to go there. From the tone of the text, it seems likely that Motolinía prepared most of this account using the earliest messages that Marcos sent back about the natives in Sonora—the messages which arrived in Mexico City during the midsummer of 1539. But he seemed not to have known much about who was involved. If he worked from messages brought back by Honorato or others, he may have been unsure who actually did the exploring and who was simply the messenger.

Half a century later, in 1596, another friar, named Mendieta, published a similar history, basically copying Motolinía's account of the Marcos venture. He must have been aware that there were two waves of information from the north. The "first wave" of messages and rumors circulated in midsummer of '39, and then Marcos himself arrived in late August, creating a "second wave" of reports with his *Relación*. Since these two waves of reports were many weeks apart, it may have seemed to casual bystanders that there had been two parties of explorers. Apparently a victim of this misunderstanding, Mendieta credited the "first wave" messengers with the actual discovery of Cíbola, and stated that Marcos made only a second expedition to the Seven Cities—thus confusing Marcos's role with that of Melchior Díaz, who had been sent on horseback after Marcos returned!

At that time the provincial of this province was Fray Marcos de Niza, a very religious man with great knowledge. In order to verify what the other friar had published, he wanted to do all the work again, and before others could decide what to do, he left with great courage. Having verified the other friar's discovery, he came back to Mexico City and confirmed what the other had seen.

Later scholars, struggling to make sense of these confused documents, handed down increasingly murky accounts. Friar Juan de Torquemada, around 1615, repeated Mendieta's version and said that Marcos "left for the new land of Cíbola, which he had heard about through the account of another friar." Friar Antonio Tello, in 1653, in his book of history, was the first to give a name to the unknown early "first wave" friar—Juan Olmedo. Tello claimed that the hitherto unrecorded Olmedo came back and reported the discovery to "his prelate, father Marcos de Niza."

This thread reappeared in 1742, when a Mexican historian named Mota Padilla published an account claiming to have examined documents left in Culiacán by one of the captains of Coronado's expedition. His account says that Ciudad-Rodrigo sent priests including "Friar Juan de Olmeda" to find Cíbola, and that Juan came back and gave a report to Ciudad-Rodrigo, who then sent it with Olmeda to Marcos de Niza, who then "set out, on foot and shoeless, taking with him the said father Olmeda." To me, this was the clue that tied everything together. According to these somewhat disjointed accounts, Juan was not only someone who arrived in Mexico City with an early report, but was also someone who had traveled with Marcos. This made sense only if Juan was an acolyte of Marcos, who went north with Marcos, and whom the friar sent back with a message from the northward march. I figured it was Juan who arrived in Mexico City with the "first wave" of Marcos's early messages and caused sensational rumors, perhaps in July of 1539. Later, people reminiscing about the great events of 1539–40 remembered that the news of prosperous northern lands first appeared when Juan arrived, and thus associated Juan himself with the discovery. They also remembered that Marcos came back later, with news confirming the discovery.

Thus Marcos suffered the final insult. The Golden Book of Great Deeds took away his original discovery of Cíbola and credited it to one or more of his messengers. Perversely, at the same time, due to the complaints of Coronado and some soldiers, the news that Marcos did bring back was called false. Meanwhile, life went on, in the sad and joyous, secretive and boisterous, self-regenerating tragedy that is history.

My Expatriate Life

The moment when I finally had my revelation about what to do with my future came after I had been working in Albuquerque for a while. It was during one of my visits to Santa Fe in 1990. I used to sit during lunch in the old plaza, and watch the cowboys and Indians and tourists and schoolchildren reading the inscription on the big obelisk that dominated the square. I went over to read it myself:

> *To the heroes*
> *who have fallen in the*
> *various battles with the* ☐
> *Indians of the territory*
> *of New Mexico.*

The blank was a word in the original inscription, but it was chiseled out some years ago. Only a rectangular depression remains. I'm told the word was "savage." The other side of the obelisk says this message was erected in 1866–68 by the people and legislature of New Mexico.

I wondered if our great-grandfathers would be angry at us for excising their epithet, out of respect for the people who were here first. It made me remember a different inscription, which Edward had showed me in one of his photographs. It was on another obelisk, in the Plaza of Three Cultures in Mexico City. I looked it up. It described the Spanish destruction of a district called Tlatelolco, in Moctezuma's capital. A battle had occurred on that site:

> *On August 13, 1521, Tlatelolco,*
> *heroically defended by Cuauhtemoc,*
> *fell to the power of Hernán Cortés.*
> *It was neither a triumph nor a defeat.*
> *Rather, it was the painful birth of our multi-culture nation,*
> *which is the Mexico of today.*

Instead of the chest-thumping, oh-so-American inscription, I preferred the Mexican inscription, with its tender and wise view of humanity.

Sitting there in the Santa Fe Plaza, thinking about the difference between the two inscriptions—that's when the revelation came to me. I needed to be like Marcos or any of the Coronado chroniclers. I needed to write down my version of the story of the golden cities. Partly it was just a desire to get all my research in order. Partly it was a way to get my mind clear about what had happened to me. And partly it was a way to fulfill Edward's dream of writing the true story of the Southwest. To do it, I needed to move. If I could get far enough away, I could be safe, and I could look back and see it all more clearly. I needed to find a new world of my own. I could do it. I still had the plane ticket, the bonus money Mr. Rooney had given me, and the money I had saved up during the job.

Joseph Conrad, in one of his novels—was it *Lord Jim*?—said you have to immerse yourself in the destructive element to survive. His metaphor was about drowning. If you fought against the water—the destructive element—you used up your energy and died. If you immersed yourself in the destructive element, it buoyed you up, and you could float with your nose in the air. Immersing yourself, you could survive. We were all immersed in the American economic system in those days; it buoyed us up. It made money for us. It gave us bigger cars and bigger houses and bigger TVs. It treated the world as a disposable commodity.

It let Mr. Rooney sign a few papers, shuffle a few blueprints, sell land for more than he paid, and then be proclaimed a benefactor of society. Everyone bought into this system, as if it were natural law. If I stayed and fought against it I would use up my energy and die. That was what Phaedra tried to warn me about. She wanted me to immerse myself, like she did, in the destructive element.

The destructive element reminded me of urban smog. Immersed in it, you didn't notice the gray-brown haze killing the colors, until you got out of town into the clear sunlight, and looked back. That's why I needed to get away, out of the land of golden suburbs and giant garages, where Thomas Jefferson's dream of building something for the future had been smothered, and where the new conquistadors were dedicated to getting rich now, and letting the future fend for itself.

IN MY LAST MONTHS IN ALBUQUERQUE, SOVIET COMMUNISM underwent its final collapse and Iraq invaded "our" oil fields in Kuwait. After everybody stopped shooting, I withdrew my bank savings and went off to see a travel agent to discuss my escape route to Europe. My friends in Albuquerque offered to stop by my post office box every so often and forward my mail. That way, I figured, Mr. Rooney wouldn't be able to track me down—if he was looking for me.

I made my reservation for a special day: On the 450th anniversary of the battle of Hawikuh I was winging my way into the sky over New Mexico. There was nothing in the paper about Hawikuh that day, no ceremonies. Out of five billion people on the planet, I bet I was the only one on that anniversary who paused to remember the poignant beginnings of the American Southwest.

SO HERE I AM IN EUROPE YEARS LATER. MARCOS LEFT FRANCE FOR America; I went the other way. I wasn't ashamed to flee to Europe. Even Einstein fled his own country when it was disintegrating around him. I figured it was no disgrace for me to do the same, once I had realized that my ancient province was being consumed to preserve the get-rich-quick ethos.

It was true that I could see things more clearly from the distance of Europe. For a few years I tried to follow the story of Arizona in the papers, and there was one story that brought it all home. According to the papers, the governor, who had risen to power through land deals, was forced out of office and sentenced to jail. Allegedly, he told the bank and other investors he was worth millions at the same time the value of his land holdings were plummeting during a recession, so that eventually he declared bankruptcy and left the investors holding the bag. In court, he indignantly maintained his innocence because, as he cheerfully explained, he was merely reporting what his holdings *should* have been worth, assuming the projections of continued growth and prosperity. It wasn't *his* fault that the economy turned down. As he always said, he was for against creeping socialism; but profit on a land speculation should be guaranteed by the government or the banks or somebody, don't you see? Eventually he was pardoned. The system was still working beautifully.

After that, I figured I had better things to do than watch the papers.

As I write this by an open window (I've come home from my café), sounds of massive bells ring out from the town cathedral, late on a Saturday afternoon. A bee flies in for a visit and leaves again. Why has southern Europe never adopted the window screen? It's as if my table is right out there in the air, and the great, deep sounds of the bells repeat and bounce off each other in endless patterns. Marcos heard these sounds, these very sounds. Embedded in the peals of the bells are resonances of Byzantine-baroque mysticism, turning out good people with spooky cosmologies about angels and demons, virgins and devils. Marcos and his friends were feeling their way out of the Middle Ages into the Renaissance, struggling at each step of the way. But the bells also celebrate God, I suppose, by which I mean Ultimate Reality. They seem to celebrate life itself, which is perhaps the same thing. Humans looking up at the stars and shouting, "Here we are."

When I arrived in Europe, I felt like Hemingway or Henry Miller. I had busted out. I would live simply, following in Edward's footsteps. I loved the downtown of every city, which was like a giant county fair of commerce, food, and art. I'd walk down the energetic streets and just marvel: pen shop, grocery, lingerie store, pizza place, shoe store, boulangerie, watch store, theater, café, bookstore, McDonalds, art museum, leafy parks with benches. Myths of right-wing American politics say that Europeans are oppressed by high taxes and socialism, and dream of escaping to the freedom of the U.S. of A., but I saw happy and beautiful people everywhere, cramming the streets, sitting in cafés, enjoying life. It made me feel healthy and safe. I enjoyed being immersed in the Great Outer World. My high school French began to kick in. Contrary to common complaint I found that Europeans have good humor about struggling with foreign languages for the simple reason that they are used to living with other countries next door. I would make a try at French, and then smile, and then shrug, and they'd come back at me with accented English.

I was a traveler, not a tourist, to use the distinction made by Paul Theroux; it meant I had no definite plan to return home. On my way to where I live now, I passed through several cities in France, Switzerland, and even the Czech Republic, where people were celebrating their new freedom. Jazz, Mozart, and hippie guitars rang out on the plazas of Prague. As my trains chugged along, I'd notice the little town centers, surrounded by agricultural fields, country lanes, hedgerows, and patches of forest. Where were the miles of car-supported suburbs? Where were the malls and treeless parking lots, baking in the sun?

I made friends easily in Europe. People sat close to each other in restaurants, and expected each other to be interesting. Along the way I told my story to various friends I made, but they couldn't understand why a town would allow anyone to buy up huge tracts of field or forest on its outskirts and tear them up to build densely packed rows of houses. A woman in Switzerland, home of the flower box in every window, said to me, "In our country, the towns control the land around them. It's in the constitution. No town would let someone buy up its countryside! That would be letting one man determine the future of the whole community!"

I said, "Arizona has this thing called private property rights."

"But there has to be a balance," she said.

Obviously, she didn't get it.

On one of my train rides, I saw a *jeune fille* reading Camus, and I realized it was America, not Europe, that built the first existential society. Europe, with its ancient cathedrals and stone bridges, and its Neanderthal ax-heads scattered in the soil, has mostly built itself around a thread from the past to the future. Americans keep snipping the thread, wandering off on new paths at random, guided by the latest entrepreneurial fad. As Mr. Rooney once said, the past has no place in the future.

One autumnal Saturday night I was walking through downtown Bern, marveling at all the people roaming the streets, and the little impromptu band playing Dixieland at the corner of the square, when I saw a peculiar trolley. Inside, everyone was seated at tables, eating. It looked like a dining car on a train. Then I saw a name on the side: THE TRAVELING RESTAURANT. My Swiss friend told me that you buy a ticket for an evening and they drive you around and serve you dinner while you take in the sights of the town—the old clock tower, the railway station square full of attractively dressed people, the riverbanks and the graceful bridges, the trees planted along the avenue, the government buildings, the cathedral, the university buildings, the house of a famous composer, the flat where Einstein wrote his papers on relativity.

I had to think about why this wouldn't work in Tucson or any of the cities built by the Southwest's land wheelers and dealers. Where would a traveling restaurant go in towns that have exploded into a thousand fragments? Had Mr. Rooney or his ilk built anything whose mere presence repays us with pleasure? Would we go downtown and watch the empty banks, the newspapers blowing in the streets, the derelicts around the Greyhound stations, and the last few well-heeled people rushing to escape the downtown in their cars at five o'clock? Or would we drive the Traveling Restaurant out to the newly built suburbs, to dine in boulevards lined with drab walls imprisoning overnight tracts of introverted houses, facing inward on themselves?

INSTINCTIVELY, I HEADED SOUTH TOWARD THE REGION THAT MARcos came from. He came to my town, I would go to his. I hung out in Nice for a while, exploring the gravelly beaches and the old hotels. Then I settled down in my village, not far away.

I like to go down the road to Nice, to visit the spots where Marcos grew up. Nice, started by the Greeks, occupies a splendid site along a curved, open bay between two hilly promontories. It is bright, open, full of sunlight, and the colors of Matisse, who came there to live. The plants are tropical, similar to what Marcos would have seen in Mexico—palm trees (at the latitude of Boston!), agaves, flowers, scattered pines and poplars. Car-filled avenues are broad and lined with mod shops that sell Givenchy to the beach-loving tourists from Germany and England, but the side streets in the Old Town branch into ever-narrower medieval alleyways that must have been here in Marcos's time.

The Old Town during his time was a triangular wedge, a few hundred meters wide, bounded on the south by the beach, on the northwest by the river (now a pipeline under a modern conference center), and on the east by the hills that divide Nice from the medieval principality of Monaco. Outside the town wall, a ten-minute walk west of the river, lay Marcos's monastery, Saint-Croix. He came there as an orphan and stayed until he left for America, around 1530. A few years later, France and Italy contended for the city. The French king hired Turkish pirates to attack the town in 1543. Marcos's monastery was an easy target outside the walls near the beach, and the Turks occupied it, and then burned it to the ground. I wondered if Marcos ever learned that his boyhood home had been destroyed.

I used to wander over there and sit in nearby cafés to write. Today the site of the monastery is a block of commercial buildings on the Rue de France, crowded with small European cars, noisy motorbikes, and pedestrians. A marble cross marks the site, not because Marcos was there, but because the pope visited in a failed attempt to forestall the hostilities over Nice. Although Marcos was the first explorer of the American Southwest, he is forgotten in his hometown.

Because so little is known about the life of the man from Nice, scholars have searched for records about him in the Franciscan archives there. The scholar I met there told me heartbreaking stories. For many years, the Franciscans, in their new monastery on a hill farther back from the beach, kept early records, possibly including archives salvaged from Saint-Croix. Some of the records ended up in the Nice library. Years passed. In 1920 the library was moved and cartons of old documents, including Franciscan records, were found to be damaged by worms. The best preserved of these were returned to the Franciscan monastery on the hill and placed with other, still older records that may have gone back to Marcos's time. Unfortunately, the records moved from the library were apparently still infested, and by the 1960s, according to some stories, the entire mass of archives had now been corrupted and unsalvageable. As a result, all the records were destroyed, some thrown out and others buried in the garden. We missed saving the last possible records of Marcos by one generation.

THROUGH A WOMAN I MET IN PARIS, I GOT A PART-TIME JOB WORKING for a French publisher, preparing a book in several languages about touring the western U.S. I did a little editing and writing of the text. It was perfect. I had income and time. After their book was done, I continued working freelance for the publisher, plus writing little pieces about travel and the U.S. for European magazines. With the help of a few permits and embassy visits, the first year stretched into two, three, four. Finally, I took up writing this memoir of the adventures Marcos shared with me.

Europe isn't cheap, as it was for Hemingway and those guys, but in any country, you can live pleasantly in the small towns if you haven't been corrupted by marketing departments. And small towns in Europe have a certain charm, rather than being bastions of rednecks and survivalists. Still, it wasn't easy, being an expatriate writer. My main problem was internal. I had to fight this fear that by moving away from the surrealistic American whirlpool, I was turning into an Oswald in Minsk, or a Kaczynski in Montana, nursing grudges in some remote place, writing in worn notebooks, pathetically coming to believe I was important. That's when you end up doing Something Really Destructive, like taking potshots at prominent citizens, in order to be taken seriously. Still, Hemingway and Fitzgerald and Miller and Bowles and Salter, the other expatriate writers, succeeded; they kept their craziness at the level they needed in order to create. If they could do it, I could, too.

ON SUMMER EVENINGS I'D PICK A CAFÉ IN MY TOWN OR GO into Nice and take my laptop to a little table with a red and white tablecloth on the sidewalk. People would come out just to enjoy the evening and drink a beer or a cider. The complete human comedy passed in front of my table every summer evening: teenaged guys sauntering by, checking out the scene; couples walking arm in arm, elderly or young; dapper old gentlemen walking funny dogs; pairs of young girls, cruising, with eyes darting around; two beautiful women arm in arm, satisfied, eyes not darting around; middle-aged men and women walking their bicycles down the sidewalk.

A YEAR OR SO AGO, WHILE I WAS WORKING ON MY BOOK, I GOT excited all over again about my notes on Marcos, and my solution to the mysteries of his trip. I decided to write a little article about it and send it to an American journal of popular western history. For the first few years, I was afraid to publish anything like that; I thought Mr. Rooney might make trouble. But now I thought, the hell with it. It's a decade later. Nobody's going to care, especially if it's published in a small historical journal. The story of my research on Marcos needs to come out. It's a valid contribution to history. It could die with me. So I wrote up my analysis of his route and the piecing together of the clues from Cabeza de Vaca, Marcos, Pedro de Castañeda, and the others. I also told how Edward and I had visited a church near Alamos, and found the journal of Marcos. I described it, but stated that the journal had been destroyed. I indicated that this had been intentional, an act by someone opposed to historic preservation. I knew that the historical journal I was writing for would not want to get into a political/criminal mess, not to mention a libel suit, and so I carefully avoided saying who it was. I figured that was clever. Get the story out, let a brouhaha start, and then let some investigative journalist figure it out and put the finger on Rooney. To be safe, I sent it through my box number in Albuquerque.

I'VE HAD SEVERAL RELATIONSHIPS HERE. A FEW MONTHS AGO I took the train up to a small town near Paris for a weekend to meet my friend from the publishing company. She took me to an open-air jazz concert. Saturday afternoon we took the walk along the woodsy path along the river, with a view across the water to the old steeples and red tile roofs. Saturday we took the train into Paris, where there were endless museums and clubs. It was a good weekend with good sex, but I'm also talking about the aura of companionship in a place where it is easy to maintain contact with friends in other cities. Just jump on one of the morning trains. We wandered the streets in the crowd, sat in parks, and gossiped about the publishing office. I showed her the article I had sent in and told her about the longer memoir I was writing. She called a week later and said everyone there wanted to see the manuscript I've been working on, about my adventures in the land of golden cities. She said Europeans are interested in the American West. So now I have a possible publisher.

NOW IT'S SIX P.M. IN MY LITTLE TOWN. THE STREET NEAR MY apartment is a walkway with more pedestrians than cars. It's a cool night with a drizzle. People walk purposefully. Broad-leaved trees with thick gray-green trunks arch over the sidewalk and drip onto umbrellas. At my little table just inside my window, I go over the draft of my memoir. I'm learning whether my story makes any sense, when it is all laid out on paper—or at least makes more sense than it did when I lived it.

This morning I had a dream, or rather a vision. I woke up wanting to build some sort of construction, an *object d'art*. It would be a four feet long, on some sort of mahogany base, if there is still any mahogany available. It would be displayed on a table. It would have foot-high black blocks at each end, with random patterns of tiny eye screws on the sides facing each other. Polished silver wires would run from eyelets at one end to those at the other. Somewhere in the middle, the wires would intersect and pass through a silver ring, a centimeter across, so that they were gathered together in a nexus. The ring and the nexus could slide slowly from left to right, so that the nexus itself could move. The ring would represent the present, sliding quietly though time. The nexus of wires would represent the known reality of the present, tight, precise, known. The fanning of wires to the right would represent the uncertainty of the future, fanning out into many possible tomorrows, each stemming from the fixed reality of today. The fanning of wires to the left would represent the uncertainty of the past, which was once a nexus, but can now be seen only indistinctly from the present—many possible pasts, fanning out backward in time. The device shows how only the nexus of the moving present is certain, and how the near future and the near past are more definite than the far future and the far past. The usefulness of this visionary device seemed very definite when I woke up, but seemed to get more uncertain as the day wore on.

THE MANUSCRIPT ABOUT MY ADVENTURES IN CHICHILTI-CALLI seems not bad. I'm trying to get the electronic files ready to send to my friend. Today it's a beautiful day with a blue sky and white scudding clouds with exotic shapes.

I have to write fast, now, because I have a new problem.

Two months ago my article was published and one month ago

the story was picked up by Tucson's arts 'n' culture weekly, which, like most such weeklies around the country, had degenerated into a mutant descendant of once-noble humanist liberalism, a sort of *National Enquirer* of the local eco-radical-nightclub counterculture, raking muck over businesspeople, the university, and political leaders alike. My editor at the historical journal got a copy and sent it to me. They did one of those "whatever-happened-to-?" articles, about the old controversy over the now-booming Coronado Estates. It told about the growing community, the museum/gift shop in the golf clubhouse adjacent to the main ruin, and my research, which had once been a *cause celebre*, and was now forgotten. In a sidebar was some text about my article and how, in Mexico, I had "claimed" to have seen Marcos's original notebook proving our ruin was Coronado's Chichilti-Calli campground. It said that I couldn't produce the book or the name of anyone who might have it, and that I "had to admit" that the notebook's whereabouts were now "unknown." The whole thing made me out as a pitiable fool, another old-west treasure hunter with yet another lost mine.

Given the placement of the article between the horoscope page and a piece on the positive effect of piercings on psychic abilities, I assumed no one would take it seriously.

But someone did. A couple months ago, I got a surprise note from Phaedra, sent to my Albuquerque box number, which is the address I had given to the history journal. She sent me another copy of the article. She said she was fine and she was still working for Mr. Rooney, and the wedding plan didn't go through after all. She also said that Mr. Rooney was livid about the article because he had always been touchy regarding my claim of finding Marcos's notebook with information about the development site. She said she remembered all our good times together, and that she was reassessing her life. She seemed not to know about my episode at Rooney's house. She gave me an e-mail address and asked me to drop her line.

Everything came rushing back. I allowed myself to miss her. I remembered the wistful quality in her voice. Suddenly it seemed that all the other women I knew talked too fast. Who else had Phaedra's combination of brains, sexual responsiveness, and interest in everything going on around them? She always seemed to combine some joy in life with some secret sadness that grew out of her history, or perhaps came from her ancestors in Mexico. Our story had never really come to a proper finish, and there had been this loose end for ten years, like a conversation cut off by a broken telephone connection. Now that the crisis was past, maybe we could meet each other as old friends, laugh about our times together, and enjoy the warm glow of the embers that might still be between us. I had the odd feeling that if we could meet again, it would close some doors in my life, and let me finish my Marcos project in peace.

I e-mailed back a hello. I told her about my life and my book.

The conversation developed by e-mail. I asked her about what Rooney had said about burning the notebook. She said he never told her about burning the book. She was horrified when I described it. She said she believed me, and saw things differently now. Her life was different. Amber was older, her sister was remarried. Phaedra had some savings, and maybe it was time for her to move on. Finally, after a couple of weeks of e-mail, she said she wanted to take some vacation and come to Europe, could she come and visit? She'd keep it secret from Rooney.

I said sure. Resistance seemed unnecessary. Maybe there'd be a chance for a new start. Or a better closure. She's scheduled to arrive in a week. The plan is for me to pick her up at the airport in Nice, but I gave her my address and phone number here in my little town as a backup, in case there is any problem.

I didn't know I'd be ending my story with a chapter about a visit from Phaedra. Jeez; a whole decade later. Meanwhile, I've been working on the manuscript, getting the files in shape to e-mail to the publisher at the touch of a key. I figured I'd wait till she showed up and we could send it off together. A romantic gesture.

*   *   *

SHE JUST CALLED ME. SHE WAS FRANTIC AND IN TEARS. BETWEEN
sobs she kept saying she was so glad I was there to get the call.

"Wait a minute. Slow down. What's this about?"

"Freddy. I just found out. He—"

"He's still there?"

"Yes. No. It's Freddy. Freddy was the one behind the murder in
Mexico. He's coming to get you!"

"Wait. What are you talking about?"

"I found out Freddy booked a ticket before my flight, for yesterday. I mean today. It's overnight. He arrives in Nice today. I think
its an hour ago, your time. I mean he could already be there."

"It takes an hour to get out to my place. But he doesn't know
where I am."

"You've got to get out of there. He's been monitoring my e-
mail. He knows everything."

"What!?"

"I started talking to people after you told me about the book. I
found out he's paid one of our ex-systems administrators to hack
into my e-mail. . . . I thought it was secure. . . ." She was sobbing
again. "He knew when I was going and you've got to assume he
read our mail about your address. So he booked a flight to get there
before me. He's obviously coming to get you."

"Rooney's sending him?"

"I don't think Mr. Rooney knows. From what I can figure out, he
just operates on his own. Mr. Rooney looks the other way. If anything comes up that might threaten the company, Freddy takes it on
himself to . . . He just goes out and does things. That Mexico trip, it
was organized to keep an eye on you. I told Mr. Rooney you had
found something, and he must have told Freddy. The ranchers were
itching to get that priest anyway. Freddy egged them into it and
went along for the ride and got the book. Maybe paid them off.
Brought the book to Mr. Rooney. Are you safe? Is your door
locked? Is Freddy there?"

I looked out my window. The street was empty.

"Listen, there's something else. I told our current sys ad what's been going on. She's on our side. Freddy's been having her look for your friend Edward. Freddy must have searched his place in Alamos after you guys left because he had some names of Spanish-language journals where Edward publishes articles. Anyway, she found him! He has an address." She mentioned a small town on the coast of Spain. "Edward couldn't find you and you couldn't find him. Listen you've got to go. If we can't make contact again before my trip, here's my plan. I'm going there, where Edward is." She gave me a box number for Edward. "I'll meet you in that town. We can find him! About us . . . I don't know. But I can't stay here. It's going to come out that I've been asking questions. We'll decide what to do. Now go!" She hung up.

I heard a car pull up. I looked out the window. The car went by, slowed, parked down the street. The door opened. It was Freddy the Fixer, looking older. I'm going to go ahead and send this file to the publisher. I'll try to get out the back. I'm grabbing the scrap of Marcos's notebook.

If you're reading this, my story got through. All our little stories will recede into the expanding uncertainties of the past. What I learned in the province of Chichilti-Calli is that money and power win in the short term, but truth keeps stumbling forward and getting stronger in the long term.

EDITORIAL ADDENDUM. THIS MANUSCRIPT WAS RECEIVED IN OUR offices 25 March, 2002. We have not been in touch with the author since that time. However, checks made out to Mr. Scott are being picked up at a Spanish post office box address, which he gave us, and they are being cashed. *Dominique Pierné, Editions Château Garvarni, Paris.*

AUTHOR'S NOTE

I have tried to portray some of the real story of the Southwest, and to use the novel in part as a forum for new research, by myself and others, on the historical mystery of Marcos de Niza and the motivations for the mighty expedition of Coronado.

As mentioned in the foreword, all the quotations in the "research chapters" (2, 5, 8, 11, and so on), where Kevin Scott searches the old records, are real. They are the actual words of the historical Spanish figures and are taken from their personal writings. This includes Marcos's own, first-person *Relación*, written or dictated within days of his return in 1539; letters by Coronado, Viceroy Mendoza, Cortés, and Bishop Zumárraga; the eyewitness testimony from Mexico City in 1539; and the various eyewitness accounts of the battle of Cíbola. The *Requerimiento*, which Marcos reads to the natives in Chapters 3 and 12, is also a real document, still in existence. I have also used accounts written by the Mexica (Aztecs) about Cortés's conquest. These were written a generation later when Spanish priests asked certain Aztecs to write their eyewitness recollections of the conquest. I drew from these when Juan Olmedo recounts to Marcos his recollections of the meeting of Cortés and Moctezuma, and *La Noche de Triste*, when Cortés's troops lost most of the treasure they had accumulated. I have made free renderings of all these documents to make them more accessible to modern readers. Quotes by modern historians (1890s to 1950) are taken directly from scholarly literature, with kind permission.

The inscriptions quoted from monuments in Santa Fe and Mexico City also exist as described.

The letters that Marcos sends back during his journey north, in Chapters 6 and 9, are from my imagination, but some of the phrasing matches that in his *Relación* and also in the rumors about the northern empire that began to circulate in Mexico City in July 1539 before Marcos got back. As now seems apparent (but as denied by Marcos's critics in the 1930s and '40s), these rumors must have come directly from the news in Marcos's letters.

The signature of Marcos, shown in Chapter 13, is authentic, and is taken from a certified copy of his 1539 *Relación*.

I have followed modern usage and spelled Cíbola with an accent over the i. The word can be found spelled both ways, with and without the accent. The original copies of Marcos's *Relación* do not have this accent, but those copies do not have *any* of the normal accents found in modern Spanish. The reason for adding the accent is that most scholars believe the word is taken from the word for buffalo in the Zuni language, which is pronounced with an accent on the first syllable. As written in Spanish, lack of the accent would throw the accent to the second syllable, which would be incorrect. Thus, Cíbola seems the least ambiguous spelling and indicates something close to the word Marcos heard—which in Zuni sounds more like SHE-bo-la or SHE-vo-la. This word was apparently widely used on the trade route to Cíbola, because, from Marcos's own testimony, the buffalo hides (or "cowhides," as Marcos called them) were a major trade item obtained from Cíbola by the Sonoran natives. I'm indebted to Coronado scholars Richard and Shirley Flint for discussions on these points and other Spanish usages of the 1500s.

Headlines and news stories used to set the scene in 1989–90 are real stories for the dates that are mentioned, taken from microfiche archives of old newspapers in the University of Arizona Library—Kevin's library.

My descriptions of the country where Marcos and Coronado traveled are based on my own travels at similar times of year. Describing plants, I have used some modern names for clarity; these names in most cases are descended from Spanish and native terms. Although Mexico City was known to the Spaniards of 1539 simply as "Mexico," I use the current name, which makes the text clearer to modern readers.

The comet seen by the Aztecs as an omen, a few years before Cortés appeared, was real and recorded in Aztec records. According to the book, *Cometography*, by G.W. Kronk (2000, Cambridge University Press), there also was a comet visible during Marcos's trek north in 1539. It was recorded in Korea, China, Belgium, and Germany, and probably even Aztec records. It might have encouraged Marcos's belief that he had discovered something of great importance, though he did not mention it in his report. Halley's comet, incidentally, had been seen a few years earlier in 1531. The true nature of comets as interplanetary bodies was not known until several generations later, and both the Mexicans and the Spaniards regarded comets as ominous portents.

A Web site containing more material about the Marcos de Niza and Coronado expeditions, along with background scholarly material that went into this book, can be found at *www.psi.edu* under "research and projects." A portion of the proceeds of this book is being used to support that Web site. In addition to the older references cited in the acknowledgments, a fascinating collection of modern research papers is found in *The Coronado Expedition to Tierra Nueva*, edited by Richard and Shirley Flint, and published by the University of Colorado Press in 1997.

The modern Tucson and Southern Arizona that I depict are lightly fictionalized; some time and place relationships, and county lines, have been altered and the modern characters are fictitious. The political/economic/environmental controversies over sprawl, land use, and water management in the modern Southwest are real. The conquest of the Southwest goes on. . . .